Olivia

No Regrets

THE ACCIDENTAL MURDERS SERIES

a novel by

Catherine Grace

LONDON LGP GROVE PUBLISHING

Published by London Grove Publishing

Cover and interior design by Catherine Adams, Inkslinger Editing LLC

ISBN: 978-1-943723-00-3

Olivia

No Regrets

THE ACCIDENTAL MURDERS SERIES

a novel by

Catherine Grace

Dedicated to my dear husband, Peter.

Neither the slings and arrows of their own misfortunes nor the outrageous ones they aim at others can permanently damage the friendship between Olivia, Mags and Janine. The three are always in the right place at the wrong time when mayhem and murders are involved, the women backing each other up—in their own fashion.

THE ACCIDENTAL MURDERS SERIES

Olivia: No Regrets (Book 1)

Book of Mags: Served Cold (Book 2)

Once upon a time,
Was always long ago,
When Happy Ever After ends,
The real story begins....

The girl that used to be,
Knew love would come along,
The usual armor, standard white horse.
Swept off her feet she'd be,
To a castle of course—to love...forevermore.

The girl that used to be,
Believed in all the magic,
She wished on stars and listened,
For the nightingale to name
Who she was destined—to love...forevermore.

Dreams are meant to fade,
Maybe love is fantasy,
Lovers think their dreams,
Are for eternity.

The girl that used to be,
Never thought that true love
Would one day...disappear.
And there's no magic wand
To dry the tears or bring back...forevermore.

Dreams are meant to fade,
Maybe love is fantasy,

Now there's one less princess,
One less castle,
And one more lady thinking about,
The girl...that used to be,
The girl...that used to be...me.

Words and Music by Catherine Grace

1

I did not look like a killer as I hurried from a Madison Avenue shop carrying my current weapon of choice: a box of Godiva patisseries. As I strode along, I thought about the previous time I had visited that shop, which was, in fact, two lives ago.

That day I had walked over to Fifth Avenue and was greeted by George, the head doorman at my destination. Adolpho, the elevator attendant, smiled and whisked me to a high floor. Bechert, the butler, opened the door and led me into a sitting room, where peace and normalcy ended.

"Are you out of your fucking mind!" shouted Mags, my sometimes scary best friend. "Oh! My! God!" said Janine, my always sane other best friend. "You need our help with this," said both. " We'll pack up what you want and truck the rest to Sotheby's. Then you can have your IKEA orgy."

We were sitting in Mags's palatial Fifth Avenue apartment, drinking our usual wine and discussing my final trip to the Park Avenue apartment I had shared with my newly former husband: "Laurence the Litigator," as we had called him in my little circle. Now he was referred to as "Larry the Liar." I was going there the following day to take whatever I wanted, which had been part of the divorce agreement, and I'd decided to go alone.

When Laurence started calling himself Larry, that should have been my first clue that something was amiss.

When I intercepted those first calls asking for *Larry,* I had wondered but thought, *Oh well.* I should have shouted, "Oh hell, not on my turf!"

So Laurence and Olivia (that would be me) turned into Larry and Sherry (that would be the bottle-blonde former assistant and new wife).

Larry seemed reasonable about the terms of our settlement. This included, for what I had thought a fair price, his taking possession of our apartment. Mags and Janine, however, pointed out that "new money" in the real estate market had much less value than "old money." Although usually astute in practical matters, I was numbed by the divorce and still trusted in the fairness of the old Laurence, so I didn't accept the truth of what they were saying. I also didn't accept his offer of an apartment in one of the Lammond Holdings buildings—Laurence's company. Probably because I didn't want to feel—in any way—under his control. Besides, I am an Aries and, for those who believe in such things, we can be a bit huffy and headstrong and not always act in our own best interests.

Then we (Mags had insisted, "You can't possibly do this without me.") went shopping for a smaller, cozier version of my former duplex pad. After weeks of traipsing through places with a hard-edged agent who could barely suppress her disgust ("Couldn't keep your man, huh?"), I realized that old money was indeed more valuable. It had bought the Park Avenue apartment for just slightly more than the one Mags finally allowed me to buy: a sunny co-op in an elegant mid-century building in the East Seventies. It had its pros and cons. The pros included a spacious living room with a marble fireplace. The library had its original wood paneling, and the dining room was large enough to hold reasonable dinner parties. The building was on a quiet street with a garage beneath for tenants only. The best pro was not having to look at yet one more place or endure more of Mags's comments, most of which began with *are you out of your f...?* The last straw was: "Why don't we just flop you on a piece of cardboard in the Bowery?" Because I suspected Mags hadn't been below 40th street since she finally finished her degree at NYU, I smugly pointed out that the Bowery was now upscale and she could place my corrugated pad outside the Chanel store on Wooster. Mags sniffed at that, but I knew her Bentley would be bumping over those cobblestones the next day. The cons were a newly renovated kitchen that included vast quantities of whatever-were-they-thinking? marble and unfortunate wall-to-wall carpeting over the old parquet floors.

Janine and Mags were justifiably hurt at my refusal of their help with confronting my former Park Avenue residence. They had been my best friends since our childhood camp days in Vermont. But I really craved quiet (which I certainly wouldn't have with Mags around) as I relived the family history in my old home. Janine understood what I had in mind, but Mags was still pouting when I left (having refused the offer to stay in one of her guest rooms) to return to the comfort of a private women's club where I had taken refuge to adjust to my new reality.

So now I arrived to find Lauren, my older daughter who was still living at home, commanding the movers to "not touch this and don't even think of packing that, no matter what she says." Since the "she" in question was me, I had a few words with her before she stormed out in a trail of accusations, including that it was "all your own fault for being such a frigid bitch."

I calmed myself with the cup of tea that Greta, our long-time housekeeper (for whom I had brought the Godiva treats) tearfully brought me as I sat for a quiet moment in the living room.

I examined the room carefully, the over-sized oriental rugs, the elegant curving sofas, the regal chairs. I envisioned the room crowded with people, as it so often had been, attending the many fund-raisers and social events where I had played the smiling hostess.

Although I had gone there with the mindset of packing a Conestoga wagon—a "what should I take into my new life?" frame of mind—it was much harder than anticipated. I don't want all this, I thought, I want a simpler life. But there were the ancestral paintings, my great-grandmother's delicate drop-leaf side table, the Chippendale mirror, the small velvet settee, her pair of Louis XVI chairs, on one of which I sat. I rose and went to the grand piano that was carefully placed in a shaded corner. It had been my mother's and the one I had sat at as a child and labored my way through Chopin's easier *études*. I picked up one of the pictures proudly displayed on the dark wood. It was of the four of us at the Hamptons: Laurence, looking a bit arrogant; Lauren, scowling; my younger daughter, Christa, smiling sweetly; and a slender, pretty me. I shed tears over the family history that stood there in silver frames.

"Ma'am?" queried the head mover. I pointed out the piano and the pictures, then took the special tabs he handed me and tagged all the other items that I had brought into the marriage.

I paused in the spacious entry hall to direct them to a pair of large ornate vases and a long narrow ivory inlaid table that my great-great-grandfather, a sea captain, had brought back from China.

The dining room was so complicated that I decided to save that for last.

I ran my hand along the carved mahogany banister as I went up the curved staircase that led to the second floor. I paused to tab some of the paintings that lined the opposite wall, then went into the master bedroom. My throat tightened and my skin prickled as I looked at the big bed and thought about what had gone on there during and after my marriage. I put a tab on my great-grandmother's painted Pennsylvania chest, the only thing, other than the rest of my clothes, that I would take from that room. I went to the closet to get the clothes and saw red. Not just the favorite color red of Sherry—whose clothes were prominently hanging there in direct violation of the agreement Larry and I had worked out, while mine were squashed to one end—but the red of fury that the brazen insult awoke in me. I grabbed the pair of her fish-net stockings draped over my boudoir chair, tied them together at the toes, slammed Sherry's clothes into a compressed group, securing them tightly with the stockings, then with a mighty heave, lifted them off the hanging bar and tossed them into a corner. It was in this frame of mind that I headed for Larry's closet.

It took me a few minutes to find it, but there—hidden behind a swing-out shoe rack—was the safe I suspected the contractor had installed as part of a renovation Larry had designed several years before. The safe had a discreet lock; I had a very indiscreet and illegal set of tools—which happened to be in my purse.

I'm not sure why I went in there, certainly not to take anything, or so I told myself. But the anger that rose from Sherry moving her clothes in early—and from Larry allowing her to do so—propelled me back and forth with packages and boxes from the safe to the Pennsylvania chest.

I closed and locked the safe and put the shoe rack back in place. The movers were taking the chest away—along with my hastily packed clothes—just as Larry and Sherry arrived. I hadn't expected her to be with him. The sight of her tall, red-clad, silicone-enhanced body, of her peroxide-blonde hair framing a smug smile as she swanned around my home, among my things, with my so recently former husband, was too much to bear. I left immediately.

2

It took a few hours for the movers and me to navigate my belongings into my new apartment. The phone rang while I was giving the moving men their generous tips, so I didn't answer, afraid it was Mags wanting to give advice and ever so grateful that a social event kept her from being there. When the men left, I was starving, so I went to order a pizza. Before dialing the number from one of the several order menus someone had left near the phone, I pressed the blinking message light, expecting to hear from my friends. Instead, my former husband—the father of my two children—screamed: "You fucking bitch! I'll have your fucking knees smashed."

This, of course, alarmed me. I ran into my bedroom and opened the Pennsylvania chest. I opened one of the wrapped packages and riffed through hundred-dollar bills. There were a lot of packages. There were also dozens, maybe hundreds—I was too numb to record what I was seeing—of several types of bearer bonds.

I was scared. The man I thought I knew so well had secrets—at least one very big secret. Where did this money come from? Why was he hiding it, and what was he capable of doing to get it back? Laurence, I had trusted completely; Larry was a stranger and possibly dangerous.

One thing was certain: this treasure and I had to get out of there—and fast. I had just unpacked two rolling, hard-sided suitcases, which I repacked as fast as possible with the contents of the chest. I rolled those bags out of the apartment, down the hall and into the elevator, then pressed the express button to the garage level where I adrenalin-humped them into the trunk of my car. The elevator had stayed put, so I went straight back up for my purse and my still-packed overnight bag—advice I had followed from sane Janine: "Pack for the night—you won't be able to find anything." I hadn't made my new bed, which was good; I stuffed the new pillows, blankets and linens into the emptied chest. I hadn't shopped for food either, which was even better—the place didn't look lived in.

I took my overnight case and handbag into the hall, locked my door, then went to the elevator and pressed the button. As the elevator door opened, I could hear my inside buzzer ring. My heart was beating at attack level as I descended to the garage. I exited swiftly, then leaned in and pressed the express button for the top floor. If Larry got past the doorman, he wouldn't see that it came from the garage. There were certain advantages in not having an elevator man who knew all of your business.

The garage exit was at the far end of my building. I inched up to the edge of the exit ramp with my lights off and saw Larry's car double-parked at the entrance. I sat there, not sure what to do. The windows of his Mercedes were tinted, so I couldn't see if Sherry was sitting inside, but the fact that he had left the motor running suggested she was. If I tried to leave, she would see me. I waited, praying that no one else would want to exit the garage or that none of the doormen, scanning the security cameras, would send someone to investigate why a car was sitting there. Larry came stomping out of the building, slammed his car door and did a tire-screeching, light-running tear up the street. I waited until his taillights were well away before I turned on my lights and drove out onto the street. I made a right turn at the corner to head uptown and out of town.

3

It was late when I got to my cottage in Connecticut, which was nestled on a small peninsula on the lake with access by one road. Two small houses—remodeled fishermen shacks really—flanked the road's entrance, my cottage sitting beyond at the halfway point. Gil Cantway's house occupied the tip, visible only in late fall when the leaves are gone, but the others were never visible whatever the season.

I got the bags into the house quickly rolling the bigger ones into the bedroom while leaving my overnighter in the kitchen. I made a cup of tea, took some bread out of the freezer for toast with peanut butter, then sat at a small table in front of the unclosed curtains. I was quivering and exhausted but there was a chance that Gil, having seen my lights, might stop by.

After a reasonable time I rinsed my cup and plate, shut off the lights and took my bag into the bedroom. I closed the curtains, got ready for bed, then lay there trying to figure out my next move. I wanted a glass of wine. At that, my next move came to mind and I went to sleep.

4

I woke early in the morning, anxiety intact from the night before. I wrapped myself in a comfortable robe, had a Spartan breakfast and curled up with a book—waiting. After a while, Gil knocked, then opened the door when I shouted, "Come in!"

I put my book down slowly and looked at him with my biggest, saddest eyes. "Hi, Gil." I motioned for him to sit. He did so, in a manner that suggested he intended to stay for a while. "I needed to be in a familiar place." At this a few tears rolled, unbidden, down my cheeks. Gil sprang up and knelt beside me, offering me a handkerchief. I brushed him away kindly and used my napkin.

"Thank you, Gil. I'm okay, really. It's just been a hard time and I needed to be alone to get my head together." Then on impulse: "I moved into my new apartment yesterday, but I couldn't bear to stay there. So I came to the only real home I have left."

"Well," said Gil, "I know this thing has happened between you two. Laurence called this morning, asked me to come see if you were here. He still cares about you, for sure."

Bingo. I have to move fast.

"Gil, I really need some alone time. I'm just not ready to talk about it. It's kind of like when you lost Vivian and took off on that camping trip in the Rockies."

Gil nodded, cowed by memories. "I understand, Livie. God, do I ever understand. Is it okay if I call Laurence and tell him you're here? He sounded worried."

"I'm touched. Do what you think is right. I just need a few days before I start my new life."

"Can I make you dinner one night?"

"Give me until Wednesday, okay?"

"Right on. I'll barbecue some chicken."

"That sounds great," I said as I rose and saw him to the door. I had no intention of being there on Wednesday and even less intention of being there with him.

Gil had inherited his place from his parents, who bought it when he was nine and I was eight. We had played together through several summers. We especially liked to be pirates, paddling over to a small island that was part of Grandfather's original property that stood about a hundred yards off shore between our houses. My father had a paddleboat—a raft really, with a bicycle mounted in the middle—tied to our small back dock. We wore bandanas around our heads, our faces scarred and whiskered with our mother's eyebrow pencils. Under their watchful eyes we paddled to the island in our orange life vests with our lunches and some treasure to bury in the remains of a small stone house that sat in the middle of the island. Gil gave me my first kiss there—which I thought disgusting—and played doctor, which was even more so. I was glad to go to camp in Vermont when I was twelve, so my embarrassing budding breasts would not be the focus of his attention. Even in later years, when we socialized as families with his wife Vivian and their strange son Jason, I had felt uncomfortable with the way Gil looked at me.

"I'm headed into town. Can I bring you anything?"

"A quart of milk, some bread and the papers would save me a trip."

I waited until I heard his truck go up the road, then put on jeans, shirt, and sneakers and headed for the root cellar.

5

Even though my grandparents had owned an elegant brick townhouse on the east side of Manhattan, they loved their little hide-away at the lake. Originally, it had been my great-grandfather's fishing camp. When Grandmamma inherited it, she had enlarged and renovated it into a comfortable rustic lodge. After Grandpapa had retired from his law firm, they had increasingly left their townhouse in the care of the staff and spent most of their time here.

The root cellar was unknown to others; Gil and I never played there and my kids never discovered it. But as a small child, I spent time there with Grandmamma, putting away the fruits and vegetables she liked to grow and preserve from her garden, a spot long ago covered by the garage and tool shed.

My grandfather also used the small dirt-floored cellar to store wine, building special wooden racks into a back alcove. I was his helper as he measured the space and the wood, and so I knew there was an old storage bin behind the racks from the days when the house had a coal furnace. After my grandparents died, my parents remodeled the house and my mother reconfigured the kitchen. She had the big, old Philco refrigerator placed in front of the unused cellar door to keep sodas, beer and other bottled goods cold. Moving the Philco would have been impossible for me if it were not now empty, and if my father hadn't invented a caster slide to put under it, as well as attached pull straps that hung down out of sight. I now put those straps to use after shoving flat cookie sheets under the casters so no marks would be left on the floor.

I was able to move the big, old box forward enough to slide behind it. Since we never went down to the cellar, the door was painted shut. But a utility knife, carefully applied, opened it.

I've always feared cobwebs and spiders, but now I feared Larry more. By the faint light of an old bulb, I edged my way uneasily through nature's lace, draping the thicker clumps on nails or shards of wood.

There were still some forgotten dust-covered bottles in the wine rack. I removed them carefully and placed them on the dirt floor. Then I removed some of my grandfather's pegged shelves. Behind the shelves, sliding door panels from an old cupboard closed off the coal bin. "Never throw anything away, Livie," he had said. "You can always use it for something." *Thank you, Grandpapa.* The wood had warped some in its frame but with a bit of jiggling and banging I was able to slide a door open just wide enough.

I bumped the heavy cases down the narrow steps in two sweaty trips, all the time listening for a truck or telephone. I was tired and had to take a break, plus Gil would be coming back. I closed the cellar door, shoved the fridge back, picked up the cookie sheets and swept the floor before I washed the cobwebs and dust off in a quick shower.

The timing was perfect. When Gil knocked on the door, I was in a robe with my hair wrapped in a towel, which gave me a good excuse not to invite him in. I took the bag. "How much do I owe you?"

"No, it's on me." This was not good. Gil was notoriously close with his money. "We're on for Wednesday, right?" he reminded me. "Unless you feel like having drinks tonight."

"Thanks, Gil. This is going to be an early night for me, but Wednesday—barbecue—I'll be there."

I watched his truck go up the road. I did not trust that man. Was this neighborly kindness between old childhood friends? Or had Larry asked him to keep an eye on me.

I certainly did not trust Larry. The man who had wanted *to have my fucking knees smashed* was not someone I even knew.

I sat at the table and had part of a soda and a sandwich made from a can of tuna I found in the cupboard that I mixed with olive oil and onion powder—not a gourmet meal, but at hand and easy. Sitting down was not a good idea—I was almost too tired to get up. But sitting there turned out to be a lucky idea as Gil's truck came back down the road and pulled into the drive. He had forgotten to give me the newspaper. Now I really did not trust that man. Figuring there were no excuses left for him to return, I put my dirty clothes back on, put the cookie sheets under the fridge, pulled it aside and went down the steps to finish the job. It was dirty work but I was satisfied with the restoration after replacing the rack and wine bottles (sprinkling a little more dust for effect). I swished a rag over the dirt floor to cover any footprints, replaced what cobwebs I could, then removed the light bulb and edged my way up the stairs, dropping webs in place behind me. I shoved the fridge back, put the cookie sheets on top of it and made a dash for the shower. I took time to blow-dry my hair, just in case I got more company. My dirty clothes went into the washing machine in the mudroom.

I was spent and needed quiet time, so I took the rest of my soda out to the front deck and sprawled in one of the lounge chairs. Some boats went past, probably on their way to favorite fishing or picnicking spots. Several circled in front of the big house across the inlet from me that had sat empty and for sale for two years. I watched them as I thought about the loot I had just hidden.

6

Larry's parents, James and Willa Lammond, had made their money in real estate. Not big-time Tishman or Trump money, but enough. From what I understood, Lammond Holdings had begun as a small company owned by Willa's mother who had died when Laurence was a child. James had become the head of the firm and built a respected business. While both participated in the wheeling and dealing, Willa kept tabs on the finances, and Willa may have been keeping more tabs than James knew about.

Laurence, along with his brother, Charles, were expected to take their families to James and Willa's for Sunday lunch every week—that was on command—and it pleased James to have this time with family. Willa tolerated this excess of flesh so she could spend time with Laurence, her clear favorite at the table. At some point, Willa and Laurence would disappear into another room for a short time. I wondered what private words were being exchanged and assumed they were about me, clearly her least favorite person at the table.

A number of times over the years, we had stopped in at James and Willa's palatial apartment while on our way to an event so Laurence could drop something off. The *something* was usually a large envelope from Willa for a smaller one from Laurence. Willa would immediately disappear into her bedroom. One time I followed her while Laurence was on the telephone. I got as far as "Willa, could I..." before she hissed at me to "Get out!" I did, but not before glimpsing Willa in her closet, on her knees, opening a metal box. I asked Laurence about the box and the envelopes. He made light of it as a private thing with his mother, inferring that he was humoring her in a little family quirk.

James was the first to go. When Willa died three years later, Laurence left the hospital before I did. I thought he had rushed home to comfort Lauren and Christa, our daughters, but when I got there, they were with their nanny. Laurence arrived later carrying two obviously heavy satchels. He mumbled something about needing to wash up, and went upstairs to our bedroom. Later in the week when I took a new housemaid through his dressing room to show her where to put the dry cleaning, I saw the bags covered with a jumble of shoes and clothes at the back of his closet area. I told the maid we needed to straighten out the mess. When we pulled things aside, I saw several of the metal boxes in one of the opened bags, which gave me an uneasy feeling. I ushered the maid out of there, telling her we would get to it later, and put everything back the way it had been. Shortly after that Laurence complained about finding a moth and said he had arranged to have his dressing room and closet custom built so he could keep things in order. I later found the empty satchels in our luggage closet. I wondered, of course, but I was the good wife who loved and trusted her husband. *Then why did you look for that safe?* a little voice whispered in my head. Had I been deliberately blind to who that husband was?

7

By now it was late afternoon and there was more work to do. I found a brush and some Elmer's glue in the junk drawer. I squeezed some glue into a paper cup, then mixed in a few drops of vanilla extract until it almost matched the color of the paint on the old door. I moved the fridge forward, just enough to squeeze behind, then brushed the glue around the door. If someone tried to open it, the door would seem to be painted shut. If someone did open it, I would know. With my last strength of the day I pushed the fridge back, then wiped the somewhat dented cookie sheets clean and put them back in the cupboard. I checked for any suspicious marks on the floor, then swept and mopped it thoroughly. I wrapped the light bulb, brush and glue cup in plastic wrap, put that in a paper bag, the bag into the kitchen trash and the wrap and utility knife back in their drawers. The place was spic and span, not a mark or a trace of dirt to give away what I had been doing. The washed clothes went into the dryer. I took some leftover pasta from the freezer, sprinkled it with garlic powder, and put it in the microwave. I sprinkled more garlic powder and oil on two slices of bread and put them in the toaster oven. That aroma would overpower any trace of glue smell. I poured a scotch and soda, sat down and thought. What the hell am I going to do now? I had to be in some kind of danger, but what?

Larry knew, or thought he knew, that I had the money. Larry would want it back, but how could he get it? He couldn't go to the police for obvious reasons—the main one being an explanation of why he had so much money hidden in his closet. This prompted two big questions: First, why did he have so much money hidden in his closet? While he'd brought metal boxes from Willa's, there seemed to be more of them now. And, second, where did Willa get so much money in the first place? This was more than just a little family quirk. Whatever she had been doing, Larry had been part of it and had apparently continued doing it after Willa's death. Whatever that was, it was probably illegal and that meant dangerous in some way. And in every way dangerous for me.

I felt vulnerable, exposed, unarmed, though the drink began to settle me down. I got up and closed all the blinds and curtains, then turned on the lights. This time last week I had been preoccupied with starting a new life. Now I was concerned about keeping the one I had. This was not a position a fifty-four-year-old Park Avenue matron ever expected to occupy. This required a plan. I mixed another light drink to have with dinner, although I would have preferred wine, but there was none in the house. Well, there were some vintage bottles in the cellar, but... I cleaned up my dinner dishes, then sat back in the big chair and thought.

Willa was the key. She had been the dominant one in that affluent but emotionally deprived household. James had come from an old New York Scottish family of almost boring respectability—a family that had once numbered in the dozens but had dwindled down to Larry and his younger brother Charles. Charles and his wife Alice had moved to Pennsylvania and I couldn't remember when he and Larry last spoke or saw each other.

Willa seemed to have sprung from the earth. In retrospect, I couldn't remember any of Willa's family or any talk about them. There was not a single picture to record her history. How strange. How much stranger that I was only now thinking it strange. Something important was missing, I needed to find out what, and that probably meant a visit to Charles and Alice.

A vehicle went past slowly. Was that Gil's truck? It seemed to pause by the drive, then go on.

8

I woke early, an uneasy feeling urging me to consciousness. Hangover? No, I'd had more soda than scotch. Alone? I had often been here alone. Laurence hated the cottage. A wooden lodge on a small isolated finger of a lake was too ordinary for his taste. He preferred to rent big houses in the Hamptons for the summer months, which usually enticed the girls, and therefore me, in that direction. But this was my house, my history, and I made sure the girls spent time here as well.

I had always been keenly aware of my personal space, my *soul's sphere*, as I had once described it to Mags, to which she had succinctly replied: "That's crap." Crap or not, I had a vague feeling of having been invaded as I threw the covers back. The feeling persisted as I filled the kettle for morning tea and put it on the stove.

"Shit!" I limped to a chair and took a sharp pebble out of my bare big toe. I rubbed the spot; lack of blood does not mean lack of pain. When the kettle whistled, I limped to the stove, turned it off and stepped on a clump of dirt. My mind played a rerun of how very thoroughly I had swept and mopped the evening before. I had come into the house only once, in leather-soled Ferragamo flats. True, Gil had been in the room twice, but I had cleaned after he left. My *soul's sphere* went tingling in its orbit.

Someone has been here.

This sent me reeling to my chair in the kitchen nook. I paused there, stunned. Then I got up and looked carefully around the big open space of the combination great room/ dining area. The big stuffed chairs, the leather sofas, the various tables and lamps all seemed to be in place. The TV, the old silver teapot were still plainly in sight; my purse was still on the counter. My purse! I got up and opened it, half hoping to find my wallet missing— that would make it a simple robbery. But it was in there, money and cards in place. So was my phone. I looked at that more carefully and realized it was not the way I always put it in—with the screen side out, so I would be more likely to see the light and remember to turn it off when I didn't need it. The screen side was turned inward.

I'm in trouble here.

Finally, I forced myself to get up and make toast while my tea brewed. I was spreading strawberry jam when Gil drove up. I hurried to get a robe and saw myself in the closet mirror. My uncombed blonde hair fanned out into a morning halo. My blue eyes, sans makeup, were not as sparkly as they had once been. The body I tied the fleece robe around had grown a little more ample. Fuzzy, that's what I've become—fuzzy. Sherry probably wore Victoria's Secret. Or maybe she got Larry with Frederick's of Hollywood—L.L. Bean versus the strip mall.

Gil knocked louder. I went to open the door and had to turn the lock. It did not turn easily—It was at half-mast. The heat of fear went up my neck. Anyone who had a key to the house knew that you made two clicks to the right when you locked it from the outside or the inside knob stuck half way. It was one of those tricks that makes houses interesting. Someone had a key who did not know that trick. That someone was not Gil, who had a key and did know and who now stood at my opened door.

"Everything all right?" asked Gil.

"I had to get a robe."

"Going to town. Need anything? The paper?"

"Thanks. I'll reread yesterday's, it's always the same." I forced a grin. "Did you come by last night? I went to bed early, but I thought a car stopped. Might have been part of a dream."

"No, I didn't. But, come to think of it, I was up late reading and thought I heard a car around your part of the road. Somebody probably got lost coming for the weekend."

This is Tuesday. "We know how often that happens," I said brightly. "I have your cell number if I think of something. Right now, I'm going to have a long hot bath."

Gil perked up at that. "Maybe some bath salts and a back rub?"

I hadn't realized that I could be appalled and flirtatious at the same time, but I also realized which one was to my immediate advantage.

"Gil, you are a bad boy!"

Gil liked that.

"Now get out of here before there's trouble."

Gil reddened happily, smiled mischievously, and left.

I put on my slippers and walked down the driveway. I paused, pulled a few weeds, spread my arms, inhaling deeply. Anyone watching me might think I was having a *Top o' the Morning* moment. Anyone close enough would see that I was examining every inch of the terrain. I went to the end of the driveway and opened the mailbox, thankful that there were some junk fliers. I took them out, stretched, looked left and right, and tried to take in everything. Then I took off my slippers and walked on the grass at the side of the driveway, shuffling and seeming to savor the feel of the earth. I tried to zero in on every stone. Squinting and focusing, I thought I could see tire marks halfway up the drive coming and going. "Get a grip, girl," I told myself. "You will see what you are looking for. You drove in, Gil's been here, how many times? You, Sherlock, are not seeing anything." And yet... The driveway had been newly graveled just weeks before—I had paid the bill—so there should have been two different tire tracks: mine and several of Gil's very distinctive studded brand, but there was that other. I could also see footprints from the halfway point.

I did not run back to the house. I sauntered to the beat of my heart, sure there was a sharpshooter in a tree somewhere with my Bergdorf Blonde head in his crosshairs. I closed and locked the door and sat at the table in shock. "Ohmigod, ohmigod, ohmigod," I whimpered. I had to get out of there and back to where there was some possibility of protection.

I cleaned the place up—made the bed, washed the dishes, put them away—just as I would do normally. I was about to empty the milk down the drain, then thought better of it and put it back in the fridge. That would give me an excuse to have Gil come in. I wanted the place to seem accessible, just as usual. Packing didn't take long and included the kitchen garbage, which I stuffed into my overnight case. I put that case into my trunk, went back for my purse, then closed and locked the door, standing in such a way that the little key trick couldn't be seen. Paranoid? Yes. Scared? For sure.

9

My new building provided parking options: the garage beneath, where I could drive in using an entry code, or valet parking. I chose the latter because 1) I wanted to get better acquainted with the staff and 2) I wanted the staff to get better acquainted with me.

Ricardo, the head doorman, greeted me.

"Any luggage, Mrs. Lammond?" he asked as I handed him my key.

"Yes, there's a suitcase in the trunk." Ricardo gave the key to Bob, his assistant.

"You have some mail and two packages. I'll have Bob bring them up with your luggage."

"Thank you, Ricardo." I headed toward the elevator.

"The telephone repairman was here yesterday," he called after me. "The super took him in. Hope everything's working now."

I stopped and turned. "The telephone repairman?"

"Ah…yes." Ricardo seemed unsure. "You called them about a problem? He had a work order."

"Oh," I managed. "Sorry, it slipped my mind."

Ricardo looked relieved, assured he hadn't done anything wrong. He went up a notch in my trust meter. I smiled at him and continued to the elevator.

I lingered by my door, fumbling with the keys until Bob brought the suitcase and mail.

"I need to get some of those coded key-covers, this gets so confusing," I said helplessly as I opened the door.

I had Bob put the case in the master bedroom and the mail and boxes in the kitchen. If there were intruders, Bob would encounter them first, which I admit was not fair to Bob. He left and I went carefully to the nearest chair and sat down.

I had to observe. I had to think. I had to breathe. Breathe! I wasn't aware of holding my breath until the first one sent me into a coughing fit.

What was the so-called telephone repairman doing here? Who sent him was obvious. That this intruder was a professional was also obvious. Larry was hiring professionals to dissect my life, my whereabouts, and possibly even me.

"Holy crap!" as Mags would say. "Give this gal a drink!" Which I wanted more than anything at that moment and which I wasn't going to get until I had observed every speck of the apartment.

I am a trained observer, you see. My training took years and it was a harsh program.

10

Lauren, my first-born child—the corn-silk yellow, July-sky blue, tea-rose pink, heartbreakingly beautiful darling—had, over what seemed like a few minutes, but which had encompassed her high school years, segued into *Lotus*, a pierced, tattooed, black tatter-garbed and chipped-polish pot-head.

From the start, I was an enabler—a word the rehabbers love to aim like poisoned arrows at parents. But I was chump change compared to Laurence's Golden Eagle.

Oh Lordie. *Laurence=Larry*, as *Lauren=Lotus*. I really wanted a drink, which is probably not the correct mind-set when one is talking about an addict.

Addict-Daughter Lauren. In defense of parents—no, in defense of me, since Laurence had so neatly removed himself from this orb of sorrow—it began so subtly, the change was so gradual. Remember, we are talking teenage girl here, first born, no template.

"Oh, it's her hormones banging around," said Janine.

"As long as she isn't banging around," replied Mags.

"Come on, girls, I'm her mother. I need help here."

It took time, too much time probably, for me to realize that she was stealing from me and for sure from Laurence. Plus when she asked—no, demanded money from him for whatever implausible reason—he handed it over without question, as long as it wasn't more than twenty-five dollars.

That, to him, was exercising responsibility. But he was so distracted with whatever distracted him that he didn't keep track of how many times he gave—at home, at the office— and did not think it necessary to report those gifts to me.

Lauren also had fingers of silk tipped with Velcro. They could slip into the pockets of any jacket or pants hung within reach and come out satisfied. One day I came home by cab and the driver gave me a five in change. He made a point of telling me to check the numbers and watch the 10 o'clock news that night, when there would be a prize drawing to match numbers on five-dollar bills. I smiled, thanked him, and forgot about it. Then a floral delivery arrived. Lauren slipped past me and out the door as I went to get the tip from my purse—the five dollar bill I knew was there, wasn't.

Parents, mothers especially, want to see good in their children. We know they aren't always good, but without the bad how can we show them the difference? We are not, by nature, objective, otherwise it would break our hearts. In our heart's eye we always see that baby whose entire universe transfers from our wombs into our arms, onto our breasts, in whose unfocused gaze we are the world. A mother watching her large, scarred, snarling killer of a son being led to the gallows still has that baby gaze imprinted on her heart.

I went into her room with the intention of tossing it, but got control just in time. I stood inside her door and observed everything. Her room was a mess, but she knew where everything was in that mess and that included evidence. The entry door slammed and Lauren returned.

The thought was like a thunderclap: She just bought drugs with the money she stole from me. That was the introduction to Observation 101.

11

But I was here now, sitting in this chair, and just as thunderous was the thought: My phone has been tapped, and possibly more than that. What if there were cameras? They would observe me sitting there, observing.

I did a total head-turning look around the room—nothing. But there should be nothing left by a pro. So then I did a Sarah Bernhardt (Do people know who she is anymore? Do people understand that phrase? It does imply something more operatic than Meryl Streep would let slip.) Rewind. I did a sad, resigned survey of my living room, ending in a prolonged sigh, then drew myself up regally and went to the bar.

Perrier in hand, I went to the telephone. I did what would be expected.

Mags answered with: "Where the fuck have you been?"

"Mags, I'm hurting."

"Oh, excuse me, Duchess! You're hurting? Does it concern you at all that my head could not get off the pillow until noon because of worry?"

"Mags, you use any excuse to get soused."

"Oh! Well! Any excuse! I will take that into consideration when my blood sister next falls off the earth."

When Mags and Janine and I were at camp in Vermont, we snuck out of our cabin one night when there was a full moon. We cut our fingers with an old pen knife and pressed our blood into each other, pledging sisterhood forever. If parents knew what went on…

"I could not stay here. I had to go somewhere to pick up my stitches."

"The cottage?"

"Where else?"

"You've recovered?"

"Not exactly, but I came in here and sat and just looked around *(cameras recording?)* and you know, this could be okay."

"Okay?" she screamed. Mags lived in a Fifth Avenue apartment with rooms she had never even seen. "You have been thrown in the trash! It's your own fault. I know it is! Men worship one god and it sits between their legs. Once you stop paying homage—"

"Mags! Stop! I have no food and I'm hungry."

"Well, you had a cook before."

"Mags, please stop."

"Out, or in?"

"I don't care."

"Have you called Janine?"

"Just about to."

"I'll call her. Just get here."

I hung up, then, possible cameras in mind, did what would seem natural. I pressed the button for messages. There were several: Mags, screaming twice; Janine, loving and concerned; one from Christa, my sensible, caring child; none from Lauren and none from Larry. Either I had imagined Larry's threatening message or it had been erased.

***

Janine was already there when I arrived at Mags, which made me suspect that she had already been there when I called. They squeezed the breath out of me in a group hug, then settled me with a glass of champagne.

"Have you heard from the asshole? Aka Larry the Liar?" asked Mags.

"Cut it out, Mags. Just leave her alone," said gentle Janine.

"Well, I never thought he had it in him."

Janine, less gently: "And you certainly are the voice of experience."

Mags was on her third marriage, with several *almosts* in between. The first, which I understood was the love of her young life, had died; the second vanished after being a long-term guest of the state; and the current, Mason, was an elegant, cynical, fun-loving homosexual who adored her bad mouth and good taste. They loved to dance and raise hell, making them the life of every party. They also loved to spend money and Mason had pots of it, both inherited and made. Mags was in the privileged position of being able to say and do whatever she felt like saying and doing. Large amounts of Mason's money and his long lineage insulated her against insults given or taken.

Mags had no half ways. If she hated you, you'd better watch your back. And if she loved you, she'd watch all sides of you like a mother grizzly. For a few precious hours I could feel safe.

"When are you going to tell us everything?" asked Janine finally.

I choked on my bubbly. "What do you mean?"

Janine just looked at me. "I thought so."

"Livie wouldn't keep anything from us."

Janine smiled, "Until she's ready to tell us anything."

My mind was in a whirl, I wanted so badly to tell them. It would be so comforting. But, on the other hand, if I were

---

in danger, could I put them in danger too? Would that be fair?

"I'm working something out."

"You're working what things out? What the hell does that mean?" shouted Mags.

Which was another reason I hesitated to share just now. Janine could be discreet, but Mags would show up tomorrow in trench coat, beret and dark glasses with two goons in tow. Give her a role, any possibility of a role, and she would out-Sarah Meryl.

"I'll tell you more next week."

"When next week? I need a day." Yes, I thought, to get her costume ready.

I picked a day. "Tuesday."

Janine rushed in for the save. "Tuesday is fine. Should we meet at your place?"

"No!" That was probably said too fast. They both looked at me, startled. "No, could we meet here? Mags always has food."

"Not to mention a cook," she said drily.

I hesitated about saying anything else and thought about it during dinner. The apartment had a private elevator vestibule and as Adolpho, the elevator man, was closing the door when I was leaving, I put my hand out to pause it and said casually, "Uh...if you call me this week...don't mention anything important. Keep the conversation light."

They were speechless just long enough for me to say to Adolpho, "Down, please—fast."

Mags screamed, "Stop! Tapped! Her phone's..." Adolpho, used to Mags's outbursts, didn't even blink and took me to the lobby.

12

When I got home, the phone light was blinking repeatedly. I thought about Dorothy Parker's *What fresh hell is this?* and considered waiting until morning to aid a good night's sleep, but knew I would think about that blink all night.

It was Larry. The voice was light and overly polite. "Olivia..." He made my name sound like a regurgitation. "There are some personal items of mine missing. I wonder if you could have packed them by mistake? Also, you seem to have taken the social telephone book. We would like to start entertaining and that information is not easily available. I could have a messenger pick the items up at your convenience."

Because I was speechless, I sat down and laughed. No, I roared. I howled, until I gasped for breath. Sherry needed my address book so she could invite my friends to my former home, to dine off my china, using my silver, and drinking wine out of my crystal glasses.

I gave the high middle finger all around for the cameras. Then god, I couldn't help it, dropped my drawers and gave the full moon too.

Sleep was not going to happen.

When I bought my address book at one of the *special clients only* sales, I had purchased three of them with the intention of giving two for gifts but had only given one away. I dug the other one out of a box.

It was a busy night.

I made myself comfortable in my bathtub with pillows and blankets and a glass of wine, hoping that no one had dared to put a camera in there.

From A to Z, I duplicated my old phone book. Well, not exactly duplicated—*fabricated* would be more accurate. I had a special code system—little checks and ticks—that only I could decipher. I particularly made sure that all the ones with two small zeros were included—minus the zeros—as those were the people Laurence had especially disliked. Some prime names I eliminated and others were doctored a bit. Under the *Mr.* and *Mrs.* lines in my book I had added the names of wives and any nicknames for all parties. That line for each entry was the most fun to alter—and the place to do the most damage.

After finishing this masterpiece, I spilled a few drops of wine here and there in the book. Then I wet the bottom of the glass and put it down on various pages and turned the corners down or up to make it look used.

It was late, but so what. I called Larry and, thankful that no one answered, left a message saying that I would leave the book in an envelope with the doorman. Also, I did not have anything of his, but there were a number of things I had been too upset to pack at the time, but would like to have now—such as my china, silver and crystal.

In the morning I called Gil to apologize for having to cancel our dinner because a very important meeting had been rescheduled. I had been looking forward to his special chicken, but would he be a darling and take the milk out of the fridge, as it would spoil. He said he would be "very happy to do anything for me" in a tone that I found creepy. The snoops who were listening could not be happy with such a lame conversation.

They certainly had more fun with the next one. Sherry called and left a message. (I thought it was Larry and, having no desire to talk to him, did not take the call.) Sherry informed me that they would appreciate getting the telephone book as it was, after all, communal property. She also requested that I not call so late, especially after I had been drinking, as she was being very careful about Larry's health, considering all he had been through. She added that I had ample opportunity to take what I wanted from "their home," and that time had passed. I should get on with my life and let them get on with theirs.

13

I did have a very important meeting, only the man I was meeting wasn't aware of it.

Women of a certain age are invisible in New York City. Unless we are among the super-rich, super-talented, or super-scandalous, most of us can go incognito as ourselves. It was a gray, drizzly Burberry day, one meant for slacks, trench coat and slouch hat, which I dressed in just like a thousand others. Then, avoiding the front entrance in case someone was monitoring my exits, I slipped out of the garage and headed up the block to the corner where, miraculously, a cab pulled up to discharge a passenger. I jumped in seconds before a man index signaled the cab and then middle-fingered me. I directed the driver to a destination on the lower West Side, halfway up the block on a one-way street.

"Do you want to make an extra five dollars?" I asked.

He did.

"Just sit here with your light on for one minute before you leave." I gave him the money, exited the cab and didn't look back. Sometimes you have to trust that the honesty of the earth rubs off on some of its inhabitants.

I walked back down the block, looking for any car that had made the same turn into that small street, then turned the corner and headed toward a building with a small brass plaque on its door reading COMMUNICATION SOLUTIONS. Smaller letters underneath cautioned: BY APPOINTMENT ONLY. I rang the bell in the required sequence and was buzzed in through the outer door into a small interior foyer. I could sense Sandy, the receptionist, looking at me through the security camera before she came to open the door. She took my purse, coat and hat and put them in a special closet in the inner foyer, then scanned me with a handheld device. When nothing *pinged*, she led me through the inner door.

Sandy went to a credenza. "Would you like black or green today? Roger will be back in ten minutes."

After we had settled ourselves with our tea, Sandy asked cheerfully, "Is this a problem or trouble?"

"Trouble. My phone's bugged, I think my apartment has eyes, and I might have been followed."

"Oh, this is fun. Roger will be so happy to see you, Livie. In the meantime, would you mind if I finish these reports? We have a rush case."

"Go ahead. I'll see what's new in Soldier of Fortune."

Sandy smiled and resumed her work. Sandy's smile, I might add, contained a few gold teeth. That, along with all the metal implanted in her body through piercings or interior hardware to repair motorcycle mishaps, would make it difficult for her to go through any security unnoticed. But then, under any circumstances she could not go unnoticed. She was a big girl—six feet at least—and brawny, not fat, but with muscle and sinew that would break the tooth of a dinosaur. Her hair was bright red and spiked; her wardrobe seemed to consist of black leather, studs and spikes. Her footwear was usually platform biker boots. It was hard to tell her age, but I knew she had to be in the middle part of life and, unlike the rest of us who fade into the scenery, Sandy chewed and spat it in your face.

While I flipped through the pages, I though of Roger and how we had met.

14

Pot brought us together. My daughter Lauren and Roger's son Marc had been almost constant companions during the start of her dope days. I first thought he was her dealer, then realized he was just her stoner buddy. Lauren tried very hard for me not to meet Marc, but I am smarter than she is and just as devious. Plus, I was sober. So I finally got his real name, which was not *Magnum P.,* as she had wanted me to believe. As the result of many careful forays into her room I had found, mixed in with all the mess of a user, the stems and buds, papers, spit cups and roaches impaled on toothpicks, Marc's home address and phone number. I called that number and Roger answered. When I identified myself, Roger immediately invited me to his office for a talk. He gave me an address that sounded strange for an office, but I found it and that was the first of many visits.

After apologizing for bringing me to this not easily accessible place, Roger explained that his wife was in the final stages of cancer and he didn't want her to know about Marc's problem, as she had only a few more months to live. There would be time afterward, before school was out, for Marc to go through his initial grief, and then Roger would take action. He asked me to go along with the plan. I agreed.

He knew who their dealer was and assured me that he had someone monitoring them as much as possible. I was to keep watch at home, and we would meet at a coffee shop on 10th Avenue in a week.

We had a number of those consoling sessions at the coffee shop and at his office. At one of those meetings I came into possession of my set of lock picks—along with a detailed lesson in how to use them—so I could find all of Lauren's hiding places. Only then did it occur to me to ask Roger just what he did for a living.

"Oh," he laughed, "when people get into trouble, I get them out."

That satisfied me at the time.

15

Roger would not be called a handsome man. His face was pitted from what must have been raging teen acne. He was square built, sturdy but not fat, of medium height and with a head of hair so thick that even with a buzz cut you can barely see his scalp through the gray-flecked black. He walked with a slight limp and, in truth, looked like a thug, but there was a confidence and kindness that emanated from him that made him not as scary as he might otherwise appear.

Now, when Roger walked into the office, I felt relief.

He was a little surprised to see me. When Sandy pointed to the security closet, he took me into his office and closed the door.

We sat looking at each other. I started to cry. He came around the desk, gave me some tissues, put his arm around me for a brief hug, then sat me up straight in the chair. "What?"

I started to tell him, trying to edit out the good part. He put a finger on my nose and pulled it away, indicating a Pinocchio moment. So I began at the beginning and told everything, including the cobwebs and the tracks in the gravel.

Roger's face had hardened at the beginning of my story. When I finished he seethed, "He said those things to you?"

I had a moment's glimpse of a Roger who was not so kind.

"And then it was gone."

Roger went back behind his desk and buzzed Sandy. "Get me Al," he said.

Roger turned to me. "Now, Livie, this is important. Tell me, as close to the minute, when you left the apartment and exactly in which order you took down the suitcases."

I closed my eyes, visualized, and recounted my two trips, one with the cases, the other with my purse and overnight bag. I panicked for a moment over the time.

"Wait! I looked at the clock when I was going to order the pizza and the message light was blinking. It was 6:20!"

"Good girl." His phone rang. "Al, got a job, need it quick. The security cameras at…" He gave my address and the apartment I lived in. "Monday night, probably around 6:30. You'll see a blonde lady, very attractive," he winked at me, and I swear to God I blushed. "There were two trips. I need the first one erased. And, Al, see if anyone else took a look."

"Sit tight," he ordered as he left the room. Sandy soon brought in my coat, hat and purse and put them on a chair.

Roger came back in. "It's the phone. Pro job, not the best work, but he hired a pro, the guy's serious."

I had suspected it, but still, when you find out for sure that your privacy has been invaded, it is scary.

Roger took a sheet of paper from the fax tray. "Draw your apartment layout, including closets, bathrooms, everything. And don't forget the windows and doors."

Since I had so recently labored over that task, trying to figure out what would fit where, I was able to do it fast.

"I want to get a guy in your place today. Was the carpet new when you moved in? Your stereo system work? Need curtains? Blinds? These are all shaky ways to do it, but since you just moved in, we can work with something here."

"Unfortunately the carpet is new, but I don't have curtains yet, just those god-awful venetians."

"Excellent! That gets us into every room. Now, I'm going to throw in a kicker." He looked at my layout sketch. "Your dining table is here, right?" He pointed to a spot in front of a bay of windows.

"It will be, I don't have it yet."

"Get with it, girl. Go shopping!" He grinned at me. "What about the living room?"

"There's a long, narrow Chinese table against this wall." I drew my great-great-grandfather's treasure on the plan.

"That should work. If there's a camera, it should take in all of that. Leave your purse on that piece. When the guy asks for a glass of water, go to the kitchen and take your time, we're going to bug your phone again."

"A bug on top of a bug?"

"Yeah, it'll be crawling in there. Throw them into a little spin. They won't know who's looking for what. I'm giving you this other phone that's clean. This one's blue, so you won't get them mixed up. After the curtain guy leaves, go into the bathroom, she'll make sure it's not bugged. Then call me."

"She?"

"Yeah, her name is Elizabeth."

16

Roger's "guy" worked fast. An hour after I got home, Ricardo rang up to announce Elizabeth's arrival. She was a central casting decorator: young, pretty, hurried, harried and lugging large sample books and a big tote bag.

I took her coat. Underneath she wore one of those leather fanny packs that fat people like to wear hanging down their bellies, usually slapping against their crotches with every step of their sandaled feet. Only hers was Prada and held a large tape measure. Elizabeth spread her books on the kitchen counter and we discussed fabrics. I rather liked several and got excited about the possibilities, until I remembered that she was one of Roger's guys.

Elizabeth went to take measurements while I continued to peruse the sample books, making notes on little slips of paper.

She called me into the living room, where we had a discussion about ruching. Then she asked for a glass of water. I went to the kitchen and got "distracted" deciding between two samples, before remembering what I was there for and got her water. By then, Elizabeth was measuring in the bedroom.

"Have you had enough for today, or do you want to look at more fabrics?"

I held my hands up in surrender. "Enough. I'm overwhelmed by this!"

"Okay," she laughed and led me back to the kitchen. "I used the toilet in your master bathroom, hope you don't mind. The faucet splashed a bit when I washed my hands, but I cleaned it up."

"No problem. I drenched myself this morning."

Elizabeth said she would write down the pattern numbers and price codes so we would remember what had appealed to me. She would call tomorrow with the estimates.

I looked at the paper after she left. "Eyes and ears: bathroom—no; everywhere else—yes. Run water in bathroom when calling."

I felt like throwing up.

I held myself regally as I walked through the crowd of onlookers in my half-furnished apartment. In the bathroom I had a satisfying pee, washed my hands, wiped my shirt where the faucet sprayed me, turned it to low, then called Roger.

"I'm going to a hotel."

"No, you're not. You'll stay there until I know who's looking at you."

"It's Larry."

"Never assume. He's at the top of the list, but we don't know who's at the bottom or in between. And don't go fingering and mooning anymore, that gives them too much. No, wait! Better yet, have a drink and do it again. Do it all the time, they'll just think you're hormonal."

"Roger!" I screamed. But he had hung up.

I left that phone in the medicine cabinet.

17

I had a few bottles of my favorite champagne in the fridge, so I opened one of them. If Larry was watching, he would know I hadn't been reduced to Night Train.

I called Janine.

"Hi," I said, knowing she would detect the uneasiness in my voice.

"Hi, my friend." She, at least, would have the sense not to be hysterical, or worse, Mata Hari as Mags surely would.

"I left messages. Didn't you get them?"

Thank you, Janine. The perfect opening.

"I had such an unpleasant message from the Larry/Sherry duo this morning that I haven't listened to any since. Would you believe he asked for my social phonebook so they could start entertaining?"

I poured some more champagne. What the hell. Live it up while I was still alive.

"You didn't give it!"

"Why not? I'm not going to host dinners for thirty in this place. I don't even have a dining table. Sherry wants the china, the crystal, the silver, and the people who go with them, and you know what? She's welcome to them."

"What are you doing?"

"Drinking champagne."

"I'll bring Chinese."

"Does that include General Mags?"

"No, they're at the museum shindig."

"I'll unlock the door right now. If you see my prone body on the wall-to-wall, I'm not dead, I'm just absorbing my new reality."

I called down to the front desk and authorized sending Janine up.

In the meantime, I took a shower, dressed myself in sweatshirt, pants and a pair of socks, grabbed some pillows from the guest room and tossed them on the floor, then lowered myself onto the living room carpet, plastic glass of champagne at the ready.

Janine walked in, stepped around me and went to the kitchen. She moved like a deer, head up, graceful, serenely beautiful. Her coloring even matched a doe: light brown hair, dark grey eyes. Several times she had been approached by modeling agents who had seen her walk into a room or down a street, but Janine could never assume that dead-eyed vapid look of the runway model—she was too interested in life and all that went on around her. She came back with her own glass. "That marble has to go and your hair looks like hell."

"Thank you blood-sister—there to count on in my darkest moments."

She took my glass to the kitchen and refilled it. "How long do we have to drink to get through this? My liver is more leathery than it ought to be."

"I'll try to keep it short."

"Maybe that's the answer to the hair—short, spiked."

"You don't spike Bergdorf Blonde—that's a color you know, not a destination."

She sprawled beside me face to face. "If you had a freebie spree— Bergdorf, Bendels, Saks, wherever you chose—what would you choose?"

I turned onto my back on the wool carpet, scrunched a pillow under my head and looked at the ceiling. A brass chandelier hung above me, one with such a pleasing patina that it would be a crime to polish it. I visualized the Waterford glowing down in my previous two-story entryway and thought about the to-do caused by the cleaning of its twelve arms and dozens of hanging crystals. This light above me now did its job, did not demand attention and, best of all, my physical or mental time. It just was. I lifted my head to sip and in the process observed what extended down from my neck: comfortable sweatshirt, pants, and socks. True, the sweats were TSE cashmere and the socks were from Paul Stuart—ones I had swiped from Laurence's drawer long ago. Perhaps I should mail them back with a note: "Are these the items you're missing?" But, sweats from the Gap wouldn't need to be dry cleaned, nor would their socks need to be hand-washed—luxuries I no longer wanted to think about. "You mean luxuries? Things I really don't need?"

"No one has ever walked through the doors of those establishments to get what they really need."

Did I mention that Janine and her husband David are psychiatrists? They have heard the dirt, disgust and desperation of most of Park and Fifth Avenues. Many people have tried to bribe and imbibe them into indiscretions, but they hold their booze like Episcopalians and their secrets like Sicilians.

I was mindful of the eyes and ears around us. I was in the unusual position (aside from being slightly tipsy on the floor) of the possible need to protect the professional integrity of my dear friend.

"Anything?"

"Anything."

"Well, I was in Saks a few weeks ago in the linens department. There were these sheets, Egyptian cotton—something like 5000 count. They felt like silk. They were delicious. And a silk comforter, all in a wonderful pinky-peach color. They were *are you kidding?!* expensive. I would get those."

Janine sat up and sort of smiled at me. "You would get sheets?"

"They were really special."

"You could have a fur coat, a diamond something, a designer gown."

"I'll take the sheets."

Janine leaned over and patted my cheek.

"What?"

"Nothing. Just thank you for being the girl I always knew."

The phone rang. An obviously disguised voice said, "Is the coast clear?"

"Mags," I sighed. "Where are you?"

"Downstairs."

I put the phone on speaker and handed it to Janine.

"The doorman won't let me up without the password."

"Just get on the damn elevator," instructed Janine. "I'll call down."

This will be interesting, I thought, trying to act normal with Mags in high drama mode. But then again, she was in some kind of mode at all times. I would have liked to ask Janine about the many hours she had spent listening to Mags's dreams—what a hair-raising movie they would make—but I knew she would deny ever doing that, as technically treating a friend would be frowned upon by her fellow professionals. But Mags would never share her secrets with anyone else: for all her flash and fury, she was painfully closed-in with her emotions and what I had come to suspect was her abused childhood. She only trusted Janine to even touch upon that, because Janine had known her when her nightmare was a reality.

The door banged open.

"I came as fast as I could."

"And why is that, dear?" said Janine. "Is the place on fire?"

"I sensed you needed me!" she said breathlessly, dropping a package on my chest as she stepped over me, heading for the kitchen. "Is that champagne?"

I sat up and opened the package, recognizing Bergdorf's lavender wrappings, and took out a pale peach satin night gown and matching robe. "Mags," I gasped, as she came back in, frowning at her plastic glass. "These are gorgeous!"

"We're throwing all your nightgowns and underwear out. I don't want you wearing anything The Liar ever touched."

Janine just raised her eyebrows. She had already surmised that Larry hadn't touched me or anything I wore in quite some time.

Mags shrugged out of her sapphire satin coat, looked around for a place to put it, and said, "When the hell are you going to get furniture in here?" Then dumped it on one of my Louis XVI chairs. She sat on the floor, fanning a strapless sapphire gown around her. The color, I noted, was stunning on her with her slightly olive skin, dark eyes and her shiny dark hair artfully piled on top of her head. Mason probably choose the gown and would never have let her ruin it with the current fashion of hair hanging down with that "just out of the shower" look. Besides, it would have tangled in the dangling diamond and sapphire earrings that perfectly complimented her diamond and sapphire necklace.

"The museum party must have been a dud."

"It was okay," Mags said. "Mason met someone interesting, so I thought I had better rejoin the unit."

Mason and Mags have, what is for them, a perfect understanding. If one of them finds someone "interesting" at a function, the other discreetly disappears, and they are each very proficient at finding "interesting" others. Because they are truly devoted to each other and intend to stay married, it saves them from messy situations. Mason isn't hounded into being a *walker* for every dowager in town and Mags, on occasion, is free to abandon herself to whatever temptation suits her.

"You haven't hung your paintings. There's no place to hide anything!"

Uh oh, I thought.

Again, Janine, thinking on her feet while lying on the floor, pointed out: "People only hid gold certificates behind pictures. If you had one now you would frame it large. It could be worth more than a Warhol."

Mags popped up. "I need to examine the walls. See where someone would put a bug."

I handed her my glass. "Open the other bottle while you're up, and if you see a bug, hit it with the newspaper."

The mention of more champagne was enough to sidetrack Mags for the moment. Janine and I looked at each other and I knew that she knew and she knew that I did.

Mags came back with the champagne and reached for the phone. "I know what to look for," she whispered as she started to examine the casing. "Do you have a screwdriver?"

"I'm hungry," Janine announced. "Let's eat. I have to leave soon—early appointment tomorrow."

We elbowed and kneed our way up. We sat on stools around the marble island top, first covering it with tea towels after Mags proclaimed, "It would be like eating off vomit," then made a production of dining on paper plates with plastic utensils.

"We are going shopping tomorrow," said Mags. "I will pick you up at ten, we'll open and close the stores." By picking me up at ten she meant that her chauffeured Bentley would be downstairs at eleven or twelve. "Eating off this stuff is indecent, not to mention how un-green it is."

Un-green? I was surprised that Mags, whose carbon footprint could obliterate Rhode Island, even knew this word.

We nevertheless managed to slurp down a quantity of food apiece, Janine setting the pace. She rose after what seemed a surprisingly short time.

"You don't mind if we leave you with the dishes?" She smiled and pulled Mags's arm. "Your car is waiting?"

"Of course." Mags surveyed the shambles. "No cook and paper plates! Your world will come to an end without my help. Tomorrow at ten sharp, and god—that marble has to go!"

I cleaned up after they left with the help of a large plastic bag. My carbon footprint felt gigantic.

18

Since the only room I could use that offered comfortable furniture (a bed) and a distraction (the TV) was the bedroom, I turned out the living room lights and went in there. I remembered the eyes watching and took my new silk nightgown into the bathroom to change and wash and brush up. I was wiping the faucet splash off my face and gown when a phone rang.

It took a few rings for me to realize that it was in my medicine cabinet. As I turned the faucet on gently, I determined that the medicine cabinet was not the best place to keep anything secret. Mags could tell you the contents of every cabinet on Fifth and Park. "If you really want to know someone, look in the medicine cabinet and bedside table drawer." I had to trust her on that.

"Hello." I could have added "Roger" because who else had the number?

"How you doing?" he said.

There was something in those few words that told me I should be asking him that question instead. So I did.

There was a pause.

"Oh, I'm okay," in a tone that indicated he was not.

Then I remembered the month and day.

"Your anniversary."

"Yeah." Too long a pause. "I'm okay—most of the time, but there are a few days…"

I threw a pile of towels on the bathroom floor to sit on and leaned against the marble bathtub.

19

When his wife Katie had died, I didn't hear from him for weeks. Then he called, brushed aside my condolences, and said it was time to move into the next step of intervention with our children. We made an appointment to meet at his office. Sandy had gone on an errand, so Roger let me in. He was as contained and controlled as a grenade with the pin pulled, but went right into the outline of a plan for Marcus and Lauren's recoveries.

"This isn't a phase, you know. They won't get over this on their own. They don't need to—they'll just con their way along until they're dead or on the streets. They are addicts, and addicts just become worse addicts, left to themselves."

He didn't look at me. He was wrapped in himself. I went around to his side of the desk. "Roger." I took that rough face in my hands and made him look into my eyes. "You know addiction." He tried to look away. I tapped him on the nose, and he looked at me and smiled. Then I watched as that impenetrable face crumbled and the tears worked their way through that moon-rocked landscape. "I know it from A to Z." He pulled away, turned away, and swiped at his face.

"Me and my buddy Zane were kids. We were wise-ass punks looking for trouble—making trouble. We didn't know each other, were from different worlds, but we were separated at birth you could say. We both ended up in Nam because two judges gave us the same choices about where we could spend our time. The state owned our asses and they sold us to the army—it was cheaper than keeping us behind bars.

"We were addicts when we went in and addicts when we came out. There's no way to describe Nam to someone who wasn't there. Drugs? We were in the middle of one of the drug centers of the world and the Congs made sure we had easy access. And Zane and I...Zane and I..." He paused.

"We had been fingered as the bad guys—the disposables—so we were sent into the tunnels. That's when I first learned how to listen. We weren't the fireworks guys, we just crawled through that hell and planted ears so the brass could hear movements. I'm claustrophobic, or was. I was locked in closets as a kid. Those tunnels...those tunnels..."

Roger lifted his head and I saw the terror, the desperation and futility in the eyes of the boy he had been.

"There was no way that I could do that without the drugs."

"How did you get clean?"

He let out along sigh.

"Zane and I got out around the same time. We got on our motorcycles and tore across the country. We did some bad things. There are some people still hurting from what we did—and those are only the ones I remember...most of the time we were stoned crazy. Then Zane's brother Cal did an *intervention*, I guess you would call it.

"Cal and Zane grew up in a biker family, and Cal was the leader of one that cops from border to border wanted to erase. Cal had enough of our shit. We were causing too much trouble. So one day his crew circled us and made us drive into the desert. We were stoned and thought it was cool, so we went along. Then they stripped us, took our bikes and left us.

"Then it got cold. We needed a fix, we needed warmth, we needed water. We needed... Whatever we needed wasn't there. We were naked, shaking, cold, hungry. We were more miserable than we had been in Nam. And we were angry. We howled and cursed at Cal and his gang, then at each other. It got dark. We crawled into some brush for warmth. The next days were Dante's rings of hell, even though things appeared: sleeping bags, jugs of water, some bread, cheese and apples. But we needed the drugs. We puked and shit streams until there was nothing left. I was delirious at one point and dreamed someone was wrapping me in blankets, then pouring water down my throat. I don't know if it happened.

"One day I woke up. I was under a tent, protected from the sun, and I was clean—I had been bathed. My clothes were folded beside me. There was a jug of water, a thermos of chicken broth and a packet of crackers. Zane was gone. I learned later that Cal had taken him away, got us away from each other for our own safety—you don't hang out with your user-buddies when you get clean. It took a while for me to get dressed, drink the soup, eat the crackers. Then I walked around the tent and there was my motorcycle, cleaned up and gassed up. The tent folded small, so I packed it and rode off into my life. I have never told this to anyone or cried since. And I have never smoked, sniffed or injected another drug."

"Where did you go from there?" I asked.

"I had an aunt in Brooklyn who'd tried to help me once, years ago. Aunt Maddy was the only person I could go to, so that's where I went. She fed me and let me sleep for a week, then told me I had to go to school or get a job. We talked about it a lot, because we both knew I could never sit in an office. One afternoon fire trucks and sirens came down the block, so we went to see what was going on. There were cops and a few of the firemen standing around a burned-out car, and we got to talking. A couple of them had been in Nam and recognized that I was drifting. They said I should get into one of their programs. One of the fire guys asked if I'd been in the tunnels. When he saw the look on my face, he told me to go to the cops because sometimes you feel like that when a building's falling around you. "You're either okay with it or not," he said. "You probably had enough."

"So I ended up being a cop. I did undercover and surveillance: the undercover got me a bullet, a limp and an early pension; the surveillance got me a lot of good contacts and this business."

20

"Hey!" Roger said. "You still there?" I snapped back from that day in his office and re-adjusted myself against the cold marble. "I'm sorry, I was drifting. What did you say?"

"Lauren hasn't called you through all this." It wasn't a question. It was a statement of fact.

"No, I'm still the enemy," I said, squirming around on the towels and wishing I had dragged in one of my two chairs.

"One day she'll realize you saved her life."

"Then one day I'll stop hurting. How is Marc doing?"

Marc was one of the lucky ones whose first intervention would also be his last. Unlike Lauren. Lauren supposedly got clean, but it took four interventions and a judge's order to do it and left her bitter and holding me responsible for the mess of her life.

"Hard to believe he'll be a doctor, if everything goes right, that is."

"Roger, sometimes you just have to trust the process."

"Yeah, trust. Right. Speaking of trust, that Mags is too loose a cannon; I don't trust what she'll let fly. Maybe you're right about going away."

"You mean a hotel?"

"No, that would look fishy."

"The cottage?"

"No. *Away* away. My instincts are thrumming— something doesn't feel right."

"Your instincts?"

"Yeah. I'd be dead by now if I didn't trust them."

"Okay. But why not the lake?"

"You're going away because your apartment is being papered, painted, decorated and whatever." I didn't ask what *whatever* meant.

"Do I get to choose the colors?"

"Elizabeth will take care of it. You'll like it."

Yes, but will Mags?

"And the cottage?"

"You need electric work, security system."

"Oh. I need to call Gil to give him a heads up. Also, there's a broken knob on one of the kitchen drawers—and don't forget the island house."

"Livie," he laughed, "my guys don't fix knobs or do windows."

"Oh," I said. Then, *"Ohhh,"* when I realized what he meant.

"What island house?"

"The cottages, mine and Gil's, are at different ends of a little peninsula, more like a thumb sticking out in the water. Halfway between there's a little island with an old fishing cabin, about a hundred yards offshore. We used to camp there as kids."

"Island. Gotcha. We'll stick with the house. Okay, where will you go?"

"I've been thinking about visiting Larry's brother and his wife in Pennsylvania. Charles is a really good guy, but he and Larry didn't get along so we didn't socialize much. I miss him and I have questions about Willa that I hope he can answer."

"That sounds okay. Take your blue phone and call me every day to check in. Leave the other one in your kitchen."

Every day?

"Can I give this number to the gals?"

"Janine, not Mags, and tell Janine to call only if she needs to. You can call whomever you want, the number won't show and a fix would be scrambled. Does Charles know you're coming?"

"Not exactly."

"I take it that's a no. Call him now, then call me back. Let him know you want to keep it private."

I re-arranged my towels again, stretched my aching back, then did just that. Charles was glad to hear from me. "Bring your riding boots," he said.

When I called Roger back, he answered with, "A car?"

"Yes, I have one."

"Don't get wise-ass. If we're trying to stash you for a week, it would be dumb for you to drive your car."

"Oh."

"Give me the info on where Charles lives and how he lives."

I did.

"That sounds like SUV country."

"Oh yes, and the muddier the better."

"Okay. Here's what we'll do…" He outlined a nifty little switch.

I packed small ("Very small," Roger had said, "you're not going to a prom.") into a garbage bag. At 10:30 the next morning I put the bag outside the service entrance door, certain that one of Roger's guys would transport it to the car. Then I left, wearing my riding boots under my slacks and took a cab to Saks. I entered through the uptown side door, then walked through the store, pausing at the La Mer counter to buy eye cream. I examined purses and gloves at a few other counters, all on my way to the door on the opposite side of the store where I exited and got into an idling, dusty Ford Explorer. I noticed a garbage bag sitting on the back seat. The driver headed west, made a few side street turns, then got out. I slid behind the wheel and got out of Dodge.

21

After maneuvering through the city and tunnel, I kept an easy pace on the Jersey turnpike. I was deep in thought about what was happening to my life, but the exit for the Pennsylvania turnpike got my attention and brought me back to the present. I was suddenly in a different world. Taking exits that led me onto ever-smaller roads and through smaller communities, I began to regain a feeling of well-being.

Charles was so glad to see me that he didn't notice the garbage bag he carried. Alice did, but just hugged me and said, "I think we'll have some interesting talks by the fire."

They settled me into a bedroom—cozy, low ceilinged, the deep walls rounding into very old windows, with a fireplace and an armoire for a closet. Not having a boot-pull, I hauled off my tall riding boots with much effort, with possibly the beginning of hiatal hernia—and a vow to have zippers installed. I pulled a pair of slippers from the armoire where they were lined up in several sizes under hanging bathrobes beside a stack of quilts.

The fireplace crackled in welcome when I joined Charles and Alice in the library. I was soon seated, sipping a glass of wine. "This is such a welcoming house," I said. "Christa had a wonderful time when she visited you. A restful time, I might add; she works such long hours at that law firm."

"And we are so glad that she got that job in Philadelphia and can come here for a weekend now and then," said Alice.

"And Lauren? What is she doing now?" asked Charles.

I could tell from his voice that he really meant: "What is she up to now?"

"Oh," I said vaguely, "she's living with Larry and Sherry."

Charles coughed into his hand and looked away.

"We're so glad you came to us," said Alice. "Charles was afraid you wouldn't."

"Why not?"

"I thought you might clump me in with Laurence," he answered. "Like a family unit."

"It never occurred to me."

"Good. I distanced myself from all that long ago."

Before I could ask about "all that," a door slammed open. The dogs began barking wildly and a voice shouted out, "Tally Ho!"

"Oh God," said Alice. "The fox is on the chase tonight."

"Where are you?" the fox bellowed, then stomped into the library. "Smelled the fire. Where's the scotch?"

Charles greeted a tall Ichabod Crane figure with a manly hug, then introduced me to Travis Johnston. Even though our friendship was five seconds old, he wrapped his arms around me for a squeeze, before moving on to Alice.

"Have you eaten yet?" he asked Alice. "I could eat the horse I came in on."

"Travis," Alice said with a straight face, "would you like to join us for dinner?"

"Oh, hey, don't want to impose, but thank you, yes. What's cookin'?"

"You'll get what you get and like it."

"Sounds delicious," he said, turning to me. "As delicious as this little lady looks."

"Out of bounds, Travis," said Charles.

I just laughed. This funny-looking brash man did not intend to offend.

"Why are you hiding her here?"

I was startled at that but settled down when Charles said, "She just now arrived."

"You bringing her on the hunt tomorrow?"

That startled me even more. "No!" I answered. "I haven't ridden in years."

"Aw," said Travis, "it's like falling off a bike. It comes right back to you."

"I presume you mean it's like riding a bike. My last memory of falling off a horse is still painful."

"You can stay in the back with the hill-toppers. You won't have to jump much."

I had no intention of jumping anything, let alone tearing up hill and down dale in pursuit of the ever-elusive fox.

Alice got up from her chair. "Olivia, would you give me a hand out here? These men must be starving."

As I followed her out of the room, Travis bellowed, "Yes, starving for affection."

"Don't mind him," Alice said in the kitchen. "He is one of the gentlest, kindest men on earth. He has seen us all through breaks of bone, spirit and heart. Do you mind if it's a kitchen night? We're just having a stew."

"Perfect. I'll set the table."

"So," said Travis, after we sat down and had paused for a simple grace. "I'm a Quaker," he explained, "place is crawling with us. What brought you out here?"

"I wanted to visit my brother-in-law and darling Alice."

"You're married to Charles's brother?" Was that disappointment in his voice?

"I was; no longer am."

He turned to Charles. "How come you never talk about this brother?"

"I don't really like him."

"Well, can't choose your family." To me, "Guess you didn't like him much either."

"Not once I got to know him."

"How long did that take?"

"Thirty-one years."

"Good! Dumb and blonde, just the way I like 'em."

Even I had to laugh.

The talk was light and mostly funny through the rest of the meal, even though a lot of the local humor went over my head. Travis rose after dessert, looked at his watch, and whistled a bar of Hi-ho, Hi-ho, a-Hunting We Will Go and to my surprise said, "Time to turn in."

We all walked him to the door, where Charles also said his good nights and went upstairs.

Alice sensed my surprise. "There's a hunt tomorrow, so we get up early. I'm nursing a pulled groin muscle, so I won't be riding, but we can follow by car if you like."

I told her I would. We cleaned up the kitchen, then sat by the last of the fire with hot chocolate.

"Alice," I began, not quite sure how to begin, "I have some questions about Willa…"

Startled, Alice asked, "What kind of questions?"

"I don't even know!" I tried to tamp down my exasperation. "Something strange has been going on and I think Willa is the Mother Lode…so to speak."

Alice sat staring at the embers of the fire. She was obviously uncomfortable, which made me even more curious. After a few quiet moments she said, "Charles has told me everything, you know."

"About what?"

"About the business."

"What business? The real estate firm?"

Alice leaned forward in her chair and stared at me. "My God, you really don't know."

"Know what, Alice? What are you getting at?"

She sank back and sighed. "This is a conversation you need to have with Charles."

"About what?" I persisted. But there was nothing more from Alice on the subject.

I didn't know what to think. As Mags would say, "My brain's on Mixmaster setting." I won't sleep a wink was my certainty.

22

The cool, country air had other ideas. I woke to Alice's sharp knock on my door. She poked her head in. "If you want to see any of the hunt, throw your jeans on. I've got coffee ready."

I splashed water on my face, brushed teeth and hair, slid into jeans, boots and fleece and met her downstairs.

We took the Land Rover, the Jack Russells in the back. Wanda, her fuzzy little Norwich terrier, snuggled on my lap as Alice, via walkie-talkie, pinpointed where the hunt and the fox were headed. We talked about the hunt, the hounds and the countryside, as she explained who was doing what.

"Most people don't know this, but fox hunting is the oldest organized sport in America."

"Not baseball?" I said in surprise.

"No," Alice laughed, "that came about a hundred years later. Farmers used to meet at each other's places for a week at a time to hunt. They did it to protect their small livestock and fowls—the fox loved the eggs and the chickens, whichever they got to first. Plus, when they got over-populated, the foxes tended to get rabies, which then spread to other animals. The farmers—George Washington was among the first—continued to thin the fox population, and following the social and hospitality conventions of the time, the hunts took on their own formality."

The dogs, other than Wanda who just wanted to cuddle, yapped with excitement at all that was going on. They clearly thought they belonged out there in the middle of the action. Alice explained that in past years, they did.

"In the past, Jack Russells' main purpose was to go down into holes and force out burrowing animals, especially foxes, to kill them or make them available to be killed. They were used in the hunts until the 1950s, but now are just farm pets. These days the foxes are rarely caught, the sport being about the chase and running them to ground. By far, most of the foxes killed now are from being hit by cars."

Alice paused as she negotiated a particularly challenging turn on the dirt road.

"In whelping season," she continued, "the mothers will go out to find food; that makes the babies particularly vulnerable. Mothers sometimes don't come back, so the hunt staff scouts out the dens to make sure the babies have a mother to care for them."

"Look!" I shouted in excitement. "Over there on the hill!"

Following my finger, she saw a beautiful red fox sitting near the crest of a hill—waiting.

"Why is he just sitting there? Why doesn't he run and hide?"

Alice laughed. "Because it wouldn't be fun. He wants to play the game."

At that point the hounds came pouring over a fence in front of us, crossed the road, then wriggled under a rather high fence on the other side.

The riders followed, jumping both fences. Near the front was Travis, his huge bay horse soaring easily over the rails. Charles wasn't far behind on a beautiful gray. The hounds were running around in circles, noses to the ground.

Alice laughed, "Look at that chaos! Mr. Fox must have run back and forth to leave a lot of scent lines. He's up there laughing."

And indeed the fox sat there, watching the show. One of the riders spotted him and shouted, "Tally-ho!" Just then, what seemed to be the lead hound picked up the scent and started up the hill with the pack following in full cry.

"That's Brandy," said Alice of the hound. "She and Mr. Fox are old acquaintances, they've run miles together." Instead of taking off at the first bay from Brandy and the pack, the fox stayed until what seemed like the last second before streaking across the field towards the woods. "Oh yes," laughed Alice, "he's looking for a good game today!"

"Will they catch him?" I was worried. I liked the fox's attitude.

"I would not bet against him," replied Alice, "that's for sure. He'll lead them on a chase through the woods. If they get too close or he gets tired, he'll go into a hole where the hounds can't get to him. The huntsman will blow *Gone to Ground* on his horn and it will be considered a victory for the hounds, who will be praised accordingly. Mr. Fox might come back out after he's rested, to stir things up again."

I watched Travis and Charles tearing up the hill and on into the woods, jumping a fence to get there. The rest of the field seemed to number about eighty, with some not so nimble of hoof and fence. We saw several "ouch" moments when horse and rider did not begin and end the jump together. Most of those riders got up, brushed themselves off and remounted their recaptured horses. A car or designated medical vehicle picked up the others.

We went to a hunt tea at the conclusion of the day's run where, after several explanations of being the ex-wife of a brother no one seemed to know Charles had, I just became *Olivia, family friend.*

When we were back at the farm and Charles was steaming out his creaks in the hot tub while Alice was planning meals in the kitchen, I went to my room and called Roger.

"Guess you're having a good time," he answered after two rings.

"I'm having a time. But there is something strange that I hope Charles will explain to me this evening."

"Yeah. I'm picking up a few things here too. By the way, you had termites at the cottage. Not too bad, we did the first treatment. Nice place, I did a little fishing."

"Termites?! Is the place going to collapse?"

"No, trust me, there won't be a bug within miles when we get through."

Sometimes I am so dense. "Oh...oh, good."

Hmmm...Roger had been up there fishing...for what? In the cellar? I was just learning how trusting and "dumb" I had been. There was a stash of money involved, and money is something that can change the best of people. I wanted to hide in the wonderfully comfortable bed and pull the comforter over my head.

"Roger, I'll call you later."

23

I woke to the aroma of a country fireplace in use, along with a hint of perking coffee. The latter pulled me downstairs into the kitchen where Charles was pouring himself a cup of the fresh brew. He looked up, then poured another one for me. "Alice is out marketing," he said. Then, looking like a boy at the cookie jar, cut two pieces of strudel, put them on plates and beckoned me to join him by the fireplace in the library.

We ate the strudel, drank the coffee and made small talk about the hunt. Finally, Charles leaned back in his chair, stretching his legs. "Alice said you have some questions."

"Charles, I don't even know what to ask."

"Olivia," he said gently, "you can go on living with the memories you have. You don't need to know more."

"Yes, I do!" I said, perhaps too quickly.

He sat quietly, looking at me. "You're in some kind of trouble, aren't you?"

"Some kind of."

Charles frowned. "You didn't, by any chance, find something when you were moving out? Perhaps you included that something with your personal items?"

My silence was loud.

"You are in more than *some kind of trouble*. Laurence is not the nice guy you think he is. He is ruthless and a degenerate, just like our mother."

"Willa?"

"Yes, Willa. This will not be easy for me to talk about."

"Then don't, Charles. I don't need to know."

"I am afraid that you do, mainly so you'll know why you should be afraid. And the fact that Lauren is living there and possibly involved...well, you're her mother. You've protected her for years, I don't see you stopping now."

This was not a promising beginning. I pulled a knit throw over me for protection. Wanda jumped onto the settee, then nestled into my lap.

"James, our father, was a very shy young man who had no success with women. His father, certain that James was a virgin, arranged a—shall we say *date* for him—to take care of that problem. That was a fairly common practice in those days, for a father to arrange his son's initiation into the mysteries of sex. What was not common was for the young man to fall head over heels for his teacher, which James did. The teacher was Willa."

This made me sit up and gape. "You mean she was a...a..."

"A whore? Yes...she was. She was also the daughter of the madam who owned the establishment—a very exclusive one, I might add."

"Charles...I'm...I'm so sorry." I didn't know what else to say.

He just laughed. "You know, people like to throw around terms, like *you bastard* and *you son-of-a-bitch*. Well, in the animal world I believe I am not the former, but I certainly am the latter."

"You can joke about this?"

"Livie, what can I do? I can't change anything. I can't blame my father for his honest feelings. Willa is another story."

"What did your grandparents do? They must have been…shocked?"

Charles pursed his lips then let out a whoosh of breath. "That's a mild way of putting it. They were very Scottish, very conservative and keen to maintain the social status they had worked so hard to reach. They also loved their only child and wanted his happiness, along with grandchildren. They sent James on a trip to Scotland to visit relatives with hopes that he would find someone there to transfer his attentions to."

Alice came in. "It's over the yardarm somewhere. I think we could use a drink."

Charles got up to pour.

Alice brought in a tray of easy food, and I sat there like a bump.

"Willa—a hooker?" I repeated. I could not grasp that.

Alice pursed her lips and nodded gravely, which told me that she had grasped it long ago.

"Hooker," said Charles, "is not really the term for Willa. She didn't go with just any customer, or many for that matter. She was a very high-priced specialist. Her mother, the respectable sounding Mrs. Martha Morgan, widow, kept Willa available for a very select, very small clientele—namely, gawky young innocents like my father—with the hope that just what happened would happen. Martha had high hopes for her daughter. Willa, in addition to being a beauty and very smart, was quite well educated, and not just in the ways of men."

I had to get up and walk around. I had to move to shake the shock that was gripping my mind. When I collapsed back into my seat, Charles continued. "James came back from his trip determined to marry Willa. His parents had to accept that or have a forever-bachelor son and no grandchildren. They invented a background for this seemingly genteel young lady and introduced her into their social circle. Willa, with her exquisite manners and gowns, had no trouble taking in those gullible people and was welcomed as James wife.

"Her mother Martha was rich and savvy. Hers was a cash business and she used most of that cash to buy property—especially derelict buildings at tax sales. She set up several small holding companies and bought cheap in areas that weren't attractive to others. She was ruthless in her acquisitions and hold-outs had a way of disappearing. Martha could see where the more refined sections of the city would need to expand and over the years she came to own a chunk of that space."

"Did James know this? I can't believe he knew this." The image of that gentle man being involved with that sordid life seemed impossible.

Charles sighed, got up and paced around. He ran his fingers through his hair, blew out some air then said, "He knew. It was the price of love.

"James was made president of one of the holding companies Martha had started. This company gradually bought out the others until it had substantial holdings. Not prime real estate at first, but James and Willa were a good business pair."

"There was also that steady stream of cash from Martha," added Alice.

"Oh yes," Charles laughed softly. "The Stream. That was handled by Willa, who turned it into a river of bearer bonds, E Bonds, jewelry and whatever could then be sold and the money diverted into brokerage accounts. Willa had a knack for picking good stocks. They became quite wealthy, and at that point, it would have been impossible to prove it wasn't all legitimate."

"But, when Martha died," I said, "There was no one to…how to say it? Run the business."

Alice laughed cynically. "Willa wouldn't let it go. Enough was never enough for her. She ran it herself."

I was beyond speechless at the very thought of Willa—

"Not quite by herself," Charles added. "Obviously the respected Mrs. Lammond couldn't hang around there; she had to have an inside partner. Someone to keep the girls in line and collect the money. A madam. But there could be no one like Martha—It had been her place and all the money was hers—she went through a string of hired madams who did not have the same point of view, so there were problems.

"One day a man came to Willa with an offer—from an organization that did not accept refusals."

I jumped up, Wanda tumbled to the floor. "Ohmigod! This is too much! You're making this up."

"No, Olivia—it sounds like a *B* movie—but I am not making it up. They would be her new partners in the business. Willa didn't have a choice. She demanded to get her share weekly, so every Wednesday a lady came for tea, which lasted just long enough for Willa to count the money and grill the girl about business. She also periodically sent one of her investigators in to check out the flow."

"And speaking of flow," Alice interrupted, "do you need a break, Livie?"

I did.

When I returned, Charles had freshened our drinks.

"Shall I continue, or have you had enough?"

"You can't stop now!" I said. "This is just mind-boggling. What about James?"

"My father ran the real estate company which grew to be quite substantial. Laurence, as you know, went into the business right after law school. I also went to law school, intending to specialize in real estate, but changed my mind."

"Why," I asked him. "Why did you change your mind?"

"I couldn't work for our company, and there was no way I could be in real estate law and not do that."

"Why not?"

"Well, for one, no other company would trust that I had their best interests in mind when I represented them against Lammond Holdings. The other reason was," Charles paused, looked down, seemed embarrassed. "While our company was well respected with James at the helm, once he was gone I would be sharing it with Laurence. He and I did not agree on just about anything. And no matter what he promised at that time about getting out of the *side business*, I didn't believe he would."

"I'm missing something here."

"Laurence continued Willa's business."

24

The human brain is the body's regulator and protector. Its neurons cushion the shocks that come with life and give us those few seconds for recovery. Otherwise, the streets would be strewn with unconscious people clutching their cell phones. I experienced that short pre-storm nothingness before managing to gasp, "You're saying…he was running a…a whore house!"

"That's what I'm saying."

I felt like I'd taken a blow to my solar plexus. My husband—the father of my children, the respected lawyer and company president who had sat at the head of my dining table, where we entertained numerous friends and people from the upper reaches of society—ran a whore house on the side. Did the profits from that business pay for those dinners and that dining table? For my children's schools? For my shoes and underwear?

I looked at Charles closely. Did he have some bizarre sense of humor that reveled in extreme pranks? This was just not possible.

"This is not possible," I said. "Laurence could not have been doing those things. I would have known, or suspected something. I can't believe you, Charles. I just can't. I accept that Willa was what she was, but Laurence—no."

"Olivia," Charles said gently, "the key word here is *was*. I saw Laurence in New York a few months ago, we had lunch together. He swore that he hasn't been involved for years."

But where did that money come from?

Charles sighed. "I didn't want to tell you all this, but if he wasn't telling me the truth, then you've done something that could put you in danger. And Lauren is still living there—that really concerns me."

There were tears now, silently rolling down my cheeks. "You're telling me that everything about Laurence was a lie? That my whole life with him was a lie? That I am the stupidest woman in the world? That…" Lauren was still living there! My stomach took another blow.

Charles leaned forward to put his hand on my arm. "You are not stupid, Olivia. You were just too innocent to imagine that Laurence was anything other then what he told you he was. He had learned a lot from Willa, but he wasn't just her student, he was her moral clone. If you had known Willa's history when you sat at her very proper Sunday lunches, would you have taken your little girls there?"

"Certainly not!"

"Laurence was as good at that part of the game as Willa. And like her, I don't think he is capable of real interest in anything that doesn't fill his endless need for more."

"More of what?"

"More of everything," said Alice. "Laurence could never be satisfied."

"But, that just isn't true," I protested.

"Let me put this in a very basic, simple way," said Alice. "How many dinner parties have you arranged where he would take the last chop, the biggest potato, the heaping portion, no matter how many others were at the table, and no matter how many portions he'd already had?"

I had arranged hundreds of dinners, both business and social, although it was sometimes impossible to separate the two, and I squirmed as I remembered some embarrassing moments.

"Well, he has a big appetite."

"How many times did you move? From one luxurious apartment to an even bigger one?"

"He's in real estate?" I said, more as a question than an answer. "It was part of the business." But I remembered, even as I said it, telling Laurence that, under no circumstances, would I move again. I obviously had not foreseen the current circumstance.

"Willa directed those moves, Livie," Charles said gently. "Laurence was her marionette to manipulate into having the life she always wanted. When she told him to marry you—" Charles stopped, pale and stricken.

"She *WHAT!* Willa told Larry to…to…"

"God, Livie, I'm sorry…I got so wound up…"

Alice sat beside me and took my trembling hand. Wanda, who had resettled herself, seemed to sense my shock and began to lick my face.

"Laurence did love you, Livie. Remember, you had all those years together."

I pulled my hand free. "That's the wrong thing to say, Alice. All those years because Willa…Willa told him to…to marry me!"

Charles said quickly, "He wanted to anyway. He just needed Willa's approval."

"Willa's approval! Like he was buying a tie or a new shirt?"

Alice stood and paced in front of the fire. She stopped and looked at Charles, then me. Charles face tightened. "I think from now on we need to be honest about everything." She sat back down beside me. "Willa chose you for Laurence: You were from the right kind of background, beautiful in a classy way, from a well-to-do family—but not so rich that you could control Laurence; and you had just landed a job at a top advertising agency. You were starting your career but had not gotten so deeply in to it that it couldn't be put aside. You were made to order."

I felt like pulling my hair out and scratching my face.

"Do you remember how you met?" Alice continued. "You were presenting an ad campaign for that new Lammond office building."

"Yes." I flashed back to an eager young me, with my sparkling new Magna Cum Laude in English. Real estate was not one of the sexy areas in advertising then, but I was thrilled to have the opportunity to *show my stuff.*

"Willa saw you and told Laurence to introduce himself. Then she found out everything about you…"

"And I was invited to join in all the meetings and go to industry dinners…"

"…where Laurence was seated next to you, or at the same table. It was only a matter of time until the very handsome Laurence and you became an item."

He was so good looking then, he had taken my breath away.

"How do you know all this?" I demanded, stroking Wanda like a security teddy bear.

"Because," said Charles, "when my father knew he was sick, he asked me to take him fishing. We sat in a boat in the middle of a lake and he told me the truth about everything, including things I had already suspected. He also told me how blindly in love he had been with Willa and the blind eye he had turned to her neurotic need for ever more money and what she did to get it. But he always knew what she was up to.

"He had worked hard to build a good company and was sorry that I didn't want to be part of it, but he understood. He had known he was dying for some time and he wanted to be fair to me and to Laurence. He couldn't break the company in half, but there were two prime commercial buildings which he owned outright." Here Charles paused. "You did the ad campaign for one of them."

"He and Willa had decided to put those two in my name, and if I agreed, the buildings would be left to me while Laurence would inherit the company. Laurence thought I was a fool, but I sold those buildings at the top of the market and invested the money well. Keep in mind," continued

Charles, "I was also a partner in a New York law firm, so we would have been fine with that alone, but the rest let us retire early and well."

The blue phone vibrated in my pocket. For a moment I didn't focus on what it meant. Roger, calling me.

Uh-oh, this could not be good.

25

"What the fuck did you do?" yelled Roger as I was adjusting the pillows on my bed. "You'd better call Janine right now! Call me back." Slam!

I called Janine—Mags answered. "What the fuck did you do? Doo-doo is what you are in."

Janine took the phone. "What did you do?"

I was at a loss—I wasn't even there. "I don't know what you mean."

Janine enlightened me. "Sherry sent out invitations for a dinner party for twenty, and it's the laugh of the week. Annabelle Trowbridge being addressed as *Bella!* Even she cracked a smile, or so rumor has it, though no one can actually say they witnessed the event."

"Oh."

"Oh! *Oh?*" Mags again had the phone. "That's not what you'll be saying when they pull your nails out and stick the hot iron up your…"

Janine took the phone back. "Where are you? Never mind, it might be safer if we don't know. It might also be best if you stay there for a few more days, let things cool down. What exactly did you do?"

I had forgotten about the phone book. When I explained, the two of them screamed with hoots and laughs.

"Well," said Mags on the phone again, "you don't have to worry about getting your china or crystal back. According to my cook, who knows their cook, she smashed most of it when everyone refused her invitations. She threw it around with such abandon that one of the maids called 911. Stay out of town, sweetie, we've got your back. Oh! And don't worry about your apartment, I've taken Elizabeth under my wing."

I called Roger.

"You like baiting bears and teasing rattlesnakes too?"

"It was funny at the time."

"Yeah, well, I've been doing some research on this Sherry broad and believe me, she doesn't have a sense of humor."

"Oh, she's harmless. She's just mad, and I don't blame her."

"A tarantula sitting on a rock is harmless, but if it's sitting on your forehead, drinking your sweat, you pay attention."

He had my attention. "What did you find out about Sherry?"

"She didn't just show up one day applying for a job. She had been making visits to Larry's office for months."

"She had her sights set on him?"

"She had something in her sights. There was more going on than we thought. Can you stay away for a few more days?"

I tried not to feel unwanted. Fortunately, Charles and Alice did want me. When I told them about the phonebook and the dinner party, they choked with laughter.

Alice gasped, "Oh Lordie, I would have paid to see that. All that china! The Baccarat!"

"You definitely need to stay here so we can protect you," added Charles. "Come on, let's go to the Huntsman for dinner."

We drove a few miles to a crowded English pub. Travis Johnston was standing at the bar. He greeted us with hugs and squeezes and said to Charles, "Our table should be coming up next."

Our table? This was not as spontaneous as it seemed. I looked at Charles, who avoided eye contact. Alice just smiled.

When we were seated at a cozy corner table, Charles told Travis that I was on the lam and would be hiding out with them until the coast was clear. Travis eyed me with even more interest. "Dumb, blonde and in trouble with the law? What more could a guy ask for?"

There was much wine pouring amid shouted small talk and insults shared with other diners—all of them horse people. Somehow, I wasn't quite sure how, it was arranged that I would go on the next hunt, riding a "bomb-proof" retired hunter in the back of the field. I decided I should probably quit drinking—I ended up in too much trouble when I did.

26

The rooster was crowing the morning of the hunt that I had so rashly agreed to participate in. Alice knocked firmly on my door with a: "Let's go! Let's go! Coffee's on."

Still a bit dazed from a lively dinner party given by neighbors the night before, I pulled on the long socks and riding breeches Alice had lent me, then overpowered my boots into the *on* position. I got the shirt on, tucked in neatly and buttoned straight; the stock tie I took down to Alice, who said, "Lift your chin." She whirled it around, tied and plumped it, then said, "Hold still," as she stuck the gold pin through the center. "You do know this tie and pin aren't just for show, don't you?"

"Yes," I answered. "When I fall off and am bleeding to death, I'm supposed to use the tie as a tourniquet and the pin to slit my wrists."

"Not exactly, but close enough. You smell terrible, those potatoes last night were loaded with garlic. You need mouthwash—or here," she handed me a hot cup, "drink this coffee. It'll kill the odor."

I gulped it down, then Alice took my cup and handed me a jacket. "They're loading the horses. Your helmet, crop and gloves are in the truck, I'll be following in the jeep."

Charles was already getting into the truck as Stacey, his groom, put the last horse in the trailer.

"A hairnet! I forgot your hairnet." Alice ran back to the house. She came hurrying out, just as Charles started the engine, and thrust a wadded thing in my hand that looked very much like a recently encountered cobweb.

"Have fun!" she shouted as we pulled out.

Having fun did not seem a possibility. My head throbbed around the road curves and my stomach churned as we bumped over ruts into the parking area. People were calling to each other; the hounds were yelping; horses stamped in trailers, anxious to get out. It was noisy and chaotic as we unloaded the horses. Haskell, my gentle, old, retired horse, turned his enormous head on his huge neck and looked at me. His eyes lit up. He grinned. You might not think a horse can grin, but this one did. He put his nose down and sniffed me, then snorted and pawed the ground like a knight's charger waiting in the lists.

"I think I'll follow in the car with Alice," I said, just as Travis walked up.

"Ah, the little outlaw! We'd better get you mounted before the posse comes over the hill!" Before I knew what happened, he had given me a leg up and I was tossed over Haskell's back and into the saddle. Then the *have fun* part began.

I had been told to stay with Megan's group, the hill-toppers who would be at the back of the hunt and jump only minor fences, if any. Megan had a bright pink helmet cover, so she was easy to keep in sight.

The hounds were let loose and swirled around the huntsmen, who soon headed off, followed by the red-coated Masters and the Whippers-in, who would fan out and keep the hounds and the hunt focused.

Haskell was twitching with excitement at being back in the game. He seemed not to have been consulted about his retirement and had other ideas: He was used to being at the front, right behind the Field Master, and decided that was where we belonged.

"Hold him! Hold him!" Megan commanded as we breezed past her.

Haskell was a few notches below two thousand pounds and could easily have worn armor and carried a similarly clad knight. Believe me, I was holding with everything I had, but his determination was fast overpowering my strength.

Megan galloped up and gave a hard yank on one of Haskell's reins, which got his attention. After he slowed down, she led me back to the group and put me between Agatha and Crowley, seasoned fox hunters well into their seventies, whom I had met at the dinner party the night before. Their horses were semi-retired and seemed to be Haskell's old buddies. After a silent conversation between the steeds, he settled down to enjoy the ride.

And it was a glorious ride. The hunt took us into territory that could never be seen from a road, up hills with open vistas for miles on all sides and into woods that were close to primeval. As we were coming out of one of the woods, I caught up to Megan.

"Megan," I said, squirming in my saddle.

"Say no more. We'll stop in that clearing." She pointed to a spot at the edge of the woods. "You can dismount on that stump, I'll hold Haskell."

I dismounted and walked back in among the trees, then dropped my breeches. Mission accomplished, I was zipping up and heading out when a voice called from above me.

"Lady, you should grab some of those dock leaves over there. You're gonna need them!" I looked up toward a hunter's stand high in the trees. "That's stinging nettle you just squatted in, the dock leaves will neutralize it."

I should have followed the advice of my unseen pharmacist.

"What was that about?" asked Megan.

My behind was burning as I stood on the stump and put my foot in the stirrup. Just as I swung my leg over, a shout came from the clearing: "Bees! Bees! Yellow jackets!"

Megan handed me my reins and took off. I managed to get my other foot settled as Haskell followed her and it was a good thing I did, as he gave a few little bucks when we crossed the clearing. At the same time, I felt searing pain on my face and hands that took my mind off the part of me in the saddle. Yellow jackets are never pleasant critters, but when their underground nests are disturbed, they are especially testy. Haskell turned and headed back through the woods at what seemed like kamikaze speed. I grabbed his mane, lowered my head so the helmet would protect my eyes and throbbing face and just hung on.

Eventually he tired into a slow trot, then a walk. We came to a stream where he almost jerked me over his head when he bent to take a drink. At this point I was mad with pain, so I gave the reins a mighty tug and kicked him across the stream. He moved obediently along, which was fine except for one thing—I didn't know where *along* was. I was in the middle of a wood in Pennsylvania, on a large horse whose good intentions could not be guaranteed—that was the extent of my knowledge. That, and very acute pain on my face, hands and butt. There seemed nothing else to do but cry, which I did, blubbering and wiping my nose on the sleeve of Alice's jacket.

Haskell looked around at me, then started off at a determined trot. I held on and just let him go. At least he had probably been here before.

I heard the hounds bay, they were at full cry actually, and seemed to be getting closer—at a very fast pace.

A fox flashed past. Then we were in the middle of the din of baying hounds and the huntsman's horn, the front riders shouting at us and the riders behind them closing in. Haskell swerved to join them, while I hung on to everything, reins, mane, jump strap, while I realized with growing horror that, along with the searing pain, my eyes were swelling shut. This was probably an advantage, as I didn't see the rise and fall of the riders in front of me when they cleared a series of fences. I began to feel numb and limp, with breathing an effort, so I hardly noticed as we went up and over and up and over. I certainly don't remember being slumped on Haskell's neck as riders on either side grabbed reins to slow him down.

Or the flip over his head that was my dismount.

27

My next memory was of dimly seeing Alice and Charles leaning over my bed on one side and a vaguely familiar face jutting out of a white coat on the other.

"Ah, yes," said Travis, "definitely the work of a swarm of angry Hymenoptera...only those ladies would be jealous enough to do that." He bent closer. "That is one ugly puss."

"I'm not sure I like you," I mumbled.

"What a thing to say! And me standing here with a needle in my hand. Well, I'll fix you." He stuck the needle in my arm and it certainly fixed me—I was out.

I groaned in pain as I awoke.

"Headache?" he asked. How long had he stood there, looking at me?

"Among other things."

"You're a bit concussed, but I checked you out and there's nothing much there." He grinned down at me. "You're pretty colorful today."

Today? How long was I out?

"I didn't know you were a real doctor."

"Well, we all have our secrets, but yours has to be a doozy. I can understand the bee stings and the header off the horse, but I'd sure like to know how, in the middle of a fox hunt, you got stinging nettles all over your ass."

Alice came in, waving some papers. "Sign these and we can spring you. They wanted to keep you for breakfast, but we have a better menu."

I sat up slowly and swung my legs over the edge of the bed. In truth, I would rather have stayed put. What didn't hurt, itched, and some places did both.

"I brought you a loose sweat suit. You won't want anything binding on your body." She started to take my hospital gown off, then turned to Travis. "Out!"

"Out?" He looked at her, eyebrows raised.

"Yes, out!"

"I'm her doctor," he protested.

"We'll talk about that later, when she's dressed. Now you're just a dirty old man."

"Old man!" He assumed the most offended face, turned and left.

"Oh, Alice, you hurt his feelings. I really don't…"

"Put the sweatpants on. What you'll be feeling will hurt more."

She was right. The ride back to their place was a patchwork of discomforts. When I finally got to my room and went into the bathroom, what I saw in the mirror was also a patchwork—a swollen rainbow spectrum mostly in the purple, green and yellow hues.

I escaped under the comfort of the comforter for a time until outside noises intruded.

"Where is that girl? I need to examine my patient!"

"Travis," I heard outside my door, "go down to the library and have a drink with Charles. I'll bring Olivia down as soon as she's awake."

There was mumbling and stomping on stairs, then Alice came quietly into my room. "Livie," she said softly, "are you awake?"

I sat up. "Are you kidding? His bedside voice would wake the dead."

"Well, he's concerned about you. You had a severe reaction to all those stings, plus the nettles. You're lucky he carries a first-aid kit on the hunt that includes epinephrine. Can you come down for dinner?"

"I could eat the horse I rode in on. Or better yet, I hope they're dining on him in Paris right now."

"Livie! Haskell is a dear! I'll pretend you didn't say that."

"Oh...I know. " I was ashamed of myself. "He really did take care of me, he just deserved a better rider. What's for dinner?"

"Will shepherd's pie do?" she asked.

"I would settle for Velveeta on Ritz and Night Train."

"We can do better than that. Let's get you cleaned up." That involved combing the grass out of my hair, spraying me with scent, putting a down vest over the sweat suit and adding fuzzy slippers.

The talk stopped when I walked gingerly into the library. Charles just stared. Travis managed a *holy moley* before getting up to gently propel me to a chair. I winced sitting down. He grinned. "You never answered my question. We had to use a whole roll of sticky tape to get those nettles out."

"A lady is entitled to her secrets. Am I allowed to have a drink?"

"Champagne?" asked Alice. "It's very curative, you know."

"Just what the doctor ordered," said the doctor.

"You stick to scotch, I only have one bottle cold," said Alice as she left to get it.

Charles made up a plate of cheese, crackers and olives and brought it to me. I had finished most of it before he sat back down.

"Appetite's okay," said Travis. "Can I get you a side of beef?"

I licked my fingers and ignored him as Alice came in with the champagne and glasses.

"It's too bad you're on the market," continued Travis. "One look at you would cool any swain's ardor."

I threw my last olive at him, which thankfully, he grabbed in midair.

"I'm sorry," I said to Alice, then for Travis's benefit, "I am not now, nor ever intend to be *on the market.*" To which he just grinned.

A bit of information caught my attention as we had our drinks and bantered: the words *Huntsman* and *video.* "What did you say?" I asked Alice.

"We're going to the Huntsman tomorrow night."

"What was the video part?"

"Oh, we have a cameraman who follows the hunt. Then the videos are shown on some nights."

"Like, tomorrow night? Will I be on the video?" I asked, alarmed with very good reason.

"I'm not sure," said Alice, then pressed her lips together to stifle a smile. Charles busied himself over the cheese tray. Travis grinned, spread his arms and blurted, "A star is born!"

"There is no way on earth or in hell that I'm going to the Huntsman!"

28

When I was pushed and dragged into the Huntsman the next night, the room got silent, then erupted into a chant.

"Livie! Livie! Livie!"

We were seated at a center table near a TV, where there seemed to be an endless loop of Haskell sailing over the fences, with the limp rag of me on his back.

There were also endless comments about how Haskell had adjusted to keep me balanced, how a natural rider (me) can do it in her sleep, etc., etc....

I, who had never done anything equine of note—who, in fact, had been a very lackadaisical rider in my Central Park lessons—was suddenly the heroine of one of the major fox hunts in the country. All because of a reaction to a few yellow jacket stings. To be honest, the image of me as this fearless, reckless sportswoman did have appeal.

Someone stopped at the table, slapped me on the back. "We'll see you out there tomorrow," he said, then taking a closer look at my face, added lamely, "Well, maybe Saturday."

The fearless, reckless sportswoman suddenly needed to pee, and I remembered how this all began. I was determined to go back to the safety of New York ASAP and would never get on a horse again.

Just then, the blue phone vibrated in my jacket pocket. I excused myself and went to the restroom, receiving high fives on the way.

"Roger," I said after he answered on the first ring—not good, "I have to call you later."

"We need to talk now." Less good. "Where the hell are you? In a bar?"

"It's a family restaurant." Well, there were a few kids present, or maybe they were jockeys, and why was I fibbing to Roger?

"We've got trouble here." Worse. "You need to come back. Vacation's over."

I let the *vacation* part slide and gladly agreed to be in his office by one the next afternoon. I could end my riding career with an important business appointment.

***

"What's so important you have to leave tomorrow?" demanded Travis later over the coffee and Alice's blackberry pie. "I haven't released you from my intensive care."

Alice and Charles were equally dismayed. I made, at least what sounded to me, like a very good case about signing papers, legal documents, deadlines. Charles just stared at me. The look on his face told me that I had committed the cardinal sin of liars: I had not kept it simple, and Charles, the lawyer, was ready to pounce.

He waited until Travis had taken his very extended leave, which included several hugs and pats and the announcement that "he would normally give a send-off kiss, but who would put his lips on that ugly mug."

While Alice tidied the kitchen, Charles steered me firmly into the library. He sat me in a big comfortable chair and pulled the matching one close, so we were almost knee-to-knee. He just looked at me, waiting, in his patient, almost cozy confessional way. I soon babbled and blurted out some, but not all, of my confession.

Charles sat back with his fingers steepled in front of his face. "Tell me more about Roger."

This was not what I had expected him to say.

I explained Roger as best I could, realizing as I did that there was so much and so little to explain.

"Are you lovers?"

This I also did not expect. "Well, no, we're just friends, fellow troubled parents."

"Uh-huh," Charles nodded. "Why this emergency meeting?"

"I don't know. Roger has been doing some checking on Sherry and has de-bugged my cottage and apartment. He must have found out something I need to know."

"Um-hmm," Charles continued in his priestly pose, then added, "I don't think you're well enough to drive. I'll take you in tomorrow."

"But I'm fine. I have to return the car. I need to…"

"I'm driving you in tomorrow, Olivia; the car will be returned later. I suggest you go to bed, get a good night's sleep, and we'll leave after breakfast."

Charles's demeanor left no doubt that I was being sent to my room. At least I already had supper. As I climbed the stairs a feeling of extreme weariness and relief propelled me quickly back to what was becoming my favorite place. I had a dreamy awareness of voices and doors closing but slept soundly until the morning light woke me.

29

When Sandy saw me, she let out a series of whoops that sounded much like some southern marsh birds.

I had forgotten about my psychedelic self as I introduced Charles as my bodyguard. "You should fire him," she said, shaking his hand.

Charles was mesmerized by this red-topped, metal-pierced Amazon. He followed her obediently as she steered him to a chair and wordlessly accepted a magazine that he surely did not have a subscription to. I suspected she would figure in his fantasies for some time, and he would have the time to imprint her on his memory card while I went in to see Roger first—an arrangement I had insisted on.

Roger gasped when I walked in. "What the hell!"

I sat down and quickly related my Perils of Pauline saga. I realized that I had never heard Roger really laugh before, but he sure did now, starting with roars and peals and ending with rocking back and forth in his chair.

"Oh, Livie, Livie," he finally managed, "what to do with you?"

The thought flashed through my mind that maybe he wanted to do something with me. Charles had planted that seed, not me. I decided to squash the little bugger right then and there. Still...

"What's been happening? Is it safe to come back?"

He gave the obvious reply. "You mean safer than your equestrian career?" which set him off again.

I took that opportunity to tell him about Charles in the outer office.

"Is this in your best interest?" he asked. "The guy's his brother."

"Trust me, they are Cain and Abel."

"Maybe so, but are you sure which one is which?"

"Funny you should say that," I replied. "Charles is really here to check you out. He doesn't trust you either."

Roger looked at me, then grinned. "Okay, let's bring him in so we can butt heads. Mine's like a rock though."

"Yeah, well Charles might look like a peach, but there's a hard pit inside."

When Charles walked in, they shook hands in a way that suggested animals circling each other in the wild. Charles pulled up an extra chair and sat down. Neither one of them seemed inclined to lob the opening salvo, so I did.

"I've told Charles everything," I said to Roger, holding one hand over the other to hide the crossed fingers: I had not mentioned all the activities of my trip to the cottage.

"And I've told Livie a few things she needs to know," added Charles.

Roger, not to be outdone, countered with, "Well, I have some information you both need to know."

Charles leaned forward in his chair and actually rubbed his hands together. Perhaps Charles was a tad bored with his idyllic life and longed for a little action. "And what might that be?" he asked eagerly.

"You might not know this, because a lot of effort was made to keep her out of the news, but Sherry—the new Mrs. Lammond—is the niece of one Salvatore Santini."

"Big Sal?" said Charles, astonished. "How did Laurence get involved with that crowd? Wait!" He held up his hands. "I can guess."

"And you probably got it right," put in Roger. They looked at me expectantly. I sat there, wondering what they were talking about until the light bulb lit in my head. "Bag Lady! Sherry was the bag lady!"

"Took you long enough," said Roger.

"Sherry wasn't just Larry's assistant, she was the go-between."

"Oh hell!" Charles was never profane, which made this outburst more powerful. "Laurence is still involved in that business. He swore to me he had gotten out of it."

"He might have wanted to, but I had someone do a run-through of his business dealings in these past few years and he was bleeding money. He made some crappy, expensive deals," said Roger.

"Including Sherry," I added in not the nicest tone.

"Yeah, well, I hear she's out buying bushels of Baccarat and Royal Dalton." Roger's look at me was of the raised-eyebrow kind. I found my fingernails fascinating at that moment.

"So what does this mean?" asked Charles.

"Livie," Roger's tone demanded direct eye contact, "you need to stay away from these people."

"Who are *these people*? I've never met someone with the name Big Sal. What a ridiculous name anyway."

"The people who helped him earn it—on his way to being a made man—" he said pointedly, "would not agree with you."

I mentally began counting my hemstitched napkins to soothe the rising panic and wished for a *do-over* on the Larry's closet caper. "But I don't want to have anything to do with them. They're the ones doing to me."

As I finished saying that, I could feel the heat glowing and growing up my neck with the *fess up* facts of the situation. Mine were the actions; theirs, the reactions. I had not for a second thought about consequences, I just wanted a little revenge. Maybe it wasn't even that noble: I acted in spite, and spite is a snake that can whip around and bite you in the ass. I squirmed in my seat and needed to scratch mine very badly.

"I think Livie should come back to Pennsylvania with me for a long country stay."

"I think so too," said Roger, "but there are some other considerations."

"Such as?"

"Such as Lauren."

"What about her?"

"She's living with them…"

"I know, she called me a frigid bitch at our last meeting there."

"And working in Larry's office."

"Working? Lauren? She can't type, she's too nasty to answer phones. What?"

Roger's straight on, nonverbal look spoke the sad truth.

"Ohmigod! She's third generation in the business."

"She appears to be very good at it. From what I hear she doesn't just transfer the envelope, she pushes it. She has a talent for bookkeeping and the *ladies* all hate her."

30

I felt a loud *thud* as my aching heart fell. I had tried with this child from the day she came screaming from my womb. Through the years of disdain and demands, I had loved her regardless of her difficult self. As I have said before, there is a special nook in every woman's heart for her firstborn, and Lauren was snuggled in there. That was the only place and time she snuggled. How can a mother say this? Admit it? That child did not love me; she tolerated me as her means of survival, but no matter how much of myself I gave to her, she gave nothing back. I had first thought that this was the way of motherhood—until I had Christa. Then I really knew how different Lauren was. Christa would look at my face and smile; if I wrinkled my nose, she laughed. Anything I did was wondrous, a miracle created just for her, and she cherished my every move.

A baby comes pre-packaged in her own skin and, like any homemade product, the ingredients inside are never exactly the same. Lauren, in spite of her attempts to disfigure herself with piercings, tattoos and whatever outrage she could inflict on her hair—was still a prize specimen of a beautiful young woman. While Christa was very attractive and pretty, Lauren was beautiful. Their childhood tests had shown that, while they were both highly intelligent, Lauren had the higher IQ. But Lauren's package was short on one ingredient: the ability to be happy, the capacity for contentment. While Christa, I feared, had a pinch too much.

It was Christa who caused me the most worry in those early years. If another child grabbed at her toy, she would smile and hand it over—the sharing and giving gave her joy. Lauren had been a grabber, but the getting did not make her smile. As a two-year-old, it made her cry. It wasn't the getting that drove her, it was the wanting, and that kind of drive followed an endless road, with no destination in sight.

Christa excelled in school, not to please her parents but because it really pleased her. Lauren under-achieved, I believe, because it pleased her not to please others. Lauren's package came with a hole in the center that nothing seemed to fill, at least nothing that I seemed able to offer.

Lauren, the troubled, cold, problem child was now a troubled, cold, problem woman. But she still held reign over that special place, and I would never abandon her to her own worst instincts if there were a single chance that I could help her. And Roger knew this; Roger knew because of what we had been through with her and with his son Marc in their drug days.

31

When we were finally able to get to the intervention stage with Lauren and Marc, it was at the end of the school year— perfect timing. We had done prep work beforehand, especially for Lauren, hers being the more complicated case.

Pre-arranged catalogs came for her from camps for writing, acting, scholastics—and a wilderness one, far, far away. That one I immediately pooh-poohed as having no value and pushed the scholastics camp. I also began coming down hard on her about summer school and chores, generally nagging her at every opportunity, as Roger had suggested I do. Several times I found her reading the wilderness catalog; she seemed to like the three-month time duration and especially the distance, which would preclude parental visits.

After one week when I had been particularly harsh, she demanded that I write a check for the wilderness camp. I objected of course, which made her more determined, and then, reluctantly, I gave in. She shopped from the provided list, packed her bags, bid us good-bye with smug relief, and got on the plane.

The camp literature stated unequivocally that drugs and alcohol were not permitted. This, to Lauren, sounded like just another opportunity to *get away with it* and made it sound like fun. What she didn't know was that, on the other end, she had been tagged as a *possible* and assigned to the users induction barracks. Or that the big tail-wagging, friendly German shepherd Chum, who licked her hand and circled her three times, reaffirmed the counselors' pre-provided information. The group in her barracks assembled with their backpacks for pre-trek instructions. In the course of the day, they and their packs were in canoes that were deliberately tipped, so any drugs not in waterproof packages were ruined.

Meanwhile, Chum ambled through all the buildings, his telltale sniffs and busy tail telling the staff what they needed to dispose of and who needed extra supervision.

Withdrawal is never easy, but it is harder and more dangerous for some. So several days of in-camp observation gave evidence of who needed to be transported to the nearby rehab center.

Lauren, somehow, made it out into the wilderness part, an experience she later bitterly described—and blamed me for—as three months of "eating shit, burying shit and doing shit-all." So much for my carefully, elegantly raised daughter. The private schools, music lessons, dancing classes, the summers in Paris and Grenoble to perfect her French—a language she never used, not even to order from a menu—a language, I suspected, from which she had mastered the correct pronunciation and usage of just one word: *merde.*

32

Marc, in the meantime, had been sent off with Zane and friends on a cross-country motorcycle tour. He was ecstatic at the thought of stoning his way through the West with this grizzled and leathered bunch of bikers. The only part of him that got stoned was his body as they rode the back roads of Nowheresville. The one time he tried to score some pot in a small town, Zane beat the crap out of him, and he never tried it again—on that trip or when he got back home. Unlike Lauren, who threw her bags in the foyer, demanded money from her father, and was out the door. Her other rehabs are too painful to recount, including that final—hopefully, final one—which had the court order attached.

33

"...Livie. Olivia! Where were you?" said Charles. "I've been talking to you."

Roger knew exactly where I had been.

"Well, she's back, so let's figure this out," Charles continued with what he apparently had been saying. "Lauren's a big girl. She's a woman now, she can take care of herself."

"And so am I, Charles. I'm a big girl too, and I'm not going to be run out of town by this Big Sal person, or anyone else. I'll give the money back. It isn't worth the trouble."

"Nu-huh." Roger looked alarmed at that suggestion. "I think you're safer if Laurence doesn't know for sure where it is or who took it."

"Why?"

"Because, my dear Olivia," Charles quickly broke in, "it is undeclared income from an un-declarable source, and once you declare your knowledge about it, some people will feel very threatened."

"I do declare," I said gaily.

"This is not the time for jokes," Roger's voice was surprisingly grim. "I don't know what Laurence is capable of, but in my cop days, I saw some of the other guy's handiwork—not pretty. Just the fact that you know about that stash puts you in danger. They'll think you'll tell someone, or blackmail them, or..."

"Testify against Laurence," finished Charles.

"I didn't count the money, but I don't think it was, like, a zillion dollars."

"That could also be part of the problem," said Roger, his arm resting on the desk, fingers kneading his forehead while the other hand doodled shapes on a pad—a sure sign of deep concern. "If he's had to tell someone that the money was stolen, then he can set that figure as high as he wants."

"While he keeps adding to his own stash," finished Charles.

"And there's something else, Livie," Roger said softly. "Something that's going to upset you."

"Oh really!" My tone dripped with sarcasm. "Like we're sitting here having tea and crumpets."

"Larry bought that house."

"What house…?" I stopped, picturing the big one across the water from me that had been on the market for so long. "You can't be serious!"

"Ah, but I am. He paid cash, closed the deal in record time."

When I had finally returned to my apartment, there was a message from Gil, confirming that Larry had bought the house across the lake from us. "What's that about?" he had wondered. It might have been a mystery to him, but not to me—Larry was keeping an eye on me.

I felt the door slam on my last refuge.

34

Mags was dramatically limp in her bath, bubbles floating, hair wrapped in a white silk turban. The entire room was mirrored, so there was no escaping the familiar look or the fact that she omitted commenting about my colorful face.

"Please sit down." She turned her head slowly as I sprawled in the ice-pink velvet chaise. Wait for it. It didn't take long.

"I'm in love."

Oh please God, I thought, not another new doorman.

"I. Am. In. Love. Truly, deeply in love. We're going away together."

I asked the obligatory: "Who, where, when?"

"I was walking along, minding my business…"

The rest of the old song refrain floated through my head: *Wham, Bam, Alakazam, Love Came And Hit Me In The Eye.*

"When something hit me in the eye. There was a doctor's office right in front of me, so I went in and Doctor Jensen kindly saw me right away. He removed a piece of granite…"

Granite? I thought. Couldn't she just have a speck of dust like normal people?

"Then, when I could see again, there we were, almost nose to nose, looking into each other's souls. He's a skier. He's going to Aspen next week 'cause there's early snow and I have my reservations."

Well, I certainly had my reservations too. "When did all this happen?"

"Wednesday."

"You mean this week Wednesday? Like two days ago?"

"It was love at first sight."

Mags did not possess the subtle humor for puns, so I didn't even try.

"I mean, Livie…this is the one. I am swept away by him." She stood up, brushing the bubbles off her well-toned, professionally trained body. "Hand me my robe, sweetie."

We moved to her palatial bedroom, where I settled onto another chaise. Mags swooned and swanned around, proclaiming her love, her rapture, her enchantment for one Louis Jensen. I was beginning to get concerned about how serious this might be when she said the magic words: "We must go shopping tomorrow." That put the retail and risqué opportunities on an equal footing. I relaxed.

"If only the real Abercrombie's was still on Madison," she sighed. "One stop, I'd have everything—mountain wear, ski clothes, the whole deal."

"What about your theme closet?" I pointed to her many closet doors, behind one of which hung every possible outfit for every possible sporting activity: shooting (big game or birds); diving (sky or sea); riding (English or Western); tennis (grass, hard court or table); and even skiing (mountain or water)—all of which she had worn with excellent results, in both the effect and the activity.

Relaxed or not, I called Roger as soon as I left Mags and gave him Jensen's name to run. He called me later with the news that Dr. Louis Jensen was the married father of four with several sexual harassment charges lodged against him.

I worried through the night about how to bring Mags safely back to earth. The next day her car pulled up to my door at noon.

"You'll never believe it!" screamed Mags as I got in. "Mason is chartering a yacht! We're sailing around all of the islands and you're coming with us! We are definitely shopping, and we are going to look hot, hot, hot!"

And so the flannel thong was exchanged for a bikini and sarong without another thought wasted on Dr. Louis Jensen—yesterday's one true love.

35

The next week was to be our summer's swan song at the cottage, just the three of us having a girl's weekend in the waning warmth of the season. A time to reenact our triumphant canoe routines from our camp days.

Mags had given me supplies to take, including a case of champagne and a bagful of products: facial and deep hair conditioning masks, hand treatment creams with special gloves to slide our slathered hands into and bottles of creams and gooes that would cover us head to toe.

But at the last minute Janine had to shepherd a patient in a life-threatening crisis to a facility in Katonah. Then Mason developed a very bad cough and Mags would never leave him if she thought he needed her. Mags cooked only one thing, and then only for loved ones who were on death's door: her *miracle chicken soup*, so called because people got miraculously better after one cup. That was out of fear that she would sit there and spoon-feed them a second one. Janine had once tactfully tried to find out if Mags knew that the chicken got plucked and the innards removed before cooking it. We shared a hilarious vision of Mags chasing a squawking chicken around her cavernous professional kitchen—like Woody Allen with the lobsters in *Annie Hall*. She had just smiled primly and said it was an *old family secret.* Since Mags had many family secrets, it left much room for speculation.

So I was alone on this beautiful exceptionally warm night, with a full moon half high on the water. I put on my swimsuit, picked my favorite from the paddles that hung on the wall in the mudroom, grabbed a flotation cushion and went down to the dock where my canoe was tied up. I whacked it a few times to encourage any visitors of the crawling or slithering persuasion to hop out, then undid the back clip and laid the rope on the dock. I tossed in the cushion and paddle, eased myself onto the seat, then pulled the canoe forward to undo the front rope.

The water was glorious, smooth as a mirror reflecting moonlight magic as I started to make the loop around my side of the finger in the lake. My strokes were quiet, rhythmic; I was one with the canoe and did not regret being alone.

My magic moment was temporarily shattered when, across the lake from my cottage, I saw lights flick on at Larry's, then music and laughter poured out. I thought of Humphrey Bogart saying in *Casablanca, Of all the gin joints, in all the towns,* and echoed it with: *Of all the cottages, on all the lakes…*

Just before the smaller inlet of water reached the wide lake center, I paddled across to the other side and felt the wind picking up. I paddled strongly and thought about the days at camp where Mags, Janine, Sly and I, the feared and fearsome foursome of the secret club MONS, had won the canoeing trophy four years in a row against the despicable Monica and her team. I was laughing at the memory of Monica trying to...

The outdoor lights went on at Larry and Sherry's and a pale figure run down the dock and dove into the water.

A cloud slid across the moon. I started softly singing Phil Ochs's version of Sir Alfred Noyes's "The Highwayman": When the wind was a torrent of darkness, blowing through gusty trees, and the moon was a ghostly galleon...

The paddling suddenly got harder. Storm, I thought.

There was a crack of lightning and the wind really began to blow—the northern storms can come in very fast. I paddled as hard as I could as the temperature dropped, aiming to get to the shortest point for crossing the open water. I was concentrating on keeping my angle just right so the wind wouldn't sideswipe me.

Suddenly, something large and pale was alongside me. Without thinking, I smashed it with my paddle, visualizing the huge carp that lived under the docks and the turtle with a head the size of a football who had recently rested that head on my dock while I was sitting there reading. I almost went over, but steadied myself enough to be able to look back. Nothing. The wind was now worse, and so was the lightning: to be out in a canoe was dangerous. Even though I hadn't reached the narrowest point, I cut across the lake, aiming toward the lights in my house and paddled as fast and as smoothly as I could in that tumult. The last few hundred yards were agony. There was no possibility of tying the canoe to the dock, so I pulled it onto the beach, flipped it over, grabbed my paddle and cushion and ran, amidst lightning cracks, to the house.

My arms were on fire, while the rest of me was freezing. I hung my paddle in the mudroom, peeled off my cold swimsuit, then got into a hot shower. I dried myself, slathered my arms with analgesic cream, then put on a warm nightgown, robe, wool socks and wrapped my head in a towel. I was still cold.

I had prepared a fire for our weekend in my best camp-girl's fashion. Logs crossed just so, kindling perfectly placed. Now I lit it and was smugly proud of how quickly it was ablaze.

"Take that, Janine," I crowed, as I went to get a glass of warming sherry. Janine thought herself the star of campfire construction and me a mere kindling carrier.

As I came back to the fire with my glass, a distant siren pierced through the claps of thunder and bolts of lightning. I went to the big window overlooking the lake. There, across the water, surrounding Larry's new digs, were flashing lights and, indeed, sirens. "What the…"

I sipped my sherry and watched as the blazing fireplace and the comforting drink warmed me. I sipped again and looked at my glass—sherry. Sherry! My mind raced back to the re-run of me smashing the carp or turtle or…

I put the glass on the counter as I went to the mudroom and pulled my paddle off the wall. It was an old paddle, my favorite paddle, one that had propelled me around this lake for years. And being so old and well used, it had a few chips and raggedy edges on its end. I examined it carefully, turned it over, and there it was—caught in one of the cracks—a single long blonde hair.

Just in time, I made it to the powder room, where I vomited into the toilet.

What does one do? What is one supposed to feel like after killing someone? Because the evidence of my crime was right in front of me. I put the paddle back on its hook, pulling the blonde hair off, which I wrapped, almost reverently, in a piece of paper towel and stuffed into the pocket of my robe.

"But your honor, I thought it was a turtle," I would plead as the jury sniggered.

I poured the sherry down the drain and rinsed the glass and my mouth. I need something stronger than this, I thought.

There was a pounding on the door. When I could finally get myself to open it, two troopers were standing there. I was frozen in terror, unable to speak, when one of them said, "Ma'am, is that your motorboat out front?"

He hadn't said canoe.

"Yes, it is. What's going on?"

"We have a woman missing in the water and we need all the boats we can get to help in the search."

"The keys are in it," I said.

The other trooper refrained from what he was obviously thinking— you wonder why boats get stolen—and kept to the crisis at hand. "Well, ma'am, we don't really know the ins and outs of running your boat, and it would be better if the two of us are in the back, one on each side, so, could you drive it?"

My skin felt like it was going to burst right off of me from my soaring blood pressure, but I said, "Just give me a minute."

I put on some spandex shorts and jersey, plus a yellow rain jacket, then went down to the dock where the troopers were waiting. I put in the code and the boat lowered on its lift. I started the powerful engine of my Mastercraft ski boat as the men settled themselves into the back and we crossed the choppy lake in minutes. Other boats were trawling along with the people in them beaming lights into the water. We stayed on the outer edge of the search, cruising slowly up and down several times. I was too busy keeping the boat steady in the wind and waves to even think about this curious situation. I made a turn to tighten our circle, which required giving the big engine a little more gas so it wouldn't stall. As I came out of the turn, there was a thud against the hull.

"STOP," shouted one of the troopers: I put the engine in idle. "GO BACK," he yelled over the wind and thunder. I gave it a little gas and did a slow circle.

"Over there!" I aimed for where he was pointing. "Stop!" Again I put it in idle. Then I watched in horror as they pulled Sherry's body into my boat.

We drove slowly to the dock where a group had gathered. There were police, EMTs, people I didn't know, and in the midst of them, Larry. Hands grabbed the boat to hold it steady as the EMTs gently and gingerly removed Sherry.

I had no choice but to climb onto the dock. I went to Larry. "I am so sorry," I told him, and I was.

Larry took my hand and held it. "Thank you, Livie...thank you." Here was the stricken thanking the striker. He was pale with shock. I wasn't sure he even realized he was holding my hand so tightly as we made our way to the house. There were people inside I didn't know, but who apparently knew me, judging from their curious stares. I stayed until the ambulance took Sherry away, all the time tightly held by Larry. Is he holding me until they put the cuffs on? Then it dawned on me that he was holding onto me for support. He asked me to go with him to the hospital, but fortunately, the officers who had come with me in the boat needed to get back across the lake to their squad car still parked at my house.

"Please come to the hospital. Please." He seemed so lost, so forlorn that I had to say I would.

And I did, after taking the officers back and dressing in something more appropriate.

I stayed with Larry and a few of his friends until there was nothing left to stay for. He held my hand again as we left the hospital, begging me to come to his house. I told him I would after a few hours sleep, and he gave me a big hug as we parted.

When I finally got back to the cottage I was near collapse, but there was one more job that needed to be done.

Embers were still glowing in the fireplace. Normally, I would never leave the house with a fire still burning, even with the full, sturdy screen in place, but tonight was not normal. I went to the mudroom, took down my old paddle and balanced it across the washtub and the dryer. With a hacksaw from the cupboard I cut it into pieces, flushing the sawdust down the drain, then carried the pieces to the fireplace, removed the screen and, with kindling, rolled paper and a few logs, soon had it blazing again. When it was roaring, I fed the pieces of my dear old paddle into the blaze one by one and watched as another crime was added to my list: destroying evidence.

I went into the bedroom and got my bathrobe, took the folded paper towel from the pocket and went back into the living room. I stood before the fire and unfolded it, staring at the long blonde hair. I felt there should be a ceremony, a last rites of some sort. I tried to curl the hair into a circle, but it was so coarse from all the bleaching it had been subjected to, that it split in two. I wrapped the pieces back in the paper and threw it into the blaze.

36

I hadn't been aware of flash bulbs popping the previous night, but the whole ordeal had apparently been recorded—according to the phone calls that began as soon as the early morning editions came out.

Roger: "I need to put you in a glass case, etc., etc."

Janine: "The front pages—all the papers, etc., etc."

Lauren: "You did it. I know you did it, etc., etc."

Mags: "Couldn't you have fixed your hair, etc., etc."

Charles: "For sure you need to come back, etc., etc."

Then Gil arrived with the newspapers. He did not try to come in for coffee as he usually did. I realized he had not been in the middle of the action last night, as he usually would have been. He just handed me the papers, an odd look on his face, and said, "You, of all people, will want to see these," and left.

Odd. But then, so was Gil.

I made a pot of tea first, then sat down.

There were pictures of me, wet hair flying in the wind, lightning as a backdrop, behind the wheel of the boat. More discreetly blurred: the officers pulling Sherry aboard; me meeting Larry on the dock; and me with Larry, leaving the hospital, hand in hand.

There were blazing headlines:

EX TO THE RESCUE

OLD SALT BRAVES STORM FOR NEW SUGAR

And whatever else they could make of the facts they knew. I shuddered to think of what they would make of those they didn't know.

The phone rang again. This time it was a call I really wanted to take; a voice I really wanted to hear. "Hi, Mom," said Christa. "I'm coming to New York this afternoon. You guys need me right now, and I need to be there. I suspect you didn't exactly love Sherry, and she and I never got to know each other well, but we are family."

Family. I had never thought of it that way, but Sherry was my girl's stepmother, wicked or not. I needed to rearrange my thinking for their sakes. Perhaps Lauren really did care for her, found her a better fit as her ideal of motherhood.

I got dressed and drove around the lake to Larry's house. The boat would have been faster, but the vision of Sherry being pulled into it nixed that possibility. The photographers were lounging around the driveway. Bulbs flashed and I could hear Mags saying, "You could at least have worn a slouch hat and sunglasses, you look so ordinary!"

But Mags couldn't know that looking ordinary was my best camouflage right now. Who would picture blood on these moon-clipped, buffed nails?

In spite of what I had so recently learned about Larry— the repugnant lie that was still his life—I filled the role that he now wanted and needed: that of wife/mother. I greeted people, organized food, made decisions and arrangements for the relocation to New York. Then I went back to the cottage and arranged myself to do likewise.

37

Before going back to my old home to be with my family, I went to Mags so she and Flore, her maid, could coif and gloss me. Mags, of course, did not like what I wore, so she dressed me from her closet. Although no doctor would approve, it became apparent that stress is the most effective diet available without a prescription. Before these last few months of madness, I had dutifully stepped on my scale every morning then gasped, moaned, and promised the fashion goddess that I would be so very good if she would get me back into a size six or size eight. Now I fit snuggly into one of Mags's ultra-sleek suits, but I fit. She fussed with a frilly scarf in the neckline, complaining, as usual, about my "excessive boobiness."

"You only had your reduction 'cause Mason doesn't care about them," I retorted.

"Mason loves tits! He would just prefer them with a penis attached. Besides, he loves dressing me more than undressing me, and high fashion is cut close to the bone."

At the door, Mags took my arm and looked into my eyes. "Olivia?"

Oh-oh…

"You are going into a situation that you must control the second you step over that threshold. You've done something—I don't know what yet…"

Double oh-oh.

"...that's holding your spirit down. So, be Olivia right now, and don't be Livie! Better yet, be me instead, and kick some ass!"

The elevator arrived. Mags hugged me and Adolpho took me to the lobby, eyeing me discreetly but appreciatively, which added to my feeling of power.

When the Mags's version of me arrived at my former home, I walked in like I still owned the place. But this place I did not, nor never would have, owned.

In her short time as mistress of the house, Sherry had done a masterful job of erasing all traces of me. Whereas mine had been a more Sister Parish style of environment, hers was Mother Nature Unbound, from the faux tortoise shell walls to the leopard print rugs—acres of them, it seemed. I wondered what had happened to my oriental rugs and antique furniture. Then I remembered what money was probably used to pay for those items and hoped they had been given to charity.

The old Laurence had been indifferent to his surroundings, as long as they were impressive and his favorite chair was in front of a large TV set. Larry, however, was proudly showing a group of people around, praising Sherry's clever eye and saying the words that drive a stake through every accredited decorator's heart: "She did it all herself."

I spotted Lauren standing on a spotted rug and went into Mags mode.

"My poor baby!" I almost screeched, walking toward her with my arms spread wide. It took a few seconds for Lauren to realize who was the sleek creature bearing down on her.

"Mother?" She had no choice but to let me engulf her in my Armani-clad arms.

"Oh, my sweet girl," I said, holding her tightly as her mother, not Mags. "I am so sorry." Her rigidity softened. Then she shuddered as she wept. I caressed her head and murmured the universal words of comfort. "There, there, we'll get through this together."

She pulled a little away, enough to look at me. "Mom, I'm sorry about the phone message. I..."

"Shhh." I silenced her lips with my finger. "You were in shock. You really cared for Sherry."

She started weeping again, so I pulled her close. She relaxed. Then Christa joined our group hug, and Lauren went stiff as a board and was about to pull away when Larry encircled as much of us as he could, what with his surprisingly enormous belly blocking his reach. Mags's proclamation at the time of their marriage that Sherry intended to "feed him and fuck him to death" came to mind.

Someone tapped Larry on the shoulder and said, "Excuse me," then whispered something into his ear.

He rolled his eyes. "I'll see my girls later." He hurried off. Christa gave me a tight hug and a kiss before we three pulled apart.

Christa turned me in front of her, looked me up and down. "Mom! You look fantastic! I never knew you were a babe!"

Lauren also looked me over. "You look...different." I chose to take that as a compliment.

Then my Olivia part took over, not for Larry's sake, but because my girls needed me to help. They didn't know, or at least, Christa didn't know, what an odious man their father was, and I hoped they would never have to find out. "Come on, girls, we need to help your father. Lauren, you and Christa stay by him, introduce people, make small talk. I'll see that the food is organized and keeps coming. And both of you watch out for those who've had a few too many drinks. Steer them to the coffee. Also, anyone with sticky fingers, point out to me. I'll handle them."

The upper reaches of society can be a hot bed of kleptomania. People who could buy anything they wanted sometimes took greater pleasure in the thrill of stealing it instead. I had become quite adept at pickpocketing over the years, retrieving many of my *borrowed* small objects from the pockets of mink and cashmere coats, bespoke suit jackets and Leiber purses. It was almost a game: one that I usually won. Mason possessed a small porcelain egg of mine that he proudly displayed on a mantelpiece. I could have taken it back anytime, but that would be considered real stealing. I had to retrieve it in the midst of a party, evading the amused, watchful eye of Mason.

I tried to avoid being a presence by staying mostly in the kitchen and dining room, overseeing the caterers. But Larry sought me out to introduce me to people I had never seen before and hoped never to see again. These people were not the upper reaches of society: These people would not steal a porcelain egg for fun. They would steal the chicken, wring its neck and roast it on a spit.

But nevertheless, it seemed that I was famous (perhaps notorious would be a better word) as they all had seen the front page pictures and wanted to meet the woman who had braved the elements to go to the rescue of "our sweet Sherry."

There were a few dark-haired, dark-eyed men who stood apart, not greeting me but giving me dark looks. I thought it advisable to leave ASAP, and after saying goodbye to my daughters, I did, with those cold dark eyes watching me.

38

Because of the manner of her death, Sherry's body had been turned over to the county coroner and could not be released until the cause of death was determined and foul play was ruled out. So the funeral was delayed.

I would have preferred to stay in New York City to take advantage of distractions and the possible extradition process, but the girls, Christa especially, begged me to go to the lake. They stayed with their father, helping him with arrangements, but would come to the cottage for quiet moments out of the spotlight. We even had dinner as a family once where Larry, unlike old times, occasionally disengaged from gorging to acknowledge our conversation and presence.

Gil kept on bringing the papers and kept on being strange. Then one morning he came in, slapped the papers down and asked for a cup of coffee. He sat down at the table and said nothing while I made one and brought it to him. Waiting on Gil was not a job I would normally scurry to accomplish, but I was not feeling normal because he had not been acting normal. He pointed to the headlines and said, "Well, well, imagine that."

I sat down and read the bold print banner: NEW YORK SOCIALITE DEATH AN ACCIDENT. CORONER JOHN RANGEL RULES THE DEATH OF… and so on.

I went numb with disbelief, relief and...fear. The way Gil was staring at me with that smirky smile told me the fear was well founded.

39

Back in New York, the service for Sherry was simple. Larry had her body cremated with the intention of spreading her ashes at a later date.

Sherry, in the meantime, resided in an expensive and gaudy urn placed in the center of the leather topped dining table that had replaced my exquisite antique one. She stood surrounded by rose petals—a bed of roses actually.

The champagne flowed freely and I drank it with abandon to the point that Mags, of all people, told me to "put a cork in it."

Gil had come to town for the service and trailed me around, trying to angle me into a corner for conversation, but I, like the champagne, kept flowing from group to group until Janine bottled me up and poured me home.

40

The early fall is my favorite time in New York. There is a slight crispness in the air that gives the feeling of a new beginning, which I suppose goes back to memories of the first day of school. I can still smell the freshly sharpened pencils and feel the scratchiness of my pleated plaid skirt. I also remembered the mixed feelings my daughters exhibited on that day: Lauren angry and defiant, Christa trembling with excitement. I had just finished setting the table for lunch when the buzzer rang, announcing the arrival of those girls-turned-women.

"Oh, Mom. I love it!" squealed Christa as she toured my apartment.

In my absence Mags and Elizabeth had battled their way through the dining room, arguing over every hue, swatch, turn of leg or anything else they could have at. They finally agreed to have the walls coated with several layers of lacquer to give depth to a lush pale peach. They also agreed on taking out the carpeting (which they had the building staff do in exchange for keeping it) and refinishing the parquet floors. The graceful Queen Anne dining table and chairs rested on an antique oriental rug, parts of which had aged to the wall color. That furniture cost more than it should have because Mags and Elizabeth ended up bidding against each other on opposite sides of Sotheby's auction room. "Money is no object" seemed to figure in Mags's decorating scheme, forgetting that it was my money she was spending so lavishly. The result was delightful.

Greta came to cook our lunch so it would seem like old times. She had been with us since the girls were little and I knew she missed having us together.

Christa was taking a mid-day train back to Philadelphia. She had missed so much time at work that she would be putting in long hours to catch up.

"How do you like your job?" I asked her, worried about those hours.

"I love it! I get a lot of grunge work now, but I don't mind. I just find it all interesting."

I was trying to think of a way to ask Lauren about her job when Christa did it for me.

"I hear you're working at Dad's office. Do you like it?"

"Yeah…it's okay."

"What do you do there?" continued Christa in a way that was acceptable from her but would have been offensive from me.

"Oh…I have a lot of responsibilities," Lauren said vaguely.

Greta brought in her special crab quiche and salad. Even without the interruption, I was sure there wouldn't be anything more forthcoming.

After lunch we sat over the remains of lemon meringue pie and sipped our coffee.

"Do you have time for a social life?" I asked Christa.

"Well," she blushed, "I have had a few dates with one of the other associates."

"And by date, you mean what?" asked Lauren pointedly.

Christa was further embarrassed. To give her a minute to recover and because it would seem a natural thing to do, I asked Lauren: "And what about you? Are you seeing someone?"

She paused, sipped her coffee then said in a slightly defensive way: "As a matter of fact, I am." Her tone left no room for further inquiry.

Then there was talk about train schedules and the flurry of leaving, which they did together.

I felt somewhat bereft after they were gone and welcomed Greta when she brought in her coffee to join me.

"Are you all right here, ma'am? My cousin Lydia has a few free days and would be glad to look after you."

I welcomed her suggestion. We sat comfortably for a few minutes, then I asked her if she had met Lauren's boyfriend.

"Oh that one! I don't like him, not one bit." Greta, ever discrete, pursed her lips, certain it was more than she should have said. Those few words were more than I wanted to hear.

41

Mags and I went to keep Janine company for dinner one night when David had late appointments at the Park Avenue office they shared. It was a lovely evening, so we dined on her terrace overlooking Central Park South. When the evening air cooled, we moved to her living room. While I was thrilled with my cheerful dining room and excited about what else my decorating duo had in mind, Janine was content with her serene, almost monochromatic surroundings. Even Mags seemed soothed in the environment and lazed full out on a taupe couch.

"I have some newwws," she teased, having saved the best tidbit for dessert.

"What!"

"Who?"

She held her glass out and looked at us archly. Janine filled it as we pulled our chairs closer. Post-summer is always an interesting time. There is an inevitable *marriage-go-round* fall-out from all the parties in the Hamptons, on yachts and at various European hideouts.

"Annabelle Trowbridge has gone to Switzerland," Mags reported smugly.

"Nooo," Janine and I breathed in unison.

"*Yes.*" Mags sat up and drew closer into our hags' circle, lowering her voice into something highly conspiratorial. "She's getting it all redone. We aren't supposed to recognize her when she gets back."

Redoing Annabelle seemed equal to redoing one of the summits in that alpine country. When Annabelle entered a room, it was like the Queen Mary sailing into port. I tried to imagine that stately vessel morphed into an agile sailboat.

Janine of course, did not waste time on such flights of fancy. "Who's the woman?"

Mags drew her legs up, leaned closer into our circle and sang: "Lester has strayyyyed."

"Lester? Who's Lester?"

"Are you drunk for God's sake—her husband!" provided Janine.

Oh…yes. I had created dozens of invitation lists for charity events and Annabelle was always at the top—in the A section. I had forgotten that the envelopes were addressed to

Mr. & Mrs. Lester Trowbridge. Annabelle was the player, Lester was the escort.

"How would he dare?"

"He didn't. But some little snip did," crowed Mags.

"Lester?" I tried to bring that nondescript man who followed in Annabelle's wake to mind, but couldn't.

"He's wearing ascots, he's wearing silk shirts, he's wearing attitude!"

"Does this gal know there's no pot of gold behind that pot belly?" drawled Janine. "He doesn't have a dime."

"Oh, but he does!" Mags's eyes radiated mischief. "An uncle died and left Lester some independence. Annabelle has to work for his attention now."

Back home I was still imagining Annabelle kowtowing to Lester as I pressed the button for my phone messages.

42

"I'll do that," said Gil, taking the kindling from me. "You start the water boiling."

I was at the cottage in response to what had sounded like a very threatening call from Gil: A *we need to talk—Now* call. I had wanted to go there anyway to do something about the canoe, something that might have involved drilling a hole in it, filling it with rocks, then pushing it out towards the middle of the lake.

I told Gil that I would bring sauce for pasta if he would bring ingredients for a salad. He thought that was a wonderful idea and offered to make bread. It was late afternoon when I stopped on my way out of town at my neighborhood Italian restaurant. I picked up a package containing a quart of their special house sauce that they had so agreeably provided—at a premium price—with instructions to simmer it for an hour.

I didn't say that I would actually make the sauce, I thought, erasing any trace of guilt when I dumped it into a pot. I turned the burner on low and was stuffing the container into the trash when Gil arrived.

He was loaded down with wine, bread and salad ingredients, so I held the door for him. He managed to brush against me for an excessive amount of time and contact. He unloaded his offerings and said, "Do you have wood?"

He rubbed his hands in satisfaction at the stack of wood by the fireplace and announced that he would start a fire and make drinks while I got the pot "a-boiling," then turned me toward the kitchen. Was that a fanny pat? He was acting so in charge, so smarmy.

I filled the pot, just because it needed to be filled at some point. The sauce was still in its beginning stage of simmer, and the only reason to boil water now would be if we were delivering a baby.

Gil had the fire going, smoking more than blazing. I could have had, with two squeezes of the bellows and a piece of paper, a martyr's blaze filling the otherwise darkening room. He had not turned on the lights and he was cozily sprawled in front of the fireplace on pillows from the sofas. He also had two large drinks in hand, one of which he handed to me while patting the floor beside him.

This was getting worse by the second. Gil's new boldness told me that he had ammunition to back it up.

I was, at that moment, in what 1950s divorce lawyers and 1750s Bavarian princedoms would concede was a *compromising position.*

43

Gil had a photographic telescope set up in a specially constructed observatory in front of his house by the lake. He had cleared surrounding trees so his view would be unimpeded. It was his *star watcher,* he told the few people who had ever been inside to see it. I was one of those people and I had also seen that the telescope was on a swivel that not only took in the stars but everything around it. He had seen something the night Sherry died. He had taken pictures of what he saw. From the way he was acting, there was no doubt about it.

As the fire blazed higher, he drew closer. We clinked glasses several times, toasting god-knows-what. I sipped daintily as mine seemed to be straight vodka.

"Let's go for a swim," Gil said, jumping up. I could see by the firelight a protrusion in his pants, one that I had never hoped to witness.

But he was my witness, I was positive about that. He had some physical proof—I was at his mercy.

"The last swim of the season," I managed to say. "I'll get my suit on."

He grabbed my hand. "Come on, Livie, let's just drop everything and jump in! Just like kids!"

Now here came the kicker: when a person is held in bondage, be it by fear, guilt, need, or just circumstances beyond that person's control, she is not the one you really ought to invite to jump into a deserted lake with you in the semi-dark of night. Especially when that person you plan to jump in there with has a lot to lose.

Gil dove into the water. I climbed down the ladder, carefully wedging a piece of pipe against the top rung.

I am not a born or trained killer. In the case of Sherry, fate had put me in the wrong place at the wrong time. Until recently, my life had been focused on things such as invitation lists for business and social dinners, teaching illiterate adults how to read, organizing charity functions and whether the cook should have Sunday as well as Monday off.

But circumstances had placed me naked, in this deserted lake, with the equally naked means of my possible destruction.

"This is wonderful!" said Gil, swimming around me. "This is all my dreams come true!"

Could I possibly think of killing him after he said that?

Gil swam out a little way. I took the opportunity to scramble up the ladder to the deck and in the process, deliberately knocked the piece of pipe into the water. What were you thinking, Olivia? I asked myself. Are you training to be a serial killer? Next you'll be buying a white paneled van.

"Where are you going? It's just getting fun!" said Gil, climbing up behind me.

I tried to get into my robe, but he was there faster than I could have imagined, with his arms around me and hands inside—one holding a breast, the other between my legs. "Livie, Livie," he murmured into my neck. "Let's not waste this chance."

At that moment I almost regretted not wasting him when I had the chance. I pulled his hands away and turned to face him—which meant looking down at him. Gil, in an eerie way, was a small Elvis: the wide facial structure, the firm jaw and full lips, the big hair, in the same dirty-blonde color natural to Elvis before he dyed it black. A number of women, according to Gil's hints over the years, found him as irresistible as the King. I did not.

"This is not going to happen, Gil. No way."

"My way," he said. The full moon emphasized the Elvis sneer on his face—did he practice that in front of a mirror? "My way from now on, for your own good."

I pushed him back. "What do you mean?"

"My scope posts everything I see into the computer. Everything. Need I say more?"

"I'm cold," I said, turning toward the house.

He spun me around. "I'm not through with you."

I reached down, grabbed his bare balls and started to squeeze. He yelped, trying to loosen my hold. "We'll talk about it over dinner." I let go of him, tightened the belt on my robe and marched up the dock, leaving him to limp along behind.

When he came in, I was stirring the sauce, which was just this side of ruined. I turned to him, "After you're dressed, you can put more wood on the fire, then open the wine." I set two bottles on the counter, which seemed to mollify him.

I closed the door to my bedroom, dressed quickly, then took a bottle of sleeping pills from my night table. I took out two pills, put them in my pocket, then returned to the living room.

Gil was opening the wine in the kitchen. He looked warily at me.

"You get to choose," I said. "Toss the salad or set the table."

He relaxed, enjoying our new domestic coziness. "I'll set the table," he said eagerly, "I was a waiter in college."

Good. This gave me a chance to pour some wine into a small glass, which, when he came back for more supplies, I poured into the sauce. "Oh, that's what I do too!" he said, happy to find common ground. "Gives it a little more body." I didn't like the way he rolled out the word *body*.

When he went back to the dining table, I poured out a little more wine into the small glass, then dropped in the pills. I handed him the rest of the bottle and two wine glasses, one with a blue rim, the other red.

"I get the red rim. You can pour."

He did so gladly as I strained the pasta and spun the salad. He handed the red glass to me and we did a perfunctory toast. I took a long sip and he followed suit. Then I handed him the cheese and grater on a plate. "Grind away," I said in a tone that would have made Mags proud.

He gulped down another swig of wine, then took the plate from me, making sure our hands touched, which reminded me of what my hand had so recently touched. This was not going to be easy, but my life might literally depend on it.

I dressed the salad, then dished up our plates and handed them to him to put on the table, which gave me the chance to pour the "sleeper" wine into his glass. When he came back for the salad plates, I was topping off mine.

"Oops," I said, handing him his glass, "they're too full to carry." I took a healthy swig and he did likewise.

The sauce had a slight char to it—not quite burned. It could have been fried dog food for all Gil cared. There was a brightness in his eyes that was more than reflected firelight: he was back to amorous.

The thought of getting into bed with Gil was odious. But if he had the power to ruin my life—to put me in jail—then it won out over sharing a cell with a two hundred-pound love-starved Amazon psycho.

We finished the meal rather quickly—mainly because I had given us small portions—but sat and drank the wine. I refilled his glass twice to my once. I could see the brightness in his eyes dimming. Time to move on. I picked up some plates and took them to the kitchen. Gil did the same while I was filling the sink. I had a dishwasher, but washing dishes together seemed to be a sexy move—at least in the movies—plus, it gave the pills more time to work. Gil pressed behind me and cupped my breasts with his hands.

"Gil, this isn't fair. I'm divorced and lonely," I whined as I turned to him. He was leaning into me, rather on me, but perked up enough to get his tongue into my mouth. I focused on my possible cellmate and tried to return his ardor. We were soon in my bedroom where Gil threw the covers back on the bed. I tried to feign some enthusiasm while undressing as slowly as possible. When will the damn pills kick in? There was much kissing and rubbing and feeling and touching, until Gil settled on what he really loved—my breasts. He must not have been nursed long enough—or maybe too long—as a baby, because that's what he did, suck away. And just like a baby, he fell asleep—I mean unconscious. I would have worried if I had time for compassion, but that not being the case, I eased out from under him and replaced my bosom with a pillow. He never moved as I crept out of the room, leaving my clothes just where they were.

I paused in the kitchen to get my lock picks and a mini flashlight from my purse. I thought about how I had used those picks such a short time ago as I took my sweat suit and a paddle off hooks on the mudroom wall. Fortunately, my canoe was still beached, so there was no noise of undoing ropes. There were probably snakes and spiders of every species curled and coiled inside, but just like pain, the greater fear overcomes the lesser one, so I did not smack the sides to encourage them to leave.

The canoe would be the fastest way to get to Gil's and the least likely to be seen. I paddled to his dock and quietly tied it to a rope hanging there, not wanting to leave a mark in the sand from beaching.

44

The observatory was locked, but with my picks and Roger's lessons, I opened it easily. I held my breath waiting for an alarm—none. With the help of my little light I could see the telescope, the computer it was hooked up to and neat stacks of paper and scrap books wedged into low wooden shelves. The room was furnished with a threadbare oriental rug, an old wooden desk and a swivel chair.

It looked like he printed everything out on a copier. In the shelves, there were dozens and dozens of albums labeled with what looked like astronomical designations. I scanned a few of the stacks and saw that some were also arranged by date. In a panic, I couldn't remember the date I was looking for. I sat down in Gil's chair and focused; Christa's birthday had been shortly before, I was sure of that, and Mags and I had gone for a day at the Red Door Spa after Sherry died, because we had talked about her death that day. I found a pile that contained that time span and quickly breezed through it. Nothing of interest, except for one day—a blank page with a red sticky marker.

Oh crap! He hid it. I twirled around in the chair and faced the old wooden file cabinet. It was locked. In went the picks, out popped the drawer. It didn't take long to find the folder with the red sticker—and there I was, paddling away in second by second dated time frames, and there I was with my paddle in the air, about to strike, illuminated by the lightning. Irrefutable proof, the judge would say. I took the folder out and pondered my next move. Did he have more copies? I'd heard that once it's in the computer, it's there forever. I could take the hard drive out, but 1) I didn't know how to do that, and 2) I didn't want Gil to know I'd been there.

Then I noticed my savior—one of those round plug-in heaters with the clear warning on the front not to put it near papers or towels or anything flammable—and it was plugged in. Even I would have had more sense than that.

I took stacks of the papers and albums and lined them up neatly to make a paper path to the computer and the copier. There were glue pots for the scrapbooks; those I opened, pouring the contents over the papers and the albums.

Gil is sure to have insurance, I told myself, to alleviate guilt for what I was doing. I pushed several pages loosely into the heater, pressed the start switch, waited a moment until it began to glow orange and the paper began puckering, picked up my folder, shut the door and locked it. I sprinted to the canoe, untied it and paddled home in record time. Looking back, I could see flames. I beached the canoe, slipped into the mudroom and out of the sweats, put the folder in the top-loader washing machine buried inside the towel I had used to dry my wet feet, along with the pick set and flashlight. I got a glass of water and went back to the bedroom.

Gil was still gone to the world. I maneuvered myself back into the pillow's place, then waited for the fire trucks.

45

The head is the heaviest part of the body, which is why you invariably hit it when you fall, and Gil's was feeling like a cement block. I was wondering how much more I could take when I heard the sweet sound of sirens. The trucks went past, screaming their emergency. Gil stirred, but slept on: one pill would probably have been enough.

I turned the light on, moved around and kicked him. Nothing. Finally I shook him hard, then harder.

"Gil! Gil!" Oh my god, did I put him in a coma? Finally he moved.

"Huh? What?" He sat up and looked blankly at me. "Livie? What the…" Memory came slowly. I didn't give him time to think. I sat up, bare breasted. He snapped awake and grinned, but I cut that short.

"The fire trucks just went by," I said urgently.

He started to really wake up. He looked around, saw our clothes all over the place, then turned back to me and pulled me down into the pillows.

"Shouldn't we go see?"

"Later," he said. "We've got better things to do now."

I let him kiss me and run his hands down me, wondering how I could get out of this when there was a pounding on my front door.

Gil groaned as I put on a robe.

"Tell them to go away," he said as I left.

Bill Lacey, the fire chief, was standing outside. "Evening, Livie. Sorry to bother you but there's a fire down at…"

"Hi, Bill." I turned, and there was Gil, a towel around his waist, coming out of my bedroom. That son-of-a-bitch. They exchanged that man thing, the invisible wink, as Bill took in what Gil wanted him to see.

"Sorry to interrupt, Gil," he grinned, "but there's a fire down at your place."

"My place!"

"Yeah, that gazebo or whatever it is in the front. We got it under control before it got to the house. It's pretty much gone, though. Saw your truck parked in the drive here and thought you might want to come see."

"I'll be right there!" He returned to the bedroom.

"See you, Livie." Bill smiled a smile that did not make me want to return it, then actually tipped his heavy fireman's helmet to me as he left.

Oh shit, I thought. Bill Lacey is the biggest gossip in the area. He would go out to breakfast and dinner on this one. On the other hand, he would happily testify how I was otherwise occupied when that particular blaze occurred. A piece of my reputation for peace of mind was probably a fair exchange.

"I'll be back," Gil said, giving me a kiss and a squeeze.

I locked the door and closed all the blinds. I took the towel and its contents out of the washer; the picks and flashlight went back into my purse, and the damning pictures I stuffed into the part of my suitcase that holds the retractable handle apparatus. I showered quickly, then dressed in clean clothes, stripped the bed and put everything Gil might have touched, including the clothes I had worn, into the washer, along with the dirty towel, and turned the settings to hot/hot and double rinse.

I had just finished when a fire truck went by and gave a toot-toot-de-toot. I knew Gil had casually mentioned to the firemen where he had been, and Bill would certainly have added details.

I took one of the sleeping pills, turned out all the lights, lay down on my bed fully clothed and pulled a blanket over me. The other trucks serenaded me as they went past, but I was past caring. I roused slightly from my artificial sleep as Gil knocked, then pounded on the door, but not enough to really waken me.

When I did awaken the next morning, the thought came to me that Gil had not used his key. Then I remembered the work Roger had done on this place, which included changing the locks and…and what? Were there cameras?

Livie, I thought, go to some desert island for the next year.

Instead, I threw the wash into the dryer, a few things into my suitcase, brushed hair and teeth, and made a hasty exit for the island of Manhattan.

46

The city was its usual chaos, but I found that comforting right now—that and the anonymity. It was nice that Ricardo, my new doorman, didn't seem to notice how casually I was dressed, unlike our snob on Park Avenue, whose eyebrows would have arched in disapproval.

The message light was blinking furiously, indicating several calls. Tough tootsie, I thought.

My bath was long, hot and cleansing. I washed my hair, wrapped it in towels and myself in a robe, got into my bed and turned on a soap opera. I hadn't watched one in years, but it didn't matter as the story was the same, just a little more risqué.

My mind numbed, I could understand how one could become addicted to living these other people's television lives, dropping your own messes and worries and replacing them with what you could watch with detachment and have some control over, even if that control was in the remote in your hand.

When that escape ended, I returned one of Mags's seven calls.

"You need to get over here—now!" I had forgotten that I would never be detached or in control of the on-going soap opera of Mags's life.

I did the best I could with my hair, then dressed in what I thought was an original and cheerful combination of clothes.

As I gathered my essentials to leave the blue phone rang.

"Hello," I said.

"Well," Roger drawled, "you are an endless source of surprises."

"You have cameras in the cottage?"

"I told you we have the place covered."

"I thought that meant telephone and burglar alarms."

"Yeah, well, the camera was only supposed to go on when someone breaks in, we'll have to fix that. You haven't told me everything, have you? What did this Gil have that you wanted?" he laughed. "And don't give me anything about *lonely, divorced* and his scrawny body. What the hell did you put in his wine?"

I was momentarily speechless.

"You really have gone too far, Roger."

"I went as far as I needed to, and so did you."

"Are all men shit heads?"

"Yeah, probably. What's in the suitcase? And Livie, this is not story hour. I need to know where you were those thirty-five missing minutes."

"You know exactly where I was."

"Yeah, I do, but I don't know why you burned down your macho man's little observatory and took what you hid in that suitcase."

"I have to go to Mags's."

"You have to be here tomorrow at noon." He hung up.

47

I felt like flushing that blue phone down the toilet but went to the living room and put it in my bag instead. While there, I pushed the buttons on my real phone to get the messages, which I immediately regretted.

"Livie, where are you, baby?" said Gil. "I might have come on too strong. Come back here and we'll start where we left off—leaving off everything, that is. Ha, ha."

I pressed erase.

"Livie, this is your concerned physician. I'm interested in examining you personally to make sure you're in good shape." Travis left his number.

I pressed save.

"Olivia," said Larry. "I really need to talk to you. You're the only one I can talk to. Do you think you could have dinner with me? I mean…if you want. Anytime it would suit you would be fine."

Now, what was that about?

I grabbed my jacket and purse, locked the door behind me and had Ricardo hail me a cab.

Bechert opened the door with Mags peering from behind him. She took one look and yanked me inside. "I hope no one saw you!" she gasped. "Who did your hair? Dagwood? And for god's sake, Livie, Gucci and Pucci together? Never! What were you thinking?"

"My creativity is offended," I pouted.

"Your creativity is offensive! The sight of you is driving me to drink."

We sat in Mags's ice-pink dressing room, sipping wine while Flore had at my hair with brushes, hot implements and sprays. When she finished and left, Mags tossed me a black garment and instructed me to exchange it for the top I had on. It was snug, but I wrestled into it.

"You're a bit fleshy," said my fashion advisor. "You can't possibly wear the really good pieces unless you have a reduction. Everyone does it."

"No. Again." We had been over this terrain so often before. "What is so urgent that I had to get here now?"

Mags closed the door and sat down. In a stage whisper that was much louder than her regular voice, she said, "This is top secret. You can not breathe a word of this or where you heard it," which would seem a contradictory set of commands coming from anyone else, but when Mags says, "I won't breathe a word about it," it never seems to include her mouth. Gossip is her coin of the realm and she keeps her treasure house full.

"Well," she settled in, "as you know, Mason is Laurence's lawyer."

"Uh huh." This was nothing new.

"His estate lawyer."

"Un huh." Again, old information.

"Well, Laurence just wrote a new will."

"With Sherry gone, I suspect he had to. And how do you know this?"

"I was dusting in Mason's office…"

Dusting? The vision of Mags as Lucy Ricardo in fluffy apron, hair bound up in a frilly scarf and wielding a dust rag sent me into choking laughter. "And you happened to see Larry's will?" I managed after she pounded me on the back.

"Yes, the new one and the old one, which was a doozy. He left her everything."

"Everything!"

"Yes, indeed. Apparently she had convinced him that she would be generous with the girls if the unforeseen happened. Obviously she hadn't foreseen it happening to her first."

"And the new will?"

"That's the strange part. It's the same, only the wife isn't named. Just *my wife* first, then if there is no wife, it's divided between Lauren and Christa. That's the condensed version, of course. It runs on and on with wherefore's and now therefore's and all that crap. Isn't that the oddest? Do you know if he's seeing someone?"

"As far as I'm concerned, the only someone he should be seeing is a shrink." Or a parole officer. "Was Larry her sole heir?" I asked out of curiosity.

"Well, of course," Mags replied. "But what did she have to leave him? Stilettos and thongs?"

"I guess. But it is odd."

"Mason says Laurence has put on about a hundred pounds and looks like hell. Sherry definitely was doing the old *f and f him to death* routine. And speaking about Sherry…Mason saw the autopsy report, which is the most interesting of all. We need more wine for this."

I was closer to the bottle, so I got up and poured, then settled in for the juiciest part, which Mags, as usual, had saved for last.

"Sherry was three months pregnant when she drowned." She sat back with a triumphant look after delivering this blockbuster.

I sat back, stunned. She thought the *pregnant* was my source of dismay, but it was the *drowned* that I was savoring. I made myself gasp, "Pregnant!" as if I gave one hen-feather damn, but I was suddenly remembering something Larry had said months ago.

"Three months!" she affirmed archly.

"Laurence must be devastated."

"Or emasculated, which rhymes with *tool*, which rhymes with *fool*," she sang to the *Music Man* line.

"Strange," I said, trying not to sound that way myself, "that she drowned. Larry told me she was a champion swimmer. He was very proud of all the medals and trophies she had won."

"Well, that was weird. There were marks around her ankles. Apparently the weeds were thick around the dock, so they think she got caught in them and was trying to free herself, but couldn't. Then the storm churned the water enough to free her body and when she popped up, her head hit the dock."

Mags's phone rang. She smiled coyly. "I have to take this." She slipped into her bedroom, which could only mean it concerned something else she hoped to do in the bedroom.

It gave me a moment to think. If Sherry had drowned before getting hit on the head, I didn't kill her. Then who did? I didn't for a moment believe that she had drowned on her own. Oh Lordie, I wanted my simple old life back, I wanted to count linen napkins, not the ways that someone could be murdered.

At that point, Silly bounded in and immediately began humping my swinging leg.

48

Mason had always wanted a dog. Mags said, "No way! Every time I would walk out of here in a black cashmere dress/skirt/pants/coat, I would feel its hairs sticking to my butt."

So Mason said, "Of course, dear," which would have seemed to be the end of the matter. Mason, however, loved to accede to all of Mags's demands, peeves and tempers just so he could find a way around them, the fun being in the end run.

He brought home a six-month-old hairless Chinese crested puppy, whom he had named Counselor, but whom we immediately dubbed Silly, as he was one of Mother Nature's extreme flights of fancy. While his speckled brown body had no hair, his luxuriously flowing white forelock, mane and fetlocks made him look genetically related to a Belgian draft horse.

His hairless condition, as Mason jolly well knew it would, distracted Mags from the fact of Silly's existence by providing her with a whole new venue of retail opportunities. The very first was her oozing motherly need to protect this naked baby with her last season's mink jacket, which she had made into a dog bed. PETA would have been horrified, and the outrage would have continued through the purchases of ever more exotic fur coats, boots and cashmere sweaters, had Silly not been such a vulnerable, pathetic looking critter that

PETA probably would have been glad to see him covered in just about anything.

Silly, at least, was house-trained. Who had done the training, and why that person had been willing to give the little dog away—or more likely, sell him for an extraordinary amount—Mason refused to say. He also refused to have Silly neutered because of his impeccable pedigree and the intent to use him as a stud. That kind of intent required attention, which neither of his people parents had for raising this dog child. Nor were they capable of being his pack leader. Silly became Lord of the Manor and all six pounds of him felt that he was entitled to whatever six pounds of dog could want. It soon became apparent that mostly what he wanted was to get laid.

Silly became very fond of a small stuffed dog Mags named Friggin'—so fond that he spent most of his puppyhood humping it. Then, as he grew, he would hold the increasingly ratty Friggin' in his mouth while he humped whatever he could mount.

Mason delighted in letting Silly loose during the cocktail hour, or at any other gathering, where he would hump himself into a lather on a footstool, then head straight for those women who were in the most receptive phase of their monthly cycles and try to tear off their pantyhose. Their gleaming-eyed escorts usually found a reason for them to leave early.

49

I was in Roger's office the next day at noon: grumpy at having been summoned, angry at his intrusion into my privacy and embarrassed at what that intrusion had made him privy to.

Certain that he would somehow find out anyway, I handed over Gil's photographs. He studied them carefully, then looked at me and said, "What the hell were you doing canoeing at night in the middle of a storm? That's a dumb, dangerous thing to do."

"But," I protested, "it wasn't raining when I started out and I've done that since I was a child."

"Yeah, well you're not a kid anymore. You shouldn't be there alone, doing those things."

I had a feeling that *those things* very much included Gil.

I did get a grudging smile out of him when I told him about thinking the pale creature I had hit with my paddle was a turtle or a carp.

"I want you to stay away from that place until we figure out where Gil fits into the picture," he said. "I have a bad feeling about the whole thing."

Roger's *bad feelings* and *thrummings* were usually correct.

"I'm thinking of going to a convent," I told him.

He looked at me, wide-eyed. "You mean, like in a black dress and everything?"

"No," I laughed. "I mean like for about five days. Just to get away and clear my mind."

"That's a good idea." Roger didn't even try to hide his relief that I would be stashed someplace safe. "Where?"

"There's one in Connecticut…"

"Oh jeez, not that damn state again. There's a big one on the Jersey shore, why can't you go there?"

But I had made up my mind, and I was comfortable with the idea.

50

I just needed to get away from the turmoil of my current life: from looking over my shoulder for someone intending me harm; from fielding Gil's and Larry's calls; from the constant feeling of being spied on. Even though I had insisted that Roger remove most of the devices, I didn't trust that he had. I needed peace.

My destination was a small convent in Connecticut that accepts paying guests for short periods of time. Five days of quiet behind cloistered walls sounded just like a doctor's order. Being Catholic was not a requirement, nor was attending the frequent services, although guests were invited to do so. Since I was raised high Episcopalian (which in these days is more Catholic than the Catholics), I would have no problem joining the nuns in religious activities. But mostly, I wanted the quiet of a simply furnished room, the ability to walk in the gardens or sit alone in a chapel to ponder my life.

There were no telephones, TV's, computers or even newspapers. In fact, no contact with the outside world was allowed. The outside world had changed for me. I needed to adjust myself to those changes.

I told Christa and Lauren where I was going. Christa was approving. Lauren seemed disinterested. Janine, a great believer in the examined life, was all for the opportunity for quiet contemplation. Mags's expected reaction was, "Are you out of your...," followed by her oft-used favorite word that I would certainly not hear for the next few days, along with her insistence that I go to their house in the Hamptons instead, as "the staff is still there," which morphed into, "It'll be just us girls, just like we were going to do when...," which was exactly the opposite of what I really needed.

I packed a small bag—basic hygienic needs, comfortable clothing, books, a writing notebook—ready for an early start in the morning.

I woke feeling out of sorts, with a headache and my joints hurting. Breakfast was tea and plain toast; my stomach seemed not to welcome the thought of anything else.

As part of my adventure into the world of the "new me," I had rented a car—not your usual traveling salesman special, but a car I had lusted after in my younger days—a Thunderbird convertible. Combining lust with a trip to the convent was probably counter-intuitive, but nevertheless, I'd called Wrent A Wreck a few days before to inquire if they had such a vehicle. Indeed they did—a black '62 with red leather seats.

I was moving slowly, with a walking-underwater feeling, so by the time I drove over to pick up the T Bird (leaving your own car in their garage space was part of the deal, a form of collateral in case you flipped the radio on to "California Dreamin'" and took off for Route 66), stowed my bag, tossed the parking receipt and documents into the cavernous glove compartment and got all the seat and mirror adjustments made, I got on the highway later than planned and had to maneuver in full rush-hour traffic. My mood soured and the epithets *jerk, loser* and *dumbass* tripped off my tongue, directed at my fellow mankind. Actually, womankind would be more accurate. I wondered what had happened to this latest generation of young females: they seemed to favor little red cars in which they swerved in and out of lanes, cutting you off or climbing your tail pipe. They also seemed to drive with their knees, as one hand held a cellphone, while the other was held up in a permanent impolite gesture.

I was fuming by the time I got out of that mess, wishing I hadn't worn a turtleneck, as I was soaked in sweat. I thought about putting the top down, but that thought made me shiver. By the time I pulled into the long driveway leading to the convent gates, I felt like crap, everything hurt, and I felt like I was burning up with fever. I stopped the car in a little cul-de-sac just short of the gates. Those nuns had little contact with the outside world—I could not morally take my fever and whatever illness accompanied it into their midst. As much as I wanted the trip to be over, I turned around and headed toward the cottage, which was less than an hour away. I could not have safely driven that tank of a car back into Manhattan.

I stopped at a gas/convenience store to fill up. That car didn't sip gas; it guzzled it like a sailor in a bar on a one-day pass. I bought milk for my tea, plain white bread for toast, eggs to be coddled, a few cans of chicken broth, a pile of gossip rags for entertainment, plus a big bag of peanut M&Ms. If I was going to be sick, I deserved some treats, and by the time I got to the cottage, I was sick. I was sicker still when I saw Gil's truck parked there. I pulled in behind him, got out and went to the door, my fever rising with anger.

51

Gil yanked the door open with a big *Hi honey, you're home* grin, as happy to see me as I was not to see him.

"Livie." He tried to bear hug me. I pushed away from him. "What a surprise! I'm so happy. I knew you'd come back." He spied the car. "Holy crap, where did you get that? Let's put the top down and take it for a spin."

"I'm sick, Gil, I was on my way to someplace else, but I'm sick."

"Yeah, right." God, how I hated that wolfish grin. "You couldn't stay away."

"Gil," I said—in this case the best defense being a good offense— "could you get my things out of the car? And what are you doing here? I thought the locks were changed." I looked around. "And what the hell is going on?"

The furniture was moved, the living room rug was half rolled up.

"I thought I heard a mouse the other night, I was looking for holes," Gil said as he swiftly put things back in order.

"Gil, please just get my things," I said, collapsing into the repositioned big chair.

"Sure I will, baby." He touched my forehead. "You really are hot," he said and did that awful Groucho Marx thing with his eyebrows that no grown man should attempt outside of vaudeville. Then more seriously, he added, "The door wasn't locked, which made me concerned. Remember I told you I would stay here sometimes because of the break-ins? I left you messages. Fever got your memory?"

Then I remembered he had left messages (which I had only half listened to) that there had been several area break-ins in the past weeks. Probably the latest crop of kids reaching their terrible teens, out looking for booze and thrills.

"Gil, please?"

"I'm on it!" He went out to the car and was gone longer than he should have been. I imagined him circling the car, examining it, salivating like it was a bitch in heat. Finally, he brought in my case and the bag of groceries. He unloaded the bag to put things away, grinning at my choice of literature and comfort food. The cans of soup, however, disgusted him. "You're not eating this stuff. Not when you've got Gil here to make the real thing."

"It's okay, Gil. I don't want you to go to any trouble."

"Trouble? Not for my Livie, it will be pure pleasure." He brewed me a cup of tea and made toast, horrified at my choice of synthetic white sponge board. "I'll make you some real bread too. I'll have to get the ingredients together. I have some at home, but I'll need to go to town for a few things. You're parked behind me, so I'll just take your car. Need anything?"

I didn't. I refrained from asking which town he needed to go to, knowing full well that once he got the top down—which at that moment I could hear happening—he would head for the open road.

So, settled in the big chair with tea, toast, magazines and clicker at hand, knowing Gil would be gone for hours, I caught up on the latest shenanigans in Hollywood and the latest outrages on Jerry Springer. I didn't hear the unmistakable sound of the big Thunderbird when Gil returned, but an unfamiliar small purr.

"You've gotta see this, Livie," he said proudly, when he came in. His hair was strangely oiled and brushed back. Oh my god, was that a DA?

I heaved myself out of the now sweat-soaked chair and went to the door. There, pulled around in back of Gil's truck, stood his newest toy—a small John Deere Gator—with a big pot and several foil-wrapped packages sitting on a canvas tarp on the back bench. He took my hand and pulled me out to the driveway.

"This thing runs so smooth, I didn't spill a drop." He slipped into the driver's seat and turned it on. "And look! You just release the brake and drop this lever into gear," he said, dropping the lever. He circled around his truck and stopped in front of me. "Easy as pie! Take it for a spin," he urged me. "You'll love it."

"Later," I said.

"Suit yourself. You're missing a lot of fun. I bought it with the insurance money I'm getting—you know, for my observatory that burned down," he said pointedly. "You deserve a ride."

I went back into the house and the comfort of my chair.

Gil brought in his supplies and arranged the kitchen to his satisfaction. He turned the oven on and soon the aroma of baking bread filled the house like a comfort drug.

Gil built a fire and made me a hot toddy, old-fashioned medicine that did make me feel better. Then came Granny's other staple—chicken soup, accompanied by the homemade bread. It was as good as it was going to get, but as the evening wore on, I was getting worse. I was drowsy from the flu medicine he had given me, and finally took myself to bed, accepting Gil's offer to clean up.

I heard him fussing in the kitchen, then turning off lights and locking the door. My hope that he was on the outside of that door was for naught as Gil turned off the bedside lamp and slid into the bed, spooning into my turned back.

"Go away, Gil," I croaked.

"Never," he slurped into my neck. "I've got you right where I want you."

He pulled me closer. "You're so hot." He pulled up my flannel gown and ran his hands over me.

"I have a fever, you jerk!"

He pinched my nipples until I yelped. "Don't ever call me that again. You think you're home free with that fire stunt?" I stiffened involuntarily. "Yeah, I thought so," he said into my ear, "but I still have copies."

His hand slid down and grabbed my ass hard. "This belongs to me."

"You're making me too hot, I need to sleep." I tried to push him away.

"You make me hot all the time." He jammed his naked body against me, moving rhythmically. At that point I didn't care what he did. If he wanted to hump my back, so be it, as long as I didn't have to look at him. Eventually, his heavy breathing stopped. I thought about getting up and washing off his leavings, but I was too out of it from the medicine, so I just fell asleep. My dreams were of heat, chaos, crashes and sudden pain that made me wake up with a scream. My arm and hip burned.

I tried to get up, but Gil's arms had me pinned. I was getting hotter, but it wasn't the fever. My house was on fire.

52

With the strength that comes when you need it most, I got myself out of Gil's embrace. The light reflecting in his open eyes told me it had been a death grip.

The pain in my arm and hip should have made me faint, but fear and the survival instinct made me get to the window, open it and perform the quick exit I had practiced so often as a teenager. I closed the window as I always had, then hearing voices, limped behind a stand of shrubs.

"All clear here," a man said into a walkie-talkie, "no one got out."

"Fan out and make sure," a voice crackled in reply.

The man went around to the front of the house. I took that opportunity to hobble down the path to the lake and wade in. Powerful lights began to crisscross the yard and house and down to the lake. I submerged. I was no longer hot—the water was freezing.

I came up under the old dock at the back of the house. There was a crash as the glass in the window I had so recently exited broke from the heat of the flames consuming the room and Gil. Lights swept the water. I thought of swimming to the island house, but even in my foggy state, realized that would not be a wise choice.

"Let's get out of here," one of the men said. The noise of the fire increased so I could not hear them leave, but I saw their car lights as they turned the bend down the road.

History has always given men the glory and laurel leaves for their bravery and strength in times of crisis. Women are not so often celebrated, from the endless cycles of births—each one worthy of a medal—through the saints and martyrs to the ordinary women. Women like those in the Donner Pass party who, in their cumbersome long skirts and with their focused determination, outlasted the men on that trek through the mountain snows to seek help.

My sister ancestors willed me the strength to not sink peacefully under that water, but to pull myself to the shore. The cozy flannel nightgown was now a freezing, dangerous weight. I struggled out of it, then limped up the path to the side of the house, the blazing fire made me choke, but it also lit my way. I could hear sirens in the distance. In front of Gil's truck sat the Gator. "Take it for a little spin," he had said. "Later," I had replied, which hopefully meant the key was still in it. It was. I took the tarp from the back and gathered it around me, then eased down onto the hot seat. Fortunately it was my left arm that had been hurt, as all the controls were on the right side. I remembered Gil's lesson. I turned the key, released the brake, shifted down and drove toward Gil's house just as fire trucks roared up the road to my flaming home. I pulled around the Thunderbird to the back door and found the key where Roger said it was hidden. "The more clever they get," I remembered him saying, "the more fun it is to find it."

"Roger, where are you?" I whimpered as I opened Gil's back door, got inside, then slid down the wall.

53

I have heard people described as a "pain in the ass" —I have been so described myself—but had never experienced it in full force. Now, my hip and my arm were in deathly combat for my full attention and it was a draw.

I so wanted to faint. I so wanted to live. I pulled the tarp tighter, rolled onto my good hip to my knees, then clawed my way up the wall, using whatever protruded, until I was upright enough to get the short distance to the bathroom at the back of the house. I knew there were no windows in there, just a ceiling light that I could safely turn on.

I had never wanted to be in this place again. It was not just physically painful, but emotionally as well.

Gil had been a better person when Vivian, his wife, was alive. You could say—and many did—that Viv was the best part of Gil. She spent the last months of her life in the small bedroom that was connected to this room and Gil hadn't removed a thing. In the linen closet, neatly arranged, were rolls of bandage wraps, boxes of institutional size sanitary napkins and bottles of medicines and antiseptics. I threw some bandage wraps and napkins by the bathtub, then carrying a bottle of antiseptic and a bottle of pain pills, stepped over the edge and sat down on the tarp.

When I recovered from that shock, I got the pill bottle open and turned on the faucet. I cupped water in my good hand to wash two pills down, then turned the faucet off and lay back in the tub until pain roused me. I pulled towels from the overhead bar and spread them across me, then got the napkins and wrap ready and took the top off the antiseptic bottle.

Which one is worse? I thought. My arm, there's something in there. I poured the liquid over my arm and clamped a napkin over the wound. Searing pain was my last memory.

54

Ohmigod, the pain, the pain. I was being moved. I was so cold, so cold, being wrapped in something thick and soft.

"Wrap everything in the tarp, rinse the tub, then spray the whole place with the solution and wipe it down with a clean towel. Don't forget to do the door on your way out. Google, follow us with her car, keep on our far side when we go past her house, then pull in front of us."

"I hope you don't run me into a tree," said Google.

"Roger?" I mumbled. "How did you find me?"

"Termites," he said. "Now be quiet, I have to close the top until we get down the road."

Then it was black. I didn't care, it was warm and softly padded. Then what seemed to be a top opened a bit and air came in.

Voices.

"I've heard of ambulance chasers, but you guys take the cake."

"Hey," Sandy said, "we got a call to do a pick up, probably some kids having fun. You think I got nothin' better to do at night?"

"Oh, sweetie," a man's voice said, "if you don't, I can think of a few things."

"Watch your mouth, captain," purred Sandy. "I'm a professional."

"I'll just bet you are." It was Bill Lacey, the fire chief. "Get this bone buggy outta here, there's nothin' to pick up and I gotta fire to put out."

"Keep your hose wet," said Sandy.

I could feel us move.

The top opened all the way. Roger was swimming around above me, fussing with some contraption.

"Tell me when you can stop," he said. "I only want to shoot this vein once."

"Now," said Sandy.

I felt a prick in my arm, then bandages being applied to hold something in place.

Then far voices.

"Slow down, Sandy, we can't get stopped."

"Who's going to stop a hearse?"

"A cop who wonders what's the rush."

Then somewhere, sometime, we did stop. A deep voice. "Pull into the bay, up to the wall. It will be easier to roll the whole thing out."

There were beeps, doors opened, then my cozy nest was rolling down a hall. Roger was at my head holding up a door.

A door over my bed? The word hearse floated through my foggy memory, chased by the word coffin. I screamed.

A hand gently patted my face. "Don't worry, Livie," said Roger, "I'm not closing the lid. Not just yet anyway," he laughed. Then: "It was the best we could do on short notice."

The deep voice said, "We'd better give her more juice before we pull her out of there." Someone fussed with the thing on my arm. "How much has she had?"

He and Roger discussed numbers. I thought about a similar situation I had been in, not so long ago. I must have thought out loud, because the last thing I heard was Roger saying, "Travis? Who the hell's Travis?"

When I woke up or came to (either one was a regrettable occurrence), I was groggy and felt elsewhere, but the pain was very real and present.

A face leaned over me—a hard face that, under the wrong circumstances, would be frightening. I focused enough to see the soft brown eyes and relaxed.

"I'm Mel Smith," the deep voice said. "Dr. Smith, you'll be happy to know. Babs," he said to someone, "crank the head up so I can get a better look."

As my sight angle rose, I could see that I was in a hospital bed placed in a regular bedroom—the pale yellow flower-flocked walls with a floral border running around the top would have gotten Oscar Wilde's attention.

Dr. Smith gently cut the dressing away on my arm. Gently or not, it hurt and I moaned. "Sorry," he said, "this is the critical time."

He peered at my arm closely, then sniffed it. Sniffed it! "Looks okay. Smells okay," he said. "Pretty sure I got it all out. Grit your teeth, girl, I have to put a little stuff on it and do a rewrap."

I gritted my teeth, turned my head to the wall and breathed as if for a contraction. It hurt about as much.

"Had children, huh?" the doctor laughed. "You never know when that training will come in handy."

He pulled a stool up to the bed so we were almost eye-to-eye. "I'll look at the hip later, that was just a graze—

nothing in there. But this," he indicated my arm, "was a fragment from a 9 mm hollow point. Now if you were fooling around with someone else's man, the wronged woman," he rolled those words out with seeming relish, "would tend to pack her purse with a little pearl-handled pistol. It looks like you met up with something more like a .357 Magnum. That's a pro's weapon. Care to tell me how a lady like yourself gets herself rolled into my mortuary not dead, but intended to be in that divine condition?"

I was fascinated by the way he spoke. His deep voice, measured and clear, as if he were reciting poetry—something from Coleridge.

"I had a fever," I rasped.

"Mouth dry?" Dr. Mel asked. I nodded. He carefully put a curved straw to my lips so I could take several swallows from a glass.

"I had a fever," I began again. "A neighbor brought me soup." I paused, not sure how to explain the rest.

"So the neighbor stayed to comfort you?" he gently suggested.

"Not my idea!" I protested.

"Um-hum. Then what happened?"

"I fell asleep. Then it was hot...I was hot. There were loud noises...pain. I couldn't move Gil. His arms were around me. I got out. There was fire, smoke. I opened the window...slid out, then closed the window...just like when I'd meet my friends Janine and Mags...we would row over to the boys' camp..."

Dr. Smith put a finger to my lips to stop me. "Later," he said. "Now go back to sleep."

We never finished the conversation. My next awareness was of being moved again, this time rolled along on a gurney. At least it's not a coffin, I thought.

"Sorry, Livie," said Roger. "We have to relocate you."

"Relocate?"

"We have to move you out of Mel's place. Once they find the remains on the bed and that hot-pants fireman remembers the hearse, inquiries will be made."

"Dr. Smith—he'll be in trouble?"

"Nah, he's golden. Even the cops use him."

"Where are we going?" I asked as the gurney bumped into the back of a van, Roger carefully maneuvering an IV drip on a pole next to me.

"For a few days, you'll be Sandy's guest."

"And then?"

"The thing about relatives…you can't choose them, but when you have to go there…"

"Robert Frost…," the English Lit major in me mumbled, "something about a hired hand." Then I woozed through my relatives: Lauren (ha!); Christa, working—too far away. Charles and Alice.

55

The time at Sandy's house introduced me to an interesting cast of characters, beginning with her cousin Chaz. Chaz was in a wheelchair, which was why my gurney could roll up a ramp into the back of Sandy's house. Chaz had been permanently injured in one of his many motorcycle accidents, which did not prevent him from continuing to ride one.

Chaz and his buddies were very familiar with pain and gunshot wounds and not the least bit familiar with sympathy. I had thought my time there would consist of me lying in bed moaning and being taken care of. Wrong. No one cared to hear moaning, and, if I wanted something, I had to get it myself. Plus I was very soon put to use. In spite of my arm being in a sling and my hip painful and swollen, I was seated on a cushioned chair at a table and taught the finer points of Texas Hold 'Em. All those hours at summer camp that Mags, Janine, our other cabin mate Sly and I had spent beating other cabins at poker when it rained were not wasted. I won so much money, one time when a whole crowd had gathered for pizza, that they made me pay for it.

After we finished the pizza, Google said he had to change my dressing, which caused everyone to show their scars. To a man and woman—the latter being Molly and Wildchild/aka Jane, who pulled up their shirts without a hint of modesty to display theirs—they all seemed to have at least one bullet hole or stab wound to exhibit. I had been initiated into an outlaw society.

Chaz and his buddies Google (named before the internet was born) and Spunk took my education in life's important matters to a higher level—not just cards and knife throwing, but in guns: how to hold them, load them, clean them, hide them and—more to the point—shoot them. There was a target range at the back of the house where we practiced, using a silencer so we wouldn't attract official attention.

Then one afternoon, in walked the fabled Zane with Roger close behind. He was everything I had expected—big, brawny, scar-slashed, scary. What I hadn't expected was an old-world gentleman. He greeted me warmly and, unlike the others, was very solicitous about my comfort. When Sandy came in, he grabbed her in a bear hug and twirled her around, one of the few men big enough to carry out that feat. When I saw them together, I immediately saw the connection—Sandy was Zane's sister.

When Roger told me later that I would have to leave within the hour, I was kind of sorry. I was comfortable with these people and, while not cared for, I was cared about, which very likely helped speed my recovery.

It was only then that I realized I had been on another planet. "Roger, ohmigod—the girls, my friends, do they think I'm dead!"

Roger shook his head. "Livie, you don't want to know how many chits I've had to call in on this one. And that includes a big one from my Aunt Maddy, who grew up with the nun who runs that convent you were going to. Well, here's the story: When you got there, you came down with the flu and fainted onto an altar rail. That's why your arm's in a sling. You were kept in isolation, away from the other nuns and visitors, with no telephone or TV. When you were notified about your friend Gil, who was looking after your house because of break-ins in the area, you went into seclusion to grieve and recover your health. You have to hold to this story, because the Connecticut police will want to interview you at some point."

If ever I had fantasized what a knight in shining armor looked like, it probably wasn't Roger. But there he stood, gleaming in that smoky room.

Then Roger asked, "Ready to roll?"

"Almost," I answered, "but there is one thing."

I looked at Zane. He laughed, understanding. "The lady wants a ride!"

Roger, resigned, helped me out the door and onto the back of Zane's motorcycle.

I hadn't really seen one up close or realized how big they were until I sat on one.

"You have no markings," I said over Zane's shoulder as he settled himself in. "It's all black. It doesn't say anything."

Zane angled his head back and grinned. "It doesn't say anything. It shouts *don't touch.*" He winked. Then we were off.

It was exciting. It was thrilling! I envied those biker chicks rolling down the highways for a moment—the moment it took me to realize it was also hard work hanging on with one tired arm and balancing on one screaming hip. Zane must have sensed that and kept the ride short.

"You okay?" he said as he helped me dismount.

"It was worth the pain," I grinned at him. "I'm ready to go again. Well, maybe in a year or so."

We went back into the house so I could say my good-byes. I was touched that they seemed genuinely sorry to see me go. Google insisted on one last inspection of my wound and a change of dressing; he was very proud of his handiwork. I thanked and hugged them all. When I bent over Chaz's chair, he lifted Sandy's big sweatshirt that I was wearing and pushed something heavy into the tied waistband of the borrowed, rolled-up sweatpants. Winking at me, he said, "To keep you safe."

Roger pulled up my shirt and yanked the gun out of my pants. "Are you out of your fucking mind?" he exploded at Chaz. "This has got to be unregistered, and probably hot! That's all she needs, to get caught with that!"

Chaz shrugged, gave a palms-up *what?* "With her history, I thought she'd need it." The others all nodded and *yeahed.*

"We taught her how to use it," Google said, as if that made it all okay.

Roger grabbed my arm—my good arm, thankfully. "Say good night, Gracie."

I gave them a big-eyed oh-oh, now I'm in for it wave as we left.

We rode in silence until the steam stopped coming out of Roger's collar. Finally he handed me a phone. "Call Charles. Tell him you're coming for a visit."

I called Charles. Alice answered. "Olivia! Thank god! What the hell is going on? You were supposed to be at the convent, where are you?"

"On the road headed toward your place. Can you put up with a visitor?"

"Just get here as fast as you can."

56

When we arrived, Alice and Charles were waiting at the door. They came to the car as I turned in the seat and braced myself with my right arm to get out. Charles, being a gentleman, took my other arm to help, which caused me to yelp.

Alice looked on in disbelief, which made me realize what I looked like: no bath or shower since my time in the lake; hair greasy and matted; pale from loss of blood and garbed in not very clean, rolled-up sweats that belonged to a giantess, with old moccasins over sweat socks on my feet. I was a mess.

Alice took my good arm. "Let's go upstairs," she said gently. "Any luggage?"

"No, I..."

"Oh yeah," Roger broke in, "there's a bag in the trunk." He looked at me and winked. "Elizabeth had to go in for more measurements." He handed Alice a plastic sample case.

"At least it's not a garbage bag," she said dryly, as she took it and me into the house.

Roger and Charles followed, Roger saying, "We need to talk," as Charles led him to the library.

"I'm sure we do," he replied as the door closed.

57

Alice turned on the shower, then wordlessly took my clothes off. She pulled the bandage off my hip, nodded to herself, looked at the one on my arm, left the room, then came back with a rubber wrap which she put around that one. Alice had been a veterinarian until her retirement several years earlier and had surely seen her share of blood and gore. She helped me into the shower where the glorious warm water finally washed away the lake residue.

"Stick your head out," Alice commanded. I did. She lathered up my wet head with a handful of shampoo. "Can you rinse yourself, or do you need help?"

"I can do it," and awkwardly, I did.

No matter how bad you feel, a good long shower, especially when you are really gamey, is such a mood lifter. Alice carefully dried me off (my modesty had washed away in the lake), plopped a gown and robe on me, wrapped my head in a towel and propped me up in a big stuffed chair.

"I'm going down to make us a tray."

I was content to just sit there, clean, and as comfortable as possible, my mind wandering. Then it settled on two sentences that had been lurking, just waiting to grab me unaware. Chaz's *With her history, I thought she'd need it.* And the voice saying, *No one got out.*

My grief and terror came like an earthquake, sudden and devastating. The scream brought Alice back into the room. The sobs that followed were so deep, so hard I couldn't breathe. Alice got me onto the bed for my own safety.

"Alice?"

"I'm here, Livie, what can I do? How can I help?"

"Janine," I whispered. "I need Janine."

At some point, Travis arrived. He must have gone to his car for his bag, because he soon produced one of his calming needles and used it.

I was awake, but not awake, drifting somewhere on the edge of the horrors I had been remembering.

Alice and Travis examined my arm. Travis said dryly, "Well, if she fell on an altar rail like Roger said, I'm glad whoever fixed her up got all the fragments out."

"What do you mean?" asked Alice.

"I was a medic in Viet Nam. I saw a lot of altar rails there—I know one when I see one. I've seen the delayed shock from battle too, and I think we're seeing that now."

I drifted in and out of a nightmare of fire and noise until the unmistakable uproar of Mags broke into it, followed by Mags crashing into my room, Silly under one arm.

"My baby! My darling sister! What have they done to you?"

There seemed to be a crowd of people trying to control her. She thrust Silly into Janine's arms and came close to me. I was waiting for the indignant reaction to what I must have looked like, the critique of my hair, face, attire, but there was...silence.

Mags took my face in her hands and looked deep into my eyes. I saw in her eyes a comprehension of pain and sorrow I had not realized she could understand.

Mags took Silly from Janine's arms, directed her to me, shooed everyone else out and firmly closed the door as she left.

Janine took off her sensible country shoes and, in her comfortable and somehow very comforting twin sweater set and tweed skirt, propped herself on the bed beside me. She took my hand and stroked it lightly in silence—two old friends there for each other.

"Janine...it wasn't an accident." I had to take deep breaths, I had to sit up. Janine kept stroking my hand. "Someone shot Gil...and me...and burned him, burned the whole house. It was my fault...it was all my fault. I was lying next to him. He was in my bed, they were after me! It was supposed to be me!"

She could have said something like, *You weren't responsible for what happened. He was in the wrong place,* etc. Instead she said, "Did you hear something that makes you think that? Now, just be very quiet in your mind, very quiet, and remember what you heard."

We sat there on the bed, not moving. Janine had a magical way of being very securely there, while at the same time being outside, an ethereal presence. I was almost in a trance when I remembered those words again.

"*All clear here, no one got out!* They knew I was there! The voice said, No one *got out!*"

"Olivia, people don't always say exactly what they mean, the same goes for people hearing what is said. But we will trust that you heard what you think you did. That being the case, our first priority is to get you well. You are in shock; you have been deeply wounded in heart and body. I am afraid that you might still be in danger and you will need all your strength for self-protection. Whoever arranged that nightmare could be a psychopath: at best, unpredictable; at worst, excited by the act. Possibly enough to try again."

"Do the police even know Gil was there?" I wailed. "The fire...I need to go and tell them."

"No," she said, "I'm not sure that would be the best action for you to take. You would not be considered a plausible witness. You have a solid alibi that says you were not there. If you tell them you were, and what happened, the authorities will see a woman who lied about her whereabouts, went to an underground doctor to have gunshot wounds attended to, and has been hiding out since without having reported a murder, attempted murder and arson. I believe you completely, but to the police, your position would seem shaky, if not criminal. You need to be healthy enough to re-emerge into your life and take charge of events. Now, let's get you up and go down for dinner."

I wondered how she got all that information. Roger would not have told Mags, but he had obviously briefed Janine.

"If you can ride on a motorcycle, you can handle Mags," she grinned.

58

They were all in the library and grew silent when I entered, which made me uncomfortably aware of who they had been talking about. Mags took care of that.

"Ohmigod, you look terrible!" she screeched, setting the Jack Russells barking furiously and scurrying around, which broke the spell. "Don't worry. I brought supplies. I'll have you human in no time."

I sat in the armchair that Janine led me to and sipped the glass of sparkling water that sat on the small table alongside. The dogs created a distraction in the silence.

Silly's appearance among Charles and Alice's pack caused some dismay. Jack Russells are very territorial and do not take kindly to strange dogs, but Silly was just too strange for them. He had been to the groomer that very morning, so he did not smell like any dog they had ever encountered. Plus his disdainful attitude cowed them. Silly simply assumed he was top dog. He had intended to claim their big round plaid bed in the library, but one sniff sent him to the sofa instead, a DMZ where he sat grandly between Roger and Travis. One by one, the other dogs attempted to take over his position of honor. Silly just stared them away.

Janine said, "Listen, friends, we have a situation here. There is no glossing over the fact that someone tried to kill

Olivia and burned down her house to cover it up. That someone might not know that Gil was in her bed."

I flinched as the pairs of eyes flanking the dog turned to me.

Travis finally spoke. "That won't fly for long. The autopsy will show the gender."

"How long do you think that will take?" asked Alice.

"They probably did the preliminary already." He turned to Janine, "Roger said Gil's truck was parked there, so his identification would have been fairly easy—but not the special circumstances." He did not use the word *bullets* and I suspected that it would compromise him professionally if he did so: I would remain *altar railed*. "The coroner will go over the results very carefully, might call in a second opinion, just to make sure."

"Then we have to move fast," said Janine. "We need to get her settled in a safe place before it hits the papers, before the press and the police come to hound her."

"What's wrong with here?" said Alice.

"I second that," from Charles. "We have a gate with a lock at the end of our drive, and if we let the dogs out no one can sneak in."

"And I can look after all her needs…medical of course," grinned Travis.

But Mags had had enough of these amateurs. "Livie's wounds need to be stabilized so she will not need outside help. How long will that take?" She directed the question to Travis.

"Well, she's in remarkably good shape." Was that a twinkle in his eyes? Yes, it was definitely a twinkle. "I can send her off with whatever she needs to care for the *puncture wound*"—the last words were enunciated carefully.

"Then we'll take her back with us to my apartment. The building is a goddamn fort. Most of the staff carries *(who knew?)* and they wet their pants at the thought of crossing me. Who better than her best friend *(Janine's eyes rolled at that)* to be her spokesperson."

Aha! Mags to the rescue! I could already see her in a dark suit—a look from the *West Wing,* hair pulled back in an elegant French twist, designer glasses in place (non-prescription; she had her eyes fixed long ago), controlling a press conference. She was born for this.

Surprisingly, Roger agreed. "She can't go back to her place yet. Not until we get a handle on what's going on. And the longer she stays away from the city, the more interesting she gets. She needs to be back there when the big news hits. She needs to make a statement about her friend Gil and go to his service whenever that takes place. She needs to be available for police interviews. Mags has the right idea." He didn't add the *for once,* but I could hear it anyway.

59

We had dinner and, in spite of the circumstances, it was quite a merry evening until Alice shrieked from the kitchen, "You little bastard!"

We pushed our chairs back in shock. She returned, holding Silly by what scruff he had on his neck. He was grinning triumphantly, and his protruding red appendage told the tale.

Wanda, my delightful little security cuddle from that first traumatic visit, was penned up in a small room off of the kitchen. The room had a Dutch door, the bottom of which was closed, because Wanda was now in heat. How Silly got over that door we will never know. He had to have been Superdog, leaping over tall buildings. Alice thrust Silly at Mags, as angry as I have ever seen her.

"Wanda is supposed to be bred tomorrow to another Norwich Terrier. They are both purebreds. I have people lined up to buy the puppies."

"Well, go ahead," said Mags, not grasping the magnitude of this earthquake. "Maybe nothing happened," although the smug, satisfied look on Silly's face indicated otherwise. If he could smoke a cigarette, he'd be puffing away.

Charles tried to soothe her. "Alice, you know Norwich girls are not easy or willing breeders." He turned to us. "A lot of times people have to use artificial insemination. Or turkey basters," he added with a grin.

"Did I close the door?" Alice sped to the kitchen, followed by the whole crowd of us curious voyeurs. The bottom Dutch door was closed. Wanda, when she spied Silly, held firmly in Charles's arms, turned her back, looked coyly over her shoulder and wiggled her butt. Yep. Wanda had given it away.

After the top Dutch door was closed, Silly was sent out for a cooling walk with Otis, the chauffeur/bodyguard. Mags had chosen to bring the Bentley for this country excursion, with the liveried Otis driving—whom Mason had hired to keep Mags safe from herself and others. We then settled back into our seats for coffee, dessert and champagne, the latter being part of the *necessary equipment* Mags had brought along.

The dog interruption over, we re-focused on the problem at hand.

Me.

It was decided that Mags and Janine would spend the night at the farm, Otis would stay in the currently empty apartment over the garage ("Our groom did a scoot, her replacement starts next week," explained Charles), and we would go back to New York the next day. "After I fix her up," added Mags. "She's not coming to my home looking like that!"

Travis, after assuring me that I looked more than fine, invited Roger to bunk at his place as it was late for the long drive back.

60

In the morning, after Otis brought in Mags's equipment, I was turned into a country-casual swan, complete with a Hermès scarf tied as a sling for my arm. That wasn't technically necessary, but Mags insisted on it for the effect. She did, however, let me remove it for breakfast. While we were assembling everything, Travis and Roger returned, bleary-eyed.

"You didn't sleep well?" asked Alice with concern.

"Well, we got to talking," Roger replied as he poured a cup of coffee from the big old-fashioned pot on the stove.

"It seems we both spent our youth in Viet Nam," said Travis, following Roger's lead with the coffee. "I was a medic. That's what got me into medicine."

"And a few other life experiences," added Roger.

I wondered what those were, but nothing more was forthcoming as we all took our seats at the long kitchen table.

Roger turned to Otis. "Maybe I should drive the ladies in—in case there's trouble…" He took a hard look at Otis: his broad-shoulders and bulging triceps, "Or maybe not," he grinned. "Pro ball?"

"Yes, sir." Otis sat even taller. "Line backer. I can assure you, sir, that I am fully equipped to handle any situation." A knowing look passed between them.

Through all the conversation and clatter and clink of plates and silver, a sound came through that shot Alice to her feet—the sound of two doggy voices in ecstasy. Silly, who had been tied up, had gotten loose to join the love of his life. All his time spent humping whatever he could reach had prepared him for this magic moment, and nothing on earth could stop him. If the night before had been a practice session, this morning was not: he and Wanda were, as they say, *as one*.

Alice just groaned. "Well, that's it: She's pregnant. Her reputation as a purebred is ruined."

Mags tried to look sorry, but you could see that she was secretly proud of Silly and had a scheme in mind. "How long does it take for puppies to be born?" she asked.

"Sixty-three days," Alice and Charles said in unison.

"Why don't I take Wanda home with me? It would be like when girls used to get into trouble and go visit their aunt out of town. She can come to Aunt Mags and no one need know."

And that was why we traveled back to town with Wanda in the front seat next to Otis, her nose against the glass partition on one side, while Silly sat unmoving, his nose glued to the glass on the other.

"Travis is very attractive," said Mags, sitting on one side of me in the spacious back seat. "You notice I didn't put a move on him 'cause I'm your best friend and he seems to have an interest in you."

And if that were the case, I thought, *what makes you think you could grab him away?* I did not say it aloud, much to her disappointment.

"And so does that Roger, but he's not nearly as cute." I knew she was just hoping to start something, like a bored kid on a trip in the back of the family sedan, but I didn't want to respond to either possibility.

But those were distractions. When the approaching New York skyline grew into full size, so did my fear. "I'm scared."

Otis glanced at me in the rearview mirror. I realized that the privacy partition was anything but. How he kept a straight face or kept driving safely while listening to our unedited chatter was amazing.

"You should be," Mags said, "someone wants to kill you."

"Mags!" said Janine, leaning across me to fix her with a warning eye. "Could you once, just once, think before you say whatever pops into that place where normal people have a brain?"

"But it's true! Those bullet holes in Livie and that blaze weren't accidents."

The car veered a bit as Otis looked at me with intense interest—excitement really. Finally something more challenging than keeping *ladies who lunch* from being mugged or kidnapped.

"If Roger had trusted me just a tiny bit," pouted Mags, "I would have come up with a more plausible story than fainting on an altar rail at a nunnery. What? Is she going to start having visions now? Will there be a line of the sick, maimed and weird outside my building waiting for her to appear? Will I have to dress her in black and white, or sackcloth?"

Janine broke in. "Why does it always come back to clothes?"

"You should know! I like being covered, since the ones I had as a kid were regularly ripped off me and..." Mags trembled, her face red with rage. She sank into the seat, her face turned to the window. I could feel her next to me as hard, as rigid as stone.

I had been caught in the crossfire of that part of Mags and Janine's relationship that was patient-client. As a result, some nagging, missing pieces of the phenomenon that was Mags started to fall into place. Now wasn't the time to ponder them, however.

This time I rose to the occasion. "Why does it always have to be about you?" I whined. "For once, I get to be the star of the play. I got shot, for God's sake, and you're hurting my arm."

"Oh, Livie! Oh darling! I'm so sorry." With this, Mags clasped me in hers, and although my arm hadn't really hurt before it sure did now. I took a deep breath and bore it, as I had brought Mags back to herself—at least the self she presented to the world.

Janine rubbed my back. "You're right. It has to be all about you now, and we have to get our stories and our plans straight."

"Well," Mags said grudgingly, "I guess I can work with the convent bit. I had thought about being a nun once myself."

This sent Janine and me into hysterics as we exchanged ideas of Mags in mufti:

"Custom-made wimples!"

"*This wool is really scratchy. Do you think we could do it in cashmere?*"

"Or perhaps, *soft moral fiber!*"

"*A silk veil would flow so much better.*"

"Have your fun," broke in Mags, "but I tried to be a good little Catholic girl, which, incidentally, might come in handy when we go to St. Patrick's."

I stopped laughing. "Why would we go there?"

"Hel-lo! Convent. Altar. Faint. Put them all together, they spell mid-life religious upheaval. We only have to go a few times to make it look good."

"And," said Janine, with a heavy dose of sarcasm, "Saks is right next door."

"Exactly. Climb the steps, walk through with bowed head and then out the little side door and right across the street."

61

When we arrived at Mags's building, Otis got out with Wanda under his arm and went to have a few words with the head doorman and handed Wanda to him. The doorman talked into a phone, and shortly, two bruisers in uniform appeared.

Otis escorted Mags and Silly to the door. The bruisers, one on each side, took me in as Otis went back for Janine. The elevator ride was a bit chaotic with the lovers finally reunited. Otis had to hold Wanda over his head and remained stoic as she dribbled something down his uniform.

Mason was there to greet us, ecstatic that he was going to be a father. He was immediately in love with Wanda, but after one sniff, immediately sent the two dogs off to the groomer with Soledad, one of the maids.

There was a faint whiff of paint. "I'm having her room prepared," exclaimed Mason. "Pale violet, a royal color for a purebred." Did he realize what strange creatures these two purebreds—one looking like Yoda from Star Wars, the other looking like something from the bar scene in that film—would produce? "I have the carpenters building her birthing bed." Then he turned on his heel, saying, "Follow me."

We followed through doors I had never been through, down a hall I had never been down, into an office—magnificent in size and furnishings—that I was vaguely uneasy about entering. Mason loved color, form and order and was a slave to the arts. While he had been seen weeping openly at an exquisite ballet performance, opposing counsel had also been seen weeping after Mason was through with them. Murder and mayhem might seem out of a trusts and estates lawyer's league, but the big league of the ultra-rich that Mason played in produced plenty of both, and Mason took no prisoners.

"Please be seated," he said, without a trace of his usual humor or deviltry. We did so obediently.

"Now, Olivia," he began, "it is my understanding that three major felonies were possibly *(how lawyerly and vague, I* thought) committed in your presence: murder, attempted murder and felony arson. Tomorrow you will be interrogated…"

My alarm was apparent, because he continued quickly, "…not downtown at police headquarters, but here in this office. Do you remember John Langston?"

I did.

"He is quite possibly the best criminal lawyer in the country. This interrogation *(I wished he would stop using that word)* will be a little talk among friends, in which John will take first chair and, at some point, I will sit in. That is, if and until it becomes apparent that any client of mine, other than you, is involved. If that should happen, I will, of course, recuse myself. At some point, John might want to talk to Roger, with or without you present, but with your permission. John will make that decision.

"The meeting will begin at six tomorrow evening. John will arrive with his wife, Kaycee, for a little dinner party. They have often been here for such events as you know."

I did, as I had sat next to John several times. He was such an outrageous storyteller and good table companion that I had not really focused on what he did for a living.

Mason grinned, the devil returning to his eyes. "We will all amuse ourselves while you get grilled."

We went from Mason's office into the smaller dining room where we enjoyed a leisurely lunch. We returned to the subject of the impending puppies.

"We have to have names!" Mags was off on a new creative bender. "We have Wanda and Silly. What about Wassail?"

"Yes, we could hoist the pup in the air as we glug," said Janine dryly.

"I like flowers," put in Mason. "Petunia, my little pet, or Violet to match her room."

"Not flowers. Jewels!" Mags was hitting her stride. "Garnet, Diamond—as in Diamonde," she drew it out dreamily.

"What if they're boys?" Janine said, which brought a silence, but not for long. Yelps, squeals and Spanish curses burst in on us. Doggy perfume filled the air, and the newly glamorous Wanda leapt into Mason's outstretched arms. Soledad, their unfortunate companion on this venture, was completely undone.

"Bad, bad, bad," she kept saying, shaking her finger at one, then the other dog. To Mags she blurted, "No more, Miss Celia say. No more." Miss Celia being the owner of the pet salon. "No more hot dog. No hot dog." Soledad left in a huff.

Mags called Miss Celia. We could hear the hysterical voice and chaos from the distance. Mags kept saying, "I'm sorry. Oh, I'm so sorry," while struggling not to laugh.

The phone call over, she could hold it no longer, tears running down her face as she hooted and gasped, "Ohmigod, ohmigod."

When she could control herself, she relayed how Wanda's appearance and Wanda's unmistakable odor of female readiness had caused every male dog to go berserk, which had caused Silly to rise to the occasion. Fights ensued. There was blood, which left one show dog with the top of his ear hanging. Several owners on the scene got into fights of their own. Several more arrived to witness Wanda and Silly experiencing bliss in the middle of the reception area.

No more hot dog translated into: *Are you out of your mind, bringing a dog in heat into my salon? My lawyer will talk to your lawyer.*

Mason tore himself away from Wanda so he could go to soothe Miss Celia and then head to his office to work to pay for the damages.

62

John Langston was one of those storybook successes. A big black giant of a man, he had been a big black giant of a kid, headed without doubt for a life behind bars until a hard-assed football coach came to his school and, on one of the few occasions John showed his face there, grabbed him and changed his life. Through the coach's slap-hard guidance, John caught up scholastically—enough to go to Iowa State on a football scholarship. John was a smart, talented player—an All American—and the professional teams came calling, offering him buckets of gold for his signature.

John followed another rainbow and, with the aid of scholarship money supplemented by busting his tail on part-time jobs, went to Harvard Law School, graduating in the top tier of his class.

John went into criminal law because he understood criminals, having spent his early years being one himself. He soon became a legend in the courtroom.

The amusing dinner companion, however, was nowhere in sight as he sat at Mason's desk. John's face was a blank, no soft smile, sparkling eyes, agreeable demeanor. He was like a still life. When he moved, it was to stand and pull out a chair for me, then to unplug the phone.

He sat back down. "Olivia, I prefer to hear a story from beginning to end. So, whenever you are ready."

I fumbled around at first, my conversational skills being of a more social kind, the give and take variety. John gave nothing—not an *uh huh, and then,* or *he did what?* I was talking to a wall. It was uncomfortable at first, but it made me go into my story without distractions.

At the end, John finally spoke. "Tell me more about Gil."

Gil?

"I've known Gil for years. Before his wife Vivian died, we often did things together as couples."

"I asked what you know about him."

"John, Gil was just in the wrong place at the wrong time."

"Was he?" John sat back in the chair, which creaked ominously from his bulk. "From where I sit, you were the one who wasn't supposed to be there. You were at the convent as far as the world knew. Your car wasn't even there."

"Are you saying Gil was the target?"

"There is a distinct possibility that he was, given the facts that we have. It is a possibility we must explore."

"But who would want to kill Gil?" Other than me on a few recent occasions, I thought but did not say. "He was just—Gil."

"We all have our secrets." John broke a grin finally. "Who would suspect that the pretty, gracious lady sitting next to you at an elegant dinner party could get herself into this situation?"

No situation is so dire that a woman won't react to being referred to as pretty. I blushed. He laughed. I wondered if a blush on someone as dark-skinned as John would show. What a great advantage if it didn't.

"We have to be prepared, Olivia, for the interview with the police. They will certainly want to hear from you personally why Gil was in your house." Here John looked at me intently. "When they ask you if you went to the convent, what will you say?"

"I'll tell them that I did go there, but that I didn't stay because..."

John held up his hand. "You will tell them that you did go there—period. You will not elaborate or add any unasked for information. You did go there. That is your answer. If they ask about your injury, you don't remember just how it happened, you weren't fully conscious when it happened. Remember, you were not fully conscious when it happened."

"Well, I wasn't! I was zonked on cold medicine."

"No elaborations! You were not fully conscious. Those are the only words you need to say. You will be distraught, wringing your handkerchief, or something like that. You will speak as softly as possible and squeeze some tears out. Now, why didn't you come right back to New York?"

I began to get into the scene. "I went to my dear friends, my relatives, to grieve in private. I knew the press would be at my door."

"Good. Good. The cops don't always love the reporters. They'll understand that. I will be with you as a concerned friend and as a lawyer if you seem to need one. They won't want to mess with me. If they ask you something that throws you, just say, *Could you repeat that please?* or *I didn't understand the question.* I'll try to hop in to rephrase it to give you a minute to find the right answer."

John took a small black notebook out of an inside pocket and handed it to me. It had a pen that pulled out of the spine, like the little gray notebooks they used to give out on the Concorde. "Any thoughts you have about Gil;

anything that drifts past, even a word, jot it down. We don't know what will be important, so put everything down. But…" We had risen and were heading for the door when he took my arm to pause me. "But," he continued very seriously, "no grocery lists." With that he let out a rich laugh, and we were back in party mode.

63

When I was settled in one of the guest rooms after dinner, I became engrossed with thoughts of Gil. How was it possible to know a person for so many years and know so little about him? And what the hell was he doing at my cottage? And was his greeting, when I arrived so unexpectedly, really so enthusiastic?

I spent a sleepless night, my thoughts like ping pong balls slammed back and forth. What did I know about anyone? I knew Roger because somehow I had asked. But that was the exception. I usually did not ask. I accepted people as they presented themselves. It didn't seem polite to pry—to interview was the only term that fit—to be a snoop. I didn't share myself. I wasn't that interesting and assumed others had their right to privacy. Is that really what I thought? Or was I just lazy? Or so egocentric that I didn't want to go outside my self-circumscribed, self-satisfied orb?

What did I really know about Mags, in whose guest bed I now lay sleepless? I knew her childhood was troubled, that her years at camp were arranged by someone called Father

Mike, and that she traveled all the way from the Midwest to come to Vermont. I had wondered why she went so far from home—so far that her parents never visited on those weekends when they were allowed to. Janine was from New Jersey and I lived in New York City, and Mags always went to dinner with Janine or me and our parents, or all of us together on those visiting days. The only mail she got was from Father Mike.

After camp we wrote letters back and forth, and when she came east, we would split her Christmas or Easter vacations between Janine's house and my parent's New York apartment.

At one time we were all in college in New York—Janine at Barnard, me at Sarah Lawrence, and Mags living the bohemian life downtown at NYU. Then suddenly there was a message that *Liam needs me*, and she left for San Francisco. We knew that Liam had been her high-school sweetheart and that their relationship had continued at New York University where Liam was a year ahead of Mags, but that's all we knew. Even though he had been her roommate for a while, we only met him a few times, the first one at a Sunday brunch they hosted. There we also met Bruce, the best looking man Janine and I had ever seen—we both angled for dates (or was it just me?)—and Calvin, an outrageous theater major. Bruce and Liam had moved to San Francisco when they graduated, and a year later Mags had joined them.

We didn't hear from Mags for months until she sent Janine a note saying that Bruce had died of pneumonia. We both wrote condolence notes, though I was miffed to get the information from Janine. She did write to both of us a month later to say that she and Liam had married. Mags made two quick trips back east, once to be my bridesmaid and then, a year later, to be Janine's. Neither time gave us much opportunity for personal talks, and thinking back, Mags seemed to avoid the possibility. Two years after that she came back, widowed, with more money than she had ever possessed before, angry, foul-mouthed, and self-destructive. We didn't see much of her those following years. She had taken up with a fast crowd that left us far behind. Then there was that disastrous marriage to Ralph and the almost-marriage to Bill.

But I was so busy with my new career, then marriage, followed quickly by motherhood, that I never sat down with one of my oldest, dearest friends and said, "Tell me what happened?" I think she never forgave me for that—and she was right.

What was she covering up with all her drama and noise? What had she escaped from into Mason's protective arms? But even those arms couldn't protect her from that short terrifying abduction she had survived several years ago.

And Mason was another book about which I only knew the cover notes—the blurbs.

And then there was Larry. I had lived with Laurence for over thirty years and had no idea of the Larry living inside him. I needed someone else to tell me who the man was. I spent my life making everything better. No, I didn't make anything better. I made things nice. I made nice. What was the matter with me? Who the hell was I?

I was someone who wanted to be taken care of, to be patted on the head and told how good I was. I needed to grow up, take care of myself and stop having my friends clean up my messes. And I needed to be a friend in return, which didn't mean just reading them as Cliff Notes, but bothering to go through the whole damn book.

By now it was early morning. I got up, took a long wake-up shower and dressed in some clothes Mags had put out for me. I went down to the kitchen where Mason sat in a sunny alcove with his coffee and newspapers. He seemed happy to see me. (*Or was he?* my new aware self asked.) Jonquil, the daytime cook made me toast and poured me a cup of coffee.

"Mason, I'm really sorry for all the trouble I'm causing."

"Oh, don't be." He patted my hand. "You know Mags isn't happy unless there's havoc around here."

I tried out my new other-awareness skills. "How do you know John and Kaycee?"

Mason folded his paper and sat back as Jonquil refilled his cup.

"John is a wonder. I love John." He looked at me coyly. "Not that way, though."

I blushed at that.

"Oh, don't worry," he reassured me. "Not my type. We were housemates at Harvard Law."

"And you've been friends since then?"

Mason considered how to answer that.

"After Mags, John is my best friend." He saw my startled reaction. "I know. What did a queen like me and a goon like him have in common? We were both outsiders; we were both unaccepted at our roots. John's family was the worst hand a kid could be dealt. The father—if in fact he was the father—was in jail, the mother a heroin-addicted hooker. Any relatives were not interested in taking on a fast growing, furious boy. He took his anger out wherever he could, including on boys like me.

"I was from a different universe. My family was top-tier. But when they saw what I was, what I was going to be, I was emotionally turned out onto the streets, while hidden away in this dump."

"You grew up here?"

"You didn't know that? Yes, not that anyone noticed or cared. There are lots of rooms here to ostracize an unwanted, queer kid. This place was a living tomb until Mags tore its top off."

"How did your friendship with John begin?"

"That first day, we took one look at each other and saw the hurt boys we had been.

"John got to stay at the house for free by acting as the cook, busboy and peace keeper. He was so driven, so hard working, he set an example for the rest of us pampered sluggards. I would not have gotten through Harvard Law if John hadn't cracked the whip. He also saved my ass in a few scary bar situations. I was a bad boy." Mason giggled.

"He seems so refined, so cultured," I said.

"Well that wasn't easy! While he kept us at the books, we taught him how to be human. He was a real ape."

"Mason! That's so, so…"

"Racist?"

"Well, it smacks of it."

"Nah. There were plenty of white apes at Harvard."

"How did you do it?"

"We all tried to have a proper dinner together, at least once a week—sit down, napkins, silver. John learned which fork to use and how to make dinner conversation. We learned what it was like in the hood, as it's called now, and how to make a shiv out of one of those knives. It was an all-around satisfying exchange of cultures."

"Where did he meet Kaycee?"

"He ran into her."

"Huh?"

"He ran into her. He was out for an early morning run and turned to look at the ass of a girl who had just passed him when Kaycee rounded a bend and he bowled her over."

"Was she hurt?"

Mason looked at me over his glasses. "You've seen John?"

"Well, yes."

"And you've seen Kaycee?" I nodded. "It was a mountain hitting a mole. Of course she was hurt. Bruised ribs, concussion. He had to carry her books for her, so to speak—she was an undergrad—for the rest of the semester— and her life—as it turned out. Kaycee did the fine-tuning in the refinement of John Langston. I was in their wedding party."

My first venture as Barbara Walters was quite successful. I liked learning about people, to see them without their costumes.

The dogs streaked into the kitchen from their morning walk. Silly, of course, mounted my crossed leg—I threw a crust of toast to distract him away—while Wanda bounded into Mason's lap, wiggling in joy, licking his face. Mason hugged her and stroked her, murmuring loving baby talk to the creature. And there he was, completely bare of the armor of sophistication and hard-edged, upper-crust exclusions: a gentle man, lavishing love on a little dog.

"Why don't you and Mags adopt?" The words were out before I even thought them.

Mason's love session with Wanda grew quieter. "I'm afraid," he said simply. "Mags's childhood and mine combined would not produce a quarter of one decent parent."

"Bad parenting is not an inherited gene, Mason. You learn from your parents' mistakes."

"True," he reflected. "John and Kaycee have three kids, and they're all great." He gave Wanda a hug. "But after all Mags has been through, I think we'll stick to dogs."

Brad, Mason's handsome personal assistant, signaled from the doorway. "Excuse me, I have to take this call."

I sat there, thinking about *all Mags has been through,* my heart hurting for my friend as I remembered the terrible time when she learned that a violent abortion forced on her as a teenager had left her unable to have children.

Mason returned, rubbing his hands in glee, a broad smile on his face.

"This can only mean someone died," I said.

"Yes!" He shot his fist in the air. "The vultures have been circling this old buzzard for ten years. Now the fun begins." He took a last sip of his coffee, picked Wanda up for a quick hug, saying to her, "Sorry, baby, Daddy has to go unleash the hounds of war!"

Jonquil came by with a tray. "You better have that car back here in an hour—Miz Mags gotta get up early to go to that meeting."

I jumped up. "Let me take it up, Jonquil. I want to see her without makeup."

"Oh, she won't be happy, no siree, she don't like the morning."

I took the tray anyway. Mason called after me, "Take your camera and snap a picture. You can blackmail her for whatever you want."

64

The heavy drapes were pulled closed in Mags's room, but three small lights burned—night lights. It was hard to imagine Mags afraid of anything, but there it was, she was afraid of the dark. I hadn't consciously known that, but it explained the memory of her at camp insisting on sleeping in a corner cot that she claimed had "better air circulation." The pole light in the compound center had shone directly through the window next to her cot.

Mags stirred as I placed the tray on the bed. "Mornin', Miz Scarlett," I chimed as I pulled the heavy curtains open.

I was shocked to realize how beautiful she was with no makeup, no artifice. How vulnerable and innocent. What had happened to her? Then she snapped back into Mags mode.

"What the fuck? Go away! It's still night."

"Rise and shine, Morning Glory. It's almost eight and you have a meeting."

"Oh God!" She sank back into her pillows. "What is wrong with those women? Nine o'clock? There are twenty-three other hours to choose from. Why don't you go instead?"

"Nuh uh, this is your deal," I said the words, but at the same time I was thinking, Why not? I should get back to meetings and organizing functions for charities and especially the Literacy Program. Mags was the driving force in a half dozen, all of them, it occurred to me, for the benefit of needy children.

Mags got out of bed, cursing with every step as she slouched to her bathroom, warning, "I'm not taking a goddamn shower. I had a goddamn bath last night and if they want a meeting so goddamn early, they can just sniff my goddamn stink."

After giving her some discreet moments of privacy, I took her coffee in and sat behind her and watched as she leaned forward on her pink silk makeup bench and peered into her ornate gilt mirror. I could see her reflection from where I sat.

"If I weren't the chair of this event, I wouldn't go, you know," she threatened as she began putting creams on her face.

"I wish you wouldn't do that," I said quietly.

She stopped. "Do what?"

"Put all that stuff on. You look wonderful just the way you are."

"Isn't that from something Jackson Brown or one of those guys wrote? Are you suggesting I face this day barefaced?"

"It was Billy Joel, and yes."

"Ha! You'd be more likely to see me walk down Fifth Avenue bare-assed. Hand me that brush, sweetie."

I did, although I wanted to swat her with it first. I sat and watched as Mags turned the face of the young girl I remembered into that of a fearsome society woman whose carefully tweezed, penciled, arched brow would wilt any wannabes.

I watched and fantasized about shooting a reality show about women and how they girded themselves for the world, which was what Mags did, layer by layer, until the finished product was as sleek and unreal—and impenetrable—as a museum statue. We create ourselves every day. But wait—so do men. Some lines of poetry ran through my mind. William Blake, I think:

> *My mother groaned, my father wept,*
> *Into this dangerous world I leapt;*
> *Helpless, naked, piping loud,*
> *Like a fiend hid in a cloud.*

The only animals born naked but not intended to stay that way, we could survive only by preying on others. We were not created with kindness in mind.

Mags was on the phone. "Otis, I needed to leave five minutes ago. Meet me in front."

But then again, Mags, in all her created self, was off to work on an event whose ultimate goal was kindness. True, it would also be a no-holds-barred occasion for a fashion slap down, but after the expensive gowns and impressive jewelry had been photographed for the society pages, society would, in the end, have ponied up some impressive money for the cause.

I would attend, of course—sitting at Mags's table or very close by, and only because Mags arranged the seating. That I would even receive an invitation otherwise is questionable given my new lowly status as an *ex* and not as part of the *Mr. and Mrs.* of my former, more exalted rung on the social ladder.

I had some decent jewelry to wear, mostly inherited, some from Laurence. In retrospect, given our place on that social ladder, he had not been overly forthcoming with celebrating me in things that shine. I have, as yet unpacked, several gowns, but Mags would be sure to shepherd me to one of the oh-so-secret charity resale shops to get the latest "lightly worn" from one of her many fellow committee women. They could not be seen in the same dress more than twice in the season, so sent it to those shops and took a hefty tax deduction for their sacrifice.

Janine and David would likely attend—Janine in the antique black Balenciaga she wore to everything. Mags didn't dare interfere with Janine's wardrobe. Besides, the dress was so simple and gorgeous, so *didn't I see Katharine Hepburn wear that in*…that it was always a pleasure to watch her walk through the doorway.

I took the tray downstairs. Jonquil bristled. "I would of got that." I told her it was no trouble and I would trade the tray for eggs, bacon and toast. She was so happy about this transaction that she made enough for two and we enjoyed the spoils together.

65

Later that afternoon, I had my official entry back into the New York world. Mags dressed me in her idea of mournful high fashion. When we left for our trip to St. Patrick's Cathedral, there were two young reporters in front of her building. Mags was thrilled to act as my spokesperson and told them how heartbroken I was over the demise of Gil.

"Was it arson?" the nervy young man demanded.

"Why was he there? Was he your lover?" the equally nervy woman queried.

We had decided on our story and Mags was sticking to it. "Gil Cantway was an old family friend." Mags then continued on to tell them about *break-ins,* ignoring their shouted questions about *murder* and *love nest* and how an act of kindness had, tragically, cost him his life. At that point, the imposing Otis ushered us into the Bentley.

We actually did go to St Patrick's, where we sat piously for ten minutes while Mags assessed the situation. After spying a reporter approaching, she decided that Saks was out for that day, but expertly angled us so the man could get the good photograph that would appear in the next morning's paper.

We went back to Mags's large dressing room to start the cocktail hour early.

As we lounged on chaise and sofa, sipping an excellent pinot gris, I decided it was time to fill some of the blank pages in the *Book of Mags.*

"You never really told me much about Liam," I began.

The look on her face stopped me: I had intruded on— no, barged into—a very private place.

She was silent for a moment, then gave me a guarded, sideways glance. "Why do you ask that now?"

I was honest. "Because I didn't ask before, and I should have done that."

Mags looked at me full on. Her face was hard. I could sense, more than see, the emotions being sorted out behind that hardness. Gradually, it softened. "Liam and I created each other. We gave each other life." She sipped her wine. "We buried Margaret and William before the world could do it to us, and we made Liam and Mags in their place. Liam was my mother, my father, my God, and I was his." Her lower lip began to tremble. "I can't say more…" Tears rolled silently down her cheeks.

I held her as she shook with sobs and wondered how she could cry so hard and yet so quietly. What kind of practice did that take? She stopped eventually, and returned to Mags.

"Oh fuck! I must look like Franken-Fuck-Stein. We have to pretty-up before Mason gets home, wanting booze and beast."

She went into her bathroom to clean up and I went to mine to do the same. It occurred to me, as I washed my hands and put on fresh lipstick, that the list of things that Liam had been to Mags, had not included the word *lover*.

Mags was especially witty and charming that night. Janine and David joined us during cocktails and neither Mason nor Janine seemed taken in by her show. They each, at some point during dinner, gave me a *What's going on?* look. Janine, skillfully, got me aside for a moment and said, "What?" When I told her that I had asked about Liam, she just said, "Ummmm." I had learned something, but I had no idea just what that something was.

66

Roger called the next morning to warn me that the dreaded interview was going to take place that day. Two detectives from Connecticut would be there in the late afternoon, and so would John. I was terrified.

Mags sat me at her dressing table and, with some light powder and a few smudges of dark eyeshadow, transformed me into a pale—if not ashen faced—grieving woman. She spritzed my hair into a frizz, then dressed me in a rather frumpy suit that must have come from her costume closet. It was a color gray that did not flatter me. Underneath I wore a lace-collared blouse that reminded me of my grandmother in her dotage. I was stripped of sparkly jewelry, had Mags's phony glasses plunked on my nose and was given a handkerchief to twist. I hardly recognized the unfortunate woman looking back at me from the mirror. I certainly did not look like someone who had been sleeping in a flaming bed beside her dead neighbor.

John arrived, assessed me approvingly and took me back into Mason's office. This was a deliberate move as he wanted the detectives to be led through the impressive apartment by Bechert. "We'll take any edge we can get," he said. He ran me through my lines, reminding me that I had gone to the convent and that I was not aware of how my wound happened, as I was not fully conscious.

The two gentlemen who arrived were just that: gentlemen. There was no good-cop, bad-cop ordeal. I twisted my handkerchief and whispered my way through their questions, experiencing such heartfelt grief for Gil that I really had to use it. They seemed to conclude that it was a robbery attempt gone bad and expressed their sympathy for my loss.

John looked at me strangely after they had left. "You were almost too good at that, Olivia. Have you told me everything?" He laughed, then we went to join Mags and Mason for drinks and dinner, but I caught him looking at me thoughtfully a few times.

67

I had procrastinated long enough. The next day, after Mags had gone to yet another meeting, I gathered my few belongings, along with all my courage, and went down in the elevator with Adolpho. He acted like I was an escaping prisoner and had the very concerned, almost unwilling head doorman, George, hail me a cab.

I went home. Through all that had happened, my new apartment, even with its beautifully decorated dining room, had not been my home because I had not accepted it as such. One of the other wonders of the human animal, along with finding ways to get clothed and warm, is the ability to adapt. I had a long-time other home that was no longer mine, so I would re-nest where I now lived, bugs and all, and I would do it with courage. Whether John was right about Gil being the possible target of the horrors at the lake, I still assumed it was me, and I was determined to protect myself and get the guys who did it.

I grew impatient as we inched through the heavy traffic and wished for a hyper-space button to push, like the one in Star Wars. That segued into thoughts of Harrison Ford pushing it. I was horny. I wanted sex, and I wanted it dangerously soon.

The cab driver was a young, good-looking Pakistani. I kept my attention focused on the photograph of two young girls he had clipped to his visor. We talked about them—he was both proud and embarrassed by their soccer prowess: proud that they were so good at it; embarrassed by what they had to wear while they were doing it. I consoled and counseled him that it was the only safe uniform—they would trip over skirts—and that it kept them too busy and tired to think about boys. The latter was not true, but it made him happy.

All the while, as we talked, I was mentally tearing through my unpacked boxes looking for Mr. Rascally Rabbit, and the spare batteries I kept with him.

Mr. Rabbit entered my life when a friend of mine came to town and stayed at the Cosmopolitan Club in the East Sixties. I had met her there for lunch and, since it was her birthday, or close to it, or at least in the same moon cycle, we had a glass of champagne to celebrate. We had the second glass because we'd had the first, careful to keep our ensuing chatter and giggles discreet as it was a very staid place. Staid, indeed.

Julia, my friend, decided we needed to go to the Pleasure Chest—an emporium devoted to exotic and erotic equipment—to get her a present. We went to the lobby and, giggling still, took the yellow pages to a quiet corner to look up the address. When she plopped the book on the table, it fell open to the very page we wanted, no doubt because the page was turned down top and bottom and filled with arrows pointing to the destination we sought, along with comments in an assortment of inks and handwriting.

It was on 57th Street and would have been a pleasant walk on that fresh spring day, but Julia snagged a cab and we were there in minutes.

I was gawky-eyed as we examined the merchandise on offer, but Julia had experience and put the Rascally Rabbit package in my hand, assuring me that it was essential and would change my life.

I hid it away when I got home, having sobered up by then, and didn't open it for at least a month. Then one rainy afternoon, a day when my skin was feeling too tight for my body (a sensation I had been experiencing often at that time) I took Mr. Rabbit out of his box and—so to speak—put him in mine. Julia had been right.

I hurried into the apartment, went directly to the carton in the guest room where Mr. Rabbit was stored and tore it open. There he was. My impatience became unbearable. But not so unbearable that I didn't take time to layer privacy sheets over the antique canopy bed that was set up in there and pop a CD into the portable player I plugged in. Bolero one might expect to hear, but Yanni poured forth, turned up loud while Mr. Rabbit and I hit the sheets—rather, the mattress—I had used all the sheets to make our love tent. Yanni and I finished together.

The phone rang and rang in the other room like a Hallelujah Chorus. I let it ring.

68

Younger people assume that the sexual desire of women over fifty flickers and dies into an afterglow, when, in fact, there is a simmering ember just waiting to flame.

They also think that the vibrator is a new hip invention made just for them. There were clinics in Victorian times where women who were having the vapors, or experiencing hysteria, went to have their symptoms relieved by a doctor's expert handling of the newly exciting use of electricity in the form of a vibrator. A number of them were known to need those treatments several times a week.

My vapors having evaporated, I crawled out of my tent, had a wonderful stretch, and got on with my life plan.

The first order was to eat something. Sex has that effect, it seems. I expected the refrigerator to be empty or disgusting, but Elizabeth, along with everything else she provided, had stocked the basics. There were even individual pizzas in the freezer, so I popped one into the microwave, popped open a can of diet soda, then sat at the table with my meal and the pen and the notepad from John. My intent was to make sense of all that had happened.

One of my teachers at boarding school had been crazed by her discovery of parsing sentences and making outlines. She would settle into that first Roman numeral like Mozart putting the first note on the staff. From there she would flow dreamily into the capital A, followed by the small numbers and letters, tripping down the page, until we finally got to capital B, at which point we students were contemplating capital murder. I never thought that agonizing exercise would be of use, but I used it now.

I. Laurence

A. Becomes Larry

a. Takes up with Sherry

b. Takes off with Sherry

B. Olivia moves on

a. Sherry moves in

C. Discord with Sherry

a. The address book

By now, I was sweating with the effort of organizing my thoughts in this mode: outlining was unnatural to me. You are an outliner, or you are not.

The phone rang. I snatched it up, not caring if it was the devil himself calling—it would be better than outlining. I wasn't far off.

69

"Hello, Olivia," said Larry, "this is Laurence." Ah-ha. "I'm so glad to hear your voice and know you're okay." Was that a quaver I heard? "The thought of losing you too…" My God, was the man actually distraught?

"I'm fine, Larr…Laurence." What the hell? I'd see what game he was playing. "I got out…" I caught myself just in time from adding "of the fire." I would have to get my story seared into my mind in block letters. I WASN'T THERE. "…of the convent to hear about the fire and Gil. I was so devastated that I went to Charles and Alice's to grieve in private. I just don't know how it could have happened." Other than you sending two goons with guns and a box of matches. "Poor Gil, he was just trying to do me a favor."

Or was he? I re-ran the scene at the cottage when I arrived so unexpectedly: the furniture moved; the living room rug rolled up. I had accepted Gil's smooth (and quick) explanation of thinking he heard a mouse the night before and was checking for any holes. But the eye is like a camera, taking quick snaps of everything it sees and storing those snaps in the brain's photo album. And just as you can pick up a familiar old snapshot and recognize what you are used to seeing there, you can suddenly focus on a dog lurking in the background, or on the grainy image in one corner, of the neighbor's underwear hanging on a clothesline. I pictured my bed and bathroom on that day. There were no traces of Gil: no toothbrush, no razor, and the bar of soap was still in its tin box in the cabinet where the mice would not be drawn to its aroma. When I got into bed, my pillows were still folded in the unique (possibly peculiar) way that I folded them—all four in half, lined up on the big flap of the bedspread, then the whole thing flipped neatly over. Gil had not slept in my house. What had he been doing there? Then I remembered Roger saying: "The cameras get tripped when someone breaks in." I had been too angry at the time to focus on that. The door hadn't been left open: Gil had broken in.

I realized Laurence had been talking. "I will be glad to take you up to the cottage so you can sort things out, see if there's anything left you want to keep as a memento. There are probably papers you need to sign, people to see. We could have dinner at that little inn you like."

What was I hearing in the midst of all those words other than *memento* and *little inn* combined with the presence of Larry? It was definitely Larry talking now. What was he up to? What was he after? Duh! The money, of course.

"Oh Laurence, thank you so much, you've always been there for me"—that my tongue didn't crumble and fall out over those words was amazing—"I do appreciate your offer. I just now got home." *Yes, home you fucking, cheating, lying, son of a bitch bastard, the home I've had to make after I was tossed out of mine.*

"Give me a day or so to sort myself out here. I really do appreciate your offer." We said the awkward good-byes of two people who had spent over thirty years together and were now on different planets.

I called Roger.

"This is not good, Livie. We need to get there before he does. Problem is, I'm out of town the next two days, but I've made arrangements with Otis to keep an eye on you."

"Mags's Otis?"

"He's a good guy." Coming from Roger, that meant, *He'll take care of you.*

Which was why the Bentley sped along the highway the next day with Otis driving and Mags, me and the dogs in the back, headed for the lake. The Bentley was not as uncommon in this part of Connecticut as it had been in Pennsylvania. Not that the folks in the Quaker state couldn't afford fleets of them, but the old Quaker mentality made non-pretentious the standard.

Pretentious or not, it was darned comfortable and spacious and the dogs needed space. Now that Wanda was noticeably pregnant, she wanted Silly to keep his distance, allowing only a paw to touch hers as long as both bodies were stretched out at opposite ends of the floor.

I didn't know what to expect when we got to the cottage, just as you can't predict where a nightmare will take you.

And it was a nightmare. I was in shock at first, as we stood there outside the yellow crime scene tape, surrounding what had been the one constant in my life—the place where I had always felt safe and cared for. The charred remains resembled nothing from my memories. Wanda whimpered and ran back to the car, but Silly stood close to Mags, a low growl coming from his chest. There was evil here. Silly sensed it and was on alert to protect his queen.

It took a while for me to get my bearings, but then I focused on the room that I was last in—the room where Gil died. I felt that I should kneel down and pray for his soul, even though his soul was very likely residing far below where my knees would hit the soil. The remains of Gil had been removed, but he was still there and always would be.

"Geez," Otis said, "something bad went down here, I'm surprised there's anything left."

But there was something left. Burned, almost melted, but lying across what once was the cellar entrance was the big old Philco refrigerator. I turned to Otis, "We have to move that," and pointed to the fridge.

Otis put Mags and Silly in the car—Mags, for once, didn't argue — took his uniform jacket off, popped the trunk and took out some tools.

I explained to him what I wanted to do and instead of telling me it couldn't be done, he lived up to Roger's assessment of him by telling me how we would do it. We carefully removed a section of the tape, then got a rope around the appliance remains. Otis, muscles bulging, pulled it away from the stairwell. Most of the stairs had been burned away and the rest looked shaky.

"I have to go down there, Otis."

"No," he replied, "Anything happens to you, there'll be no safe place to hide." He jerked his head back at Mags, who was sitting at full attention, hands over the window's edge, watching us. "Whatever you hid down there has to be real important, so just tell me where to look." My choices seemed limited to one, so I described the cases behind the wine rack.

Otis backed the Bentley as close as possible to the remains of the house. Then he took a workman's safety belt from the trunk and strapped it firmly around his waist. He pulled a long coil of rope out, opened the other back window, moved Mags to the front seat, then ran it through the car. He made some quick knots and fastened it around the thick protective belt on his waist. "Hope this reaches," he said. "If I get stuck, I'll give a holler and you move the car forward. Gently," he added.

I watched in fear as he got himself down the charred stairs. There was creaking and groaning as the remains of the house shifted above him. I heard a crash below and Otis coughing. It seemed forever and I was at the point of moving the car to drag him out when he appeared below, covered in dirt and gasping for breath. He untied the rope from his waist and made a sling for one of the cases.

"Can you handle this?" he coughed, "Maybe you should get Mags."

"I'm here," she said from behind me. We pulled up the case—the fabric had been scorched from it, but the metal beneath was intact. I tossed the rope back down and we repeated the process for the second one. Then Otis secured the rope back around his waist, and took a firm hold. "I'll brace myself on these stairs," he said, "but they won't hold me, so ease the car forward."

Mags got behind the wheel: she had been to racing school after all, so had more expertise than me, or so I thought. Otis came popping out of the hole like a champagne cork.

"I'm so sorry," Mags said, wringing her hands as Otis shook his. "I didn't expect it to have such pick up." His dark hands were bloody now, and I'm sure his ribs were bruised, but he ignored that and, wrapping his hands in napkins from the car bar, concentrated on getting the refrigerator remains back in place and covering any tracks we might have left behind.

Otis stowed the rope, belt, and cases in the trunk, then cleaned himself up as best he could with the gallon of water Mags had brought for the dogs. He swiped his hands with something from the first-aid box and wrapped them in gauze. He put his pristine jacket on over black sooty trousers, donned his cap, covered his lacerated hands with his gloves, and drove out of the drive. He stopped, got out and replaced the tape. There was an anticlimactic silence—for a time.

"I won't even ask what's in those cases that's worth risking Otis's life for," Mags finally said.

"Thank you for that," I said simply.

Mags squirmed and flung herself around in the seat so she could peer directly at me. "I won't ask," she continued, "because I expect my best friend not to have secrets from me, and you, dear girl, have been very naughty—so you'd better 'fess up."

"Mags, there's nothing I can or will tell you right now."

She banged the partition open. "Otis, give me your knife." His look was either denial or dismay, I couldn't tell. "The one you have strapped to your leg. Now! Give it!"

Otis reached down and did what was demanded. Mags took the folded switchblade, flicked it open all too expertly for my comfort, then grabbed a handful of my hair and held my head up with the knife dangerously close to my throat.

"Mags," I gasped, "for God's sake…"

"Tell me, you little shit. I can't believe you've done this to me."

And there it was—*done this to me*—in the back of a car speeding away from the crime scene at my childhood home, which was burnt to the ground with the ashes of Gil still blowing in the wind and mine not joining them by mere chance, but it was *done this to me.*

"Damn it, Mags, cut the crap. I'll tell you if Mason says I can."

She paused for a moment, then let go of my hair. Delicately closing the knife, she handed it back to Otis and slid the partition shut. She opened the door to the bar, took out a chilled bottle of champagne, popped the cork, poured two glasses, returned the bottle to its holder, handed one glass to me, touched hers to mine and said, "To friendship."

She sipped. I gulped.

She fingered my hair. "It's very dry, you know. You haven't been using product, have you?"

70

When we got to Mags's building (I had wanted to go home, but there was no possibility of that) she directed Otis to go "below," meaning the very secure garage beneath the building. The three of us, along with the dogs and the strange looking smoke-infused suitcases, crowded into Adolpho's elevator and were whisked up into the startled arms of Mason.

Mags hit the ground talking. "Mason, make her tell me what's in those suitcases."

Mason immediately grasped what was afoot and knew it was something he couldn't and wouldn't step into. He instructed Otis to bring the suitcases and follow him, which he did, with us close behind—Mags looking forward to the unveiling and me dreading the exposure.

Instead of going to his office, Mason veered off down a small corridor and stopped at a steel door with a peephole—the kind you normally find on an outside apartment door in Manhattan that let's you see if it really is the pizza delivery man and what he's doing with the hand not cradling the carton.

Mason thanked Otis, who left, then put his eye to the peephole, which opened the door. Behind it was another steel door. He did something with a keypad and that door slid open to a vault that would have done a small bank justice. Mason rolled the cases in, then came out. He had to physically move Mags out of the way so the outer door would close.

"I could snatch your eye out and use it, you know," howled the loving wife, "and I bet I can figure out the code."

"Yes, dear, but you wouldn't and you couldn't," Mason cooed as he ushered her back along the hallway with a pat on her butt, her muddy Jimmy Choos stomping out her anger.

Back in the drawing room, she paced up and down. "I will find out, you know." Maybe.

"You can't keep anything from me." Usually.

"I'm smarter than you." Not likely.

"Enough of this, Mags," said Mason in a voice you dared not ignore. "You sit down and listen."

She did both.

"Let's just play with a hypothetical because, if it could possibly be true, which it isn't, it would put Papa Bear, who happens to be a lawyer, in a very compromising position. Now in this fairytale," he arched an eyebrow at that, then returned to serious, "Momma Bear and her good friend Polly

Panda go for a drive in the country. They come to a place where they think a honey pot might be hidden, but around this place is yellow tape with words printed in black. Since neither one of these bears seems able to read—" he put special emphasis on that word— "they don't know whether it says HONEY POT FESTIVAL—YOU ALL COME ON IN *or* CRIME SCENE—DO NOT CROSS. They also seem not to know that if it were the latter, it is a crime to cross it."

Mags brushed some mud off her shoe.

"But they do not notice these things as their sniffly noses are all a-wiggle with scents of the honey pot, so they leave their senses behind and go after the scent. If it came from behind the Festival tape, what a treat they have uncovered! If, however, it came from behind the Crime Scene tape, why, they have committed a crime! And they would be in big trouble. What a dilemma. They want to share this honey pot with Papa Bear. What do you think Papa should do? Other than put it away for safe keeping and never talk about it again?"

He sat down. There was silence all around.

"Why don't we go upstairs so I can do something with your hair?" said Mags, turning to me. "And I really need to change these shoes."

71

"You know I'm gonna find out," she said into the mirror, as she stood behind me. I was seated at her movie star-sized vanity table, a fresh towel around my shoulders as my hair, newly washed and fluff-dried by Flore, was now being combed by Mags.

I knew what she was up to—setting the scene for the intimacy between hairdresser and client that seems to be a natural part of an appointment. A hefty sum of unreported income is enjoyed by the top people in the top salons in the city—money proffered by columnists and P.I.s looking for the juicy tidbits that seem to trip off tongues when the heads that hold them are being massaged, brushed or back-combed. It might be a reflex action. I had never been in the top chair league, as neither my hair nor me were considered interesting enough to warrant it. Until, that is, that front-page picture appeared of it flying wet around my face as I drove my boat in the attempted rescue of Sherry. Then there had been several messages on my phone from shops trying to woo my hair and my story into their chairs.

"There," she cooed, working some tropical-island smelling goo in as she massaged my head skillfully, "you just relax and let Mags do her thing."

Dracula probably used those very words and I was as relaxed as I would have been if he were hovering, fangs bared, over my exposed throat...which brought another scene to mind.

"You could have cut my throat in that car, bumping along!"

"But I didn't now, did I?" she said in a soothing tone, massaging faster with yet another enticing aromatic product. But as hard as she tried to ease me into a nirvana state of relaxed body and loose tongue, I held fast to the image of the knife at my throat.

"Knock, knock," said Janine as she came in. "What's been happening?"

"She tried to kill me today," I dutifully reported.

"I did not. She almost got Otis killed and all of us arrested for invading a crime scene."

Janine arranged herself on the chaise and smiled. "Just another normal day."

"I'm not kidding. She held a knife to my throat in a moving car."

"Well, you just ask her what's in those two suitcases she made Otis haul out of the cellar of her burnt down house— suitcases we never knew existed that are now locked in Mason's vault."

"Children, children, I'm glad to see you've been playing so well together. I had a few words with Mason on my way in and he asked me to deliver a message."

"I am not talking to that man," pouted Mags.

"That man's message had to do with talking. Explicitly, that you two should button them, zip them, snap them closed, or he will duct tape them all around. In other words, not one more word will be spoken about today's events. And his secretary," she directed this to Mags, "has canceled your hair appointments until further notice."

72

As John had directed, I jotted down words and random thoughts about Gil in the little book he gave me for that purpose. "Put everything down," he said, so I handed it to him *as-is* at our next meeting, which Roger attended. John read words and phrases out, which Roger wrote into a column on one side of a sheet of paper. When John finished reading, Roger took his completed sheet and made two copies of it, eyeing me with raised brows as the machine whirred away. The Connecticut Caper, as he enjoyed referring to it, was fresh from the telling and he was both angry and amused by the tale.

He and John sat on opposite sides of the desk, making lines and arrows and jottings like they were sitting an exam, while I played with my pencil.

"What have you got?" John finally said.

"Not what I expected." Roger sat back, tossed his pen on the desk and cupped his hands behind his head. "Gil was a lot more interesting than I thought."

"I'm with you there, brother." John also leaned back, hands behind his head. Maybe it was a man thing. "Were those packages he mailed always the same size?" he directed to me.

"I recall those boxes you pay twelve dollars or so for and mail about seventy pounds," I said. "Oh! And he said they were blow-ups of his sky photos, so the box probably had to hold an 8x10, but I think they varied."

"And it was at least once a week?"

"I think so. I didn't really pay attention, it was just part of Gil's routine. He would stop when I was at the cottage and ask if I had anything to mail. I saw them in his car the times I was outside."

"And those trips he took?" asked Roger, "Were they always out West? Was he visiting family?"

"The only family I know he has is Jason."

"Yeah, right, the son," Roger said thoughtfully. "Where's he now?"

"Well…Jason could be anywhere."

As hard as Lauren was to raise, Jason was worse. Poor Viv, she was an angel and tried so hard, but she was the model for the mother in that song "I'm The Only Hell My Mama Ever Raised."

"You know he dealt to Lauren and Marc."

I didn't know, but I should have realized her trips to the cottage had nothing to do with family and everything to do with tripping.

To John's questioning look, Roger said, "Lauren and Marc, our kids," he paused, reddened a bit, "I mean, her daughter, my son, used to drop dope together, and this Jason kid was one of their suppliers."

"He hasn't claimed Gil's remains yet. Does he even know what happened? We need to find this guy," said John, "and find out who received those packages."

I flipped open my phone and punched speed dial for Lauren's private number, hoping she wouldn't edit and ignore me.

"Hi, Sweetie," I said, trying not to sound surprised when she answered, "I've been worried about you." Paused for her usual *I'm fine, Mom.* "I'll be near your office tomorrow. What about lunch?"

After we set a time, I threw in the casual question. Perhaps it was devious, but I had learned from the master to whom I was now speaking. "Oh! Someone asked me about a service for Gil. Do you know if anything has been arranged? Have you heard from Jason? I don't want to step on toes, do anything without Jason's say-so, but Gil was a family friend, and he died in our house, so I really want to help. Do you know how to reach him?"

I must have registered surprise at Lauren's answer, because Roger and John sat up in their seats in anticipation.

"You will? That's a good idea. You were friends and he probably needs one now." More words from Lauren. "Yes, it was horrible…horrible, I'm still in shock. Oh he does? Tomorrow? Will you come too? Then let's have lunch the day after. Okay, I miss my girl. Bye."

The men got the gist of the conversation. "So she's kept in touch with him." Roger did not sound happy. "I don't like the feel of this."

"Did she say where Jason is now?" asked John.

"No, and I didn't dare ask. She is so suspicious of anything I do."

"What's happening tomorrow?" asked John.

"Larry wants to take me to the cottage so I can pick up some mementos, as he put it."

"Does he know you were there yesterday?" said Roger.

"I certainly hope not."

"Should you be going there alone with him?" John seemed worried.

"I second that question," added Roger. "You should take someone with you."

"Mags?"

"Hell no!" Roger almost shouted. "There's no way she won't blab about yesterday. You need someone sane, someone to protect you."

73

Otis and I picked Larry up the next day in the Bentley.

Mags protested our taking the car, and especially taking it without her in it. Mason had put his handmade Italian leather-shod foot down, which I was learning was very heavy indeed where Mags was concerned. "You biked across the country, you'll survive one day without a limo." Another piece of information to add to my *Book of Mags*.

Larry was pleased with the arrangement, both for the comfort of being in such a car and of not having to drive one himself. I was pleased about not being in a car with Larry driving. He is one of those people who looks at you when he has something to say, heedless of the fact that he might be hurtling down the highway at seventy miles an hour. Plus, his certainty of entitlement—to rules not applying to him—would, for instance, send him speeding along the shoulder past a line of waiting cars that should have included his.

Frankly, I wasn't sure what we would talk about—what we could possibly have to say to each other once we got past the girls. But Larry, it seemed, was trying very hard to turn back into Laurence. He said more words to me than he had in a number of our past years together, but my mind was not in it, so, like a dog, I heard my name—*Olivia, blah, blah, blah, Olivia, blah, blah, blah*—while I tried to figure out what to do when we got to the cottage. Then I *boinged* back to the present.

"What did you say?" I asked.

"I said, do you think we could get back together? I really miss you."

"Larry, I..."

"Please call me Laurence. I'm past that crazy stage."

"But, Laurence, Sherry just died. Have you even buried her ashes? How could you be talking like this?"

"I'm a piece of shit, I know. Sherry was this *thing (he made the quote marks with his fingers)* that happened. I don't know how I got into it. I had no control. Sherry wanted to get married, so we did."

I sat back in silence, thinking about his *I'm a piece of shit,* which would imply something inconveniently stepped into, then casually scraped off on a curb. No, he had been more than that. The removals from all the stalls at Churchill Downs might cover one of his little toes.

"Larry...Laurence, let's just sit quietly for a while. I have to think about this." And I did think and I did try to be fair to this man. I had heard many stories about women of a certain age being dumped for the next best thing. The men seemed to be puppets manipulated by younger women, their strings pulled by the panic of middle age, of being the next generation to face those furiously riding Four Horsemen. They weren't strong, these men. I thought of a few lines from a country song:

> *The world sees me as a man of steel,*
> *But you know, sometimes I feel*
> *I'm just a boy with silver hair.*

I took a good look at Laurence, his silver hairs covered by that shade of red-brown that the salons seem to favor, his jowls hanging over his collar, his sagging eyelids (if Sherry had been around longer, he would have had the procedures to lift those lids and his forehead frown lines for that wide-eyed deer-in-the-headlights look) and I looked at his enormous gut, not as disguised as he probably hoped by the hand-tailored, double-breasted suit. He wore a lavender shirt under the navy pinstripe with a well-chosen tie. He looked spiffy. He also looked very unhealthy.

Did I feel compassion? I should have felt compassion, but I really felt nothing. He had physically left my life and I had filled in his space: I didn't miss him; I didn't want him back. I thought of the handsome young, prince-of-a-man I thought I had married, and realized, with great sorrow, what a shallow fool-of-a-girl I had been to so easily give up the smart, eager young woman that had once been me. I had been absorbed into a comfortable life and been turned into one of those perfect, brittle, empty shells that some beetles leave behind when they move on.

We arrived at the cottage. Without the frantic activity of the previous day I was free to grieve and cried openly for the loss that lay before us. I grieved for Gil. He had been a man, a fellow human who had been kind to me most of the time and had shielded my life with the very last of his.

I grieved for the family memories, for my childhood years spent here fishing, swimming, helping my grandparents, learning so much from being their helper. All the love my parents had given me was also mixed in with those charred remains.

Then suddenly Jason was beside us. I put my arms around him to comfort him, but he wasn't in a comforting mode.

"Why was my father here with you, Olivia?" Not *Hello, Mr. and Mrs. Lammond* from the young man I hardly knew and faintly disliked, but a steady glare from the hardened face of a man I did not want to know and instantly feared.

"Laurence," he said—the way they shook hands gave the distinct vibe of two people who were friendlier than I would have thought. Then, directed to me: "What's this bullshit about him sleeping here because of break-ins?"

I had once witnessed a golden falcon land on a deck railing, holding his prey. As he devoured the small creature, his eyes darted around taking everything in—eyes that made me shiver. They held not a spark of soul. Jason looked at me with those very same eyes and—I began to shiver. Otis came from behind us with my jacket, possibly for my benefit, but probably to be closer to the action.

"Who's the goon?" snarled Jason. "Your protection?"

"I...I don't need protection," I stammered.

"Yeah? Well, why did my dad take two slugs while he was in your bed?"

"Olivia!" rasped Laurence. "What the hell is going on here?"

"I don't know! I have no idea," I lied with my burgeoning expertise.

"Oh, I think you do," Jason said evenly, eyeing me with those unblinking falcon eyes, "and I will find out what happened here."

"Jason, " said Laurence, "how do you know this?"

Jason waved a piece of paper. "It's a little thing called a coroner's report. I just picked it up from the medical examiner's office. I have a right to it, seeing as how I'm the last of kin. I have a right to a lot of things now, and believe me, I will use those rights to my advantage. I'll see you, Laurence." Then he turned and got onto the Gator that I had used to my advantage not so long ago.

Jason knew that I had been there the night his father had died. I don't know how, but he knew.

74

"What was that all about?" Laurence asked, as we drove to the inn for lunch.

This was another one of those forks in the road, a time for choosing: I don't mean telling the truth—that was out of the question—but rather taking the low road of reminding him how Jason had always been a strange kid, a heartbreak for his mother etc., or the high road, which I stepped gingerly onto. "Laurence, he just lost his father in the most horrible manner, he's crazed with grief. We must be patient with him, help him through this."

The words were mostly true: Gil had died in a horrible manner, and Jason was crazed—he had been so from the day he was born. It was the *patient* part that had my *vibes thrumming* as Roger would have put it. Jason and patience were not words normally used together in one sentence. He would do something, and soon. Pondering that *something* sent me scurrying for the ladies room as soon as we got to our destination.

I called Roger.

"Yeah, I know," he answered. "Otis already called. He doesn't like this kid, says he's trouble—every letter capitalized. Thinks he's a pit boss or dealer—as in cards—says the eyes give him away. Are you at the love nest yet?"

"We stopped for lunch!" I snapped.

"That's the way these things start. He put the move on you?"

"Well…" I said uncomfortably.

"There you go. Don't push him away too fast, we might need to embed you in that household," he laughed hard, "so to speak."

I hung up without pleasantries and was glad to see that Laurence had already ordered drinks. Hell, I wasn't driving and a little mind numbing could help get me through this day.

It being lunch time I ordered a salad plate, which the young waitress ("Hi, my name is Tiffany and I'll be your server") wasn't sure how to balance against everything Larry (no matter how I might address him, he would now remain Larry in my mind) ordered, which was cream of corn soup (bowl, not a cup), shrimp cocktail, followed by a large rare steak with fries and apple pie à la mode. Yes, he even ordered dessert. Since mine would be the only salad on the table, Tiffany wasn't sure when to bring it.

"With his steak." I relieved her of that problem. Then I watched Larry eat. He was a real trencherman. Tiffany had to refill the breadbasket twice and I only had one piece to keep him company while Larry had at his food. I pictured his wild Scottish ancestors squatting around a log, as wenches brought them halves of barbecued beasts and giant stone-baked breads. I could see him breaking off a hunk of the bread, filling it with the slab of meat he had hacked off the carcass, then swiping the whole thing through the bloody grease on a stone platter. They didn't order salad then either. If they needed greens, they went out to a field and grazed.

This man is obese, I thought. This man is a beast. But maybe all men are until love morphs them into the shining knight we want to see.

I turned the conversation to our daughters, a seemingly natural thing to do, but my intent was not entirely motherly; I wanted to find out what Lauren was up to. So I started with Christa—how proud I was of her landing such a great job with a top Philadelphia law firm. How worried I was about her working so hard, not having enough time for a social life or her family.

Larry was having none of that. "Philadelphia—that's bull crap. She should be back in New York, working in the family business, just like her sister."

"But her specialty is trusts and estates, not real estate," I protested.

"Yeah, just like her uncle. He high-tailed it for the boonies as soon as he could sell his buildings. What is it about that place? What's it got for Christ's sake? The Phillies? The Eagles? And those goons, the Flyers? What's so special about that place when the family is here?"

He went on about Christa, using words like ungrateful and loyalty. He really resented that she had not stayed in New York.

"They would be a great team, the two of them. Lauren's really into the business end. She's got a good head on her shoulders. Doesn't take crap from anyone. And Christa, she could handle the rest."

The rest, I feared, would be keeping them out of jail.

"I've made my will," he said suddenly. "I did just what my folks did. Christa will get two tall buildings and Lauren will get the lot." He laughed at his own pun.

A trickle of fear went down my spine. I looked at this obese man, the table before him holding the wreckage of his heart-stopping meal, and thought about mortality tables.

Christa would do fine with two buildings. She might even do better without them. She had a solid career as a lawyer and she had comfortable trust funds from both sets of grandparents. She did not live on a grandiose scale, but she was able to buy a modest apartment on Rittenhouse Square. She was happy.

Lauren had raided her funds the second she was eligible. Where the money went was not apparent, if one chose to ignore her constantly runny, suspiciously sore nose. She lived with her father and from all accounts, off her father. Lauren made me so furious, so frustrated, that most of the time I wanted to wring her haughty tattooed neck. But in spite of herself, I would not abandon her to the disaster that was riding on Larry's large, life- threatening pot belly.

When we got into the car, I moved closer to him and put my hand on his arm.

"Laurence," I said with carefully formed care in my voice, "you seem tired. You work so hard and you've had so much turmoil in your life of late, we really shouldn't talk about us right now."

Which opened the floodgates for him to talk about us, sometimes weeping in the process, for the rest of the trip back to town. By the time we dropped him off at Park Avenue, he was besotted in the way straying men are when they go back to their comfortable, comforting number ones.

Otis looked at me quizzically in the rearview mirror as he took me to my place. I slid the partition open and said, "If you say one word of this to Mags, I'll cut your tongue out."

He grinned big, saluted, and I knew we were cool.

75

Larry and I had dinner several times that week while I geared myself up for what I had to do. Although I tried to steer us to out-of-the-way places, it was just a matter of time before the calls came in.

"What the fuck are you up to?" as expected from Mags.

"Okay, you're flying on your own here. Tell me when you need back up," from Roger.

"I understand what you're trying to do," said Janine. "I'm here to listen."

"He's going to die. I can't let Lauren have that business," I said, sitting across the desk from Roger in his office. He bonged his pen back and forth, then finally threw it on his desk. He leaned forward, scratched his neck, perplexed. "Are you sure you can get the wills set up?"

"We're either each other's sole beneficiaries or I won't marry him. He did it with Sherry, so that gives me leverage."

"So you're gonna finish what Sherry started? What'd Mags say—fuck 'em and feed 'em to death?"

"Roger," I looked straight into his eyes, "he can go fuck himself. I'll just be there to provide the food. He's going to kill himself anyway, I need to protect Lauren."

"That kid—ounce for ounce—has been more trouble than anyone I ever met." Then he looked up at me from under his eyebrows. "Except for the mother, of course." We laughed. "Is she worth it?"

"She's worth it," I answered.

"So's the mother," he said far too seriously.

76

The wedding was very small. A suspicious Charles repeated his role as best man, accompanied by a disappointed Alice and their sons and families. Mags and Janine had a slap down over who would be Matron of Honor and who would be Flower Girl. I never quite knew who won, as they were both crowded so close to me. Mags was mollified that the event took place at all by several exhausting shopping trips and by being given free rein on arrangements.

Christa was so happy by the family being reunited, she was comfortable enough to bring a date—Jeff, a fellow lawyer she had been seeing for several months—whom Lauren immediately put the move on even though she had brought a date of her own—to my horror—Jason. Roger, accepting my invitation, just accepted what was happening and drank too much, while keeping an eye on Jason, who kept his falcon eyes on me.

The wedding ceremony and banquet took place in a set of elegant private dining rooms at the University Club, compliments of Mason. Mags did her usual spectacular job with the flowers and food, especially the food. And especially the *fois gras* that Larry loved and spread thickly on slabs of bread, rather than daintily on the crackers provided. We were suitably merry and consumed great quantities of whatever there was to consume.

My girls were also taken care of. Mason arranged for Christa and her friend Jeff to have adjoining rooms at the club for the night. They would return to Philadelphia the next afternoon. Meanwhile, Roger had brilliantly suggested that I give Lauren the keys to my apartment so the honeymooning couple (I had to think who he was talking about, until I remembered that it included me) could be alone. Lauren, with Jason in tow, was eager to get into my place so she could snoop through my things and find something interesting. Roger, of course, had the place "swept" before they got there. I, however, could not resist replacing my comfortable cotton undies with padded lace bras and matching thongs and leaving large-sized condoms in the drawer of my bedside table.

The honeymoon was this bride's dream: Larry, overfed and over-boozed, snored like the little engine that couldn't in our former bedroom while I slept peacefully in a guest room.

To make up for my wifely short-comings of the night before—and even though Greta, our housekeeper, insisted it was her kitchen—I cooked him a breakfast to make his belt pop: an omelet with five eggs and cheese sautéed in some of the fat from the six slices of bacon, plus four slices of toast slathered with real butter. He was ecstatic with our new domestic arrangement and eagerly asked, "What's for dinner?"

Monday morning I called Larry's doctor. Dr. Sloane was very happy to hear from me and to hear that I was back in charge, as he was worried about "Laurence's expanding girth and rising numbers." I asked him to have his secretary call Larry's secretary to schedule an appointment for a complete physical—and was thus officially on record as The Concerned Wife.

As a wedding gift I bought my new/old husband a membership in a very exclusive gym—exclusive because it was impossibly expensive and included private lockers equipped with personal sweats, towels, shoes, everything the client could want or need. All Larry had to do was walk through the door. This astronomically costly gym membership included two other things—a *care car* pick-up and a personal trainer. While at the establishment arranging this gift, I chose his trainer—a gorgeous, toned, bronzed muscular girl—one whom Larry would never want to see him with his bulk bulging out of shorts and a T-shirt or a form-fitting sweat suit. For a moment I felt almost righteous about my seemingly good intentions.

Was there any guilt? Yes, there was. I was contemplating a despicable, hell-rotting undertaking and I wasn't sure I could see it through. But the more I was around him, the more I got to know what he was and had been up to, the more I listened to him, the more I wanted to exchange Larry's lies for Here lies Larry.

And he lied about everything, almost as though he didn't know how to tell the truth. Now that I was looking for it, I caught him out in large-scale lies and in teeny fibs that were of no gain to him. His mind had been trained, twisted in that direction, and it could only have been steered there by Willa.

Three times a week the *care car* picked him up at home. Three times a week, with the air of a knight in full armor off to do daring deeds, he pecked me on the cheek with a heroic "off to the gym" and left. Three times a week the car dropped him off at the Greek diner close to his office for a second breakfast.

How do I know? I asked Otis to follow him. Mason went to the office early. Mags didn't ordinarily leave the house until noon, so Otis was glad to do this favor for me. He also talked to one of the drivers—they were mostly college kids making a few dollars—and was told that they often got paid off to drop the client someplace other than the gym. Mostly, I suspected, at hotels where the client got his workout with a stacked young hottie, not with the hot stack of pancakes covered in syrup, bacon on the side, that Larry was most likely working his way through.

77

About that peck on the cheek… That and a few hugs seemed to account for our sex life. I didn't have to worry about the *fuck him to…* part. It didn't seem to occur to Larry that sex would be a part of our marriage. He was very content to have me sleep in the other room as long as I was in the kitchen when he got there. Mr. Rabbit and I were equally happy with the arrangement.

But my curiosity drove me back to Dr. Sloan's office. He had been our family doctor for years, so it would not be out of place for me to show up with *my problem.* I acted embarrassed and hesitant, but he finally got it out of me that I thought there was something wrong with me because we had no sex life.

Dr. Sloane laughed and asked, "And how much sex life did you have before the divorce?"

"None," I replied truthfully, "but I thought it was because he was seeing someone else."

Dr. Sloane shook his head. "I don't know what that was all about." He clasped his hands on his desk and leaned forward in a professorial manner. "You are close to full menopause, Olivia. Your hormone levels have dropped considerably. Men also go through an adjustment stage—some earlier, some later. Laurence's testosterone levels are exceptionally low—have been for several years—which helps to account for some of the weight he has put on and the lack of sexual impulse. Now, I can give you both replacement treatments which will help, but I hesitate to give Laurence anything until his weight is under control."

I am not a born banterer. The clever phrase does not trip off my tongue until three in the morning when I wake, snap my fingers, and think I should have said that! I chose that moment to develop my skills.

"But what if I want to get pregnant?" I simpered.

Dr. Sloane, it seemed, had even less talent. "You have a twenty percent chance. Laurence is at zero. So don't even think about that." He had taken me seriously and in the process had given me some very seriously incriminating information: Larry was not the father of the fetus that died with Sherry.

"How is Laurence's weight?" he asked.

"Dr. Sloane (we were social friends, but in the office I always called him by his honorific), I wish you would see him again. He goes to the gym three times a week and I try to watch every bite he takes." (The hell-fires were burning my toes, but I hadn't really lied. I did watch almost every bite he took: steaks, fries, eggs, cheesecake, banana cream pie...) "But he still seems to be putting on weight. I'm very worried."

"So am I, Olivia." He patted my arm as I left his office. "I'll get him in here next week and give him a good going over and talking to."

That task accomplished, I went to my office. Yes, my new office at Lammond Holdings.

78

And then Mason called at midnight. "I'm sending the car. Please come." And there I was, with Janine, in Mags's bedroom. But it wasn't Mags's room; it was just a piece of real estate. Mags's spirit wasn't flowing there: It was bottled up into a tight ball of being somewhere in her bed, like a black hole pulling us into something dark and frightening.

Mason wept, wringing his hands. "Do something. Please. Do something. Help her. Bring her back. Please. Please!"

If Mags had been shot, pierced, burned or in any way bodily harmed, she would have been moaning in that bed, asking for help. But she wasn't. She was turned away, turned in, blocking out the world.

Janine slipped off her shoes, climbed around Mags and inserted herself on the far side. I was reminded of another time, not long ago, when she had settled herself onto another bed with me. I eased myself onto Mags's other side. We didn't speak. I did not know what words to use and Janine knew better than to use them. We didn't hold her. The rage flowing from her told us that would have met with resistance.

Janine signaled me with her eyes; I knew what she wanted. I slid off the bed and went to Mason. "Champagne, quick. Then leave us."

It must have been piped into every room in the apartment, like the old money containers that would hydraulically whoosh through the J.C. Penney stores. A bottle and glasses on a tray were put into my hands shortly after the words were spoken.

Janine placed the tray over Mags's scrunched-up being. She popped the cork on the bottle and poured our glasses. She clinked hers to mine, "Cheers," and started drinking. I had no recourse but to imbibe. Janine talked about the dinner she and David had attended the night before, dishing some mild gossip, adding to the general store of information we all fed on. I followed her lead and sat back against the headboard, sipping my drink and chatting, almost forgetting about why we were there, until why we were there reared up, scattering tray, bottle and glasses.

"Oh! Don't let me disturb you! Just go on drinking my best champagne over my almost dead body. I'm so glad my best friends are here celebrating my pain!"

There was a moment of suspense.

Janine slapped her. I don't mean a girl kind of *oh you bitch* slap. She clocked her.

Mags's head bonged back and forth. There was a moment of silence, then Mags started wailing, holding her hurting jaw. Janine had given a little hurt to let loose the big one.

"You fucking bitch!" Mags picked up the champagne bottle and swung it around, smashing the glass in my hand. Blood came out of Janine's cheek where a shard of the glass had stuck close to her eye.

Shit! I thought. People complain about not having real friends. Well, have I got one for you!

We wrestled the bottle out of Mags's hand and finally had her on the floor and let me tell you, it took the two of us. She was kicking, biting and being a whole-hearted hellion. We got her down and that's when Janine really let her have it. I mean, her hand was going to hurt the next day.

The thought flitted across my mind that Janine was a psychiatrist. Was this a new kind of therapy? She gave a final resounding slap and Mags let out a wail like a banshee. Only it didn't stop. It went on and on through octaves into shuddering screeches and sounds that finally formed recognizable words. "She called...to tell me...tell me he's dead. I didn't get to kill him...I didn't get to kill him...I didn't get to..."

When Mags finally lay silent, she was spent. I felt she was gone—that some of her had died. I didn't know how much and was fearful about what was left.

I didn't need to ask who the *she* was, or the *who* Mags didn't get to kill. So much of Mags fell into place in those early morning hours.

Mason, who had been sitting by the door, came in and picked Mags up from the floor—I was surprised by his strength—threw the covers back with one hand, scattering bottle, tray, glasses and glass, put her in the bed and, still in his suit and shoes, climbed in beside her. Holding her close, he pulled the covers over them.

Janine and I went to the kitchen to ice down our various injuries.

"This is really bad," I said.

"No, this is the breakthrough I've been hoping for," replied Janine as she pressed a cold compress to her face while waiting for Otis to take us to her doctor's house for stitches.

"Are you always into hitting people?" I asked.

"No, I just try to save people from themselves."

That's when I decided not to kill Larry.

79

"Road trip," said Mags. "Three days; bring comfort and entertainment," which I interpreted as casual and with my Kindle and iPod.

There was little conversation as we covered the miles to the Midwest. Mags was deep inside herself, so I read or put in my earplugs and listened to Etta Baker's blues or Tony Trischka on banjo.

When we finally got to our targeted little town I was expecting to visit some relatives. Mags, however, directed Otis to a cemetery on the outskirts of town and told him where to stop. Then she ordered him to pop the trunk and to stay in the car. I asked if she wanted me to come along.

"No, but suit yourself."

Mags took a shovel and a plastic bag out of the trunk and walked up a hill, threading her way between grave markers. I knew this was not going to be something I would enter in my diary.

We arrived at what seemed to be a fairly recent grave. Mags walked around the grave, stomped around actually, then appeared to measure off from the headstone to what I would imagine would be the head in the coffin below. The outfit she wore to do this stomping around in was quite astonishing—starting with the bow in her ponytail, down to a white short-sleeved shirt tucked into a pleated plaid skirt, and ending with black Mary Jane shoes over white socks.

"You better turn you head, Livie. You aren't gonna like this."

I turned aside half way. I did and didn't want to see this, but I also didn't want to drive a few thousand miles and miss the production number. I should have tamped down my curiosity and walked away and not be forever burdened with memories of what followed. Mags, using the shovel, dug a hole where the head probably was. She took a pair of rubber gloves from the bag and a pile of what appeared to be personal wipes. She pulled on the gloves, then, lifting her skirt, squatted over the hole and let loose with what ever was in her bladder and bowels. She took the wipes, cleaned herself off and threw them on the pile, then took off the gloves and did the same.

"Goodnight, Daddy," she said, and worked up a nose-clearing, honkering spit to add to the offering. She took off the blouse, skirt, socks and shoes and added them to the pile.

I followed her bouncing dark hair—beating out a black rage from her bare-footed, bare-assed being—back to the car, where she put the shovel in the trunk, then took out and pulled on a purple cashmere sweat suit and matching Uggs.

Not quite knowing what to say on this intimate family occasion, I blurted, "Will we stop to see your mother?"

"No...I couldn't bring my gun. State lines, you know," and we headed home.

80

We rode in a heavy silence for many miles. Finally I took her unresisting hand and asked, "Do you want to talk?"

"I'll talk when I start talking to Janine again. That stupid bitch broke my jaw," she said, working her jaw.

"She broke your chops, but your jaw seems fine. Janine, on the other hand, has a scar on her cheek. It took three stitches."

"A scar!" Mags perked up at that. "You mean she won't be Miss Perfect anymore?" In an obviously happier mood, she took my iPod from the seat and plugged in the ear buds—briefly. "What is this shit? You some damn hillbilly?" She tossed it aside, slid open the partition and demanded Otis's iPod. "You know, the one you have plugged into your window-side ear where you think I can't see it, so you can listen with the other ear?" He passed it back.

We spent the night at the same highway hotel we had stayed in the night before. Otis stowed our meager luggage in our rooms, then joined us in the dining room, wisely changed out of his uniform, as it appeared to be a local hangout. Mags was on her second serious drink.

"Livie," she said, "there is so much bad in the world, it behooves us to do as much good as we can." When Mags, or anyone else for that matter, uses the word *behooves* in a barroom setting, their legal limit has probably been exceeded.

I envisioned us dressed in our designer Sisters of Mercy outfits, sitting in the back of the Bentley while Otis drove us to our designated needy sites to deliver the bounty.

"I mean something really good," Mags continued. "I can't have children, but I can help those kids other people shouldn't have had." I didn't react when she said that, just acted as though I already knew. Maybe she thought I did, that Janine had broken her code of silence.

She was serious—very serious. "Mason has the money. He'll finance a—what?—a foundation? You can get us a building. We'll look for runaways, for kids who've been abused." At this she looked away, her eyes glistening. "We'll call it *Father Mike's.*"

"We won't have to look far," said Otis. "We can pick them up at the Port Authority before the pimps do, right when they get off the buses."

We talked about it over our meal, Mags getting more and more excited and alive, real, no façade. I thought about my grandmother's saying: Out of everything bad comes something good. I silently reaffirmed my decision not to actively participate in the death of Larry.

81

Graveside good intentions aside, it was not easy to save Larry from Larry. I hired a cook—who was renowned for her skill with diet cuisine—away from the newly svelte Annabelle Trowbridge. Annabelle crossed our names out of her social book, but I frankly didn't care since she now made it a point to not "overfeed" her guests. You were lucky to get two carrot sticks for hors d'oeuvres and you were guaranteed to leave her table hungry and hankering for a good glass of wine.

Olga was very happy to come to us, mainly so she could escape the constant meddling of Annabelle in her kitchen, and also so she could enjoy the hefty raise I gave her.

The food was delicious. We really were not aware that Olga had counted every calorie that went into the dishes she prepared. Even Mags had no complaints. I watched her across the dining table at one dinner, as she was torn between sidling into the kitchen to proposition Olga and the thought of confronting Victor, her brawny evening chef, to tell him he was fired as he stood there with a cleaver in his hand.

No one seemed surprised to see me seated, once again, in the hostess chair. But then, this was New York where marriage was a game of musical chairs and most people wrote their address books in pencil.

Olga did her best. Larry got his omelets some mornings, made with egg whites and even served with three slices of turkey bacon. She also packed him well-planned lunches. Still, he gained weight, probably because he stopped in for his usual breakfast at the Greek diner after he left our table, and his secretary, in a thoughtless moment, told me how much she was enjoying the lunches.

I began to wonder, did he want to kill himself, with or without my help?

82

I got more comfortable going into the office, ignoring Lauren's hostility and suspicions.

"What do you want here, Mother? Can't you find someone to go to lunch with?"

After the wedding I had taken over a small office as my own. The size and location could be interpreted two ways: the first, that it wasn't an important corner office with an expanse of windows, so therefore, I wasn't important. The other, my view of the deal, was that anyone going to the important offices had to pass this one.

I called in my personal decorator, Elizabeth, to redo the long corridor outside my office with much-needed new carpet and new artwork.

"At least that gives her something to do," I heard Lauren snipe to one of the secretaries.

The new artworks were large painted-on-glass creations, quite attractive actually, spaced along the walls, with one hanging outside my office. That one was "hung" in the dead of the night, as it required removing a chunk of wall so the picture could be connected to one of the same size that hung directly behind it inside my office, the whole thing being a one-way mirror. I could see Lauren walking past, giving me the finger without her knowing I saw it.

I also saw whoever went to Larry's office and that was an interesting parade indeed, many of their scowling faces captured by the implanted camera.

One face I wasn't expecting to appear was Jason's, a knowing smirk on his face as he peered right at me with those eerie eyes. I had been at the picture, preparing to press the sequence of colored dots that were part of the design, to turn the image ability off, as Mags and Janine would be arriving for a foundation meeting. I looked into those eyes and knew damn well that he knew he was looking into mine. I pressed the sequence and scooted back to my desk where I busied myself, my back to the door. Lauren, without knocking, brought Jason in with a "Jason wants to see your office," which would have startled anyone, but at least gave my momentary panic a bit of cover.

"Hello, Olivia," he said. "Nice art work."

"Elizabeth, the decorator, will be happy to hear that," I replied.

"She the same one who did your apartment?"

Was that a sneer?

Thankfully, Mags and Janine arrived and crowded in, so he could not get close enough to my picture to press the dots I suspected he knew were there.

"Hello, Dr. Hadley," he greeted Janine. "Nice to see you, Mrs. Morrison," to Mags. Only I was "Olivia," but then again, mine was the only bed his father had died in.

"Jason," said Janine, "I want to compliment you again on what a nice service you arranged for your father. Gil would have been proud of you."

"Thank you, Dr. Hadley. Lauren helped me pull it all together."

"Are you in town for a while?"

"Yes," Jason said, trying to get closer to my picture. "I have some business and some people to deal with." At this, he gave me a look.

"Well, we shouldn't delay you any longer," piped in Mags. "We have a meeting going on here. A board meeting," she added importantly. And Mags, in her pinstriped suit and white silk shirt looked important. The two left, with Jason throwing me a final *I'll be back* look.

"I don't like that kid," said Mags, hopefully after the door had closed completely. "He reminds me of a weasel."

"Mags," Janine reminded her gently, "we're here to talk about helping kids, and he's one that could have used our help. A lot of them will not only look like, but act like animals."

"Well, I still don't like him," said Mags, taking her *Mrs. Chairman's* seat.

83

Two detectives arrived at my door the next day—not the same ones who had interviewed me in Mason's office. When we were seated in the kitchen sunroom—it was morning and they had accepted my offer of coffee—they assured me that it was for routine follow-up questioning, but their demeanor was harder than that of the other detectives. These two intended to be intimidating. I wondered if it was because John wasn't sitting beside me.

I regretted not ushering them into the sitting room where the softer lighting would have offered a little more protection. In the bright sun-filled room, I felt vulnerable—and I was. They were going to ask me the same questions—hopefully the same questions—the other two had asked. And I was going to give them the same not-quite-a-lie answers, in light as bright as any used when giving the third-degree and without John running interference. I thought about calling him, but on the TV crime shows the perp usually calls his lawyer just before making a full confession. I could throw myself at their mercy and sob, "Yes, I was there—in that bed!" but where could I go from there? Other than straight to jail? I needed to talk to Roger.

There are times when you just have to believe in guardian angels.

Greta came in and announced—almost as a question—"Mr. Roger is here?" I went out to the hallway, barely keeping myself from hugging him. "There are two detectives from Connecticut here."

"Detectives? From Connecticut? Where are these guys?"

I led Roger into the kitchen. The two men stood and shook hands as Roger introduced himself, adding his full NYPD credentials to his name. The demeanor of the two men immediately changed. Before they had been intimidating. Now they were deferential.

"Detectives?" Roger asked.

"Oh, no sir. Mrs. Lammond must have misunderstood us."

I did not.

"We're investigators looking into the recent death of Gil Cantway."

"Is that so?" Roger was in full bullying mode. "Who hired you?"

"I'm afraid that's privileged information, sir," said the lead liar.

"Yeah?" Roger got close to the man—really in his face—the guy would have been able to identify his toothpaste brand. "And I'm afraid this is private property, and you're trespassing."

"The lady invited us in," protested the lesser liar.

"No, she invited two detectives in. Did you card her?"

They were uncomfortably quiet.

"Well, card her now."

Reluctantly, they took out their wallets and each handed me a business card. Roger took them, studied them, then said to each in turn, "Now, Private Investigators Nolan and Weiss, here's my card." He handed one to each. "If you have any more questions, you call me. I have the answers."

"Yes, sir," the younger Weiss snapped to, revealing a military background.

Roger propelled them out. "You know, we could work together on this."

When he returned, we just stood looking at each other.

"Roger," I finally said, "why are you here?"

"Hell if I know. I was driving down Park and a car pulled out up in front of me. A parking place—on Park Avenue—never happens. And in front of your building? I knew I had to take it."

I couldn't help myself. I hugged him. The hold he gave me back was tight and lingering.

"Roger, if I weren't married..."

"Yeah. Well, you are." He released me. "Got any coffee?"

"You know this is scary," I said, looking at him over my cup.

"Yep...it is," he said, gazing back. But then he went back to business. "And so is having those two bozos showing up at your door."

"I was an idiot to let them in."

"No, you weren't," he said reassuringly, then popped that comfort balloon with, "You were an idiot not to ask for and examine their badges and ID. I'm gonna have a little talk with your doorman about letting people through and not even calling you first. But that's then. We have to be more aggressive now about finding out who sent those guys."

"Will that be hard to find out?"

Roger fingered the cards the two men had given him. "These two guys...there's something about them, something familiar...I don't know..."

He pulled out his cell and called Sandy, giving the names and P.I. license numbers and asking for a *quickie,* which I assumed meant a fast check, but set me wondering about the nature of Sandy and Roger's relationship. Was I jealous?

"Who they are, or probably who they are not, will be easy. The real question is who sent them. That's what we have to figure out."

"There are only so many people on that list," I suggested hopefully.

"There are more than you think," replied the spoilsport.

"There's Larry," I offered.

"There's Jason," he countered, "followed by Sal, Lauren, and Mr. X."

"Mr. X?"

"There's always a Mr. X, and if there isn't, you make him up. Keeps you from going in circles with the ones you know about. Besides, he's probably the one who pulled the trigger, or gave the orders."

I involuntarily rubbed the scar on my arm, pondering this Mr. X person and his possible invasion into my life—and in the ending of Gil's.

"We have to really lay this thing out and come up with some answers. The Connecticut cops can't find these guys because they don't have all the facts. It's only a matter of time before they come back with more questions. I'm hanging on an ethical thread here. We all are." Roger rose from his chair. "I'll call John— set up a meeting. You sit here and write every thought that comes to mind. We have to go over every possibility and think of a few more."

I walked Roger to the door. He gave me a brief hug. "Don't worry, I've got your back." I did worry that maybe I wanted him to have more than my back.

84

I got my little book to do my assignment, but had to clear my mind of things I couldn't write down before I could get to the task at hand. Having already proven my lack of skill at outlining, I wrote down thoughts randomly, which better suited my way of thinking.

1. Larry was almost sure I took the money.

2. If Larry knew, Sherry probably knew.
3. Why did Sherry marry Larry? (Now that was a biggie. Why did she? Love? Status? Or Loot?)

I quickly crossed off the first. The second held some appeal, but the third was a *bingo!* That will of theirs still stuck in my craw. Sole beneficiaries? What was that about? That was so not Larry.

4. Did Larry kill Sherry? He would seem, as sole beneficiary, to be the only one to benefit from her death, whatever assets she had to leave.
5. Or was he?

By the time we had our meeting, my mind was in such a whirl that I viewed everyone as a suspect.

"Why are you looking at me that way?" demanded Roger.

"Innocent here," said John. "This happens when you start making lists and writing it all down. Just about everyone has a toe-hold in the top motive categories."

"Which, as we all know," added Roger, "are money, love and revenge. You can usually find your perps hanging out in one of them." When he said the *revenge*, he nodded at me.

"It wasn't revenge!" I said, perhaps a little too huffily. "It was in the closet, so it was part of our joint marriage assets."

"Doesn't matter if it was buried under the apple tree," said John. "You took it—all of it—which brings us to another motivator that rears its head often in my cases—greed."

"But I didn't really want it. I just wanted to take it."

"Uh huh," murmured John. "Every department store security team hears that a hundred times a day. Olivia," he said seriously, looking me directly in the eye, "did you take the money?"

"Yes, sir," the *sir* just coming out on its own.

"Did you kill Sherry?"

"I didn't mean to. I mean…I don't think so. I didn't plan to. I thought it was a turtle."

John, unlike Roger, maintained his composure. "That would require a yes or no answer."

"No, sir."

"Good. That eliminates one suspect. Now, let's get on to the others."

When I reported the previous day's events at the office to them, Roger said, "I'm not surprised the kid recognized one of those things. It makes me even more sure about what's going on."

"What is going on?" I asked.

"Something very clever, very neat. Jason suspects the mirror because they use those in the casinos. That's where he spends his time."

"Casinos? Where?"

"Out west," said John, "strung out along every highway and back road."

I recalled seeing some in New Mexico—pathetic, grim places, seemingly surrounded, 24/7, by rusty pickup trucks and old cars.

"There are a lot of them," he continued, "and they would be the perfect cover."

"For what?" I asked even as it began to dawn on me.

Roger anticipated my *a-ha* moment. "For getting the money into circulation."

"And you think Jason is part of that?"

Roger nodded. "And so was Gil. Those packages he mailed weren't photographs, and he wasn't sending Jason chocolate chip cookies. We think he was sending money."

"Unmarked, of every vintage, nothing sequential," added John. "The bills could have been worked into the system with ease if the right people were in place."

"But where does Larry fit into this? And Lauren? Is it still Willa's scam going on? Who killed Gil? And who killed Sherry?" I blurted out.

"Whoa!" said John, putting his hands up. "This is all speculation. We have no proof of anything. Something smells in that whole business and we're just following the odor."

"What makes you think someone killed Sherry?" asked Roger quietly.

"Because," I imitated his voice as best I could, "something's thrumming."

"Yeah, me too. But you left one very important question out of your lineup: To the *who killed Gil?* add—was he the only one they were after?"

I didn't like the implication of what he said, but it didn't keep me from being a smart-ass. "I vote for Mr. X," I said smugly, like that annoying girl in fourth grade who had all the answers.

"Just hand over your notebook." Roger was not amused.

They passed it back and forth, but instead of writing my scribbling on a sheet of paper, John, whose office we were meeting in, flipped over a picture on an easel to reveal a hard felt chalkboard. He took chalk from his drawer, then drew a circle in the center of the green board and labeled it with a big money symbol.

"This seems to be where it all began," he said. Then, like rays spiking off the sun, he drew lines out and labeled them: Larry, Sherry, Lauren, Gil, Jason, Sal, Mr. X—he nodded to me at that, looked at me more closely, then added Olivia. Under Sherry and Gil's names he wrote in *deceased* and added the dates.

Roger got up, took another piece of chalk, erased *deceased* and replaced it with *murdered* in both cases.

"You're sure about Sherry?" I asked.

"Absolutely," answered Roger. "I got a copy of the coroner's report, ran it by my New York guy who knows what to look for. Someone grabbed her by the ankles and yanked her down. Had to have been one strong person, or two of them, she was a big girl, she wouldn't have gone easy. When you hit that turtle," he directed to me, "it was already dead, for sure."

"We have to start somewhere," said John. "We need someone to stick a pin into." With that he took a box of bigheaded multi-color stickpins from his desk and stuck a red one in Sherry.

Maybe it was the idea of sticking a sharp object into someone that brought another name to mind.

"Wait," I said. "Somebody important is missing from that circle—Willa."

"You're right," said John. "She should be writ large," as he wrote WILLA in capital letters. "Why don't we start with her?"

I retold the exchanges between Willa and Larry, about Willa on the floor with the box, about Larry rushing from the hospital to retrieve those boxes. Then I went over what Charles had told me about Willa being strong-armed into a partnership with Sal, but on her own special terms and how Charles was convinced that Larry was still involved.

"You're right," said John. "Willa was the cornerstone of this whole business."

"We know Sherry was connected to Sal, but it doesn't get us to Gil," said Roger.

John nodded his head. "But they are connected—I feel positive that they're connected."

"Sherry wasn't the original bag lady." I introduced what Charles had mentioned. "Willa had several—all gotten rid of one way or another when they tried to rip that little old lady off. But Charles thought there was someone on the inside as he put it, to keep tabs on the business. What if that someone was Sherry?"

"Crap," said Roger, hitting his head with his hand. "Just suppose Sherry started to make the deliveries to Willa—and maybe met Larry in the process—but she was also keeping the books for Sal. You remember I told you she wasn't someone to cross? That's because she wasn't just a member of Sal's family: She wanted to be a member of the family—you know what I mean? Sherry was very ambitious. Word is, she wanted to be the first made woman. The cops think she'd already made some hits—nothing you could prove—but some bad things happened when Sherry happened to be in the vicinity."

"Could she have been ambitious enough to try skimming from Uncle Sal?"

Roger raised his eyebrows and blew out a long breath. "That sure would have made enemies. And there could be others—from the hits, for instance—that we don't know about."

"You mean Mr. X." I tried not to be smug.

Roger ignored me. "We need to find out how Sherry was connected to the houses. Maybe it's time for a little raid."

"Do you mean we'll go in with guns blazing?" I asked.

"Livie," he sighed, "just sit back and watch the process." To John, he said, "Those places get raided periodically—almost on a schedule. Nothing much happens. The lawyers meet, work out the fines, the ladies get a week's vacation. They're pretty much left alone otherwise if nobody gets hurt or files a complaint."

"Something the customers aren't likely to do," John added.

"Exactly. I have some friends in vice—ones who've managed to live long enough to climb the ranks—who won't care if it's this place instead of another place they drop in on. We can pull in a couple of the girls, older ones who've been around for awhile, and ask a few questions."

"They'll be lawyered up," said John.

"What if their lawyer is detained, or delayed in the middle of the night, and you happen to be on hand?"

John grinned at that. "I really like the way you think, Roger. I really do. But, you know I can't do that. I'm too well known. If I'm hanging around a precinct at night, there will be flashbulbs popping." John paused, grinned again. "But I've got just the person for the job. He's a real weasel, but if we give him the questions, he'll get the answers. It won't be free."

"Whatever it costs," I jumped in. "I've got money."

Of course, a lot of the money would come from Larry, and the fact that it might be used to convict him of a major felony didn't seem to bother anyone in the room.

"You'll have to dig deep into your stash, Livie," said Roger. "The other thing that's got me thrumming is this Jason kid. I need to send a couple of guys out to look those casinos over. We need to get a fix on what Jason does out there."

"Whatever you need, Roger." I was pretty sure that I had met *the couple of guys* at Sandy's house and was also sure that their motorcycles would blend in with the pickups.

"Well," said Roger, rising, "I've got things to do."

John rose from his desk chair to shake Roger's hand—a kind of a seal-the-deal shake. "And I have to attend to some paying clients…"

"Oh John," I was embarrassed at my oversight. "Please! You're on retainer. I expect to be billed."

"You didn't let me finish." He put a reassuring hand on my shoulder. "I was about to add *so I can afford to play*. This one's on me. This one's for fun."

85

"The meeting will come to order," said Mags, banging her gavel on the boardroom table—not the foundation's table, we didn't have a building yet—but the one in the Lammond Holdings headquarters down the hall from my office, which had gotten too crowded for our meetings with the two new board members attending. They were Muriel Goldfarb and Penelope Smith. It would be close to impossible to find two women more different. Muriel, in her youth, had been every parent's nightmare. If there was a hint, a wisp, a possibility of trouble to be mired in, Muriel would be found, stuck in the middle. Her parents were very rich, which was a good thing, because extracting Muriel from some of her exploits was expensive indeed. She had been expelled or forcibly removed from so many boarding schools that she had to be shipped off to Switzerland when the stateside supply ran out. There is a lack of written proof that she ever did receive the equivalent of a high school diploma. Muriel simply was not acquainted with any part of N or O, which is why Mags asked her to join the board. She was put in charge of fundraising.

In truth, Muriel seemed to have calmed down after a series of disastrously expensive failed marriages finally led to one that lasted long enough for her to reproduce. Those twin spawns of Satan were miniature Muriels who finally made their mother realize what hell she had put her own parents through. In an attempt to atone, and possibly be given some miraculous relief from the uproar of her home life, Muriel had turned to *good works* and Mags had snagged her.

Penelope was one of those women you would have hated as a child—the one about whom your mother would have said, far too often, "Why can't you be more like her?" Penelope never wrinkled, dewed, ran at the nose or had a misplaced anything, be it keys, notebook, pronoun or spinach on tooth. Penelope was a wholly complete package of preciseness, primness and proper deportment. She made you want to surreptitiously sniff your pits to make sure you were still socially acceptable. Janine had brought her on board. I secretly hoped that Penelope was one of Janine's more outré patients who had an axe hidden in her handbag or was at least sitting there primly sans underpants.

Penelope was put in charge of the production of our upcoming fundraiser—a job that meant dealing with caterers, florists, sound technicians, linen and china suppliers, etc., all of whom could be prickly and could sabotage an event with the first wrong-colored napkin placed on the first wrong-sized table. This was a job that required diplomacy, and, looking around at our group, she was the only one possessing that asset, other than Janine.

At subsequent meetings, Muriel would arrive with astonishing amounts of pledges, along with checks and outright cash.

"How do you do it?" I asked.

"Easy. I have a lot of old friends who are now in high places. We grew up together. Hell," she laughed, "we threw up together. I just go in and say, *Remember when we…*and they whip out the old check books."

"Are you blackmailing them?"

"Good heavens, no," she said all too primly. "Their companies have *gimme funds*—you know, for charities. They have to give the money away. Why not to us?" Muriel, it seemed, was very light on her feet when it came to treading that fine line of legality.

Mags threw out idea after idea for our ball theme, including Dyngus Day. That one gave us pause and required explanation, but we quickly out-voted her on the grounds that 1) it was really a Polish National holiday and we didn't want to use red and white as a color scheme, 2) Easter would be long past, and 3) to give the New York women license to beat the men and each other about the head with pussy willows would require us to carry such a huge liability policy that the premium would wipe out what we took in.

Mags reluctantly agreed to Penelope's previously suggested In the Pink theme. I happened to have been at Mags's the previous week when a ball gown was delivered, which Flore took out of its wrappings while Mags steered—no yanked—me out of her dressing room, but not before I had a glimpse of something stunning in peony pink. We had been *played*, of course.

86

On the way home from the meeting, I stopped at a pastry shop on Madison Avenue and bought two of Larry's favorite little Godiva chocolate cake concoctions. All the diet plans say that the dieter, just for his effort, earns an occasional treat. Larry had been trying, well, lying about trying, but in his mind and the minds of all who would listen to him, he was on a diet. So a treat would not be out of the question.

Besides, I wanted to question him about Sherry and there was nothing more likely to loosen his tongue than to feed his face with something sinful.

We had a very nice dinner, starting with a creamed soup (Olga had the night off and Greta, a solid meat and potatoes cook, was filling in), going on to the heavy stuff with plenty of wine in-between, and ending, much to Larry's delight, with the cakes. He inhaled his with gusto, then sat like a dog eyeing his master's food as I took a nibble of mine. I pushed my plate a little toward him, but held on as I queried coyly, "Laurence, how did Sherry get you away from me?"

Like a dog, he was salivating, looking at the cake. "I don't know," he said. "She was delivering some, uh, business receipts every week or so, and assisting me with, uh, some things. Then," he wiped the drool off his chin, "she needed an office. Didn't see any harm in that. Then, you know, one thing led to another." He looked at me—an accusing look.

"She wanted me. You didn't." I let go of the plate and watched, my heart hurting, as this overgrown boy wolfed down that poison.

"Laurence," I took his hand. "I'm so sorry. We should have talked more."

"Yeah." He patted my hand. "That whole thing with Sherry and me? It didn't amount to much. My mind went crazy for those months. Whatever she said, whatever she wanted, was okay. I couldn't say no." Then he took my hand and caressed it. "I'm sorry, Olivia. I hurt you. I hurt the girls, and I'm really, really, sorry." I had a flashback to the very handsome young man he had been and to the love I had felt for him.

That night, for the first time since our remarriage, we shared the marital bed. It wasn't physically easy, given his bulk, but the old moves, the old favorite spots, were still there, so we managed some kind of intimacy.

I slept quite well and woke late. I stretched languorously, like the elderly Chinese woman in the Pearl Buck book, one toe at a time, working up to my head. By the time I got to my fingers, I froze. I had slept very well. Larry hadn't kept me awake with his snoring! I lay still, listening. There wasn't a sound. Then my nose began twitching. There was definitely an odor. Urine? And... I jumped out of that bed, horrified. His mouth was agape, his eyes open.

I ripped my fouled gown off me, went to the door and screamed for Greta.

By the time the EMTs arrived, Greta had helped clean me up, brought clothes from my room and helped me to get dressed.

Greta called Mags and Janine. Janine called Charles and Roger.

I sat numbly and called Lauren, who was still staying in my apartment. She was there in seeming minutes. We huddled together and dialed Christa's number. Thankfully, Jeff answered. She wasn't there alone. "This isn't good news, is it?" he asked.

"No. No, it isn't."

87

In every society, the ritual of death and the closing of a life varies, mostly in how the remains are attended to and the accouterments used in the rites. But in general the preparations are invariably carried out by the women. And so it was here. Mags, Janine, Greta and Olga became the traditional womenfolk who shifted into high organizing gear.

And Mason, dear Mason, with Charles at his side, did the manly part with the minister and the funeral director.

"You are not wearing the same suit to his funeral that you wore to Sherry's," Mags instructed me.

"Leave her alone," said Janine. "She can wear whatever she wants to wear." So there was some normality in the middle of the upset.

There was a crowd of people at Larry's memorial service and I greeted them all, with Lauren and Christa flanking me. Fortunately, Dr. Sloane was one of them, and he spent several minutes, within everyone's earshot, praising me—in his precise, carrying voice—for all my efforts trying to improve Laurence's health by overseeing his diet and getting him the gym membership. "Olivia," he finally intoned, "you did everything you could."

Yes, I did. And I was overcome with guilt. On-lookers mistook it for grief, but I knew what I had done.

"Well, well," said Jason, as he leaned into me, ostensibly to give a cheek kiss, but really to hiss into my ear, "the black widow. Is it condolences or congratulations?"

It hit me full force: Larry was the second man who had died in my bed within an uncomfortably short time span. I excused myself from the girls with a call of nature ploy. I needed to escape. But really, was there anyplace to go that didn't set me in the role of a Jessica Fletcher in her unquiet little town of Cabot Cove? Like Jessica, if I was around, someone was going to die.

I went into the powder room and searched the mirror for signs of evil. The face that looked back seemed rather nice: blonde hair—chemically enhanced, but close enough to the original color to be acceptable; blue eyes—not ice or sapphire—just blue. Janine's calm gray ones were probably more interesting, and Mags's big dark ones were certainly more compelling. At camp we had all craved emerald green eyes, with either masses of unruly red curls or masses of ebony locks, which was what the heroines of the bodice-ripper novels we hid under our mattresses all seemed to possess.

I leaned in closer and tried a smile. The lines around my mouth and eyes didn't bother me—at least not enough to take action against them as Mags had suggested I should consider doing. I didn't look evil, and more importantly, I didn't feel it. I had guilt, for sure, but even if I were indulging in a binge of rationalizing, Larry was going to do what he did and I had provided him with opportunities to make different choices.

Larry had been cremated, so we had one more urn to reverently place. His, at least, was of a tasteful plain sterling silver, unlike Sherry's overwrought creation that now resided in a closet—the broom closet, to be exact—which is not as heartless as one would think, as it had been placed in a very safe cubby hole with a closed screen door.

Some well-meaning soul suggested that I put Larry's urn in our bedroom so he wouldn't be lonely. I found the suggestion to be excellent and did so, ignoring the intended reason as I never intended to sleep in that room again. In fact, there was no bed. I had that and the carpet disposed of immediately after they took Larry out of there.

88

The next days were controlled and filled in by friends, starting with Mason who believed in reading the will as soon as the lid was clamped down or the urn screwed tight.

Larry, as we had agreed, had left the girls each a half million, after taxes. Christa was almost overwhelmed by her father's generosity. Lauren was equally underwhelmed by his Scrooge-like behavior and glared at me through the rest of the reading.

"I suppose you'll take over his office," she said before slamming out of the room. "That'll be a laugh," trailed after her.

I tried to rest in my room after that, but her words haunted me. With all my hanging around the office spying, I hadn't really learned a damn thing about the business. The little shit might have been in a snit, but she had hit the nail on the head: it was going to be a laugh. I would need help.

Christa and Jeff, along with Alice and Charles, were staying that night, so Greta made us a comfort-food meal of meatloaf and mashed potatoes. I enjoyed spending time with Christa and her obviously adoring beau and seeing how much they enjoyed each other. If I had the world to choose from, I could not have picked a better man for her.

Jeff, it turned out, was a rider and had hunted with Alice and Charles several years before. Alice knew his aunt and other members of his family. The whole thing made for such a comfortable fit. The only nagging raw spot was the absence of Lauren, who thought a night on the town with Jason suited her more than a quiet dinner with the remainder of her family. I might even have accepted Jason at the table, just to have Lauren there. But then, it would have been such a different, tense evening. Christa deserved her time in the center, having so often been pushed aside by her run-amok squeaky-wheel of a sister.

89

I would have liked a month alone on a deserted island before going into the office, or even two weeks on the oft-delayed yacht cruise with Mags. Mason, however, picked me up the next morning at seven. "We want to get in there early and do a lock down," he said as he handed me a cup of coffee in the back of the limo, introducing me to a strange-looking man right out of Central Casting. His wispy tufts of sparse hair stuck straight up—the same color as his gray suit, and for that matter, his skin. He looked like he lived in a tomb. But Edgar Wedgecomb—that was his name—enjoyed a fine reputation as a forensic accountant. He was regarded with fear and loathing by half of the moneyed world—and was, therefore, loved and adored by the other half.

"I need to look at the books," was the extent of his conversation.

Roger and another man were waiting in the lobby. Mason had given strict orders about who would be allowed in that day, and apparently, I had given most of the staff the day off.

Roger introduced his companion—a man named Parvis Kamali. This man was four times the size of Edgar, also with gray hair, but his looked like nails sticking out of his large head. His skin was swarthy and his eyes didn't believe anything they saw. Roger later told me, "If you want to find out where the money is, you bring in Parvis."

We went up to Larry's office. "You okay with this, Livie?" asked Roger kindly. "We can start this without you, if you want to stay in your office for now."

I was okay with it. They pulled a large comfortable chair over to a sunny corner and sat me in it. Then they started going through the filing cabinets. Anything that seemed of a personal nature was placed on a table beside me, and Larry's desk drawers were left for me to go through. Other files were sorted on a big conference table.

I listened as Edgar and Parvis spoke the strange language of their special world. They seemed to get on well together.

Mason left to attend to some business, saying he would be back shortly. Roger went to my office to make phone calls.

The desk phone rang. Edgar picked it up, listened, then brought it to me. The head of the security desk described some very irate people downstairs who needed to get to their offices. I recognized some of the names of top executives, so told him to send them up.

Parvis was not entirely pleased about that. He told me—yes, told me—to come with him. We got Roger from my office, then went to the elevator. As I walked behind the men, I had a good look at Parvis and came to the conclusion that he did forensics accounting for fun. The rest of the time he probably spent in dark dangerous places doing deeds that supplied the real forensic labs with interesting material.

Three men burst out of the elevator, mad as hell and not going to take this anymore. They calmed down to greet me and to reiterate their condolences. Roger led them into a conference room, apologizing for any inconvenience. He had the coffee cart brought in—the company could function for one day without the executives, but not without the coffee lady. There was the bustle of getting coffee and donuts and settling around the table. Roger explained that an accounting was taking place in Larry's office.

They did not like this situation and began to get more and more agitated. Fortunately, Mason arrived and took the situation in hand. He informed them that not only was this the usual procedure, but as executor of the estate, he was required to oversee its performance. He then queried each man about his position in the company and assured them that he did not intend to disrupt the workings of the company and would be glad to have them stay, under certain conditions: they would work in the conference room; they could go into their offices, one at a time, accompanied by

Mason or Parvis to retrieve files; and nothing was to leave the building.

Two of the men, Robert Ridge and Alex Modesky, reluctantly agreed to the plan. Gino Sergio did not. "You can't fucking do this! I'm going into my office—alone! And no one's gonna stop me!"

Mason picked up the phone and spoke one word: "Security."

Gino got up, ready to barge out of the room, but soon discovered that would mean going through Roger and Parvis. He thought better of it, then roamed the room, running his fingers through his thick hair and muttering words like *lawyer, Gestapo, fucking nightmare,* and *I'm outta here.*

I sat back and watched—petrified. I was going to have to deal with these people on my own, and hundreds more. Lauren was right: "What a laugh." I was ready to pee my pants, but didn't dare ask permission to leave the room.

Security arrived and Gino had his choice: He chose to stay. Mason and Parvis took Robert and Alex to their offices. Roger walked security to the elevator to have a few words. I was left with this raging maniac. But he wasn't. He came over to me and apologized. "Geez, Mrs. Lammond, I'm sorry. This is a mess…no one's in charge. You can't just close a business down for a day. Not this kind of business. The other guys will be dancin' in the streets, goin' after our stuff. I'm gonna lose thousands today."

"Olivia," I said. "Call me Olivia. I'm really sorry about this, but I was assured it was necessary. I will try to see that you're made whole. You know, Gino," I gestured for him to sit down, "I'm going to need a lot of help here, a lot of patience and advice." I looked him full in the eye. "I don't know a thing. You guys are going to have to teach me."

He liked that. He relaxed.

Then I added, "There's Lauren, of course." He visibly stiffened. "She must know how some things work," I finished lamely.

"Yeah, well…we'll discuss that someday." He was no longer looking me in the eye.

The object of that little discussion burst into the room. "What the fuck's going on here?" she screamed.

I remained calm. "If you would bother to answer my calls or listen to my messages, you would know what's going on here."

"I'm not putting up with this shit! I'm going into my office, and you can go fuck yourself."

Gino got to his feet. "Listen here, you little—"

I shushed him, then looked at my raging daughter. "Lauren Lammond," I said, "you're fired."

"Who the hell do you think you are?" she said in my face. "You can't fire me!"

"Oh, but she can," said Mason who had returned in time to hear that exchange. "She's the boss."

"Boss of what? She knows fuck-all about anything." Then she looked at me venomously. "Other than about killing people and getting away with it."

There was dead silence in the room. I rose, went to the phone and repeated Mason's one word: *Security.*

Lauren was quiet, shocked by her own outburst. She left between the security guards without a backward glance.

I had to start being the boss—now! "Okay, gentlemen," I did a chop-chop with my hands, "let's get to work." Then I fled to the bathroom.

I stood numbly in front of the sink, pressing a wet towel to my face. There comes a time, I thought, there comes a time, and Lauren's was long overdue. Of course it was unfair to shut her out like that, just after losing her father. Of course it was. But there's me! I wanted to shout. I'm here. I need you!

To continue to allow her to treat me in that contemptuous manner was no longer an option. To let her address me in that outrageous way in the office was more simply just out of the question.

90

In the midst of all the death and mayhem, there had been birth: Wanda and Silly had become the proud parents of *Ohmy* as in *Ohmigod! What is it?*, which was the usual reaction when people saw him. Depending on whose side you took, Ohmy either had the best or the worst of both parents in an eye-popping mix. He was short-legged, like his mother, naked like his father, sporting his father's elegant long nose protruding from Wanda's fuzzy face and with mane and forelocks that Silly could envy.

Alice fell in love with Ohmy when she came to get Wanda after the weaning period, but, with Mason crying and beating his breast about losing his "little Wandy girl," she relented and left the baby in Mason's custody. Privately, she told me that it was in Ohmy's best interest to stay in New York, where anything was acceptable. In the country, his bizarre looks would probably excite too much interest from the Jack Russells, not to mention what it would do to Wanda's reputation.

Still, Mason moped for months truly mourning the loss of Wanda. He loved that little lady, and the strange and aloof Ohmy did not replace her in his heart.

Then Mags called. "Come! Come! Mason is bringing home a baby."

Mags's *come, comes* were getting harder to heed with all that was going on at the office, but I couldn't let this new part of my life consume me.

I got there in time for cocktails. Janine was there, and Muriel, our fellow committee member, who had eased her way into the group and was vying to become a new BFF.

Otis came in first, carrying a large and furry dog bed, which I was glad to see, as Mags had not made clear what kind of baby Mason was bringing home.

Then Mason walked in, shyly, like a father bringing his daughter to her first ballet class. He held a violet leash in his hand and, walking regally at the end of it, was the most beautiful creature I had ever seen. She was blue. She was blue-gray velvet. Her lashes—which had to have been fake, they were so long—outlined impossibly violet eyes. And, she was a bit large to be called a *baby*.

"Her name," Mason said proudly, "is Princess Prussian Blue."

Mags was taken back by the size of Princess, but was soon more taken with her beauty and the possibilities of matching outfits: hers involving Persian lamb, no doubt.

Princess retained her regal demeanor through all our handling and petting and was nonplused when Silly came to raise his nose up to her privates.

Janine, who was sitting beside me, nudged me, holding her sides in silent laughter, and whispered, "Look at her paws, she's half grown."

I did, then nudged her back, my silent mirth making it more of an elbowing than a nudge, that caused her celebratory glass of Dom Pérignon to spill over her gray Brooks Brothers pleated skirt.

"Mason," I gasped, "this is a…"

Mason put a finger to his lips. But I had seen what were, without doubt, the biggest paws ever assigned to a puppy. Ohmy sat gazing up at her in awe. I looked at poor Silly and thought you'd better sniff her while you can, because those goods will be out of your reach very soon. Princess was a Giant Great Dane.

91

Christa and Jeff came as often as they could for weekend visits. Even if just a day trip, they made the effort, and those were the bright spots in my otherwise darkened life. One day Jeff asked to speak to me alone. He was very nervous as we settled ourselves in the library. Then he began explaining his life plan, his goals, laying out his prospects. My heart was almost in tears over this earnest young man.

"Jeff." I put my hand on his arm. "Are you asking me for permission to marry Christa?"

"Yes!" he beamed, relieved. Then he spewed out a garble of *love each other, not right living together,* and so on.

"Why don't you go get Christa?" I suggested.

A few minutes later they returned, Christa holding out a hand sporting her new ring. There was not a diamond ever pulled from the dark earth that could possibly shine brighter than my darling girl's eyes at that precious moment.

I had already planned a little dinner party for that night, so we celebrated the couple with champagne and good wishes and kisses.

Mags was into the wedding production as soon as the ring hit the finger. Christa, shyly, asked if I would be hurt if the wedding was at Charles and Alice's farm. They wanted a small Valentine's Day ceremony, and it would be easier for their co-workers and friends to attend if it were at the farm.

Mags answered, "Oh yes! Valentine's Day! We'll have a red theme!" And apparently that was settled.

Alice was thrilled with the idea. "The place has needed some freshening up for years. This will make me go ahead and do it."

The place, their home, is one of those beautiful, rambling houses that can be glimpsed most often in Pennsylvania and Connecticut. The original house was built over 230 years ago; an addition, a hundred years later. Then came the new part, fifty years after that. The house has a large, open center hall entry where a graceful staircase spirals down from the balcony above—a perfect place for a bride to descend.

Charles, an avid gardener, had the grounds exquisitely laid out and maintained. The big side patio would easily hold a tent that would have kitchen access. In other words, a perfect setting.

To say I was completely happy with the idea would be disingenuous. I was happy in concept, but also sad that our elegant Park Avenue apartment did not hold that same appeal. We too have an entrance hall with an even more magnificent descending staircase, plus multiple rooms fanning out from the entryway that could easily provide a beautiful setting for their wedding. But there was something lingering in this place, something bad, an underlying uneasiness.

92

Mags, Mason and family arrived in full bark for the wedding. Silly and Wanda headed for the hills, Ohmy engaged in a standoff with the quietly gaping Jack Russells as Princess ambled into the kitchen. She was later seen strolling to the barn with a large bottle of cola held gently in her mouth. A groom reported, swearing to have been sober, that Princess shared her drink with one of the horses.

Princess seemed to have tripled in size in those few months, but not only was she a giant, she was a smart lush of a giant: she had learned to get caps off of anything, along with opening cupboards, drawers and the refrigerator. Mason was convinced that she mixed her own drinks, because more than once he had gone into the library and found the liquor cabinet door open with Princess snoring loudly from behind a chair, her paws cradling gin and tonic bottles with caps missing, along with the contents. Alcohol is poison for dogs, but Princess apparently hadn't read her manual.

This, of course, is the preamble to the shocking event.

I had thought long about Larry's urn and had decided to give it to Lauren. It probably wasn't the best idea, or in the best taste to do that at Christa's wedding, but I had brought Larry along because it was Christa's wedding.

Janine had no words to say—just a *you really are crazy* raising of the eyebrows. But, nevertheless, I brought the urn and put it on a table in a corner of the grand entryway—a sentimental thought that Larry would be there when Christa walked down those stairs. It was a good, caring, sentimental idea.

Sometime during the party part of the evening, a canine commotion arose out at the far back edge of the garden. Alice came to me, white-faced, gasping, "You'd better come."

Mags was by my side at the moment and tagged along too. When she saw Princess, she cooed, "What has my baby been up to? Have you been a naughty…"

Princess stood there with Larry's urn—rather, one half of Larry's urn—in her mouth. Around her, the other dogs, especially the Jack Russells who can smell a kill a hundred years old, pawed and dug and raised their legs over a small mound.

Alice, Mags and I just looked at each other. We tried not to laugh, we really did. But in the end, what could we do? After we got control of ourselves, we pried the urn half out of Princess's mouth, filled it with what dirt was not frozen to the ground, and having found the other half, screwed it together. Oh what the hell. It was sterling silver. Lauren would probably end up consigning it and its contents to a pawn shop anyway, and if the proprietor noticed those faint, evenly spaced marks on the outside, he could never dream that they were left there by a blue velvet, violet-eyed Giant Great Dane.

It was fitting for Larry to be spread in Charles's beautiful garden, even if the ground was frozen, the spreading involved many paws, and the watering down of his dust done in the most natural of manners.

93

Other than that dramatic event, the wedding for my daughter Christa and my new son Jeff was as perfect as it could possibly have been. The early afternoon sunlight streamed through the tall windows and French doors, illuminating Christa like an angel. She descended the staircase to take her Uncle Charles's arm, who walked her out through the open doors to face the guests seated in the heated tent. Jeff was trembling and awed as Charles handed her into his care.

Mags had kept the decor simple, using hundreds of fairy lights hidden in creamy silk swathed over the tent's ceiling and sides and in puffs of dangling baby's breath lightly twined with thin red ribbon. Nothing was to outshine the bride. She had also insisted that the couple face their guests so we could see their faces as they exchanged vows, which was almost too touching for this mother's heart.

Yes, my daughter Christa's wedding was perfect—except for one flaw—my other daughter Lauren.

Lauren and I had managed to avoid contact after I fired her—giving her a hefty severance package to ward off a lawsuit—while she still lived in my other apartment rent-free. Christa, aside from wanting her sister to be her maid of honor, hoped to reunite us as part of the ceremony. That was not going to happen.

Up to this point I had always thought—no, *thought* isn't a strong enough word—I had been convinced that a mother's love was a bottomless pool. Well, it isn't. The part of a woman that is the pool of motherly love is always there, always belongs to her children; otherwise children would never survive the rather nasty, sticky business of their early years. They certainly overdrew from it in their teens. But they are supposed to stop the draw-down and do some replenishing as they become adults. Lauren had just kept siphoning out until there was just moist muck left at the bottom.

Oh, I could give her money, material things, at arm's length and preferably through an attorney, but I did not really like the person she was, and I wasn't sure anymore about how to love someone I didn't like. I was no doubt carrying over some of my confused and bitter feelings about Larry and attaching them to the daughter who so resembled him in his way with the world, but I could not control the feelings.

And that was before the wedding. Then things got worse.

Lauren and I managed to greet each other in a civil way, even indulging in a perfunctory hug. I did, however, overlook Jason's proffered hand. Jason was her accomplice. Most people would refer to him as her date, even her *beau*, but Jason was ever an accomplice.

Lauren was dressed in a stunning red silk sheath dress, worn under a matching mandarin-collared shorter coat, which she had kept partly buttoned. Later in the evening, after the ruckus in the garden, Lauren and Jason stood in front of me in the great room. It was a seemingly casual encounter, but my antennae were on full alert. Lauren had unbuttoned her coat. She pulled it aside and there was the unmistakable bump of my first grandchild. As I stared, the bump was covered by the hand of Jason, whose falcon eyes glittered at me as he did so. The very size of Lauren's stomach told me that they had been more than *just friends* for several months at least, and confirmed my fears about Lauren's involvement in whatever Jason had been doing.

"We have some news," he said.

"I can see," I replied, riveted to the spot.

"We're gonna need to talk about some things soon—real soon. This kid will need to be taken care of."

The sly smirk on Lauren's face sent me fleeing into the powder room where I threw up.

Any woman of my age, seeing that bump on her first-born daughter, should have been overjoyed with happiness. I was overwhelmed with anguish. That baby wasn't conceived out of love—that baby was implanted out of spite, or worse, as a business asset. What kind of monster had I conceived those years ago?

When I finally cleaned myself up and could breathe, Travis was waiting outside. He took my arm and steered me into Alice's small office behind the kitchen. He gave me a glass of water.

"I know, in the movies you'd be getting a shot of booze," he said gently, very gently. "But you need to hydrate." I drank the water. I was in shock, and he knew it.

"You saw?" I asked him.

"Yes, I did. I surely did."

"What should I do?"

Travis took my hand and caressed my palm and my fingers. It was incredibly erotic, this simple gesture. What kind of monster am I, to be sexually turned on at a moment like this?

"You can't do anything," he said simply. "Well, yes you can. You can turn yourself inside out, rip your heart out and hand it over to them. You can watch while they break it and see that it won't do a damn bit of good for anyone. Or you can disengage, let them live the lives they choose. Either way, there will be collateral damage, and you are in the drop zone. For now, I would advise you to run for cover."

I sat there for a moment.

"Thank you, Travis." I took the hand that had been caressing mine to my lips and kissed it. "This is Christa's day. I will not let Lauren and Jason take that from her and I know that is what they intend to do." I got to my feet. Travis rose.

"May I escort you back to the party?" he said as he proffered his arm.

Christa, protected from close contact with Lauren by her alerted Aunts Janine and Mags, left for her honeymoon shortly after with the besotted Jeff's arm around her.

Lauren and Jason, with Larry's urn tucked casually under her arm, left soon after, the screech of their tires sent to warn me of their displeasure. It also pointed out the disregard Lauren had for the fetus under her seat belt, a disregard that the grandmother's heart she had created in me would compel me, no matter what other feelings I harbored—along with the natural primitive need to keep the seed blooming through generations—to protect that baby.

But, not tonight. Tonight I went home with Travis.

94

Through all this busy-ness, there had still been the business to attend to and that was a nightmare. It hadn't taken Edgar and Parvis long to discover Lammond Holdings teetered on the edge of financial insolvency—bankruptcy some would say—but that would imply that the banks owned everything and that wasn't the case. Larry, it seemed, took the term *A Wholly Owned Company* at face value and tried to make it just that, by astonishing means. Uncovering those meandering financial machinations took the two money sleuths several months and many *what the hell!*

They finally came to me with their report, which opened with: "We wouldn't have believed it if we hadn't seen it," which is not the way one would like to hear such an important analysis prefaced. Parvis added, "He was either the smartest guy in the business, or the luckiest dumb schmooze on the planet." I feared it had been the latter.

Larry had been running his own internal Ponzi scheme with the buildings, taking from the pool to buy or prop up whichever building needed it most.

Not that he didn't have mortgages, that would have been impossible, but as Edgar so delicately put it, "Not the proper amount." Along with that, Parvis informed me, "There had been a river of cash under those buildings that's dried up."

Which brings us to another problem—Sal Santini—Big Sal, and the fact that no one had delivered any proceeds from the other business, not to mention the rent, since Larry died. I didn't want the "business" money, but I did want the rent. I suppose he thought I wouldn't notice or was too afraid to ask. I did notice and I was too afraid to ask.

"Olivia," Parvis interrupted those unwelcome thoughts, "you need to sell some buildings. You need to sell them now."

After we discussed just how much was needed to stay afloat, they left me to contemplate this new business world I inhabited. The numbers were so large, the world they encompassed so Brobdingnagian, that it had become unreal, like playing Monopoly. I did not want to spend my life doing this. I wanted out. But first, I had to sell some buildings and I knew just which one would be first on the block.

I called Gino Sergio to come to my office. Yes, that Gino, the one I was afraid to be alone with, who had now become my right and left hand man. He and Alex Modesky really ran the business while allowing me to enjoy the view from the big corner office.

When I told him what I wanted to do, he rubbed his jaw and rolled his eyes. "That could be a little...ah..."

"Dangerous?" I provided. "Gino, I know what was going on. It hasn't been going on these past months, I can assure you."

"Can you?" He looked at me with those black Sicilian eyes and I felt a chill. "When did you last see Lauren?" he asked.

I sat speechless. I understood him exactly.

He then said, "You know, Jason is still making trips out west."

"This is bigger than I think, isn't it, Gino?"

"Oh it's big—it's real big. You could call it a monster."

"Are you in it, Gino?"

"Just 'cause I'm Italian? Don't lump us all together."

"I'm sorry. I had to ask."

Gino massaged the anger from his face and sat back. "You want to get out of this. We both know that. You think because Sal Santini's people haven't been around that you're off the hook. What you don't know is, it's been business as usual, only they've cut you out of the deal. They figure they don't need you, Olivia, and maybe you don't want to give them a reason to think they don't need you even more."

This should have scared the shit out of me, but it made me even more determined to rid myself of that building, to make the whole business clean.

"Would someone buy it?"

"Hell, yes! The WestProp Group have tried a dozen times to get them. They've put together most of the block to tear down so they can put up a monster high-rise. Those four brownstones sit right in the middle of their holdings. That area was a slum when Larry's grandmother bought in—now it's prime real estate."

"Four buildings?"

Gino leaned back and laughed at my ignorance. "You'd better start reading those reports that land on that big desk."

There had been so many.

"It's four of them, in a row. I heard some walls were opened and some secret doors installed, so there's a convenient flow between them."

"How much are they worth, Gino?"

"Well, since they're holdouts and the WestProp guys are sitting on a lot of property that's costing them money every day, probably fifty."

"Fifty? Fifty what?"

"Mil."

"Fifty million?"

"Yeah, though we could probably hardball them up some more."

I nearly fainted.

"And there's no mortgage, you know," he added.

I recalled that Edgar and Parvis had said the same words in accounting wonderment.

"Larry's mother made him promise to keep them free and clear, which has become a very expensive promise. The taxes have sky-rocketed, but the buildings," he chortled, "get this! They're rent controlled! Those ladies might have the cheapest rent in New York!"

"Can Sal Santini buy them?"

"No way. He can't get that kind of money and he sure as hell can't get a mortgage. That's why this is such a sweet deal for him and why he's not gonna walk away from it without a fight."

There was a loud knock on the door, a second before it burst open, then Muriel invaded the space.

"I was in the neighborhood and thought I'd grab you for lunch," she said to me while eyeing Gino, the one she clearly wanted to grab. "Am I interrupting something?" she asked, all innocence.

The effect of her actually opening her coat, which she did with a practiced swish, displaying her very rounded curves packed into a knitted suit—perhaps a size too small—flattened Gino into his chair. She fluffed her red-hued hair—definitely not a gift of nature—over her collar. She licked her lips, and said, "Can you come?"

"Now that you mention it, I'm starving...."

Gino got up, mumbling and blushing.

Oh-uh.

"Muriel, nice to see you," said the suddenly gawky teenage Gino.

Ohmigod—she was fluttering her eyelashes! I couldn't wait to tell Mags.

"And we have committee business to discuss…" I turned to Gino. "Gino, think about this, we'll talk more later." Although I wasn't sure that he heard me, I was equally sure that he would be thinking about something as we followed Muriel's powerful mix of pheromones and perfume to the elevator. Gino pushed the button, then went on to his office.

"He's cute," she said as the door slid close and I knew that Gino had pushed another button.

95

Over lunch we talked about the foundation, the upcoming fundraiser ball, how much we had raised toward a building, amid her little probing questions about Gino. Once she discovered that he was long divorced, Muriel relaxed and devoted herself to the business at hand.

"But you must have a building you can give us," she pouted.

"Well," I heard myself saying after the second glass of Pinot Gris, "as it happens, I have four you can choose from."

I turned on my coffee maker as soon as I returned to the office, then called for Gino, along with Parvis who had taken to hanging out in my old office.

"What if I donated one of the middle buildings to a charitable foundation?"

They knew which buildings I was talking about.

"You mean, to sell?" asked Parvis.

"To do whatever they want with, which I assume would be to sell."

"Well," he pondered, financial wheels churning, "we could take the tax deduction over a period of years."

"You're sly, Olivia," said Gino. "Give a middle building away? That would muddle the works. What's the charity?"

"It's a foundation for troubled teens. A safe house for runaway girls, and abused kids, generally. We're working out the details. Muriel is in charge of fundraising," I added casually, knowing this would raise Gino's interest level and give the project priority. "First I need Roger to have some old friends carry out that long-overdue midnight inspection."

96

Roger didn't like the idea, especially after hearing that Lauren and Jason were doing business without me.

"I'll send Edgar over. I want the guys to take a really good look, see if anything has changed these past few months."

That Roger was willing to continue helping me was a wonder.

"Do you ever think about what you're doing? Or do you run off with the first guy who asks you?" he had shouted—shouted—at me several days after he had somehow found out about Travis.

Well, no, I hadn't thought very long about it. I just let my horny, needy self be tucked into Travis's car and Travis's bed. But I obviously had some doubts and guilt that fueled my shouting back, "At least he asked!"

I had been sidestepping Travis's pleas to return, and threats to come and get me ever since. I yearned to go on Mags's and Mason's oft-delayed cruise, allegedly leaving in two weeks, for what, in comparison, would be peace and quiet.

97

The raid took place several days later at an early morning hour. All four buildings were hit at the same time, which was unusual, so the top women and madams couldn't scoot through the hidden doors into one of the other buildings.

It turned into something far bigger than vice doing a routine raid. The mayor's people had gotten wind of what was going down—and, it being an election year, there he was in front of the cameras as the ladies were led away. One o'clock in the morning had been chosen by vice to make sure that the mayor's buddies, if not the mayor himself, would be long gone by the time the cavalcade of squad cars closed off the block.

The next day, Mags and Muriel, jockeying for top spot in front of those very same cameras, waved a deed around and announced that Lammond Holdings had donated a building to the Father Mike's Foundation, to be used as a safe haven for runaway and abused girls. The public loved the poetic justice of the story—it made good press, until it was replaced by:

SHE WASN'T THERE!

Gretchen Mayer, a devout communicant and frequent participant in holy retreats at the Connecticut Convent, never saw Olivia.

Followed quickly by:

SAVE HER OR SINK HER?

SHERRY WAS MURDERED!

This featured a reprise of the picture of me, wet hair blowing in the wind, driving the boat the night Sherry died.

AN UNNAMED SOURCE SAYS THE LATE SHERRY LAMMOND WAS MURDERED!

POLICE HAVE INDICATED THAT OLIVIA LAMMOND MIGHT BE A 'PERSON OF INTEREST'

And the best one:

THEY DIED IN HER BED! BLACK WIDOW? PREYING MANTIS?

Followed by never-before released details about Gil and Larry.

The combined details could only have come from one source—and that would be the tag team of Lauren and Jason.

98

I was sitting in my office, reading these very exciting efforts in journalism, when my office door banged open.

I looked up, expecting Muriel and Mags in one of their snits. It was many degrees worse, in the form of Big Sal Santini and two of his hefty supporters.

Sal came to my desk and splayed his hands on it.

"Well, Olivia," he rasped, "you don't seem to know the rules of the game."

I said nothing, not because I was playing it cool, but because fear had glued my tongue to the roof of my mouth.

"Sammy and Joey here," he nodded toward his acolytes, "thought you could use a lesson in good sportsmanship." Joey locked the door and Sammy moved in closer.

Now, among the interesting items that Larry had left in his desk was a Smith & Wesson. I had meant to mention it to Roger, if not to turn it over to him on several occasions, but forgot. How one could keep forgetting about this big honking hunk of metal, I leave for Janine to interpret, but there it was.

Then somehow, there it was—in my hand—safety off, as Google and gang had so patiently instructed me should never, ever, be the case, unless you *intended to use the motherfucker.*

Sal and Co. were backing carefully away when there was a loud banging on the locked door. The sound startled me, or rather it startled my finger, which had been lying lightly on the trigger, into an involuntary reflex tightening.

A Smith & Wesson firing in a closed office, even a big corner closed office, makes a sound that brings to mind a blast off to the moon.

Sal grabbed his arm. Sammy and Joey went for their weapons, then stopped, noting that I was still holding mine. They were very familiar with how many bullets were still in the gun.

Then Sammy, who realized that I was frozen in shock, came around my desk, put the safety on and removed the gun from my hand. "Lady, you're dead," he said as Joey unlocked the door for their escape.

Parvis, a weapon like a cannon in his huge paw, yanked the door open, pushed past Joey and Sal and burst into the room. Sammy, thinking better of taking that on, put my gun into his pocket and got Big Sal out of there.

Parvis took in the situation immediately. He went into my private powder room, pausing to smash the butt of his gun into the glass coffee pot that sat on the burner in the built-in credenza.

How light on his feet he is, I thought dreamily, just like a ballerina.

"Olivia!" Parvis shouted, as he came out of the bathroom, "snap out of it!"

He dropped a hand towel on the burner. It began to smolder just as security arrived. Parvis snatched it up, cursing in Persian for their benefit, threw it into the little sink in the credenza and explained that the pot had exploded. He quickly took some paper napkins and dropped them over the spots of Sal's blood on my rug, warning, "Careful, there's glass everywhere."

After I assured security and everyone else who came to investigate that I was fine, hoping the smoldering towel smell covered the cordite odor enough to dispel suspicion, Parvis closed the door and called Roger.

It was then I realized Parvis hadn't just been hanging around, using my office space: he was one of Roger's *guys* and was using the one-way mirror in there to keep track of things.

Roger must have told Parvis to put the phone on speaker, because his voice was suddenly jarring the room.

"You shot Sal Santini?" he sort of screamed.

"I didn't mean to…"

"You didn't mean to!"

"It just…happened."

"Nothin' around you *just happens*. What'd he say? How many did he have with him?"

"He said Sammy and Joey wanted to give me a lesson," I stammered.

"Yeah, in what?"

"Sportsmanship. He said I didn't know how to play the game," I finished lamely. "But I didn't mean to shoot him!"

"Like in, *you didn't know the gun was loaded* crap?"

"I didn't!"

"Mrs. Lammond," Debra my secretary came in breathlessly, "security desk says there are reporters in the lobby, wanting to know about gunshots heard from your office. What should I tell them?"

"Fuck!" shouted Roger over the speakerphone.

Debra dropped her notepad and her jaw. "I will not be talked to that way!"

"Sorry," said Roger. "Go back and tell them…what?"

Parvis told her. "A coffee pot exploded—end of story."

Debra left, her sensibilities still offended.

"A coffee pot exploded! I didn't know the gun was loaded! I thought it was a turtle! Where does this end?" Roger shouted. A pause—then—calmly, "Parvis, give her the keys to your car, put her in the back elevator."

To me he directed, "Livie, go to Sandy's."

Parvis gave me time to grab my purse, then put me into the back service elevator—car keys in hand—so fast that I only had time to get make, model, and instructions to "take the G. W. Bridge, then get on to Route 4, it's a right turn…" before the doors closed.

99

I got across the George Washington Bridge and, still in a dither, almost missed the exit for Route 4, but hung a screeching last-second right onto that road. I stayed in the right lane with no idea of where I was going.

Suddenly, some motorcycles whizzed up to me and began to pass. I saw a face peer into my window, then talked into a mouthpiece.

Oh my god, it's the police! But the one who came up next to me wore a matte-black bucket helmet that looked familiar.

When he pulled in front I recognized the long gray hair tied in three places with leather thongs that hung down over the worn leather jacket. I followed Zane, as Google followed me, to Sandy's house.

"Man, you sure do get into some heavy shit," said Chaz, as he popped a beer and wheeled it over to the table where I'd now slumped, repeating the homey vignette from not that long ago. This time in trouble for shooting, not for being shot.

Zane, being the strong and silent type, just shook his head either in disgust or wonder.

"Good thing we're back from that Western trip. Man, that was a haul," said Google. "I almost lost my damn bike at the craps table. If Zane hadn't—" Zane gave him a look. "Well, never mind."

Roger arrived. He looked like he wanted to grab me and hug me. He also looked like he wanted to grab me and choke me. He put his hand over the top of my head, squeezed and sighed: "Livie, you're killing me. Once you got let out of your cage…"

I probably should have taken umbrage at that, but having so recently taken on Big Sal and lived to tell the tale, I had nothing left.

Google was beside himself. "You shot Big Sal Santini? Wait till I tell the guys!"

"Google," said Zane quietly, "you like having your tongue attached?" Google nodded. "Your eyeballs in their sockets?" Google nodded again, terror growing in those eyes. "Then shut up. Now, tomorrow—forever."

When I finished my recital of events, a thought came to me, something that should have occurred much sooner.

"Did I kill him? Ohmigod—is someone else dead?"

"No," said Roger. "Doc says you just winged him." I assumed he meant the same *doc* who had attended to me when I was *winged* myself. "A few inches to the right, though…" He tilted his flat hand back and forth. "The problem now is, he's looking for you. So are the cops, a boatload of reporters, and just as bad, so is Mags."

"We know why Sal wants to see her," said Zane. "What do the cops have? A warrant?"

"Not yet. All those headlines brought up some questions that they would like answered. Plus, guess who owns the buildings they just raided?" Roger nodded toward me. "And if you think they haven't heard about Sal Santini—you can bet our little lady is a *person of interest.*"

100

Because of my somewhat questionable legal position, it was decided that I should stay out of New York. But John had information from his *weasel* lawyer friend, who had interviewed some of the ladies the night of the raid. Zane also had to report about their casino crawl. John, reluctantly, agreed to drive out to Sandy's during rush hour so it would be almost impossible to tail him.

The usual pizza was waiting when he arrived in an ordinary car driven by Otis—and also containing Mason as a surprise companion. If the threesome were startled by the grizzled bikers, they did not show it.

John started the discussion. Besson's, the Weasel's, ability to get information was aided by the fact that all the women had been caught in the raid, something that had never before happened, which both scared them and gave them a measure of anonymity in numbers.

No one could be sure who had said what.

One sentiment they all shared was their hatred of Sherry. A few said that, given a chance, they would have "popped" her themselves. They were also, to a woman, scared of her and did not entirely believe that she was really dead. They were also convinced that Sherry, along with picking up the receipts "and doing a few other jobs," had been an enforcer for her uncle Sal.

John looked hard at me. "You're a lucky lady," he said. "Why she put up with you, why you didn't step off a curb and get mowed over..." He left that thought dangling amid the aroma of pizza and beer while he helped himself to another slice.

"One gal in particular," John continued, "one who seemed to have some authority, according to Besson, flat out said that Sherry had been skimming the proceeds."

"If that were true," said Mason, "then there would be good reason for Sal to get rid of her." Mason, jacket off, sleeves rolled, drinking beer out of a can and eating pizza off the cardboard box seemed surprisingly normal. But then, the only things different between him and the regular denizens of the room were that he was gay and incredibly rich, both of which came to him at birth and without his personal invitation.

"Well," John continued, "everyone would like to know where that money went. It didn't just disappear."

Mason and I looked at each other, both wondering if it was sitting in a safe in a certain Fifth Avenue apartment.

Mason decided to steer the talk of money in a different direction. He turned to Zane. "Did some of it go out west, do you think?"

"Oh, I think so," said Zane, "and I'm sure that Jason was and still is the one who spreads it around. Some of my friends hit those casinos regularly—dumbasses still think they can beat the house—and they've seen Jason at all of them. He never gambles, just goes to the back office, talks to the managers, things like that. My friends know him 'cause he doesn't like bikers, looks at 'em like they're dirt."

"Then that could mean Jason works for Sal Santini..." put in Roger, not looking at me.

I finished it for him: "And so does Lauren."

John took charge. "We seem to have a possible reason for Sherry's death, but how do we account for Gil?"

Roger turned to me. "What did Gil say? You know, the night he died, when he was in your bed?"

The biker boys sat up and looked at me with new interest.

"It's not what you think," I protested.

Roger went on. "Didn't he say he had more copies of the pictures?"

I could still hear Gil saying as he grabbed my ass, *This belongs to me. I still have copies…*

"He said he did."

"What if the pictures weren't just of you bopping Sherry with the paddle?"

"Whooee!" shouted an excited Google, as Chaz slammed his hand on the table and laughed. "This girl's got history!"

Roger held up a hand for quiet. "What if he had pictures of who killed her before you did? I mean—"

"You mean, before I accidentally hit her with my paddle?" I finished vehemently.

"Exactly," he replied. "What if she was already dead when you hit her? What if someone had been in the water, maybe in a wet suit, waiting for her to take her nightly swim? What if Gil didn't just have pictures of you canoeing past?" He looked at John. "We need to find those photos, they're probably still in Gil's house."

"And Jason has the keys," I added.

There was a commotion outside, a small crashing sound, slamming doors, then Sandy came in, followed by Mags.

"I had a flat on 78," Sandy announced. "This nice lady offered to bring me home. I never rode in a Bentley before!"

Roger put his head down and groaned, while Mags surveyed the scene triumphantly.

101

"I won't even ask how you found us," said Mason. " I don't want to know."

"Oh, it was easy—" began Mags, eager to show off her detective skills, when Zane broke in.

"There are too many cars in front of the house. If you're trying to keep a low profile, you're not doing it."

"Zane's right," said Roger. "We need to move on and figure a way to find those photos." He turned to Sandy. "You didn't have a spare?"

"I do. It was flat too."

Roger looked questionably at Mags, who assumed a very questionable innocence. Roger and I exchanged looks.

"Do you have another spare in the garage?" Roger asked her.

She did.

"We'll put it in my car and I'll take you to yours and help you change it."

"I'll follow along and give a hand," said Zane. "There's a lot of traffic now."

Zane left, then immediately returned, ashen and almost speechless. Almost. "My bike," he gasped. "My bike!"

"Oh—I'm so sorry," squealed Mags, putting her hands to her face as though she had committed a naughty little girl sin instead of almost taking the fender off one of the most respected pieces of machinery from coast to coast. "I'll have it fixed right away. You'll never even see the difference."

Zane left like a zombie in response to honking from outside.

"If it's okay with you, John," said Mason, "I'll go back with you and leave Otis to drive the ladies."

John thought that was a good idea, as they had plenty to talk about.

102

Our departure was delayed while Mags used the facilities, then, much to Otis's agitation, delayed even more while she showed Sandy how to properly backcomb her flaming red hair.

The sound of motorcycles drew near, then stopped. The door was soon thrown open to reveal two women in motorcycle leathers. I remembered them from my last visit: Molly and Wildchild/Jane.

"Hey," said Molly, "guy down at the gas station heard Sal Santini's got cars cruising around here, looking for someone."

"There's a Bentley out front!" said Jane. "I never touched one before. Bet they're looking for whoever came in that."

Chaz was glad to inform them that we had come *in that*.

But their attention had landed on Otis.

"Uh, ladies," Chaz said. "This isn't good, you need to get out of here."

"But if they see me in the car..."

"Ohmigod," Mags said, "they'll shoot us! We can't drive around in that thing!"

"I'll drive around in that thing," laughed Jane.

"Yeah, me too," seconded Molly. "Can you ride a bike?"

"Yes, I can," said Mags firmly—as I was saying, "No, we can't."

"Mine's a Harley low-rider," said Molly, "rides two easy. You ever ride a Harley?"

Mags went on to recite a surprising amount of credentials and exchanged information about equipment and specs and things like that, providing me with a clue to still more of her history. Mason had said that she "biked across the country." At the time, I had envisioned two wheels and pedals, now I realized what he had really meant.

"Mine leans a little heavy right when you stop. Kick the stand or put your foot down quick."

"I got it," said Mags. "Uh, we can't ride like this," indicating our clothes.

"Oh, I'll trade ya," Molly said. Then surprisingly added, "Looks like Prada to me."

Jane nodded toward Otis. "Is he part of the deal?"

"Otis—and only Otis—drives the car," said Mags firmly.

"Good," said Wildchild/Jane, happy at that. "That means he's with us at all times."

"Can you ride the bitch seat?" Molly asked me. Before I could answer, Mags piped in, "Oh, you bet she can," in a tone I didn't particularly like.

"We better get started," Jane said, whipping off her red leather jacket. "Those guys must be getting closer. We need to get a move on," which was easy to interpret: "Hot damn, let's hit the road with the hunk and the Bentley."

Molly followed suit by taking off hers—Chaz and Google, as well as Otis, were sitting at the table watching— moaning and shouting when the girls dropped their pants: there was no backup.

Mags and I looked at each other, telegraphing visions of what was swarming around in those leather pants. I tried to think of a subtle way to swab them down with a bucket of bleach, but the truth is, you can be choosy and condescending when you have the goods. When someone else has them—and you need them—those are luxuries you can't afford.

We stripped and pulled on their pants, Mags with her *La Perlas* and me with my more ordinary *Barely Theres* firmly in place.

"Won't be as comfortable," said Jane, "they'll ride up your crotch."

We got their tight T-shirts over our bras—Molly and Jane were also not encumbered with those apparatuses—and zipped into the jackets. The outfit was not as uncomfortable as I had expected, probably from being so well oiled from the inside out. We had a snag with the fit of the boots but settled on Mags wearing Jane's, which were slightly too big, and me in Molly's, which were way too small.

"I need the comfort," Mags said, "I'm driving." A thought that didn't really penetrate until we were all in the driveway where Molly and Jane, prancing around in Prada and St. John's, were giving last minute instructions. Otis, dismayed at the dent in the Bentley's fender and very unhappy about letting us out of his sight, made Mags promise to "just circle the block a few times."

Chaz's phone rang. He listened, then directed Otis to roll Jane's bike into the garage. Then Google took us out to a back path that led through a neighbor's yard onto a different street. He attached an EZ pass to the windshield, then handed me my phone and wallet. "Took these from your purse." He stuffed something heavy and metal into the back of my waistband and pulled my jacket firmly over it. I thought he did the same to Mags before he showed us how to use the intercoms in our helmets.

"Now, you girls just ride around while Otis takes Molly and Jane for a tour of the neighborhood. You can bet they'll make sure everybody sees them, and we hope Sal sees them too. He won't mistake them two for you. Keep in touch, we'll tell you when to come back."

He waved to some friends sitting on their bikes in the yard, who all revved their engines in reply.

Mags revved hers in turn. We dropped our visors and she took us out into the street, turning so wide that my boot rapped against a parked car. If they hadn't been so small I might have lost a toe.

Mags breezed through two stop signs, me shouting into my microphone, "Stop! Stop!" and her shouting back the discouraging words, "I can't, I can't."

From my estimation Mags's motorcycle career must have peaked at least twenty years before, so all I could do was pray that she was just getting her bearings, remembering *the feel* of the thing.

She kept taking her hand off the handlebar to push her helmet back—the fear that she couldn't see now added to my growing list of worries. Finally, she slowed for an approaching red light and came to a stop, shouting, "Right foot down!" as she stalled the engine. We endured the hoots and hollers from the Jersey boys in a car next to us and the toots from the one behind us as Mags, very deliberately, started the engine and got herself together.

She executed a few more stops with growing expertise, then pulled into a gas station. We came to a full stop by a pump and put our right feet down as she kicked the stand. Mags took her helmet off. "We have to switch helmets," she said. "This thing is too big for me. And I don't know what the hell Molly was doing at the gas station 'cause we're almost on empty. You have any money?"

103

Thanks to Google's foresight I had my wallet. I got off the bike—even after that short time aboard I felt like a sailor disembarking after a long voyage—and handed her my helmet. A young Pakistani came out to pump the gas. I was grateful that New Jersey was one of the few states that required an attendant to man the pumps as I had no idea where you poured it into something as small as a motorcycle and didn't really want to know if it was the fat round part below my seat. I had just finished paying him when a black TransAm cruised by.

There was a screech of tires as it braked halfway down the block. It began a U-turn, backing into a parked car and shattering glass.

"It's Sal!" I shouted, pulling the helmet on that should have been masking me in the first place. I leapt onto my seat as Mags gunned the engine and we tore out of there.

Mags was loving it. It seemed not to have flitted through, past the drama of the outfits and the roar of the big engine, that there were people speeding along behind us with the intent to kill.

But I had to admit that Mags, after a few almost fatal tilts, could handle the bike. She squeezed us through lanes of cars and then, at the toll booths, through the lines using the possibly—make that probably—hot EZ Pass that Google had provided.

104

For what seemed like a trip halfway around the world, Mags kept up our thrilling pace, until she shouted into the speaker, "I'm pooped and I gotta pee," to which I rapidly agreed.

We coasted into a Burger King compound. "The bathrooms are always clean," said Mags, who had been riding deep inside Molly's very personalized leather pants. We parked in a shadowed spot, then went into the bathroom and helped each other peel off the, by now, second skin pants.

"Talcum powder," I remembered a rock star saying about his own tight leather pants. "We need talcum powder."

"Just pull!" demanded Mags. "We need to get out of here."

We bought a couple of Whoppers and drinks and gulped them down while we stood beside the Harley and thought about our next move.

Once again, we were headed in the direction of the lake. I was beginning to think all roads led either to there or to Rome.

"Your cottage, in case you forgot, is burned to the ground. And I'm not going to Gil's," said Mags.

"There's Larry's house," I reminded her as I reminded myself. I now possessed it and had done nothing about relieving myself of that burden, so there it sat. I had every right to go there and besides, as I pointed out to Mags, it was on this side of the lake, meaning the nearer side, so we could get there faster.

That appealed to both of us, so we were soon carefully cruising the winding road that took us there. The winding road, though a little scary at night, also gave us chances to pause to see if we were being followed.

We found the house and parked in the back.

"Do you know the security code?" asked Mags.

Unfortunately I did: Sherry's birthday.

"Okay, I'll open it, you run in and punch in the code." Mags picked up a good sized rock, smashed a glass panel in the back door, undid the lock, then threw the door open and stepped aside to let me dash in to the security pad.

Nothing. No one had set the alarm. No one had cleaned out the refrigerator or put out the garbage either, and as we dumped everything into big black trash bags, I realized that *no one* was me.

Since I hadn't cleaned out the closets either, we were soon showered and dressed in Sherry's lounge wear, of which there was plenty—all of it interesting.

Since the only things worthwhile in the fridge were champagne and some unopened, mostly un-moldy cheese, which we supplemented with a tin of crackers from the cupboard, we were soon relaxed enough to get past the creepy feeling of the clothes and started snooping around.

I told Mags about the possible extra set of photos. Why not? We might die together soon—this was no time for secrets.

She threw out the thought, "What if they're here?"

As far-fetched as it seemed we started a casual search— more from plain old nosiness than from any real thought of finding anything.

Well, we did find things, some of them really, really interesting. Sherry, it would appear, experimented with any and everything and had introduced Larry to a whole catalogue and several Internet sites of new experiences that relied heavily on little whips and clips. The thought alone sent Mags into laughing hysterics.

At some point—just because Larry was Larry and didn't have that much imagination—I looked in his closet and pulled out what appeared to be a recently installed shoe rack. And behind it, was a safe.

I called Mags in, bemoaning the fact that it was a combination lock.

"We can handle that," Mgs said and headed for the kitchen with me trailing behind. "Why don't you freshen our drinks," she said, "while I have a look around."

She started going through all the drawers, throwing things on the counter, including an ice pick, hammer and screwdriver. "These are if we have to do it the hard way. You go see if Sherry had any hairpins or clips—" The word sending her into a spasm of mirth. "We know she had those, for sure! Look for tweezers too."

I went toward the master bathroom, then on impulse stopped in Larry's closet and tried Sherry's birthday on the combination lock. Nothing. Then, while I was squatting there, trying to figure out their wedding day, I twirled my birthday numbers in and the door clicked open.

105

"Mags!" I screamed.

She came running. "If it's a mouse or a spider, you're on your own!"

We stood looking at the safe. I gingerly opened the door. There were packages inside. I started handing them to Mags, who dumped them in the middle of the king-sized bed and came back for more.

"I'll get the rest of the champagne," said Mags, heading for the kitchen.

"Wait! Make sure the door is locked and set the security while you're there." I gave her the code. "And turn off the lights."

I quickly closed the blinds and the heavy curtains in the bedroom, having realized—hopefully not too late—that lights in this particular house would be of great interest to particular people.

Mags came with the half bottle, a cold new one and a bag of pretzels.

"I told you I'd find out," she said smugly. "This is more of the stuff that's in Mason's safe, right?"

I hesitated, mainly because her tone of voice and the fact that she had found out were just downright annoying. But we were going through this stuff together—unless Mags lured me out of the room and slammed the door shut, which I should have thought of sooner.

We slit some packs open, using Sherry's nail files.

"This is money," said Mags quietly. "This is big money. People kill for this, you know."

"People have killed for this, and we need to find out who did it."

"You don't think it was Sal?"

"I don't think it was Sal. I have this kind of thrumming…"

Thrumming! Roger! Phone!

"Oh hell! We haven't called anyone. No one knows where we are! I have to get my phone."

"Use the one in here," said Mags, lifting the receiver. "Speaking of dead—" she dropped the phone back into its cradle—"somebody didn't pay the bill."

My leathers were still spread around the master bathroom. I went in and unzipped every zipper, and there were more than seemed decently necessary. No phone.

We turned out the bedroom lights so they wouldn't radiate outside the room. Mags crawled into the guest bathroom and, using a flashlight from the night table, amid grunts, yowls and curses, searched through hers.

"Nada," she announced on her return. "Maybe you dropped it when we got off the bike here." But I had a sudden visual flash of something popping out of a pocket amid the trauma of us getting back into our uncooperative sticky leather pants.

"It's behind the toilet at Burger King," I said with great certainty.

"Oh, well," said Mags, "at least Roger won't be bothering us all night long. What is it with you two? Why don't you just get it on and get it over with?"

I didn't have time to sit there and think about what she said, because Mags was going at the packages like a sugar-high kid at a birthday party. At one point, she actually threw an opened bundle into the air and let large bills rain down around her.

One package I opened was different from the others, and it was a good thing that I opened it, as Mags was not careful with her nail file. This one contained not only photographs, but a CD. I stared at the series of pictures. I brushed money aside and laid them out. Mags had gotten quiet at my quietness.

"What?"

"We are in worse trouble than I thought."

The pictures showed a black zodiac boat drifting near the dock right in front of this house. Two men were in the boat, both in black wet suits and caps. All that showed in the pictures were their black-smudged faces. Something was familiar, but it took me a minute of staring to recognize Nolan and Weiss, the *detectives* who had come to visit me that sunny morning on Park Avenue.

"Tell me! Tell me!" Mags demanded.

I showed her the pictures. "These are the men who killed Sherry." Then I told her the rest.

"How dare you! How could you think of going through all those things without my help!"

Of course, it was Mags here—the *me* girl. But then, Mags had gotten us here, on a big red Harley with a carload of stone-cold killers in hot pursuit.

106

We argued over the guns.

We had decided to share the big bed, feeling safer together in one room, but I did not feel safe sleeping with the guns under our pillows, which was what Mags proposed we do.

"They always do it in the movies," she declared, which did not make me feel one iota more comfortable with the notion. We agreed to put them in the nightstand drawers, safety locks on, and I checked hers to make sure.

I awoke to movement, a rustling in the room, then a blast from a gun. Was this *déjà-vu?*

The light went on. Mags sat there, the proverbial smoking gun in her hand.

"Hot damn!" she said proudly. "Even in the dark, the girl's still got it!"

I didn't bother my head thinking about where she had *got it* from. I just looked around the massive bedroom in which at least one of us had so recently been asleep.

The room contained a large fireplace, which apparently, in the absence of any other use, had become home to a family of raccoons. The family was now smaller by one member, who lay splattered against a wall.

Unfortunately, that family member was the mother and there was a litter cowering in the shards of a nest in the fireplace. I jumped out of bed and stretched the screen across the front to keep them there and stepped in something gooey. No good ever came from using a gun, I thought as I hopped to the bathroom to get towels and clean a piece of Mother Raccoon from my foot.

I returned to find Mags in tears in front of the fireplace.

"Murderer! I'm a mother killer! I didn't know there were babies." She started to remove the screen.

"Leave it!" I shouted.

"You don't have to be so pissy," she pouted. "They're just babies."

I handed her the towels and pointed to the recently deceased mother. "You killed it, you clean it." Then I made sure the screen was firmly in place and all possible exit points were blocked.

"We should call the Animal Rescue Squad," suggested Mags. "I saw them on TV—real nice people—they'll take the babies to a shelter."

"And while you're calling—if you could call, that is, seeing as how we have no phone—why don't you notify the police? So they can come out here and ask a few questions about the gun you used and where it came from and what we are doing here? Why don't you just do that!"

I was steamed at the mess of things, the haphazard piles of money and papers and the untidy bits and guts of raccoon on the wall and carpet.

"It could have been an intruder," said Mags. "I could have just saved our lives, you know."

She was right. It could have been one of the guys in those pictures splattered all over the wall.

The baby raccoons were making "I want momma" noises. Mags went to them, cooing, "There, there," and started to remove the screen.

"Mags," I warned her, "unless you intend to breast feed them, don't move that screen. We'll deal with them later." I went to a window and cautiously pushed the curtain aside. Thankfully, dawn was upon us. "You prepare the mother for burial while I check out the house. I'll see if there's any food we can give them. And we've got to put that money back in the safe."

I unlocked the bedroom door and, gun in hand, safety on, quietly scanned the rooms. It was actually a really nice house with beautiful lake views. There was one glassed-in half-round room, where I noticed a telescope bolted to the floor in the middle.

In the pantry, I found cans of tuna, sardines, anchovies, things I felt young raccoons would like since they seemed to be born knowing how to open every garbage can invented to keep them from getting to those empty containers. I opened a can of each, put them on a tray and carried it into the bedroom.

"That looks good," Mags said. "I'm starving."

After feeding our new family, we went back to the kitchen and fed ourselves.

It was fully light, so we were free to explore the whole house. I went back to the telescope room.

"Mags!" I called. "Come in here!"

She came in behind me. "What!" And I had the sure feeling she was armed.

"Look at this." I got out from behind the telescope. Mags put her gun on a small table, slid into the seat, and put her eye to the scope.

"It's your house. There's a small tractor or bulldozer in front." She moved the instrument slightly. "And there's Gil's house. Someone's there." A pause. "Jason's there, and so is Lauren."

"So while Gil was watching here," I pondered out loud, "someone here was watching Gil."

"There's stuff all over the place, looks like they're moving, or something."

"Let me look." Mags gave up the seat reluctantly. "It's the *or something* I'm worried about." I peered into the powerful scope. I could see boxes and papers scattered around the house. I could almost read the print. I could see the mole on Jason's left cheek. Lauren came into view, I could see...

"That son of a bitch!"

"What?"

"Look at Lauren's face."

Mags pressed over my shoulder and looked. "She's bruised! She's crying!"

"He beat her!" I said in disbelief. "She's pregnant and he's been hitting her!" As I looked again, I could see tears rolling down her cheeks, the desperation in her eyes.

"Get dressed," commanded Mags. "We're going over there."

There was no question about how we were going, as there was no question about what getting dressed involved. We found talcum powder in the bathroom, which really did speed the process of getting into the pants.

Mags was already on the Harley when I went out, after cracking open a window and pulling away the fire screen and hoping the little guys would find their way out.

She had turned the bike around and there on the ground behind it was my phone.

107

With an angry Mags driving, we swung around the lake like something loaded.

On the way, I called Roger. I told him where we were and where we were going. I also told him about finding the pictures of Nolan and Weiss. He was less than an hour out, having finally decided that we must have gone in that direction. All the other words he used are not necessary to recount. I dialed Mason and held the phone to my interior microphone while Mags shouted the same message to him and told him to send Otis, which he might not have completely heard, as the battery on my phone went dead.

A car was parked at the place where my house had once stood. Jason was on a small bulldozer, working at moving the Philco refrigerator. He seemed not to notice us ease past him, probably from a combination of the sound-deafening earmuffs and the goggles he wore, along with the noise of the machine. We pulled by the side of Gil's house and went in.

The place was a shambles. Whatever could have been pulled out was. Every book, dish, paper, piece of linen, was piled in the middle of the rooms. Lauren sat amidst this wreckage, looking defeated and scared.

She looked up listlessly. As two visor-helmeted visitors in red, we must have looked like creatures from another planet, but she didn't seem to care. I slid my visor up and, for the first time in years, my child was glad to see me.

"Mommy!" she wailed, and started sobbing. "He's a monster! He's crazy," she sputtered out the words.

Mags and I both rocked her and said our many *there, there* and *we're here* and *everything will be all right.*

But everything wasn't all right.

"I'm bleeding," Lauren said. "The baby—"

"We have to get you to the hospital, I'll call an ambulance."

"Do you have a phone?" she asked hopefully. "He took mine and—"

Mags held up the phone base with its cord ripped from the wall.

"I'll go get the car," I said.

"No!" Lauren was alarmed at the suggestion. "He has a gun. He'll shoot you! I know he will."

"Not if I shoot him first," said Mags, brandishing her favorite new accessory.

"You're not doing any more shooting. Maybe we—"

"Shhh!" Lauren held up her hand. It was quiet outside; Jason was no longer using the bulldozer.

I crept cautiously out to the screened-in porch. Our houses were not that close together, but with most of the leaves gone and all of my house gone, I had a clear view.

Jason was not alone. Nolan and Weiss, the two pseudo-detectives, were talking to him. They all seemed angry.

Jason reached for something, but he never got to it, because the man who had called himself Nolan shot him. When Jason's forehead exploded, I screamed. They looked in my direction, then ran to their car.

From behind me, Mags said, "I'll lead them away. You get Lauren to the hospital."

108

The motorcycle revved up and roared out of the driveway, then Mags streaked down the road. The men were in their car, heading towards us, when she sped around them. They did a U-turn and went after her.

I ran up the road as fast as my too-tight boots and sticking-together pants would take me. The keys were not in the car. Then I saw Jason's jacket hanging on a post and went through those pockets. By the time I found the keys, I knew too much time had been wasted.

When I got back to the house Lauren was sitting, holding her stomach, rocking and whimpering. I made her stand and helped her to the car. I couldn't carry her, but I draped her arm across my shoulders and propelled her as best I could to the back seat where she lay down. I went back into the house and grabbed some pillows and blankets to put under her head and knees and to cover her.

That motherly act was a time-consuming mistake. I had just closed the back seat door when I heard a car coming down the road—fast.

I went back into the house and found my gun on a table. Running out, I positioned myself behind a rock wall, away from Lauren. The car slowed, less than thirty feet away.

Despite what might be said to the contrary, the crime and adventure series on TV are not a total waste of time.

There are things to be learned—one of them being to steady your weapon and hand on something.

I crouched there with my arms firmly planted on the wall, my visor pulled down for protection, the gun steady in my hands. I fired off two shots. One went somewhere, but the other went through the windshield. The car swerved and the passenger side came to rest against a tree.

I shook so hard I could barely hold the gun. I thought about my helpless child lying not far from me, possibly bleeding to death and, in every sense, got a grip. The driver's side door opened and I was ready. The man edging towards the back of the car might have had a machine gun or a flamethrower, but I had a mother's anger and need to protect, so we were even.

Something showed over the trunk and I let off some rounds.

The man stood to shoot at the position I had just given away with my wild shots.

"Mom! Duck!" shouted Lauren.

Now he turned in the direction of Lauren. I stood and shot him.

109

"Shit!" he yelled and disappeared behind the car.
I was stunned.

I inched around to the edge of the stone wall. The passenger door was opening, the other man's foot searched for the ground.

How many bullets do I have left? I had used two on the car, at least two on the man and—Is this my gun or Mags's? I pictured the raccoon on the wall and tried to remember how many shots she had taken.

The wounded man, Nolan, got back into the car and turned on the engine. I was sure he was going to come at me. He never got the chance. Jason's car started up and drove straight into its side, inflating the air bags.

Lauren was slumped over the wheel when I got to her. Fortunately, the impact had not inflated her air bag, so I pushed her over until she was half straddling the center console, and I drove us out of there.

We didn't get far before motorcycles surrounded us. I pulled over when I saw Mags.

Two big bikes came behind her and the riders dismounted. One walked toward the car with a slight limp. Roger took off his helmet, yanked the door open and pulled me out. He held me tightly. I could feel him trembling.

"Livie, you're killing me…"

110

I so liked fairy tales as a child, but was always a little skeptical about the endings. I always had questions. Wouldn't Cinderella's stepmother and stepsisters go to live with them in the castle? What about Prince Charming's parents? If he was just a Prince, didn't that mean there was a King? And a Queen? What if they didn't like Cinderella?

A real spoilsport and worrywart kid I was.

It would have been so nice to dissolve into Roger's trembling arms and have everything taken care of by writing *The End* or *And They Lived Happily Ever After*, but real life is messier than that.

After a quick check on Lauren and an overall assessment of the situation, Roger told Google to park his bike down the road behind a closed-up house, drive Lauren and me to the hospital emergency entrance, then *ditch the car*. He and Zane took off down the road, soon returning with Google riding behind Zane.

Roger, in the meantime, handed Mags his "scramble" phone with instructions for her to call for an ambulance and tell them there had been a shooting on my road. I watched Roger, helmet on, visor down, ride his bike back to Nolan and Weiss's car.

He looked inside, said something to the still dazed and now trapped occupants, the airbags not having fully deflated, then ran into the house and came back with the cord of the useless telephone. He tied one end of the cord around something in Nolan's side of the car, which I later learned was his hand to the steering wheel, then stretched the line across the top of the car and tied Weiss's hand to something in the other side. He talked to them both again, then slapped things on either side of the car, things that looked very much like Viv's old kitten magnets from the refrigerator door. Later, Roger confirmed that was exactly what they were, but Nolan and Weiss thought they were *wired plastique packs,* and unless they wanted to become *one with the tree* the car was resting against, they had better not move.

111

Mags and Roger sat with me in the emergency waiting room, all of us looking like the bikers we currently were. The other people in the room crowded to the opposite side, especially after Zane and Google joined us.

I expected a much longer wait, but fairly soon a young doctor came into the room and asked, "Lauren's mother?" I detached myself from the group and followed him into a hall, aware of Mags velcroed to my back.

He introduced himself as Dr. Crowley, but he could just as well have said Dr. Doogie Howser because he looked like the sixteen-year-old doctor from the TV show. But he was serious and to the point.

"Your daughter was beaten up by someone. Is that the only trauma she's suffering from?"

"No, her boyfriend was murdered."

I realized, as I said it, that this good young doctor probably thought he was in the middle of some biker gang war.

"But her mother here," Mags indicated me proudly, "shot one of them and Lauren took care of the other guy. They're probably in an ambulance now."

I knew she was trying to be helpful—either that, or she was trying to get the good-looking young doctor to focus his attention on her—but the poor man paled at the thought of what might be in store for him if Lauren and child didn't suddenly become healthy.

He pulled himself together to tell me that, while he didn't like to give drugs (he stumbled over that word, no doubt convinced that Mags and I were walking repositories of every controlled substance known to woman) to pregnant women, Lauren was so traumatized that he had put her into a "twilight sleep" to calm her and bring her blood pressure down. She would need quiet and complete bed rest for at least two weeks.

"She's resting in the ward now."

"She's in the ward!" shrieked Mags, in a voice that raised the blood pressure of everyone within hearing distance.

Mags still had Roger's phone, which she used—in spite of all the prominently displayed signs forbidding such activity—to call Mason, apprising him of the situation. Within the hour, Lauren, whether she was aware of it or not, was wheeled out to the hospital helipad for transport to what I assumed would be a New York City hospital.

Within that same hour, and before the helicopter arrived, Molly and Jane sashayed into the waiting room in our much worse-for-wear clothes, followed by a very exhausted and guilty-looking Otis. We four ladies took over the restroom for quick changes, so I was reasonably attired to accompany my daughter on the flight.

Mags took Otis back under her command and the whole group scooted out just as ambulances brought in Nolan and Weiss, whose wounds and claims of *terrorists and aliens* were not as interesting to the police as the guns they found in the car. Forensics would later prove that one of them had been used to kill Jason.

112

We did not fly into the heliport in New York City as I had expected.

Mason, with reasoning I had not yet figured out, sent us to land at a hospital compound in Delaware, where an ambulance then transported Lauren a short distance to a state-of-the-art Obstetrics Center. There she was folded into the arms of top-notch medical care.

"Mason," I said into my phone from the waiting room, "why here?"

"I didn't want to bring her into the packs of news hounds that will be circling. By the time they find Delaware on the map, she'll be out of there."

And I thought Mags was devious. He could have sent us to Philadelphia—there were excellent medical facilities in that city—but when Alice and Charles joined me in the waiting room, I figured out some of his plan.

"We're taking her home with us as soon as she can be moved," said the overly eager Alice. "We'll make sure she gets the quiet she needs."

This was exactly what Mason had in mind. They lived on an unmarked country road; you had to know where you were going to get there. The few other residents on that private road would notice anything unusual and the Jack Russells would not quietly let strangers approach.

Mags called. "I was coming with Otis to help, but Mason grounded me! He said I can't use the Bentley this week, it's in the shop. Bullshit! *I'm grounded!*"

I silently thanked Mason and kept just as quiet about suggesting there were other modes of transportation than the Bentley, praying she would not reprise her motorcycle career.

Mason did provide me with wheels however—a nondescript dark sedan with a burly driver, whom I was instructed to sit next to. We were to drive into New York City, looking like your ordinary non-communicating couple. Mason informed me that Jerome, my driver, was to take me everywhere I went and that I was paying the tab from my *stash*.

Before we left, I went to see Lauren, where I discovered another cause for depleting my so-called stash. The door to Lauren's private room was closed and a nurse informed me that I could not go in as Dr. Hadley was in consultation with Lauren, and they could not be disturbed.

Janine, I thought. Janine is here?

I sat in the nearby waiting area, keeping an eye on the door and wondering why she hadn't called to tell me she was coming here—and who had called her in the first place.

Finally, the door opened.

"David!"

Dr. David Hadley motioned me to follow him into a small empty consulting room.

"Olivia," he said, "I'm glad you're here." He could have fooled me, judging from the look on his face. "Mason called us. Janine and I agreed that Lauren might view her as being too close to you, that her input would be diluted."

"Why are you here, David?"

He looked at me quizzically. "Your daughter has been through enormous trauma, physically and emotionally—"

"I know—I was there."

"And she wants to terminate the pregnancy."

This I did not know. I thought about the circumstances of the child's conception—bred in spite—and Lauren's bruised, teary and terrified face saying, "He's a monster." I thought about a tiny baby staring at me with those falcon eyes.

"She has her reasons."

"Livie, as a psychiatrist I am required to put aside my own religious views when treating a patient, so they do not figure in what I hope to help Lauren understand. Aside from it being late in the pregnancy for a safe termination, I hope to help her see that erasing the child is not going to leave her with a clean slate. In fact, in this case, I believe it would leave her more permanently damaged then anything else that has happened to her."

"But, if she hates the child?"

"She doesn't have to keep the child herself if her feelings are so negative that the child's well-being would be at risk."

"You mean, give it up for adoption?"

That was when my grandma button got pushed for the second time.

"In this case, giving the child to strangers wouldn't be the best path to follow for all those involved."

"All those?" I looked around, expecting a small army to materialize. Then the pieces fell neatly into place.

"Oh! No! You can't be serious! Mags as a mother!"

"Offset by Mason as a father. The whole family would have free access to the child and if Lauren were to succumb to the motherly instinct—which, between us, does not seem to be very strong in her—then Mason would be agreeable to shared custody."

113

On the trip back to New York, I shook so hard that the stoic Jerome asked if he should pull over. After that, I tried to control myself, as the shaking was suppressed laughter as I conjured up images of Mags with a real live baby. I saw her, along with two nannies, pushing the Rolls Royce of baby carriages in Central Park. I saw her emptying out the Madison Avenue children's boutiques after she had decimated Saks. I saw the baby girl—it had to be a girl for its own sake—in a little fur coat…

What I didn't see was me. What about me? I was the grandmother. Why shouldn't I have the child? I sighed, then shook softly, but no longer from laughter, as I dabbed at my eyes. There were several reasons:

1. Lauren hated me.
2. Lauren hated me.

3.   Lauren hated me.

I called Janine as soon as I got into the apartment. She answered on the first ring.

"I thought you would call from the car. Are you home?"

"Yes," I sobbed.

Janine might have been waiting in the lobby, she was there so quickly. Either that, or I was in too much of a daze to keep track of anything as trivial as time.

In the end her advice to me—and because we were talking as friends she could give direct advice and not wait for me to discover it somewhere in the depths of my mind—was to get back to work, to save what I could of the business and, most importantly, not to let down my guard. I needed to remember that there was still a missing link in all the mess of the past months. Whether it was Sal Santini or somebody else, that person was very likely still interested in buried treasure and, possibly, in burying me.

With that sobering thought, we opened a bottle of champagne and called Mags.

114

The first glass had prepared us for her arrival—or so we thought. She tried her damnedest to keep the secret that Mason had likely sworn her to. But when she came through the door, Janine and I just looked at each other and choked on our laughter.

Where she got her hands on a Peter Pan collar, who could say, but there she was with a scalloped collar fitted into the neck of an all-around pleated tent dress. The loose-flowing charcoal silk dress just grazed her knees, in direct conflict with her two-and-a-half inches above rule. Her dark hair hung girlishly loose, pulled back with a black velvet band, her makeup confined to an apple-cheeked blush. She had on semi-sheer stockings and, for her, sensible shoes. True, while they were Mary Janes, they were Christian Louboutin's version with four-inch wedgy heels. She even wore a circle pin—diamond encrusted, but a circle pin.

"Expecting, are we?" Janine said archly.

"Whatever do you mean?" Mags replied, sitting demurely on the chair meant for her and pointedly ignoring the glass of champagne on the table beside her.

"You're not grabbing my grandchild," I said flatly.

"Why, whatever do you mean?" she repeated, putting her hand to her chest in a Miss Piggie Mo*i?* pose. Then I realized just how far Mags was prepared to go: she wasn't wearing nail polish.

"I mean, you are not taking Lauren's baby."

"How could you be so ungrateful! Why, here we are, your best friend and her upstanding husband, prepared to give shelter to a child in harm's way—"

"Is that another form of protective custody, dear," said Janine, just so pleased with her front row seat.

"I suppose one could phrase it that way," replied the newly sainted Mags, eyeing her glass with laic longing.

"And from whom would you be protecting her?" I demanded, pouring more champagne into Janine's glass, replenishing mine, and pointedly ignoring hers.

"The family history is a little troubling," Mags replied, examining her bare nails as if she didn't quite understand what they were doing there on the ends of her fingers. "The authorities—looking at a list of recent activities—would certainly choose to whisk the child into safer hands."

"Safer hands!"

"Yes," she said demurely, no longer able to keep one of those safer hands off the glass of booze. "Hands that, for instance, have not stolen large sums of money, not to mention having shot two people—so far—" sip, sip—"as far as we know—" sip, sip—"that is."

I was speechless.

Mags sniffed, inhaled deep breaths, then took a lace-edged hanky from her sleeve to dab at her dry eyes. She pulled herself together, sitting taller and straighter in her chair, sighing deeply. "This is very difficult," she whispered, deep sigh, deep sigh, sip, sip. "But I am prepared to make sacrifices too."

"Too! As in also? As in—what?"

"I don't want you to be alone now, and even more—" sip, sip—"I need to know that you're protected, so...I'm going to give you Princess."

Blank. Several seconds of complete blank.

"Princess?" I finally gasped. "Princess? You want to give me a two hundred-pound dog? In exchange for my tiny, yet-to-be-born grandchild?"

"Princess is not just any *dog!*" she huffed. "She's a Great Dane!"

Janine jumped up and grabbed my arm, removing the empty bottle from my hand, a bottle held as high as my arm would reach and one whose trajectory would have had a linear conclusion with Mags's head.

"Oh good," said Janine, "I'll put this in the recycle bin and get a fresh one."

I momentarily wondered if Janine was able to spend all those hours in the crazy world she was professionally subjected to—quietly, without emotion—because we gave her so many opportunities to interact in an even crazier one.

115

The next weeks were a whirl of trips to the farm where Lauren was recuperating. She did not want to discuss her plans for this child with me, and I couldn't push her to confirm what David had told me because, technically, he shouldn't have told me. But I also couldn't forget his words that "the motherly instinct does not seem to be very strong in her." Whatever her ultimate plans were for this baby, I was sure they would be most beneficial to the mother.

On one occasion Roger went with me to check things out, and we were invited to stay for dinner. Travis joined us that evening, which could have been uncomfortable, but he made sure it wasn't. He and Roger got on very well, and even told some funny, non-violent Nam stories. Travis caught me in the hall behind the kitchen when I came out of the powder room and took me in his arms. "Relax, kid," he whispered. I did. He kissed me softly, then said into my ear, "Thank you for a night of love." He turned me back toward the dining room, giving me a pat on the behind to send me on my way.

116

I had been following Janine's advice about throwing myself into work and generally getting in everyone's way, but at least I was starting to learn what the business was all about.

One afternoon I was sitting in my office, trying to feel like the head of a company and wishing I had something to do. There was very little for me to do, however, even if I knew how to do it, as Gino and his newest hire, Muriel, had everything in hand and ticking along smoothly. Muriel, under the protective wing of Gino's adoring eyes and his realtor's credentials, had rented out just about every square inch of commercial space we had available. I had learned from our committee meetings not to ask Muriel how she accomplished what she did, afraid she would describe every questionable sales pitch she had made.

Gino had also sicced her onto some laggard rental payments with immediate, amazing—bordering on frightening—results. He told me privately and proudly that we should be paying her commissions, but if we did, she would be pulling in more than anyone else in the company.

So when Debra, my secretary, buzzed me to announce that a *Mrs. Betty Reynolds* would like to see me, though the name rang no bells, I was happy for the company. "Show her in."

Mrs. Reynolds—"Call me Betty"—and I shook hands across the desk, just like men. As she walked into the room, however, I noticed those long, tan legs below the discreetly short skirt of a well-tailored navy suit. The jacket and silk blouse encased a waist that was a little too small and a bosom way too large for the ordinary mortal. Betty's luxurious upswept hair was a little too blonde, her lashes too long and lips too pouty in her evenly tanned face.

Showgirl, I thought. Then, with alarm: Vegas!

"Olivia," she said in her low, velvet voice, "I'm going to put my cards on the table." She opened her Hermès bag—and from where I sat, it looked like the real hundred-thousand dollar croc Birkin deal—extracted a deck of cards, which she slapped down on my desk. Then reached in again and, next to the cards, gently placed the prettiest little engraved mother-of-pearl handled pistol.

She broke the seal on the box, took out the deck and shuffled it. Casually, with one hand, she fanned the cards.

"Your call—aces high or low?"

"Low," sort of dribbled out of my mouth.

"Draw."

My shaky hand extracted a card.

Betty did likewise. "Well, aren't you the lucky one?" she said, slapping down the ace of spades.

I turned over the queen of clubs.

"Now, instead of just shooting you, you get to answer some questions."

I nodded in agreement, although I had no idea why.

"What all did you take from Larry?" she asked matter-of-factly.

"Do you mean from the apartment?"

Betty laughed as she rolled the cards, with one quick flick of her hand, back into a neat deck. "Yes, the apartment. I've already seen the mess at his lake house. What the hell were you doing there? Those raccoons were crapping out hundred-dollar bills," she laughed. Then seriously, spine-chilling seriously, "Now back to you. Describe exactly what you took."

I did the best I could. When she didn't seem satisfied, I blubbered on about the lake house safe and the photographs.

"You mean of Nolan and Weiss?"

I nodded yes.

"You did some people a favor—those two seemed to think there were three sides to every deal."

I noted she hadn't said *me*, but *some people*.

"What about a long leather box and some felt bags?"

She noted my unfeigned dismay. "No, nothing like that. Just packets of money and the bonds."

"What were you going to do with the money?"

I told her about the Father Mike's Foundation and the safe haven it would support.

She studied me for a moment with her piercing blue eyes. Were they a little too blue? I felt that she could see everything about me, like x-ray vision, like she could see what I had for lunch.

"I like that. I'll let it go as a finder's fee in exchange for the other items. I'm going to give you a card—keep it in a very, very safe place. When you figure out where those other items are—the long flat leather box and the felt bags that tinkle when you shake them—do not open them. Do not even think about doing anything other than calling the number on the card. And," her throaty voice continued, its even, velvety timbre as threatening as the hiss of a cobra, "you will want to be calling me soon."

Betty put the deck of cards and the pistol back into her bag and took out a pale lavender business card that was printed in raised dark purple ink. It read BETTY and had a telephone number—nothing else.

"Is your name really Betty?" I asked.

"Yes," she laughed. "Can you believe it?"

She rose and strode out with the grace of the chorus girl she, no doubt, had once been, leaving me relieved and thinking that Roger had been almost right—his Mr. X was, in fact, *Ms.* X.

117

I didn't call Roger because I was meeting him for dinner.

We had never been, just the two of us, to a restaurant for dinner. It had started out with Roger saying, over coffee at our old diner hangout, that he'd had the best calamari ever the night before.

"Raw or fried?"

"Oh fried, deep fried."

"I love fried calamari!" And before I knew it, we had agreed to meet at that very restaurant for "the best Italian food on the West Side."

Was I nervous? Like a schoolgirl. I tried on four different outfits. I would have liked Mags's input, but, well, I couldn't call Mags because I didn't want the rest of her input any more than I wanted Janine's concerned caution.

I could tell that Roger was nervous too. He had on a suspiciously new-looking navy blazer over a white shirt and jeans. He looked sexy as hell.

We inhaled our first glasses of wine to settle us down, then had what I have to assume was a wonderful meal. I wasn't as focused on the food in front of me as I was on who sat across from me. Roger was a sexy eater: He caressed his food; he enjoyed it slowly, savoring every bite. He drove me home, and when we got to Park Avenue, he said, "There's that parking space again."

"Guess you'll have to take it."

118

As soon as we were inside the door, Roger took a very willing me into his arms for a kiss.

It might have been the longest kiss on record. At some point, it included being on the leopard carpet (just when did I have time to redecorate?) amid piles of clothes.

We woke up in the morning entwined on my bed, looking at each other and smiling. Roger surveyed my face with a wonderful smile on his—that suddenly changed to shock.

"Oh, jeez, Livie, oh jeez, I'm sorry," he gently touched my chin, which caused me to yelp.

Yep: my chin was whisker-burned raw. That, along with a few obvious hickies, made up for the good teenage girl I had been in the backseats of cars.

"I'm not sorry," I laughed as we examined ourselves in the bathroom mirror, Roger rubbing his heavily stubbled chin and me holding a cold wet washcloth to mine. He kissed me on the back of my neck and it tickled. I tried to turn to him, but he held me in place, and we again looked at each other in the mirror.

"We have to think about this," he said, "not get crazy. Maybe this was something that needed to happen—once. Let's give it time."

"I don't need time—"

But he put a finger to my lips, and as our eyes locked, I realized he was thinking about Travis and Gil and Larry and wasn't entirely prepared to trust me.

I wouldn't trust me either.

Greta had cooked breakfast for two, which wasn't surprising as she had picked up articles of two people's clothing from the floor and had neatly hung a navy blazer over a chair. This could have been a very awkward time, but Greta simply handed me an ice pack for my rapidly inflaming face while Roger looked sheepish.

Then I remembered Betty. Greta got my purse for me. Not being a total angel, she casually mentioned that she had found it on the floor, under a table.

I took out Betty's card and handed it to Roger while recounting every detail of her unusual visit.

"Betty?" he replied when I asked if he knew of her. "Every cop has heard Betty stories, and they don't usually end as gently as yours."

We mused about that, then Roger got an *a-ha* look. "The Father Mike's Foundation. Betty came from somewhere in Minnesota. Word is, she left as a kid, leaving something ugly behind. Took the first bus out and ended up in Vegas. But, she has New York history too."

"The leather case and the bags? I assume they contain jewels—what's that about?"

"I think this whole thing just got more complicated." Roger leaned over and gently pulled a strand of hair away that had caught in my ice pack. My stomach fluttered. "On the other hand, it starts to answer some questions. But, Livie." He gently cupped my inflamed face to hold my head so we had direct eye contact. "Betty is as cold as they come. If you find anything…"

I took the card back from him and put it in my wallet. "I'm the one who sat across from her. Trust me, I don't ever want to see her face again. But where did the jewels come from?"

119

"People go to Vegas to win," Roger mused as he drank his coffee. "The big rollers usually take their wives, or girlfriends or hired arm-pieces, who are all dolled up, wearing their best jewelry. When the guy wins big—and at first, a lot of them do—the little lady gets some bling as a souvenir. Then the guy goes back to the casino—about ninety percent of them aren't smart enough to take the money and run, the other five percent come back later—and they lose it all, plus another big chunk—the house rarely loses, and when it does, it's usually to the other chosen five percent. The guy is mad—or panicked—and needs to win it back. He's always sure that one more toss of the dice or fall of the cards will do it. Where to get the money? The little lady's new bling is an easy place to start, plus a piece or two from what she arrived with. Let's say the store that sold him her trinkets won't take them back, but suggests a little shop down the street—a classy pawnshop—that will bankroll the guy. If he wins, he can get the stuff back, paying a hefty interest for the loan. Usually the guy loses and slinks out of town, leaving an unpaid bar tab and the jewelry behind. Even if he gets lucky, the pawn shop earns a high interest rate."

Roger paused while Greta, all ears and nodding in agreement with this tale, poured more coffee. I wondered about Greta's history.

"The gambling part of Vegas is a small town, so as soon as the guy scoots, an insider tells the pawn shop—you have probably guessed that Betty's group controls them—along with the jewelry stores. They don't want a lot of Aunt Tillie's broaches or Grandma's engagement rings displayed. They keep some for customers who like that stuff, but most of it gets cut. The jewels are removed and the gold or platinum melted down. Then the goods get refashioned into new pieces that go back to the store. They have people who do it out there, but the best ones are here in Manhattan. Plus, a lot of the stones probably get sold to dealers here. And, sweetest of all, part of it is legit. All-in-all, it's a nifty business."

"Part of it?"

"Yeah, the part that's declared as income. I suspect that the best stones don't show up in the receipts. And the New York people are paid off with New York money, if you get my meaning."

I did. "But why does Betty think Larry had the stones?"

"They had to get to Manhattan. You don't just stick that stuff in a FedEx box. Someone had to bring them here so they could be distributed."

"Someone like Jason—or Gil?"

"They are looking like the usual suspects."

"And Larry and Sherry?"

"They would have been involved, for sure."

120

Since I couldn't stay in town, lest my inflamed face be seen by my friends, and I couldn't go to Charles and Alice's because I would be seen by a whole crowd of people, beginning with my hosts, plus Lauren, Christa and especially Travis, I decided to go to Larry's lake house and clean up the mess that Betty had so recently reminded me that Mags and I had left. A cleaning service was out of the question, for obvious reasons.

Easing a needling conscience, I called Lauren all the same.

"Oh, that's okay, Mom," Lauren said when I called. "Mags is here."

She was there already! I had visions of her on her way there, sweeping in, loaded down with presents. She quite obviously got handed the phone and had the decency to fumble for words:

"Oh! Ah—hi, Olivia! I happened to be in the neighborhood..."

Since I, for somewhat awkward reasons, happened not to be in the neighborhood where I should have been, I had to give her that one. There was happy chatter in the background. Christa? My younger daughter was next on the phone, sounding so joyful to be there with her sister.

Something I had longed and hoped for—that my daughters would one day experience sisterhood—had come to pass with Lauren's pregnancy. Christa, with or without Jeff, went to the farm at every opportunity, and the two sisters would talk. They talked! Something I couldn't remember happening in the past fifteen years. I understood the basis for their new relationship: Lauren finally had something, finally had done something better than, or at least before, Christa—something Christa could envy. It wasn't the best foundation for their new closeness, but it got them there.

I also knew what got Mags there. She saw the baby slipping out of her freshly scarlet-taloned grasp: she feared Lauren had begun to like the idea of motherhood and all the attention that it generated. Somehow, she and Mason were going to be an important part of raising this child, and she was there, staking her Jimmy Choos in the territory. That baby would need to cover a lot of territory to keep the growing crowd happy.

Lauren was back on the phone and actually asked when I would come to see her. Then she told me that Mags and Mason had invited her to stay at their apartment when she could travel in a week or so. Lauren was going after the best deal.

Time had taught me to choose my battles. When one is faced with a well-equipped large force encamped on a hill, one does not try to climb up there, slingshot in hand, to do battle.

Instead, I would get out of town before Mags came back with peace offerings. It was still morning when I packed a few things, including Sherry's urn, and went down to the garage. Jerome, no matter what Roger and Mason would prefer, was not taking me on this trip.

121

The house was pretty much as Betty had described it—a mess.

I stowed some groceries I had stopped to buy, then deposited my things in the guest room. Even though Mags and I had stayed in the master bedroom that thrilling night, I did not want to sleep in Larry and Sherry's bed. It was near the end of winter now and most of the houses were still closed for the season. Fortunately, whoever had built this one had installed a good automatic heating and cooling system and had buried the pipes deep in the ground, or they would have burst by now, leaving money and bonds floating in a half frozen pool of water.

I spent the first hour gathering up the money, cursing Mags as I envisioned her throwing it in the air and it raining back down. At least Betty, and whatever muscle she brought with her, had chased the raccoons out, but their poop was still around, poop that contained identifiable bits of chewed-up currency.

When that was cleaned up, I called Hal Jennings, a glazier I knew, and asked him to come out to replace the glass Mags had smashed. We had duct-taped cardboard over the opening, but that had crumbled in the weather and the missing glass was just an invitation for break-ins, especially with the area now so deserted.

While I waited for Hal to arrive, I put on my boots and parka and carried Sherry's urn down the path to the water's edge.

Several times Altagrazia, our Mexican-born cleaning helper, had asked me what I was going to do with Sherry's urn. I had assumed that Sherry's family would show some interest in claiming her remains, but she still sat in the broom closet.

I knew that Sherry had been rude and abusive to Altagrazia during her period as the lady of the house, and Altagrazia could hold a grudge. While she made it seem that it was the ornate urn she coveted, I could picture Sherry's ashes being strewn over the floor and Altagrazia stomping around in them before she pulled out the Hoover.

The dock had been partly pulled in to protect it from the ice. It had been such a mild winter however, that there was only a fine crust of ice at the edge. I spotted the Styrofoam top from a cooler wedged under the dock, which I was able to pry loose. I climbed out onto the dock as far as I could, then got on my stomach and put Sherry's urn on top of the foam, pushing its little feet in to secure it, then lowered the whole thing carefully into the water and gave it a shove. Even Sherry deserved a proper burial and the place where she had died seemed to be the right choice.

122

Hal must not have been busy because he was there within the hour. He replaced the glass, checked around for other damage, and because it had been a mild month with little snow, was able to go up on the roof to put a new mesh cover over the chimney after I told him about the raccoons.

When he finished, I made him coffee and we sat and talked. Hal told me how really sorry he was about my old place burning down. As a young man just taking over his father's business, he had put in all the new windows in that house when my parents redid the place.

"And all that funny stuff with Gil...." He shook his head. "There were strange things going on for years. And that kid Jason? He was always trouble."

"Strange things?"

"Oh, yes-sir-ee," said Hal. "Gil had visitors that didn't come from these parts. And those packages he was always mailing? Got people to wondering, I can tell you."

Hal left, assuring me as he did that he would "stop by the police station to tell the Chief you're here alone." The chief of police being his brother, Ray.

Then I got to wondering about what he had said. I went to the telescope, but dark had begun to set in, so I didn't expect to see anything. I didn't, just hazy dark images. I fiddled with different knobs and buttons—I didn't have anything else to do—and then, suddenly, I could see.

Everything had a greenish cast, but I could see the ruins of my house. I turned the knobs gently, practicing, and could soon focus the scope quite clearly. I saw a deer nibbling on a bush. He stopped, alert, head up, looking in my direction: I was looking directly into his eyes. He must have sensed it, because he took off.

This was fun! I swung the scope around and spied on all the neighboring houses.

There was movement. Three young men, kids, were prying open a window on the Jacksons' house. I recognized two of them. They weren't bad kids, probably out doing their teen ritual. The Jacksons were big drinkers: the kids were no doubt looking for booze.

I thought about calling Chief Ray at the police station, but then, would the boys get a mark on their records? They would be applying for college soon, would that mark keep them out of where they wanted to go—change their lives forever? But what if they got drunk and drove their car into a tree, or into another car? That would certainly change their lives forever. It wasn't easy, just sitting there, playing God. I was saved from the decision: the Jacksons, having been targeted once too often, had installed an alarm.

When it went off I could see the incredulous *holy shit!* on the boy's faces. They peeled out of there and minutes later a patrol car arrived. The officers assessed the situation, laughed and shook their heads. The younger one had probably done the same thing a few years before. The senior officer was on the phone: He talked, he listened, then nodded and turned to scan my house. Chief Ray must have told him that I was there and to patrol my road during the night.

"This is fun!" I said, rubbing my hands together in a secret glee. But then I rethought that: No, this is not fun— this is creepy.

And then I thought about me canoeing and singing one night: I thought about me canoeing and burning down Gil's gazebo observatory another night; I thought about me, wounded and bleeding, driving Gil's Gator away from my blazing house. Who had been watching?

123

I had a microwave dinner—no wine—I was already high on adrenaline. I got into bed with a book and my cell phone: the book to distract me, the phone to protect me. I momentarily wondered if I had been too hasty in my dismissal of Princess as my proposed consolation grandchild.

Out of politeness I had turned the phone off while Hal was there. I switched it on: I had a number of messages.

Christa: "Mom, are you all right? You never let Mags get here alone. Call me."

Lauren, of all people: "Hi, Mom, you okay? Listen, if I want a break from Mags, can I come home for a while?"

Janine: "Hi, sweets. Just let Mags run with it. You know what a short attention span she has—Mason will be another matter. Call me when you can."

Roger: "I understand if you don't want to talk to me, but I gotta know where you are. Your car's gone—you and Jerome have a falling out?"

And finally: "Oh! Lauren looks just soooo beautiful! Let's go shopping tomorrow."

There were also calls from Alice and Mason. I did not listen to those just now, but called Roger instead.

"I don't like this, Livie, you can't just disappear. You're supposed to take Jerome when you do."

He didn't feel any better about things after I told him where I was and about the telescope's capabilities.

"I don't like that, I should come up there."

"No, Roger. The alarm is set, the police will be patrolling. Besides," I giggled, "you know why I had to get out of town."

The last was designed to make him feel better and worse.

"Ah, jeez, Livie. Next time…" He paused. "If there is a next time, I promise to double shave."

We did our first billing and cooing over the phone. Before we hung up, I promised to call him and Chief Ray if I heard so much as a mouse squeak.

I opened a book to read but that was hopeless. What I really wanted to do was think.

What kind of people would have a device like that telescope in their home? The previous owners who had built the house? I envisioned the room where the telescope was installed, bolted to the middle of the floor. It was a semi-round extension on the edge of the house that resembled a silo. There were built-in cushioned benches below the windows, circling the lakeside view. I doubted that the occupants of those benches were supposed to sit there watching someone use the telescope. It was a room meant for conversation, for book club meetings, for having drinks while watching the sunset. Larry and/or Sherry had installed the device. But why? This was meant for people watching. Me? Gil?

124

In the morning, I made my tea and toast with peanut butter and took them on a tray into that bedeviling room. It was a very cozy room, the sun streaming in from the side. There were tray tables in a holder. I took one out, set it in front of a bench seat and made myself comfortable.

Without that thing bolted to the floor in the middle, it really was a delightful spot with wide views of the lake. I could imagine spending time here, reading, thinking, talking to… I wasn't ready to fill in that blank.

It had been a foolish, impetuous night after Christa's wedding when I went home with Travis. He had been a gentle, giving lover. He was such a good man that the thought of hurting him hurt my heart. But he hadn't sent me into hiding because an endless kiss left my face an embarrassing mess. My heart was in a flummoxed condition. Maybe I wanted a do-over on everything.

I got up and sat in the seat behind the scope. I adjusted some knobs so it was on a more or less daylight setting, and began to scan. This could be really addictive. I found a cardinal couple, his scarlet easy to spot, her protective brown, not so, and followed their activities.

But the scope and I naturally swung back to the houses, mine that wasn't there, and Gil's that was. I studied each site, scanning back and forth between them. Something was eating at me. The answer was there, I knew it was. I just couldn't see it.

Did I have to go over there and rummage through Gil's house? That thought was repugnant. I scanned idly between the places again, then stopped to watch a large bird circle, then dive down on its prey. Dive down to the island. Yes. Of course.

At that moment there was no doubt in my mind about where the long flat leather case and the felt bags that tinkled when you shook them had been stashed. It was as if a big *X* hung over the island, like the mark on a pirate's treasure map.

What to do? Go over there? Look for myself to make sure?

I didn't need to look—I was sure. Besides, I didn't have a boat to get there. The thought of a boat brought my attention to two bass boats that had whizzed past several times. I had always found them annoying, especially in season when there were fishing contests that sent them roaring up and down the lake like a pack of gnats. Did they ever catch anything? Or did they just buzz from place to place—boys with their toys? One of them came slowly past again and I could hear the other one coming back down the lake.

When is bass season? I set the scope on a spot where the second boat would pass. It did, with one man driving and another person sitting in the fishing seat, looking at me through binoculars.

Do not even think about anything other than calling this number, Betty had said. The pale lavender business card was still in my bag. I fingered it as I sat back down with another cup of tea.

I should just call, I thought, and knew that I would. But first, I had to think. I was pretty sure I knew the location of something that Betty wanted, really wanted, enough so that people who got between her and her treasure had died. I had a mental image of Betty in full pirate garb, like a glamorous Anne Bonney—and just as lethal.

The boats buzzed by again, but I was not going to be intimidated. I was going to make this discovery work for me. I had something that Betty wanted, and I was sure that she had something to give in return—information. What I had to decide was: What did I want to know, and if I really wanted to know it.

125

"Hello, Olivia," said the throaty, velvet voice.

I never liked caller ID and continued to view it as an affront to my privacy.

"Good morning, Betty."

"Are you enjoying it there at the lake?"

Bitch. "Oh yes, it's a lovely morning, the sky is clear, the fishermen are out." That quieted her for a second.

"What can I do for you?" she said, but really: *What can you do for me?*

"It's more like, what we can do for each other."

"How so?"

"I have information that you want," I replied. "And I think you have some that—well, maybe I don't really want to know, but think I should."

Betty went quiet. Hello, are you still there?

"I believe you have a fresh cup of coffee," she finally said.

I looked down at the tea in my hand and was about to correct her, but stopped myself—she didn't have to know everything.

"What is it you think you want to know? No, wait, that's too open-ended. You uncorked this bottle, so I'll be the genie and give you three questions."

I noted that she didn't ask for her information first, but then, the bass boats were idly circling in front of me, and there was, without a doubt, a car at the end of the driveway, so Betty, in card terms, was holding a full house.

"But you know, Olivia," she cautioned, "once the genie is out, it's like toothpaste, you can't put it back in. There are things that might be better left in the tube."

"I know that, Betty, and thank you for warning me. In the past months, I've discovered that the man I spent over thirty years of my life with was someone else."

"Oh, yes," she sighed, "Larry. I assume Larry is your first question?"

"He is."

"Don't be too hard on him. He was a very flawed man. I had a career in flawed men, and at least he wasn't mean to others."

"Others?"

"Yes. Larry was mean, you could say cruel, but it was mostly to himself."

"I don't follow."

Betty took an audible breath. I could almost see her settling back in a chair.

"You knew Willa?"

"I certainly did."

"The world is a better, safer place because, one, she wasn't a man, and two, she's dead. Willa ruined Larry. How the other brother came out sane, I don't know, but she ruined Larry."

"Ruined him? How?"

Betty's voice turned hard. "It never stops amazing me how wives can see just what they want to see and are either blind to, or blindsided by the rest."

"But I knew Laurence," I broke in hotly.

"Oh, yes. You knew Laurence. What did you know about Larry?"

I had to admit that, until recently, I didn't know he existed.

Betty continued, "There's a line from a musical: *We wear our costumes/ We play the people we mean to be.* I was never sure which costume Larry wore. Did he mean to be Laurence? Or did he always want to be Larry? At the houses, they called him Larry."

"At the houses?"

"Yes, Olivia. That row of houses you now own—the whore houses? Did you think Larry didn't go there when he owned them?"

I was silent.

"Larry grew up in those houses, dropped his cherry there. So did his brother. Charles stopped going when he went off to college, but Larry had developed...other needs."

"Such as?"

"This will offend your proper sensibilities, but to be blunt, he was a masochist. He needed to suffer. The older he got, the more successful he seemed to the outside world, the more he needed to be humiliated at the houses. Even Willa got concerned, tried to keep him out of them, but she understood those needs. Hell, she had made a fortune providing those services, so—I think she figured that he'd just go someplace else—and at least her places were clean. By the way, have you been tested for STDs?"

"What? No!"

"For God's sake! Grow up. Especially now that you're screwing around."

I covered my chin with my hand.

"Larry got worse when Willa lost total control of the business—then out-of-control when she died. The girls were getting tired of smacking that naughty little boy around, I can tell you."

"How do you know that?"

"I still know some of the girls, I spent time in the trenches there." Betty paused to laugh. "I even bagged for Willa a few times—that woman was a greedy bitch. I made my contacts in the jewelry trade there, before coming back to Vegas."

"You're saying Larry was a...a pervert?"

"Olivia." She rolled out my name like a sigh. "Don't throw words around that you don't understand. You like champagne—are you a drunk? You live the good life—are you a dirty capitalist pig? You've slept with a couple of men you aren't married to—are you a whore?"

"How do you know these things?" I asked in dismay.

"Knowledge isn't just power, it's safety."

She went on. "Larry wasn't born wanting to be strapped into devices that caused him pain while being told what a bad boy and the worthless piece of shit he was. Willa marked him as her successor. He wasn't strong enough to say no, but he was too strong to say, *Yes, this is a good thing to do.* I'm not a shrink, but I think he was trying to block out his mental pain with the physical stuff."

"What about Sherry?"

"Now, that I consider question number two. Should I go on?"

"Yes."

"Sherry, as one of her duties for Uncle Sal and the family, was overseeing the take at the houses. You remember I said some of the girls were getting tired—bored, in fact—with smacking Larry around?"

Unfortunately, the thought had seared itself into my imagination. "Yes."

"Well, Sherry happened to be there one time when they were complaining about it, and she thought she'd like the opportunity to inflict some pain on a man. You wouldn't know this, but Sherry was trying to break into the club, to be a made woman."

I did not correct her assumption.

"Most of the guys in the family had given her real shit over that and tough garbage jobs to do, so she was up for putting the screws, literally, on some guy."

"I don't need to know all the details," I broke in. I was beginning to get really freaked out with the images rolling around in my head.

"Fair enough. I'll stick with the bare facts," she laughed, "so to speak. My grandmother—sadistic, crazy bitch that she was—was right about one thing: For every pot there's a lid. Those two, Larry and Sherry, really fit each other's needs to a T. Then Miss Sherry got an idea: Here was this guy who owned the business plus a lot of other real estate, and if she got control of it, she could tell those goons in the family to go fuck themselves, then really be able to put the screws to anyone who got in her way."

"But," I broke in tentatively, "there was me. Laurence and I were married."

"Oh, yeah," Betty's rich laugh rolled out. "You're like a cat. But you've gone through a few of your nine lives recently, starting with Sherry letting you continue to have one. That's still a mystery to me, it's not like she hadn't already processed a few people to the other side. The only thing that makes sense to me is she wanted to flex some ego to show that she could take him away from you. Don't know why you just gave her that touching burial, but it was sweet."

I flinched and looked at the binoculars on the boat below. I was so tired of being spied on.

"And incidentally," she continued, "you were one dumbass girl about the settlement. If you're ever in that situation again, don't go to a Yale guy in a three-piece suit, find yourself someone named Mavis from Brooklyn Law. You'd have got the apartment, half the business and at least one of his balls."

"It was enough," I said. "I wanted a simpler life. I wanted to go on to other things."

Betty laughed loud and long at that. "Like getting shot with your house burning down around you and a dead man beside you? Or tearing down the highway, clinging to that nut case friend of yours? With Sal and his gun-toting goons right behind you? Yeah, and I'm Betty Crocker."

"Let's get back to the story," I said.

"You're trying to get a twofer here," she said, "but, okay, you played me. When you left the apartment, you took more than grandma's teacups, right?"

"There might have been a few things—"

She did not hedge. "For brevity's sake, I'll refer to the happy couple as S&L, and that doesn't mean as in Savings and Loan Association, although, in a way, they were."

"Like in running money through the casinos? And paying for the jewels to be reset and put back in play."

"Oh, yes…my friend Roger figured that one out, huh?"

My friend Roger?

"He's a good man. You don't want to do anything to hurt him."

Was that a threat? Or a warning?

"Your sticky fingers put a kink in the pipeline," Betty went on, "but, mostly it made Sherry really mad—and suspicious. Or more so, I should say, Sherry was raised to be suspicious, not to trust anyone. And besides, they weren't positive that you took it."

"So they bought the house I'm sitting in now to keep an eye on me?"

Betty didn't answer right away. Then: "I think you've pushed the second question to its limit. Think carefully, be like St. Teresa, about what you ask for next."

Yes: *Be careful what you pray for.* Was she warning me? About what? Lauren—it could only be Lauren.

126

"Why did Larry kill her?" popped out.

"Way to go Olivia!" Betty almost squealed. "I'm impressed! I thought you'd ask me about that pain-in-the ass daughter of yours."

I should have called her on that, but the fact that I didn't need to ask which daughter she was talking about meant we were dealing the truth here.

Betty continued, "We can never know what goes on in that tangled mess that passes for a man's brain, but we can guess at some possibilities."

"Such as?"

"Such as the wee wifey proudly announcing that they were pregnant when he knew she was more likely to get in that condition from the guppy in the fish tank than from him. Or, maybe finding out that the mommy was skimming off more than usual from the money the daddy was shipping out west."

"Gil!" I gasped.

"Oh, well, that's a freebie, I'll give you the rest. Sherry and Gil had their little game going for quite a while. They couldn't have done what they did without each other. Or maybe Larry had a feeling—and rightfully so—that Sherry, who soon after the marriage got tired of seeing to his special needs, was getting just as tired of his presence on this planet."

"So he did her before she could do him?"

"That would be the answer I would choose, along with all of the above."

"And Gil had the photographs."

"Now you're pushing."

"They bought this house to watch Gil! And Larry sent those men to kill him because he was afraid of Gil, and they burned my house down and—" Suddenly, the little nagging bubble of memory that had been floating around in my subconscious popped up and burst. Out of it spilled the words, *Fan out and make sure*. It was Larry's voice.

"Ohmigod...ohmigod..." I was blubbering. I looked at the telescope...No one got out...Larry had known I was there. He had sent Nolan and Weiss...he was getting rid of evidence.

"Olivia! Livie," Betty said sternly, yet kindly, "pull yourself together."

"But, why did he marry me again?"

"Maybe to get back the money you took, maybe he had a conscience, or more likely, maybe he wanted to make sure you couldn't testify against him. It seemed you weren't easy to kill. So who knows? But you finished what Sherry couldn't."

That last was not said kindly.

I pulled myself together, remembering that we were not two ladies having tea. "And Jason?"

"You've had your three—plus some. Jason was my business," she said, all cold business. "I've run out of words to say, now I'm in the listening mode."

127

I told her where I thought the jewels were hidden. The bass boats tore around the end of the small peninsula and approached the little island. I told Betty where the boats should pull into the shallow cut-in that I could just barely see. I felt like the director of a movie.

I looked through the scope and watched the men anchor the boats and struggle through the thin layer of ice near the shore.

Then I described to Betty the remains of the little stone house and the tin-lined box, built-in under the floor so critters couldn't get at supplies, whose pull handle had long ago disappeared. With the dirt, leaves, and now snow that naturally blew in, you wouldn't see the outline of the opening unless you knew it was there.

I was not surprised when the men came back to the boats carrying something.

Would Betty live up to her end of the bargain?

I was jolted with the realization that the bargain had been answers from her, and treasure from me. No one had said anything about my life. I had made a very foolish and dangerous assumption.

There was a loud knock on my door. I looked around for a weapon and settled on the most dangerous at hand—a cleaver hanging on a pegboard on the kitchen wall. I took it in my hand, grasping it like a lifeline. What that would do against the guns waiting outside, I didn't know, but I would put up a fight; I wouldn't just stand there and let them shoot me.

I slipped out the deck door and climbed down a short trellis to the lower deck, then down the stairs to the side of the house, where I crouched by some winter bushes and assessed my options.

My cell phone rang. I had closed it and stuffed it into my pocket without turning it off. I answered to keep it quiet.

Betty was laughing. "Olivia—you are a piece of work!" Then she started singing "I Shot the Sheriff, but I Didn't Shoot the Deputy." She laughed again and hung up.

I looked around. The bass boats circled away and started speeding up the lake. I flattened myself against the corner of the house, raised the cleaver and peeked around, my face coming against the chest of Chief Ray.

128

I had my suspicions, so prepared myself.

Sandy was more than happy to lend me one of the voice changers from the office and not only showed me how to use it, but pre-set the rasping voice I asked for without questions.

When the early morning call came, I clamped the device on before answering.

"Livie!" screeched Mags, sounding like she was on Jupiter, rather than a private plane heading south where the yacht was waiting. "We had to leave early—" *mumble...rustle*—"weather changing...meet us in—" scratching—"on the—" static.

"I can't, Mags, I'm sick," my newly edited voice answered.

Suddenly her phone was very clear. "My god! You sound terrible! What can I do? I'll send over chicken soup."

"No, no," I rasped more forcefully, fearful that she had some of her homemade catastrophe in her freezer. "Greta will take care of me. It's a good thing I didn't get there in time," I said pointedly, my new voice sounding so authentic that I began to feel a chill coming on.

"Oh. Yes. What with Lauren's condition and all..." Was there a hint of remorse in her voice? Probably not. "I'll call you when we sail for Aruba—oh!"

She hadn't meant to tell me where their first stop would be in case I hopped on a plane. And I had thought of doing just that when I suspected what she might be up to. I'd had the phone in my hand.

But I had stopped and thought more about it. If I were on board, it would be non-stop plotting and maneuvering to show a disgusted Lauren who would be the best, most caring grandma/auntie. With me not there, I would actually have more face time. Mags would have a captive audience to regale with her recent exploits and, like it or not, I was the cause of and companion in those happenings. Her thrilling recital of our adventures would have to put the spotlight on me—and Janine, who would be on board, would keep her honest about that—so Lauren would hear, from a source she trusted, about the actions we took to protect her and the baby and the horrors we experienced from the people she had gotten us mixed up with. One on one, she wouldn't have given me the chance to tell my story, and in truth, I wouldn't have told it.

But, after Lauren was cooped-up on that yacht with Mags for two weeks, I stood a better chance of reclaiming my daughter, and eventually my grandchild, than if I had sailed with them at dawn.

Besides, Mags would owe me. Big time.

Besides, besides, Roger and I were going fishing.

Acknowledgments

My sincerest gratitude to Catherine Adams of Inkslinger Editing LLC, who slid open that drawer full of meanderings and manuscripts and thought we could have a little fun. She might have re-thought that while buried under a mound of excess commas but Catherine always managed a smile, even when ripping scenes apart and killing characters: A perfect editor and friend.

To my friend Sarah Hankins, PhD, for her support and prodding over the long haul and for her insightful editing and suggestions during the critical early stages.

My sincere gratitude to James Hall for his assiduous fact-checking and keen memory of events that kept page six in sync with page two hundred sixty-six and for acquainting me with the intricacies of New Jersey by-ways.

Thank you to Patricia Laurence, PhD, for suggesting the series title ACCIDENTAL MURDERS.

About the Author

Catherine Grace has lived large from outhouse to Greathouse and fortunately, for some people, never kept a diary but remembers it all.

Visit Catherine Grace's website and sign up to be the first to hear of new adventures for Olivia, Mags, and Janine.

www.catherinegraceauthor.com